LADY *of*
MILKWEED
MANOR

LADY *of* MILKWEED MANOR

a novel

JULIE KLASSEN

BETHANY HOUSE PUBLISHERS

Minneapolis, Minnesota

Published by Bethany House Publishers
11400 Hampshire Avenue South
Bloomington, Minnesota 55438

Bethany House Publishers is a division of
Baker Pubishing Group, Grand Rapids, Michigan.

Printed in the United States of America

Library of Congress Cataloging-in-Publication Data

Klassen, Julie.
    Lady of Milkweed Manor / Julie Klassen.
       p. cm.
    ISBN 978-0-7642-0479-1 (pbk.)
     1. Children of clergy—Fiction. 2. Physicians—Fiction. 3. London (England)—Fiction. I. Title.

PS3611.L37L33   2007
813'.6—dc22

                                     2007034144

To my dear parents,
whose unconditional love
paved the way.

To the Milkweed

NONE call thee flower! I will not so malign
The satin softness of thy plumëd seed,
Nor so profane thee as to call thee weed,
Thou tuft of ermine down,
Fit to entwine about a queen . . .
. . . Ah me! Could he who sings,
On such adventurous and aërial wings
Far over lands and undiscovered seas
Waft the dark seeds of his imaginings,
That, flowering, men might say, Lo! look on these
Wild Weeds of Song—not all ungracious things!

—Sonnets by Lloyd Mifflin

PROLOGUE

When first I knew her, I thought her an amusing scrap of girl, silly and a bit grubby from her mornings spent in the gardens. When not pottering about out of doors, she seemed always to be reading some poetic nonsense or other and loved nothing more than to pose the most disturbing questions. Still, I liked her even then and, I think, she admired me. But her father took notice and pronounced me unsuitable, effectively pruning our young friendship before it could grow into anything. I soon forgot about Miss Charlotte Lamb. Or so I convinced myself.

Years passed, and when I saw her again she was altogether changed. Not only her situation, which had changed from privileged to piteous, but also her very substance. At least it seemed so to me.

Others would look at her with much different eyes. They would see, perhaps, a fallen woman at the deepest point of humiliation. A woman to be flicked off one's sleeve like a disgusting worm. Or an insect to be tormented. Cruel, overgrown schoolchildren that many are, they seem to delight in ripping off one wing, then another, watching in morbid glee as she falls helpless to the ground.

To the gentler observer, she is a creature to be scorned at worst, ignored at best, but certainly not one to watch in hopeful anticipation. Day by day to witness her transformation amid the grime and cloying weight of her surroundings, not to wither nor shrink, but to unfurl, to become all that is sun and wind and flower and grace.

I, of course, can only watch from a safe distance—safe for us both. For me, now a married man, a physician of some note, a man of standing in town. And for her, whose reputation I am determined will suffer no more—not if it is in my power to prevent it.

Yet, as I watch her there among the milkweeds, I confess all these thoughts fade away. I think only of her.

How lovely she looks. Not abstractly beautiful, but perfectly fitted to the landscape, etched into a painting of purest golden glow above, and mad, overgrown garden below—gold, green, purple—heaven and earth. And there at the center, her still figure, looking not at me but at the distant horizon, where the sun is spilling its first fingers over the milkweed, over her milky skin, her hair, her gown.

The light moves toward me and I am stilled, speechless. A sharp barb of waiting fills my chest and I can barely breathe. If I don't move, the light will touch me, the painting encompass me. If I step away, retreat into the shadows, I will be safe, but I won't be there to see her when she finally flies away. . . .

Dear God. Please guard my steps. And somehow bless Miss Charlotte Lamb.

PART I

That exquisite thing, the seed of milkweed,

furnished abundant playthings.

The plant was sternly exterminated in our garden,

but sallies into a neighboring field provided supplies

for fairy cradles with tiny pillows of silvery silk.

—ALICE MORSE EARLE, *OLD-TIME GARDENS*

Alas! And did my Saviour bleed,

And did my Sovereign die?

Would he devote that sacred head

For such a worm as I?

—ISAAC WATTS

The common milkweed needs no introduction.

Its pretty pods are familiar to every child, who treasures them

until the time comes when the place in which they are stowed away

is one mass of bewildering, unmanageable fluff.

—19TH CENTURY NATURALIST, F. SCHUYLER MATHEWS

CHAPTER I

Twenty-year-old Charlotte Lamb laid her finest gowns into the trunk, pausing to feel the silken weight of the sky blue ball gown, her favorite—a gift from dear Aunt Tilney. With one last caress, she packed it carefully atop the others. Then came her promenade dresses, evening dresses, and gayer day dresses. Next were the coordinating capes, hats, and hair ornaments. Finally the long gloves, petticoats, and the new boned corset. Definitely the corset.

Turning back to her rapidly thinning wardrobe, her hand fell upon a plain muslin in dove grey. It showed wear in the elbows and cuffs. She tossed it on the bed. Then a thought came to her and she stopped her packing and left her room, stepping quietly down the corridor to her mother's room. Looking about her and seeing no one yet awake, she pushed the door open as silently as she could. She stepped into the room and, finding the shutters closed, walked to the windows and folded them back, allowing the grey dawn to illuminate the chamber. Then she returned to the door and closed it. Leaning back against the wood panels, she closed her eyes, savoring the stillness and peace she always felt in this room. It had been too long since she'd been in here.

From somewhere in the vicarage she heard a noise, a clang, and she jumped. Though why she should fear being caught in here she had no idea. Most likely it was only Tibbets lighting the fires. Her father would probably not be awake for hours. Still, the thought of someone up and about reminded her that she needed to hurry if she wanted to depart with as little to-do as possible. She stepped purposefully to the wardrobe and opened its doors. Yes, her mother's clothes were still here. She raked her fingers through the fabric, the lace and velvet and silks, but did not find what she was looking for. Had her father or Beatrice discarded it? She pushed the gowns aside and looked at the bottom of the wardrobe, at the slippers lined up neatly in a row. Then a flash of brown caught her eye, and she reached down and pulled out a crumpled wad of clay-colored material that had fallen to the bottom of the cabinet. She shook out the simple, full-cut dress—her mother's gardening dress.

Tucking it under her arm, she ran her fingers across the books on the bedside table. She didn't dare take the Bible her mother had used, knowing it was from the vicarage library. Instead she chose the *Lady's Pocket-Sized New Testament and Psalms*, as it was smaller and lighter. It was a lovely edition with a canvas cover embroidered with birds and flowers worked in silk and metallic thread. It had been a gift from her mother's sister, and Charlotte didn't think her father would object to her taking it.

With one last look at her mother's things—hairbrush and combs, cameo necklace and butterfly brooch—she left the room and walked quickly back to her own. She rolled her mother's dress as tightly as she could and stuffed it into a leather valise. Then she shoved in the worn grey gown, shifts, stockings, slippers, drawers, and a pair of short stays. Into a carpetbag she placed a shawl, dressing gown, gloves, and the New Testament. Two of her most service-able bonnets went into her bandbox. Handkerchiefs and what little money she had were secured in a reticule which would hang from her wrist.

She looked at the trunk, filled with her beautiful years, her happy vain youth, and firmly shut the lid. Pausing to secure a traveling hat over her pinned-up brown curls, she left her room with only her valise, carpetbag, reticule, and bandbox—all she could carry. She quietly made her way down the stairs and glanced at the silver tray resting on the hall table. Yesterday's letter lay there still, unanswered. Their cousin had written to tell them of her "blessed news" and how she looked forward to the "great event to come this autumn." Beatrice had curled her pretty lip and said it sickened her to read of such private matters, especially from a woman of Katherine's advanced age. Charlotte had said not a word.

Now Charlotte paused only long enough to run her fingers over Katherine's elaborate script and the smeared London Duty date stamp. She took a deep breath and walked on. She was nearly to the door when she heard her father's voice from the drawing room.

"You're off, then." It was not a question.

She turned and, through the open doors, saw him slumped in the settee by the fire. His greying hair was uncharacteristically disarrayed and he still wore his dressing gown. She felt her throat tighten. She could only nod. She wondered if he would soften at this final moment. Would he hold out some offer of assistance, some parting words of conciliation or at least regret?

In a voice rough with the early hour and disdain, he said, "My only consolation is that your mother, God rest her soul, did not live to see this day."

The pain of it lanced her, but it should not have. He had said the like before, worse even. Willing tears to remain at bay, Charlotte stepped out of the vicarage, quietly shutting the door behind her. She walked through the garden, committing it to memory. There were the neatly trimmed hedges that Buxley still coaxed into the shape her mother preferred. There, the exquisite flower beds with their cleverly mixed color palettes, graduating heights and varying textures—delphinium, astilbe, cornflower, Canterbury bells, lemon lilies—all of which Charlotte had tried to maintain in her mother's honor, at least until now. She took a long deep breath, then another, savoring the dew-heavy fragrances of sweet violets and purple pincushions. She had no intention of picking a flower to take with her, a flower that would wither before she reached her destination, but then she saw it. A vile milkweed in the border of sciatic cress, which Buxley called Billy-come-home-soon. How had she missed it before? She strode to the weed and pulled at it with her free hand, but the stalk would not give. She set her bags and box down and pulled with both hands until the whole stubborn thing was unearthed, roots and all. She would leave her mother's garden in perfect order. But for how long? *Who will tend your gardens, Mother? Buxley will try, I suppose. Though he is not getting any younger. With the horses and all the heavy work falling to him, the garden suffers. And Beatrice has no use for a garden, as you well know.*

On nostalgic impulse, Charlotte snapped off a cluster of small purplish flowers from the milkweed plant and held it briefly to her nose—it smelled surprisingly sweet—then slipped it into her reticule. She tossed the stalk onto the rubbish heap on her way down Church Hill. Glancing over her shoulder at the chalky white vicarage, a face in an upstairs window caught her eye. *Beatrice.* Her sister wore a stony expression and made no move to wave. When Beatrice turned from the window, Charlotte turned as well, wishing for a moment that she had turned away first. Two minutes later, just as she knew it would, the post wagon approached.

"Hallo there, Miss Lamb," the driver said as he halted his horses.

"Good morning, Mr. Jones."

"Care for a ride into the village?"

"Yes, thank you."

He took her bags from her and helped her up. "Off to visit your aunt again, are we?" He settled her carpetbag beside her.

She did not wish to lie any more than necessary. "I am always so happy in their company."

"And why not. Such fine people your aunt and uncle are. Never knew the better."

"You are very kind."

She clutched her carpetbag as the wagon started off again, her generous pelisse shielding her from the damp morning wind, from curious onlookers—and even from the full brunt of her father's farewell, such as it was. She would not cry—not now, not here, where villagers she knew might see her and guess she was leaving not on another holiday but rather on a much darker journey.

When the driver helped her alight at Chequers Inn, she took not the coach headed for Hertfordshire and Aunt Tilney, but rather a coach bound for London.

❧

The black enclosed coach bumped and jostled its way to the west side of London. When the driver called his "whoa" to tired horses, Charlotte arose from her seat, clutched her belongings, and pushed her way out of the conveyance before the coachman might help her alight.

She stepped down and made haste up Oxford Street, past the stationer and paper hanger, china and glassman, and linen drapers. Walking north on busy Tottenham Court Road, she passed silversmiths, chemists, and dwelling houses that were clearly less than fashionable. Then she stepped off the cobbles and crossed the damp and narrow Gower Mews. At the alley's end, she paused between market wagons and rubbish carts to look over her shoulder, assuring herself that no one was watching. Then she slipped in through the rear door of the Old Towne Tea Shoppe and, with an apologetic nod toward the proprietress, stepped out the front door onto Gower Street, opening her black umbrella against the slight mist and any prying eyes. Head lowered, she stepped over a refuse-filled gutter, then walked crisply on. Coming upon a sign bearing the name Store Street, Charlotte checked the directions her aunt had written down for her. This was it.

Charlotte glanced up and immediately saw an old manor house looming against a border of shadow and trees. It was a grey hulk of a building with two dark wings at right angles to each other, a boxy garret at their apex, standing guard over a formidable, arched door below. Perhaps a great house a hundred years ago, the structure looked sound but bleak—mottled stone, severe lines, the absence of adornment save a hedgerow lining the edge of a mossy stone walkway. She saw no sign, no plaque naming the manor, and somehow that made her all the more sure she was in the right place.

It was only then that she allowed the tears to come. Here, the street behind her streaming with people who knew her not and cared less, she felt the sting of her father's rejection and the loss of her home. But she could not agree with his assessment. He might be glad that her mother was not here to witness this day, but Charlotte was not.

She thought of her dear mother, the well-loved Lillian Lamb, who had brought warmth and moderation, cheer and steady calm to the vicarage, and especially to Reverend Gareth Lamb himself.

Charlotte hoped her memories of her mother, gone these five years, would not fade in this absence from all that was familiar—her mother's room, her portrait, the far-off look in Father's eyes that meant he was thinking of her. His parting words echoed again through Charlotte's mind, and she flinched—envisioning the disappointment that would certainly have clouded her mother's face—but yet she wished her mother were here with her, walking this rutted path, consoling her as she always had that all would work out in the end.

I wish I had your faith, Mother. I wish I were half the fine lady you were—or half as proper a clergyman's daughter. Would you have forgiven me, even if Father will not?

As Charlotte drew closer to the looming grey edifice that was to become her temporary home, she could not help but notice the secretive shuttered windows of the ground floor.

Then she noticed the milkweeds.

No formal gardens here, or if there once were, they had long since given way to islands of tall grasses and unchecked patches of milkweeds running the length of the wall facing Charlotte.

Her father would be horrified, and even her mother would not have approved of the tangled mess. Charlotte sighed. She supposed that for the women within these grey walls, the gardens outside were the least of their problems. *And the same is true of me.*

But milkweeds? What a bane they were to gardeners, their stubborn roots sending out crafty runners, the offspring only slightly easier to pull than the mother plant herself. And they spread not only by runners, but by their prolific seeds that filled the air every autumn. Apparently that was what had happened here—milkweed had been introduced and, left unchecked, had taken over most of the lawn.

Couldn't they at least hire some boy with a scythe to come and cut the pests down? Charlotte wondered. Milkweeds were pretty enough when the flowers bloomed, but when the grey-green pods aged to a dull silver, the reedy stalks held little aesthetic value at all.

Perhaps that solicitor friend of Uncle's had given false information about this place. Or Aunt Tilney had gotten it wrong somehow. Her aunt had confided in hushed tones that this place was of better quality and more discreet than others like it. Charlotte gathered their London solicitor had procured the recommendation for her. Her father knew nothing of the arrangements, other than to exact Charlotte's promise of secrecy and anonymity for as long as possible. Otherwise he seemed to care little of where Charlotte was to go or how she was to provide for herself. It was clear he could barely wait to get her out of his sight.

Charlotte wondered if her mother would recognize the man she had been married to for so many years. Not that Gareth Lamb had changed so much physically, except to grow a bit grey in his side-burns and a bit paunchier around the middle, but his demeanor was markedly changed. He had been stern—self-righteous even—before this happened, and now was all the more. The whole of his concern revolved around two points: how such a thing would likely ruin his career and how it would ruin Bea's chance at a suitable marriage.

I am dreadfully sorry for it. I am. I suppose Father's anger is right and just. But it does not feel like it. If only you were here to soften him. To accompany me.

But her mother was dead. So Charlotte walked alone.

A single knock brought to the door a thin, plain-faced woman a few years Charlotte's senior who quickly led her from the entry hall, through a large dining room, and into a small study with the words, "The matron shall be in directly." And, indeed, not two minutes later, a severe but attractive woman in her forties wearing a dark dress and tightly bound hair walked in, her officious air proclaiming her title. The woman's stern appearance brought Charlotte some disquiet, but when she settled her gaze on Charlotte, there was grim kindness in her expression.

"I am Mrs. Moorling, matron of the Manor Home. May I be of assistance?"

Charlotte arose on shaky legs and pressed a letter from the London solicitor and a bank note into the woman's hand. This was her only reply.

Mrs. Moorling slipped the money into her desk drawer without comment or expression, then glanced briefly at the letter the solicitor had written at her uncle's request. "I see. I'm afraid we haven't a private room available at the moment, but you shall have one as soon as possible. In the meantime, you will need to share."

"I understand."

"Your name is—" the woman scanned the letter—"Miss . . . Smith?"

"Yes, Smith. Charlotte Smith."

Mrs. Moorling paused only a moment before continuing, again with no change in her expression, though Charlotte had the distinct impression the woman knew she was lying about her name. "Before I can admit you, there are a few questions I need to ask."

Charlotte swallowed.

"Is this your first occasion availing yourself upon such an institution?"

"Yes, of course."

"Not 'of course,' Miss Smith. There are many who do not learn from experience. I must tell you that the Manor Home for Unwed Mothers is a place for deserving unmarried women with their first child. Our goal is to rehabilitate our patients for a morally upright life."

Charlotte looked down, feeling the heat of embarrassment snake up her neck and pulse in her ears. She heard the sound of paper rustling and knew the matron was again reading the letter.

"This letter attests to your character and background, though I haven't the time to verify it at the moment."

"Mrs. Moorling. I assure you. I have never been in such a predicament before . . . never conceived myself in such a predicament."

Poor choice of words, Charlotte thought grimly.

She forced herself to meet the older woman's eyes. Mrs. Moorling looked directly at her for a moment, then nodded.

"Gibbs will find a place for you to sleep."

Gibbs, the plain, painfully thin young woman, led her back through the entry hall and to the right, to the street-facing wing of the L-shaped building. Hurrying to keep up, Charlotte followed her through the long corridor to a door midway down its length. Charlotte looked into the dim room—once a portion of a fine drawing room, perhaps—with a high ceiling and broad hearth. The bedchamber held only one narrow bed, the width less than Charlotte's height. A small table with a brass candlestick sat on either side of the bed, and one chair stood against the nearest wall.

Three simple wooden chests lined the opposite wall, no doubt used to store the belongings of the room's temporary lodgers.

"You'll be sharing with Mae and Becky. Both slight girls—you're a fortunate one. They must be off visiting in one of the other rooms. They'll be in by and by. We have a water closet below stairs. But there's usually a wait for it. Chamber pots under the bed for late-night emergencies. We know how you lying-in girls get toward the end. You're responsible for emptying your own, at least until your ninth month or so. Our physicians believe activity is healthy. All the girls have duties, long as you're able. You'll get your assignment at breakfast tomorrow. Eight o'clock. Any questions?"

Charlotte's mind was whirling with them, but she only shook her head.

"Good night, then." Gibbs let herself from the room.

There is no sense in crying over spilt milk.
Why bewail what is done and cannot be recalled?

—SOPHOCLES

CHAPTER 2

S he is dreaming or remembering—she isn't sure which, but the sensation is delightful. She is dancing with a young gentleman at Sharsted Court, a gentleman whose name she can't recall, or perhaps never knew. She feels the polite pressure of his hand on her gloved palm and sees the warm admiration in his shy glances. In fact, she feels admiring glances follow her as she moves effortlessly through the patterns and steps of the dance. She feels not, she hopes, bloated vanity but rather surprise and pleasure at the attention paid her. Her sister, Beatrice, is not in attendance this night. Beautiful Bea, home with a cold. She is sorry, but really, how heavenly to feel so sought after, so desirable, all loveliness in her sky blue silk. Suitors aplenty, all her life ahead of her.

The music ends, and the young gentleman, golden eyelashes against thin pale cheeks, escorts her from the floor. She catches a glimpse of green eyes and rust-gold hair, but when she looks again, another partner has already taken his place. This one boldly thrusts his hand toward her, his brown eyes gleaming confidently, impudently. She turns away but feels his hand fall against her shoulder and turn her back around. She wants to flee, to refuse the presumptuous hand.

Instead, she wakens.

There, in the dimness before Charlotte's eyes, dangled a hand. Someone in bed beside her had thrown an arm across her shoulder. Bea? *No,* her mind told her. *You're not home any longer.* Dread and black fear swelled and sank deep within her.

Please. Please, let it all be a dream. Oh, God, please . . .

She reached under the blanket and ran her hand across her midriff, hoping it would still be smooth and flat.

Please.

Her hand found the hard rounded mound and she winced her eyes tightly shut.

It cannot be. It cannot be.

But it was.

Charlotte, lying on her side on the edge of the droopy bed, again opened her eyes. The hand was still before her, eerily like the one in her dream. Gently, she pushed the arm off her shoulder and scooted farther still, until she feared she might fall off the bed. Her back ached. Unable to get comfortable, she turned over again, the effort creaking the bed and taxing her more than imaginable a half year before. She found herself nose to nose with Mae, who had obviously eaten onions for supper. Another young woman clung to the opposite edge of the bed. Three women, six souls, in one small bed. Like sausages being turned, one after the other in a pan, Mae turned over to her other side, and the third woman followed suit without waking. Charlotte couldn't recall the younger woman's name. A girl, really.

Charlotte had met Mae not long after she had gotten into bed, plumping, then folding the pillow to try to get comfortable. The pretty, petite woman, near her own age, Charlotte guessed, had come in, mumbled her name, and promptly climbed in beside Charlotte as though they had been sharing a bed their whole lives.

Charlotte surprised herself by falling asleep soon after. She did hear the second girl come in some time later, but was too tired to acknowledge her. All she wanted was sleep. Because in sleep she could return to her old life.

Charlotte was just drifting back to sleep when she heard a scream in some distant part of the manor. She sat up so suddenly that Mae awoke beside her and groaned.

"Lie still, would you?"

"I heard something."

"What?"

"Someone screaming."

"Better get used to it." Mae turned over, her long auburn plait landing on Charlotte's pillow. "Babies always gettin' born in the night here."

"What?"

"Never heard a woman in childbirth afore?"

"Oh. No, I haven't."

Mae didn't respond, and Charlotte surmised that the woman had fallen back to sleep already. Charlotte sat still, listening. But she heard no more and lay back down for a few more hours of fitful rest.

※

In the morning, Charlotte awoke to find herself alone in bed. She arose and dressed quickly in her grey day dress, then followed the sound of footsteps and feminine voices through the entry hall and into the large room she had passed through yesterday on her way to Mrs. Moorling's study. The room had doors on either end and was filled with tables—serving, apparently, as both dining room and workroom. At a long table against one wall, Charlotte followed the example of the others and filled a small plate with bread and a stringy hunk of cold mutton. She also poured herself a cup of weak but, thankfully, warm tea. She sat at a table alone, dreading the questions that would undoubtedly come from the other girls.

She had barely eaten half her bread when Gibbs, the assistant who had shown her to her room the night before, stopped before her, a ledger of some sort in her hands. She spoke with cool efficiency, her dull eyes glancing only briefly at Charlotte before returning to the bound ledger before her.

"What use are you, then?"

"Pardon?"

"What are you fit for? Laundry, cooking, sewing . . . ?"

"I am skilled enough with needlework, I suppose. Embroidery and the—"

"Very well. Mending stockings for you, then. Second table— off you go."

Charlotte took another bite of bread, skipped the congealed mutton altogether, and drank the rest of her tea. She took her time returning her cup and utensils to the sideboard and then, when she could think of no other excuse, stepped toward the table Gibbs had indicated. As she walked, she looked at the women's heads, pulled in close like a tightly cinched drawstring purse. She heard their whispers and laughter and feared they were talking about her. The first to raise her head and look in Charlotte's direction was a fair-haired woman with a long, angular face and surprisingly kind eyes.

"Here you are, love. Have a seat." She moved her darning things, clearing a place for Charlotte beside her.

"Thank you," Charlotte said quietly, eyes downcast.

"You're a new one."

"Yes." Charlotte forced a smile and bent to her task, trying to find a stocking with enough sound material left to mend.

"I'm Sally. Sally Mitchell." The blond woman smiled a toothy smile, her prominent front teeth protruding and not quite straight. Still it was a friendly smile. Unlike the narrow-eyed scrutiny she felt aimed at her from the others.

"I am Miss Charlotte . . . Smith."

"*Miss* Charlotte, is it?" a second woman broke in.

Charlotte glanced up quickly and took in a mop of tight brown curls, a sharp nose, and thin mouth.

"And I'm *Lady* Bess Harper." The woman affected a haughty voice and dramatically extended her hand as though for a kiss.

The other women laughed.

Bess slumped back in her chair and gave Charlotte a hard look. "I wonder you're here at Milkweed Manor, then, and not up the road."

"What do you mean?"

"Queen Charlotte's up the road at Bayswater Gate. I would have thought you'd go there, what with your name and all."

"Queen Charlotte's?" Charlotte repeated, confused.

Mae, her pretty bedmate from the night before, said, "Maybe she thinks one queen is enough in a place, and she wants to be ours."

"No, I . . ."

At this, Bess Harper leaned in, her thin lips disappearing in a frown of disdain. "Queen Charlotte's Lying-in Hospital. Telling me you never heard of it?"

"No. Should I?"

Bess looked pointedly at her middle, and Charlotte fought the urge to look away in shame. She threaded her needle and said weakly, "It is my first time."

"Sure it is," Mae said, "just like the lot of us."

Bess grinned wickedly, "Oh, me too. You never heard me say otherwise."

Sally leaned toward Charlotte and explained gently, "They only takes girls what haven't gotten themselves caught breeding before."

"They aim to reform us here," Bess said. "Put us on the straight and narrow and all that."

"One fall they can forgive." Sally sighed. "But two and you're done for."

"Yes," Charlotte said. "I believe the matron said the Manor Home was for 'deserving unmarried women with their first child.'"

"Deserving? I'm deserving all right," Bess said. "How 'bout the lot of you?"

Mae nodded her head. "Very, very."

"I believe we're all deserving a cup o' tea about now, don't you agree?" Bess said.

"Aye." Sally grinned and rose to fetch some. "And jam tarts besides."

From time to time, Charlotte glanced around the workroom, taking an inventory, of sorts, of the two dozen or more girls. She was curious as to why she hadn't seen the young girl who had shared her bed last night. Surely her time had not already come.

"Mae, might I ask the name of the other girl who shares our room?"

"Young Becky, you mean."

"Yes. I don't see her about, do I?"

"No. It's her morning, I'm afraid."

"Her morning? She's delivering right now?"

"Nay. Her morning to be examined by one of them blood and bone men, you know."

"Oh . . ."

"Better her than me." Mae shuddered.

"What do you mean?"

"You'll find out soon enough."

Gibbs approached the table and tapped her ledger with a blunt, ink-stained finger. "Miss Smith, you will be seen next."

"Pardon me?"

"For your examination. All the girls must be seen by one of our physicians."

"Oh. I see."

"He is just finishing up with another patient. Wait here, and I'll call you when he's ready." Gibbs strode briskly away.

Charlotte sat without moving, watching her go.

"Why, you look frightened half to death." Sally laid her hand on Charlotte's. "'Tis nothin' to be scared of."

"Unless she gets Dr. Preston," Mae said. "That man's like an orphan in a candy shop, all eyes and hands and lickin' his lips."

"S'pose he figgers, why not—ain't the jar been opened already?" Bess's sharp face was expressive. "A bit more used up won't do any harm."

Charlotte swallowed. "Are you suggesting this . . . Dr. Preston . . . takes advantage of the girls here?"

"I'm not suggesting a thing," Bess said. "Only sayin' you best watch your backside, underside, and all the rest like."

"He's never bothered me," Mae said.

"Well, you're not half the looker I am, are ya?"

"Well, then, I'm thankful I'm not."

"Have they no midwives here?" Charlotte asked.

Bess smirked. "Oh, a country girl, ey?"

"They once had some," Sally answered. "But not at present."

"Do they . . . ? I mean, I have never been 'examined' before. Not . . . like that. Do they . . . ? I mean, will I be asked to . . . ?"

"Take off your drawers?" Bess grinned.

Charlotte inclined her brow and swallowed nervously.

"I hate to break it to you, birdy, but when the babe comes, you won't be wearing drawers or petticoats or much of anything else for that matter."

"Hush, now," Sally interrupted. "Don't scare her more than she already is. Don't fret, Charlotte. They let you wear your nightdress, though 'tis likely to be spoilt."

"As for the examination," Mae said, "it depends on which man you get."

"Are there two physicians?"

"And a surgeon."

"The young physician is real gentleman-like," Mae said.

Bess snorted. "Green, you mean. He's barely more than a boy. I don't think he's ever seen a woman in all her natural glory."

"'Course he has," Mae said.

"Can't tell it the way he turned red as a robin when he looked me over last month." Bess crossed her arms smugly.

Mae ignored this. "But if you get the other, Dr. Preston, I'm afraid you're in for it," she said. "He seems to like dressing us girls down."

"Undressing us down, you mean."

Just then Charlotte recognized young Becky as she walked quickly through the room, head down, face flushed red, shawl and arms pulled tight across her bosom like a shield of wool and adolescent muscle. Sally followed Charlotte's gaze and clucked sympathetically.

"Becky, poor girl, come sit with us," Sally called. "Can I pour you a cup o' tea?"

But the girl only shook her head swiftly, eyes on the floor, as she walked past them and out the other door.

"Whatever is the matter?" Charlotte asked. "Is she ill?"

"She was right as rain before her appointment," Mae said.

Gibbs reappeared in the doorway and Charlotte's heart began thudding in her chest. The needle slipped in her sweating hands and she set her work down, wiping her palms across her lap. If this man did not conduct himself properly, she would give him a piece of her mind. Just because she had made one mistake did not mean she would make another. She took a deep breath. Still she could not calm herself. She felt so vulnerable, so removed from those who would protect her.

Gibbs walked toward her, and Charlotte took another deep breath. The woman's face was a mask of somber efficiency, but Charlotte thought she glimpsed some darker emotion there as well. Anger? Annoyance? Had Charlotte done something wrong? When Gibbs stopped at the table Charlotte rose from her chair.

"You may return to your work, Miss Smith. Dr. Preston has been . . . called away suddenly and cannot see you this morning after all. We shall reschedule for tomorrow."

"Oh, I see." Charlotte exhaled. "Thank you."

Gibbs turned on her heel and strode back toward the offices. Charlotte sank back into her chair, feeling foolishly relieved. Across the table, Sally winked at her.

Charlotte returned to her stitching but found herself thinking about her mother, who had spent a great deal of time in the company of surgeons and physicians in the final years of her life. Her mother had enjoyed a friendly camaraderie with her physicians and never feared their presence. Portly Dr. Webb, a respected and kindhearted doctor, had called on her so often as to become nearly a friend to the family. The only thing Charlotte had feared from him was a final diagnosis for her mother.

Dr. Webb had brought to the Doddington vicarage a succession of colleagues and apprentices. The colleagues were stuffy older men—Cambridge professors or renowned London physicians come to offer their opinion on her mother's condition. These men offered benign greetings to Charlotte in passing. The apprentices were young men who seemed determined to prove themselves, so most rarely condescended to speak with a young girl, and of course, Charlotte was never examined by any of them. Actually, Charlotte had been such a healthy girl that she had rarely been treated by anyone. Her mother had cared for her minor ailments, and she had never broken a bone. The only time she had seen a surgeon was when she had fallen into a fox hole while running through the sheep pasture behind the churchyard. Her parents had feared her ankle broken, but the surgeon—she didn't recall his name—declared it only sprained.

There was one apprentice who did speak with Charlotte, though granted, he was a bit older than most of Dr. Webb's apprentices. Daniel Taylor was his name. He was tall and very thin, with reddish-blond hair and the palest of skin. She could not think of him without both a smile and a painful wedge of guilt pressing against her stomach. She always seemed to say the wrong thing, and inevitably his boyish face would blush a deep apple red, a brighter hue than his rust-colored hair. But still, he must have admired her. She was certain he did, at least until her father made his disapproval so mercilessly clear. Mr. Taylor left Kent with barely a good-bye and, she feared, the impression that her own opinion of him matched her father's. Something the vicar had no doubt implied.

Charlotte pricked her finger with the needle and gasped. Eyes from around the table rose up in question. She held up her finger, the spot of blood growing big as a beetle. She smiled dolefully at the others. "One should never daydream with sharp implements in one's hand."

Bess rolled her eyes and the others returned to their work, but Charlotte found herself morbidly fascinated with the mounding blood. She lifted her finger and watched the blood run down into her palm. *Life-giving liquid,* she thought oddly. *God's milk.*

Poor woman! how can she honestly be breeding again?

—JANE AUSTEN, LETTER TO HER SISTER, 1808

CHAPTER 3

The next morning Charlotte awoke before either Mae or Becky, driven by nerves to prepare herself for the visit with the dreaded Dr. Preston. Would he really require her to remove her clothing? She shuddered. Worse yet, would he question her about how she came to be in this place?

She bathed herself with a rough cloth and cold water from the washbasin, cleaned her teeth, and brushed and pinned her hair. It crossed her mind that she should attempt to make herself appear as unattractive as possible, considering the girls' comments about Dr. Preston's character. But she doubted anyone could find her attractive in her present condition. Rather, she felt the need to arm herself with good grooming and her best dress, as though to show the man that she was not just another poor, uneducated girl he could manipulate. The thought pricked her conscience as surely as the needle had pricked her finger. Did she feel herself above the other girls? Yes, she admitted to herself, she did—even as she acknowledged the hypocrisy of the thought. *Forgive me.* Wasn't she just another poor—though not uneducated, certainly naïve—girl, alone in the world and at men's mercy? She shook off the unsettling thought. *Please protect me, almighty God.*

After breakfast, Charlotte again joined the other women at the sewing table. She glanced around nervously and was relieved when she didn't see Gibbs anywhere about. Perhaps the doctor was still indisposed. But no sooner had she begun her second stocking than Gibbs and her ledger appeared before Charlotte.

"The doctor will see you first this morning." Gibbs glanced at the clock on the mantel. "He is expected directly. I will let you know the moment he's ready."

Charlotte swallowed and nodded.

Bess and Mae exchanged knowing looks. Bess snorted and Mae covered a giggle with her freckled hand.

"Hush, now," Sally admonished gently. "Dr. Preston is gentleman-like most of the time. If you ask me, 'tis that other doctor what gives me the shivers."

"The old one or Dr. *Young?*"

"Young. He looks at you with those cold eyes and 'tis as if they've got no feelin' in them. Ice like. Like he's . . . gutting fish instead of tending people."

"Better cold eyes than warm, roamin' hands," Bess muttered.

"Here he comes," Mae whispered.

"Which one is it?" Bess shifted in her seat to try to see past Sally.

"Young," Mae supplied.

Charlotte turned her head with dread to look at the man entering. She took in a tall, thin man in coat and hat, with hard, pointed features and somber expression, neither much softened by the small round spectacles he wore. Even before she could get a good look at his face, something about his demeanor made her stomach clench. He removed his hat just as he pulled open a door partway down the passageway. When the sunlight from a nearby window shone on his rust-blond hair, a jolt of recognition stunned her. Mr. Taylor.

It had to be. Mr. Taylor, here? Now? To examine her? It could not be! She pressed her fingers to her brow and groaned as he swept out of view.

Sally leaned close. "Did I not tell you? Ice."

"At least it's not Preston," Mae said.

"I cannot," Charlotte whispered.

"You 'ave to, love," Sally soothed.

"But I . . . know him."

"Know him?" Bess asked sharply. "Biblically-speakin', you mean?"

"Of course not."

"I thought you said you hadn't been here before," Mae said.

"I haven't."

"Then how'd you know him?"

An inner plea for caution rose up in Charlotte and she changed tack. "Perhaps I am mistaken. Perhaps I do not know him." Perhaps her eyes had played tricks with her mind. After all, no one had actually mentioned the name Taylor.

"Dr. Taylor will see you now, Charlotte." The matron, Mrs. Moorling, appeared and her no-nonsense voice dampened Charlotte's spirit yet pulled her to her feet. "Dr. Preston has yet to appear this morning—I've sent Gibbs to find him. Come, come, we haven't all day." The woman should command armies rather than this sorry gaggle of expecting females. Hurrying to catch up, Charlotte followed the older woman down the passageway.

"Mrs. Moorling. I am sorry," Charlotte said, struggling to keep pace, "I don't mean to be difficult, but I really cannot be examined by Mr. Taylor. . . ."

"And why not?"

"Because I . . ." She hesitated. What would be gained by telling the matron that she knew Daniel Taylor? Would that somehow risk her anonymity? Would the matron ask more questions than Charlotte wanted to answer?

"It does not seem, well, proper. He is so young, and I . . ."

"Miss Smith. Dr. Taylor may look young, but I assure you he's well educated—more than most. He is also a married man and completely respectable. Again, more than most." Her voice carried a hard edge.

But Charlotte was still striving to grasp what the matron had just said. Mr. Taylor was married. Somehow that both troubled her and eased her mind greatly, for the present predicament as well as the past.

"If it were another physician, I might offer to stay in the room with you, but I have a long list of duties that require my attention and, I assure you, you are in perfectly good hands."

Terrifying choice of words, Charlotte thought.

Mrs. Moorling opened the office door for her, and taking a deep breath, Charlotte stepped inside.

He was sitting at a plain but large desk, reading some documents on its surface. She took a few steps forward, then stood silently before the desk, waiting for him to address her. He squinted at the paper before him and did not look up.

"Miss Smith, is it?"

"Ah . . . um . . ."

"Miss Charlotte . . ." He glanced up at her then, and his lips parted slightly. ". . . Smith?" The question in his tone was obvious, and in that moment in which he sat there, unmoving, staring at her, she saw the ice of his expressionless blue-green eyes melt and then freeze over again.

"Miss Smith. Do sit down." His eyes fell back to the papers, and he picked up his pen and dipped it into the ink.

She sat and primly folded her hands in her lap. Did he not recognize her after all? She felt relieved yet mildly hurt at the thought. Was she so changed in the years since they had last seen each other? He had changed but was clearly the man she had once known. His hair was a bit thinner at his forehead, the rust-brown stubble on his cheeks more noticeable, the shoulders broader, but his face was still as angular as ever. What had changed most were his eyes. Gone was that teasing spark she remembered so fondly, and all warmth with it, or so it seemed.

"Age . . . twenty?"

She found her voice. "Yes," she whispered.

"And this is your first pregnancy?"

She cringed with shame at the baldness of his words. "Yes."

"When was your last monthly flow?"

Never had a man broached such a topic with her! Never had a woman, for that matter. Such things were not spoken of. She was too stunned to speak.

At her obvious hesitancy, he rose to his feet, but his eyes seemed trained beyond her. "Look here, I heard your little conversation with Mrs. Moorling. If you'd rather wait and see Dr. Preston, that is perfectly all right by me. I shall tell Mrs. Moorling myself."

"No!" The urgency with which she spoke surprised them both, and he silently sat back down. Embarrassed by her outburst as well as the whole mortifying situation, Charlotte sat staring at her hands, yet felt the man's silent scrutiny.

She took a deep breath and whispered, "The second of January."

She heard the scratching of his quill.

"And Smith. That is your . . . married . . . name?"

She swallowed, completely humiliated. This man who, she believed, had once admired her was now—if he recognized her at all—thanking the Lord above that her father had so thoroughly discouraged him. And she couldn't blame him. "I am . . . not married."

Dr. Taylor hesitated, eyes on the paper, then put down his pen. He looked up at her, his professional facade gone, his expression earnest.

"Good heavens, Charlotte, what on earth are you doing here?"

Charlotte sighed. "I should think that painfully obvious."

He winced. "Forgive me. I only meant this is not a place for you, a girl with your family, your connections."

She opened her mouth, but the words "I no longer have either" wouldn't form over the hot coal lodged in her chest and the tears pooling in her eyes. She bit her lip to try to gain control over herself. She would not seek pity.

"As bad as all that, then?"

She bit her lip again but only nodded.

"I am very sorry to hear it. I suppose your father, being a clergyman, took it very hard."

Again, she nodded.

"Still, there's not a one of us who hasn't made some foul error or other. All like sheep astray and all that."

She could only look at him, speechless.

"I've had a taste of your father's rejection, if you remember. I mean no disrespect, but I cannot say I'd wish that on anyone, much less you."

She managed a slight smile through her tears.

"I don't wish to insult you, but I assume that every attempt has been made to garner some arrangement, some responsibility or recompense?"

"Please. There is nothing to be done, and even if there were, I should not like to pursue it."

"Still, there are legal actions in such cases, if the man—"

She shook her head.

"You claim no injury, then?"

She closed her eyes against the shame her answer brought with it. "I cannot."

"Still, though you be a party to it, there remain courses of action to secure your support."

"Please. I do not wish to speak of it further. You can be assured that my father and my uncle, a solicitor himself, have discussed these matters with me thoroughly. Exhaustively."

"I am sorry."

"Everyone has urged, even begged me to reveal the man so they might *work* on him."

"You have not told them who the man is?"

She shook her head.

"Why on earth not?"

"Because it will do me and my child absolutely no good . . . and it will harm others."

"A married man, then?"

She swallowed. "He is now."

"Miss Lamb. Charlotte. Have you considered—"

"Mr. Taylor, excuse me, *Dr.* Taylor, I have already told you far more than I should. More than I've told anyone else." She looked up at him, then back down at her hands. "You always did have that effect on me."

"Make you chatter on? I'd rather have had a different effect on young ladies in those days."

She smiled in spite of herself. "Then let us speak of it no more. Though I do appreciate your concern."

"Yes, well." He cleared his throat. "We have an examination to conduct."

"Yes," she murmured, feeling her heart begin pounding again.

"Well, first of all, I need to ask you a few questions about your medical history and the like."

"All right."

"If I remember correctly, you were a most healthy girl. Any medical problems since? Illnesses, serious injury?"

She shook her head.

"And, since your . . . condition. Any pain, light-headedness, swelling of extremities?"

She thought of her ankles, not as thin as they once were. "Nothing to speak of."

"You have been seen by another physician prior to coming here?"

"Only one time."

"Dr. Webb, was it?"

She shook her head again. "Father wouldn't hear of me seeing anyone local. He was sure word would get out. I saw a surgeon, a Mr. Thompkins, when I was in Hertfordshire with my aunt."

"And how long ago was this?"

"Three...nearly four months now. He was brought in only to confirm that I was indeed, well, as I am."

"Well, here we examine patients weekly once they're as far along as you are."

"I see."

"Now, I notice that you are showing surprisingly little for someone as progressed as you are."

"Which has been a blessing until now."

"Yes, I can understand that. But, have you had difficulty eating, keeping foods down?"

"I haven't much appetite lately, but I do try to eat."

"All right. Now I do need to do a physical exam. To start, I will auscultate you."

"Pardon me?"

"Sorry. Listen to your heart."

He tapped the tall table. "Please, have a seat here."

She complied and sat as straight as she could, rearranging her skirts around her, self-conscious of her bulging middle, her plain dress, her hair escaping its practical pinning. She had a sudden flash of memory, of peering through the keyhole as a young girl and seeing Dr. Webb lying over her mother's body, head on her chest. Charlotte had been quite shocked and had burst into the room, ready to defend her mother's honor.

"What are you doing?" she'd cried, her affront ringing in the room. Dr. Webb sat up quickly, stunned at her outburst. But mother only smiled gently. "It's all right, my dear. Dr. Webb is only listening to my heart, to see if the old thing is still working."

Understanding dawned on the man's kind face and he, too, smiled gently at her. "Come here, if you like, Charlotte. Would you like to listen to your mother's heart?"

She nodded, all seriousness, and walked to the bed. She sat beside Dr. Webb and laid her ear on her mother's bosom.

"A bit higher—there. Do you hear it?"

Charlotte had closed her eyes and listened, and there, a dull *ta-toom, ta-toom, ta-toom.* "I hear it!" she'd declared proudly, relieved in more ways than one.

As delightful as the memory was, when Charlotte imagined Dr. Taylor pressing his head to *her* chest, her palms began sweating.

From his case, he extracted a wooden tube, a device she had never seen before.

"A physician friend of my wife's made this. He's still working to perfect the design. Still, it's amazing how much better I can hear with this simple tube than I can with my ear alone."

He stepped closer and bent near. He looked into her face. "It also lends a bit of propriety, which patients seem to appreciate." He lifted one side of his mouth in an awkward grin, then bent to his task. Charlotte took a deep breath and held it, aware of his nearness, aware of the strangeness of the situation—to be alone with Daniel Taylor, unchaperoned, so close to him—all of which would be highly inappropriate in any other setting. She felt the tube press against her chest, just above her left breast, and she involuntarily started. The device was not terribly long, so he had to bring his head to within six or seven inches of her body to listen. She released a ragged breath and drew in a shallow one in return, finding it difficult to breathe.

"Fine. Now I will attempt to hear the heart of the fetus as well. Has the babe been active?"

"Yes, quite."

He pressed the tube with firm pressure against her abdomen and listened intently. He repositioned it slightly and listened again. "There he is." He listened a moment longer. "Strong and steady."

Charlotte smiled. "Do you call all unborn babes 'he'?"

"I don't know. Don't think so."

"I do think it is a boy. Just a feeling I have. I suppose all ladies in confinement say such things?"

"Yes, and they are often right."

"Are they?"

He grinned. "About half of the time." Then his grin faded. "Well, next I would normally palpate the"—he waved his hands over her abdomen—"uh . . . area. And examine . . . other areas as well." He swallowed, "However, I think, considering your general health and the quickening of the babe, that this has been sufficient for today." He stepped back, and Charlotte slumped a bit on the table, relieved.

A soft knock sounded at the door, and Dr. Taylor leapt eagerly to answer it. Charlotte couldn't see whom he spoke with through the partially opened door, but she could hear much of the muted conversation.

"You're wanted above stairs."

"Is there a problem?"

"I'm afraid . . . quite upset."

"I see. I shall be up directly."

He shut the door and looked back at Charlotte. "I'm wanted elsewhere, Miss Lamb—excuse me, Miss Smith."

Charlotte lowered herself from the table.

"Gibbs will alert you to our next appointment."

She nodded.

"Good day," he said, and turned to leave.

"Good day," she answered, but he was already gone.

The poor collect milkweed down and with it fill their beds,
especially their children's, instead of feathers.

—PETER KALM, 1772

CHAPTER 4

Charlotte read the letter in the garden, which, mess though it was, offered her a bit of privacy—something sorely lacking within the manor itself. Gibbs had handed it to her with a simple, "Letter, miss." And while Charlotte should have been pleased to receive it, especially because the fine, feminine handwriting was clearly her aunt's, she trembled as she carefully peeled it open. Somehow she knew it bore ill tidings. What else could she expect at present? Surely her father hadn't forgiven her, asking through Aunt Tilney for Charlotte to come home. She knew this, and still her hands trembled as she read.

My dear niece,

It is with deep sadness that I write to you today. Your father has asked that I sever all connection with you, something I am loathe to do. You know I hold you in the highest esteem and dearest affection, positions unaffected by recent revelations. I hope you will in time learn to forgive your father. He has always held the good opinion of others too dearly, as you well know, and I fear this has laid him very low.

There is some small hope, I believe, that your sister may secure the affection of a certain gentleman, whom you well know, before news reaches the ears of those who would compel him to withdraw any connection with your family. Your sister, especially, longs to conceal the unhappy truth as long as possible.

It pains me to write so plainly, but there it is. Your father bids me to beseech you to confine yourself away from the public eye, and to conceal your identity until an engagement is secure. It is too much to hope this could extend past a longed-for wedding date, but all put every confidence that the gentleman's long association with your sister might withstand, nay, even overshadow, other less happy events.

Do not give up hope, my dear. There is goodness in your father, and I will fervently pray that he will soften toward you in time. For now, I have little choice but to abide his edict. Perhaps if your dear uncle stood with me, but alas, he feels it is not our place to come between father and child. You know he would do all he could to assist you were he only allowed to do so.

Still, I cannot rest without at least offering this olive branch. Likely you have been too upset to think too far into the future, but I am plagued with worry over your situation. I offer you this—while not grand nor fashionable, it will at least assure a roof and bed and food to eat once your time in London is at an end.

As you may recall, I have in Crawley an elderly aunt. You can well imagine how old she is if I, your aunt, describe her thusly. Still, she lives in a snug cottage a short distance from the village proper on Crawley's High Street. I have not seen her these many months, but at Michaelmas she was in good health and spirits. I have every confidence she would welcome you and that the two of you would get on well together. I daresay she would be quite happy for some companionship. Her own grown son lives in Manchester and, as I understand, rarely visits. I shall write her directly and introduce you.

If some impediment to this arrangement arises, I shall find some way to let you know. Otherwise, my dear, this must be my last letter, at least for the foreseeable future. My heart aches to *think of it. Rest assured, you shall never be far from my thoughts or prayers.*

Your Loving Aunt

Charlotte wiped at the tears with her free hand, then quickly refolded the letter and tucked it into her dress pocket. She strode back inside the manor and into the workroom, determinedly putting on a cheerful face.

"What is that you're working on, Becky?" she asked, sitting beside the young girl at a fabric-strewn table.

"'Tis a swaddling blanket, mum."

She eyed the square of coarse cotton. "How nice. Will you have it done in time, do you think?"

"Oh! 'Tisn't for my own babe. Least I don't think 'tis."

"Oh?"

"Same as your mending stockings for the girls here, I'm stitchin' blankets for the foundlings next door."

Charlotte looked in the direction of the girl's nod.

"You didn't know about the foundling ward?" Becky asked.

Charlotte shook her head. "I did wonder what was in the other wing."

"Sure and what did you think happened to all the babes born here?" Bess asked brusquely, coming to the table with a teacup in her hand.

"I don't know. I had not thought . . ."

"They just keep infants here 'til they're weaned," Becky explained. "Then they're moved to the big foundling hospital up on Guildford Street."

"Don't some girls take their infants home with them?"

"Is that what *you're* going to do?" Bess asked skeptically, sitting down across from her.

"No. Not home. I am not . . . quite sure where yet."

Two other girls walked to the table together, tall flaxen-haired Sally towering over petite auburn-haired Mae. They sat down on either side of Charlotte.

"Well, I know where I'll be," Becky said. "Back in the workhouse soon as my time's up."

"But . . . what about . . ."

Bess broke in, "Don't you be judging her or any of us."

"I did not mean to. I am only surprised."

"Some of us haven't any choice," Sally said quietly, eyes on her tea.

"But . . . to leave one's child in the care of strangers. It is something I could never do."

"Oh, don't be too sure," Bess said. "Never can tell what a body might do for love or money."

"Or to keep body and soul together," Mae added.

"My mum can barely feed my brothers and sisters," Becky said. "She sure don't need another mouth to feed."

"How old are you, Becky?" Charlotte asked.

"Fourteen."

"So young."

Becky shrugged. "About my mum's age when she had me."

"And you, Sally," Charlotte asked, "what will you do?"

"I already had me boy two months ago now. I'm a wet nurse in the foundling ward. Didn't you know?"

"No, I . . ."

"Guess I haven't me figure back if you thought me still in my lying-in! I best lay off those jam tarts."

Bess and Mae laughed.

"Forgive me, Sally."

"Never you mind, Miss Charlotte. I've been a big girl me whole life—I'm used to such."

"Your boy, is he . . . ?"

"I'm blessed to have a sister who looks after my wee lamb. I'm nursing here until I find a better post."

"A post?"

"Wet nurse, o' course. Pays good, sleepin' in the nice warm nursery of some fine house. Yes, that's the life for me."

"But who nurses your own child?"

"I told you. Me own sister. She's always breeding and has a little ankle-biter right now what's got her milk flowin' but good. 'Tis no bother to her to nurse another."

"You're lucky," Mae said. "My sister had to put her child out to take a wet nurse post. One of them baby farms, like, where the nurse had three or four others to feed. Poor thing near starved to death."

"Then why would she do it? Why leave her own child to nurse a stranger?"

"A bit daft this one," Bess murmured under her breath—but loud enough for all to hear.

"The *money*, dearie," Sally explained. "If she don't work, she starves—and her own child with her."

"I'm sorry. I suppose I have never known that depth of want. I could never do that, leave my own to nurse someone else's baby."

"Careful what you say, Charlotte," Sally warned gently. "I'll wager a year ago you never thought you'd find yourself in a place like this either."

"You are quite right."

"How . . . did . . . you end up here, Charlotte?"

"Same way as everyone else I suppose." But she could feel her face heat with a fierce blush.

"Somehow I doubt that," Mae said. "Who was the bloke? A baron, was it? Some scheming lord what promised you a wedding?"

"Maybe she fell in love with the footman and her father forbade them marry," Becky said wistfully.

"Girls, don't tease Charlotte so," Sally urged. "You can see plain as anything she's a lady."

Bess snorted. "*Was* a lady more like."

Sally put her hand over Charlotte's. "Don't listen to her, Charlotte. You're still a lady in my eyes. All your handsome words and polite ways . . ."

"Handsome words and polite ways won't get her very far 'round here," Mae said.

"Won't make a bit o' difference when her time comes neither. I can just hear her now." Bess began imitating an upper-crust accent. "I say, Dr. Preston, would you be so kind as to remove this melon from my middle?"

Mae joined in. "Pardon me, but the pain is such that I fear I must yell my fool head off."

The others laughed good-naturedly, and Charlotte couldn't take offense. She did continue to blush, however. And the first prickling of fear for the delivery itself began to work its way through her being.

%

Charlotte was just about to blow out the bedside candle that night when the sound of a scream snaked beneath the door. Beside her, Mae groaned and young Becky slept on. Pulling her dressing gown around herself, Charlotte arose and stepped tentatively out into the passageway, holding the candle before her. She paused, listening. The draft in the old manor led the flame in an erratic, swaying dance. She heard no more screams, but she did hear footsteps approaching. She hesitated. Should she duck back into her room? How foolish! She was doing nothing wrong. No doubt some girl was in the pains of labour somewhere in the manor. Dr. Taylor appeared at the end of the passage his face drawn, rust-stubbled and weary.

"Is everything all right?" she asked.

"Miss Lamb. You startled me."

"Forgive me. . . . I thought I heard someone crying out."

"Did you?"

"Yes. Is someone delivering?"

"Um . . . no. False alarm as it turns out."

"Oh, I see. Are you quite all right, Mr.—excuse me—Dr. Taylor. I'm afraid that will take some getting used to."

"That's all right. And . . . yes, I am well, thank you. And you?"

She nodded. "Are you always here this late?"

"Yes. Though not always awake, thankfully. I keep a small apartment above stairs here. Makes night duty less interminable."

"You are very dedicated."

He looked at her sharply, as though weighing the sincerity of her statement.

"Truly." She smiled to reassure him. "It is a comfort to know there's a physician about the place."

He smiled then too. "Even if the physician is me?"

"Yes. I have heard some things about the other man that are not comforting in the least." She said it lightly but saw his eyes widen and his mouth set in a hard line.

"What are you implying? Wait. Let us step into Mrs. Moorling's office, where we won't disturb anyone."

"Very well." She followed him to the matron's office beyond the workroom.

"You were saying?" he prompted.

"Well, from the sound of it, the girls here do not trust him, in fact they are quite frightened of him."

"Frightened? That is absurd. He isn't perfect, I realize, but is certainly not as bad as all that."

"I'm sorry, I am only repeating what I've been told."

"Well, in the future I suggest you don't besmirch a man's reputation based on rumor alone."

She looked at him, stung. His reaction seemed too strong, and she wondered if there was more at play here than collegial loyalty. "You are quite right. But I had no reason not to believe them. In fact, I saw one young girl shaking when she took leave of Dr. Preston."

"Preston?" he asked, clearly surprised.

"Yes." *Who did he think I was referring to?*

He hesitated, seeming to study his shoes.

Charlotte felt compelled to continue. "Forgive me—are the two of you friends?"

"Colleagues certainly. Are you implying that he behaves . . . inappropriately with his patients?"

"Yes, or at the very least humiliates them."

"Well, humiliation is no crime. It's difficult to maintain modesty in such situations. As far as the other . . . well, I'd wager it's just gossip, but if you personally have any difficulty whatsoever with Dr. Preston, please let me know immediately."

"Thank you. I shall."

The tension in his face faded, and they stood there for a moment in mildly awkward silence, Charlotte trying to think of a way to excuse herself, when she saw the side of his mouth lift in a boyish smirk.

"And what do they say about *me*?"

She smiled at him, then said imperiously, "Oh, you are the worst of the lot. Ice, they say. Distant. Impersonal. One girl compared your bedside manner to that of a man gutting fish."

His brows rose. "Dreadfully sorry I asked."

She regarded him a moment, then said tentatively, "You do seem changed. Though I suppose that is only natural after so many years."

His expression became somber indeed. "If you had seen the things I have—death, piteous creatures, loved ones lost . . ." He hesitated, seemingly adrift in thoughts too bleak to share. She guessed he was speaking of more than his medical duties alone, of losses infinitely more personal.

"Yes," he continued, "perhaps I have distanced myself. Become harder."

"Colder," she added helpfully. "More aloof."

"There are worse things." He looked directly at her, and Charlotte ducked her head.

"Miss Lamb, I did not mean . . . I was not referring to you, to your condition."

And there he was again. The Mr. Taylor of old, teasing but reassuring, comforting her.

Charlotte kept her eyes lowered. "I confess when I first saw you here, I was quite mortified."

"I can imagine."

"I think now the worst of the shock has passed, I shall be glad to have a friendly face about."

"A cold face, you mean."

"One that improves upon acquaintance. Or in our case, reacquaintance."

"I am glad to hear it."

Charlotte suddenly had the disquieting thought that he might think her forward, so she asked, "Might I have the privilege of meeting Mrs. Taylor sometime?"

"Well, I . . . I don't think . . . ."

"Of course. Forgive me. I am in no position to be introduced to anyone. How foolish of me."

"Miss Lamb, I—"

"It is Miss Smith for now. Good night, Dr. Taylor."

She left the office and walked quickly down the passageway, embarrassment burning at her ears. *Stupid girl*, she remonstrated herself. She imagined Dr. Taylor saying to his wife, *My dear, please meet the ruined Miss Charlotte Lamb. Can you believe I once admired her?*

If the milk of a wet nurse could give a child a loud laugh
or a secretive disposition, what kind of influence
would be derived from the milk of a goat or a cow?

—JANET GOLDEN, *A SOCIAL HISTORY OF WET NURSING IN AMERICA*

CHAPTER 5

The next few weeks passed slowly and Charlotte grew weary of stitching. She stood before the matron's desk, feeling like a wayward schoolgirl.

"Mrs. Moorling. I wonder," she began, "might I help in the foundling ward?"

The matron's eyes narrowed with near suspicion. "Why?"

"Well, I . . . I am sure sewing is no doubt beneficial. It is only that I thought . . . well, with my own child on the way, some experience with infants might do me good."

Still the woman stared at her.

"I might enjoy it, actually."

Mrs. Moorling shook her head, an odd bleakness in her eyes. "I would not plan on it."

"Then I may not—?"

"You may. I only meant that you should not plan to enjoy it. You really are naïve, aren't you?"

"I suppose so. Still I see no harm. . . ."

"Go on with you, then. Use the entrance through the scullery. Be sure the door latches behind you."

"But what shall I do once I get there?"

"Just ask for Mrs. Krebs. She oversees the foundlings and is always in need of another pair of arms."

Charlotte thanked the matron, then walked through the dining room and down the scullery passage. The large white door with an old-fashioned swing bolt stood at attention, its X-shaped cross boards reminding Charlotte of a guard with his arms crossed, barring the way. She swallowed back the silly notion and reached for the bolt, only to have the door swing open in her face. Charlotte stepped back quickly as Sally and another girl came through the door, Sally balancing a tray of used plates and teacups in her hands.

"Oh, Miss Charlotte! Sorry, love, nearly ran you down."

"Hello, Sally." Charlotte looked up at her. She had never known such a tall woman.

"You're not thinking of goin' in, are you?"

"Yes. I was."

"Well, I suppose Mrs. Krebs might need some mending done, or some cleaning."

"Could I not help with the children? I have never been around babies and I should like to learn."

Sally stood silently a moment, studying Charlotte seriously. Then swiftly, she swiveled and placed the tea tray in the other girl's hands. "Take this into the kitchen for me, Martha. There's a love."

The girl disappeared and Sally was still staring down at Charlotte, her frequent smile noticeably absent.

"If you're set on it, I had better go in with you."

"All right . . . thank you," Charlotte murmured, but she was confused.

Sally took Charlotte by the arm and led her through the doorway, latching the door firmly behind her. Then she escorted Charlotte down a whitewashed passage, through a small galley, and into an entry hall.

"This is where the babies first come in. Admitted, they calls it." She pointed to an odd revolving shelf built into the outer wall. "See that turn there?"

"Yes. It looks like one we had at home between the galley and kitchen. The servants used it to pass through dirty dishes."

"'Tisn't dirty dishes passing through there. 'Tis babies what no one wants. This way the poor mother don't even need to show her face. She puts her baby on the shelf and rings the bell. Then Mrs. Krebs turns the shelf and the baby comes inside."

"Poor things."

"Yes. 'Tis a desperate girl who abandons her baby."

Charlotte had meant the babies left behind were the "poor things," but she didn't argue.

"Sometimes mothers what's starving leave their babies in the turn, then come to the front door soon after, asking for work as a wet nurse, hoping to feed their own babe and get food and some small pay in the bargain."

"But why would they do that?"

"'Cause they's starvin' or have no place to live, no money, no job. How can they work with a newborn to feed every few hours?"

"Oh."

"Come on."

They walked down the long passageway, past a dim room on the left filled with cribs and another room filled with rocking chairs. On nearly every one sat a woman nursing an infant, sometimes two babes at once. Charlotte had never seen a woman do such a thing, and though most were fairly well covered with blanket or babe, Charlotte felt her cheeks redden at the intimate sight.

"And see them doors on the other side of the passage? That's where we nurses take turns sleepin'."

"Sally! Good, you're back. I need your help." An older woman in her late fifties stepped forward, her ash-grey hair in a loose knot at the back of her neck and a large stained apron over her ample figure in a simple black dress.

"Mrs. Krebs, this is Miss Charlotte Smith."

"How do you do, Mrs. Krebs." Charlotte stepped forward, offering her hand. "I would like to help too, if I might."

Glancing back down the passage, the woman didn't seem to notice her hand. "Well, you're just in time to help with the goats."

"Goats?"

"Yes, yes, follow me."

Charlotte looked at Sally, who sighed and nodded and followed Mrs. Krebs, who was already marching purposefully toward the end of the passageway.

"You were brought up on a farm, weren't you, Sally?" Mrs. Krebs asked over her shoulder.

"Aye."

"And you, Miss Smith?"

"No, I'm afraid not."

"No matter, a pair of willing hands is always welcome." She stopped at a small table beside a closed door. "But do put on these masks and gloves. Dr. Taylor's orders."

Sally began pulling tight leather gloves onto her long fingers and explained, "This is the syphilis ward, Miss Charlotte. All these babies have syphilis and must be kept away from the rest."

Mrs. Krebs handed Charlotte another pair of gloves and began tying a cotton mask over her own nose and mouth.

Charlotte hesitated.

"Is it safe? For my own baby, I mean."

"Dr. Taylor assures me the nasty business is only transmitted by direct contact with the sores," Mrs. Krebs said. "'Course these poor lambs caught it from their own mothers afore they was even born."

Mrs. Krebs pushed open the door and walked in. Sally and Charlotte paused at the threshold, taking in the scene.

Cribs filled the room and cries filled the air. In one corner, a nun was standing hunched over a crib, trying to get an infant to suckle from some sort of tube. Dr. Taylor stood beside her, arms behind his back, quietly instructing the woman. He looked up when the door opened. His eyes narrowed for a moment when they lit on her.

A knock came on a wide, stable-like door on the other side of the room.

"That's Rob now, I wager."

Old Mrs. Krebs strode with impressively youthful vigor past the cribs with their pitiful infants. She opened the door and a young man came in with two goats, one black and one white, at his heels.

"What are they doing with the goats?" Charlotte whispered.

"You'll see," Sally said and stepped into the room.

Charlotte, still concerned, stood in the doorway and watched a sight she would never forget. The goats pranced with seeming eagerness into the room, bleating as they came. The black one trotted down one row of beds, the white down the other. Suddenly, the white goat jumped nimbly up on top of the first cot and gingerly straddled the infant. Charlotte gasped. Sally stepped forward and helped lift and position the waiting infant onto the goat's teat. The hungry babe latched on and began nursing. Charlotte was stunned, horrified, yet fascinated at the same time. She stepped forward tentatively and stood behind Sally, peering over her bent back.

"Why in the world . . . ?" Charlotte began.

"No one will nurse these poor souls. The syphilis is catching that way. They try to feed the babes by hand, but it ain't natural like. This ain't either, but it seems to work a bit better."

Mrs. Krebs, who was helping another swaddled infant suckle the black goat, said from her position a few strides away, "I was as stunned as you no doubt are, Miss Smith, when Dr. Taylor first suggested it. Thought he was off his bean. Said the Frenchies do it all the time and it might be worth a go here as well."

As Charlotte watched, the white goat jumped down and moved to a cot at the end of the row and eagerly hopped up again. Sally followed, again helping the waiting babe reach the goat's teat with her gloved hands.

Dr. Taylor came to stand next to Charlotte. "It's as if the goats actually know and remember which babes are hers to nurse. The white one always feeds these and the black the others. Even if we put the babe in a different crib, the goat finds her own to feed."

"Amazing."

"It is, isn't it? Still, it's a pity. Most of these children have little hope of seeing the month through."

"Really?" Charlotte felt herself take a step back even before she realized what she was doing.

"It's a sad business. But we try."

Charlotte's cheery visions of singing lullabies to healthy pink babies seemed foolish now. She felt as though she might be ill.

"Can nothing be done?" she asked.

"Well. Pray, of course. And thank God for goats."

The [milkweed] root, which is the only part used, is a counter-poison,
both against the bad effects of poisonous herbs
and the bites and stings of venomous creatures.

—NICHOLAS CULPEPPER, 17TH CENTURY HERBALIST

CHAPTER 6

A few hours later, Daniel was standing in the manor hall directing the flow of volunteers bearing crates and bundles of donated supplies. He looked up and saw Charlotte walking toward him, coming from the direction of the foundling ward. He immediately stepped forward, hoping to shield her from view.

"Miss Smith," he said, keeping his voice low, "might I suggest a sojourn in the back garden? A horde of ladies-aid types are swarming about the place, and I understand several are from Kent."

Her eyes widened as she glanced at the hall beyond him, expression sober.

"Thank you, I shall."

She turned at once and quickly retreated the way she had come. But not quite quickly enough.

Daniel turned and nearly collided with a thin-faced socialite in burgundy velvet and plumed hat.

"That woman you were just speaking with—that was Charlotte Lamb, was it not?" She craned her neck to see past him.

"Lamb? I do not believe we have anyone here by that name."

"Yes, yes, that was Charlotte. I am sure of it."

He shrugged. "There are so many here today, with your group, as well as our staff and volunteers . . ."

"But you were just speaking with her."

"Was I? I believe the last lady I spoke with was a volunteer, donating blankets. She is not with you?"

"No."

"Well, we are blessed to have so many generous souls such as yourselves come to visit. I cannot keep track."

She opened her mouth to speak again, her expression clearly skeptical. But instead of questioning him further, her mouth curved in a feline smile. "I know what I saw. Or shall we say, *whom.*" She turned on her heel and swept across the hall.

❧

Charlotte walked through the manor's garden, breathing in the outdoor air, forcing away the images she had seen in the syphilis ward. Reaching into her dress pocket, she ran her fingers over the letter from her aunt, which she carried with her as a comfort, a sort of lifeline. She knew whom her aunt was referring to in her veiled reference to Bea's "gentleman" suitor.

Charlotte remembered well the first time she had met William Bentley. That is, the first time in many years. She had seen him on several occasions when they were young children, but not for a number of years since, when he unexpectedly appeared at their drawing room door three or four years ago.

"Mr. William Bentley," Tibbets had announced and then backed from the room, pulling the doors closed as she went.

The young man who stood before them was slight and not much taller than the maid who had shown him in. He was about eighteen, Charlotte estimated, a year above her own age at the time, though he bore the confidence of someone far older.

"How do you do?" he asked, hat in hand. Tibbets had forgotten to take it.

Charlotte glanced at Bea, saw from the frown line between her brows that she had no idea who the young man was. Charlotte glanced next at her father, whose place it was to greet the man and make introductions, but he wore an expression that would have been comically similar to his daughter's, were not the situation so awkward.

"Bentley . . . Bentley . . ." he began, obviously trying to place the mildly familiar name.

"You remember, Father," Charlotte offered. "Mr. Bentley is nephew to Mr. Harris."

"Is he now? Oh, yes, I think I remember hearing something of a nephew. Let's see, Harris has an older brother . . ."

"Sister, actually, Father. Mrs. Eliza Bentley. Of Oxford."

"That's right, thank you." The young man smiled at Charlotte. "You seem to know the family quite well, Miss—?"

"Charlotte Lamb."

"Of course." He nodded, his eyes widened in a knowing expression that left her feeling unsettled.

Her father stood at that moment, casting a disapproving glance at her. "I am the Reverend Mr. Gareth Lamb, Vicar of the Parish Church of Doddington, Dedicated to the Beheading of St. John the Baptist."

Mr. Bentley's eyebrows rose. "How unusual." A hint of a smile lifted the corner of his mouth, but her father did not seem to notice.

"Yes, it is. One of the rarest dedications in England, shared only with the Church of Trimmingham in Norfolk."

"Ahh . . ." Mr. Bentley uttered the universal sound of the duly impressed. When her father's grave expression remained fixed, Mr. Bentley continued, "I am very pleased to make your acquaintance. My uncle speaks highly of you, sir."

"As I do of him. And may I present my elder daughter, Miss Lamb."

Beatrice merely dipped her head.

"And Charlotte has already introduced herself," her father added as he reclaimed his seat. He tossed a sour smile toward Charlotte but did not quite look at her. "Do sit down, Mr. Bentley."

"I thank you."

"Of Oxford, sir?" her father asked. "The university or environs?"

"Both, of late."

"You must know my friend Lord Elton, then. He is quite the patron of Pembroke."

Charlotte winced at her father's boast. Lord Elton was Uncle Tilney's friend, not his.

"Who has not heard of him? His son is also quite well-known. I have not had the pleasure of meeting either man, I'm afraid. My studies keep me quite occupied."

"Excellent. And what will you take up?"

He hesitated, then oddly looked at Charlotte, then Beatrice. "I have yet to make up my mind, sir."

"The church is as noble a profession as you might aspire to, sir, if you have a taste for servitude and humility."

William Bentley smiled, clearly amused, then straightened his expression into sobriety. "I'm afraid I haven't your fortitude, good sir. Nor your modesty."

"Well, you are yet young." Her father sighed. "I'm afraid the church calls to me even now." He pushed himself cumbrously to his feet. "I'm to meet the churchwardens to discuss repairs to the south chapel and nave. If you will excuse me."

Mr. Bentley rose.

"No need to get up on my account. Do stay and have your visit with the ladies. Beatrice, perhaps you could play something for Mr. Bentley?"

"It seems a bit early in the day . . ."

"Oh, would you, Miss Lamb? I'd be delighted to hear it."

Bea looked at Mr. Bentley as if gauging his sincerity. "Very well."

Their father left and Bea walked slowly across the room and sat at the pianoforte. She flipped through some pages of music on its ledge and began playing a moody piece, the somber tone darkening her already stern countenance. Then, seeming to remember her guest, she stopped.

"Forgive me, that's not quite fitting."

"Quite powerful though," Mr. Bentley said, his eyes full of admiration.

Tibbets knocked once and entered. "Begging your pardon, Miss Charlotte, but Digger says it's time."

Charlotte rose, but Bea answered for her. "Tibbets, we have a guest, as you know. Tell him to wait."

"Actually, I will go," Charlotte said gently. "Thank you, Tibbets. Tell young Higgins I shall be out directly."

"Very good, miss."

Bea shook her head in disapproval. She spoke to Mr. Bentley but her gaze remained narrowed on her sister. "Charlotte seems to love nothing better than playing with dirt and plants all day. She spends more time out of doors than in."

"Your grounds here are lovely," Mr. Bentley allowed. "But why go out of doors when there is so much beauty to appreciate within?" He smiled significantly at Bea.

Charlotte bit back a wry smile of her own. "I am sorry, Bea, but I did ask Ben Higgins to fetch me just as soon as the tree arrived for the churchyard. Forgive me, Mr. Bentley. You must think us terribly rude, first Father rushing off, and now me."

"Think nothing of it, Miss Charlotte. My visit was unplanned, after all."

"Thank you. Perhaps you might come again. Are you staying with your uncle long?"

"I'm not sure. A few days at least."

"Then please do call again." It wasn't Charlotte's place to invite him, she knew, and she could feel Bea's silent censure from across the room.

But the young man smiled brightly. "Thank you. I shall."

He bowed to Charlotte and she smiled at him. Bea glared at her over the man's bent head. Charlotte simply shrugged, then left the room.

Charlotte sat down in the entry hall, on the bench between the drawing room and the outside door. She leaned down to remove her slippers and begin the arduous task of fastening all the buttons on her calfskin gardening boots. From the nearby drawing room doors, she heard Bea run her fingers experimentally over a few keys.

"Please excuse my sister, Mr. Bentley," Bea said. "I don't know what she could be thinking, leaving on account of a tree."

Charlotte started. She had not realized she would be able to hear their conversation from here. Evidently Bea did not realize it either.

"What is so important about this tree?" Mr. Bentley asked.

"Oh, some tree she wants to plant by our mother's grave."

"That is very sentimental of her."

"I suppose." Bea began playing a cheerful quadrille.

William Bentley spoke more loudly to be heard over the music. "You know, my uncle has often described what a lovely girl Miss Charlotte Lamb has become. So, when I first entered the room, I thought you must be she."

A sour note, a half step off-key, reverberated through the doors as Bea abruptly stopped playing. "Mr. Harris finds Charlotte . . . lovely?"

In the hall, Charlotte froze mid-button.

"I suppose that's what he meant, a lovely girl, a lovely young girl. But you, Miss Lamb, are a beautiful woman."

Charlotte expelled the breath she'd been holding. She could imagine Bea's reaction, the red-cheeked pleasure that must be coloring her face.

"I believe Uncle is quite fond of your sister," Mr. Bentley continued, "though it must be tedious for a man of his age to always be warding off the infatuation of one so young."

Humiliation filled Charlotte, and she quickly pulled on her other boot without bothering to finish buttoning the first.

"Did he say that?" Bea sounded as appalled as Charlotte felt.

"No, no, heavens no. I am only reading between the worry lines as it were. Fret not, beautiful Beatrice, Uncle holds you all in great affection."

Charlotte did not wait to hear more. She made her way quietly out of the vicarage and strode across the narrow lane to the churchyard. Ben Higgins, a lad of fifteen who assisted his father with grave digging and upkeep of the church, was waiting for her. He had already maneuvered the young tree, its roots bound in a ball of dirt, to a spot near her mother's grave. Charlotte picked up a shovel and thrust it into the ground with more vehemence than necessary.

A few minutes later, William Bentley came walking across the churchyard. "Your workman desert you, Miss Lamb?" he called.

Charlotte looked up at him from the hole she was digging. She paused in her work, leaning on the shovel with one hand and pushing a stray hair from her face with the other, though she did not realize until later that her muddy glove had left a smear of dirt on her forehead. Nor why Mr. Bentley had bit back a smile as he drew near.

"I sent him to ask our gardener for some manure. He shall return directly."

"Manure? Lovely. You could wait and let him do that, you know."

"I do not mind a bit of work. Do you?"

"I confess I am not really the digging-in-the-dirt type."

She grinned. "I cannot say I'm surprised."

"Really?"

At his feigned chagrin, she felt her smile widen.

His eyes danced with pleasure. "You do indeed have a lovely smile, Miss Lamb."

"Thank you."

He nodded toward the sapling resting beside the hole. "What sort of tree is that?"

"A French lilac. *Syringa vulgaris.*"

"Looks like a stick to me."

"I suppose it does. But in year or two, it will boast the most fragrant lilac blossoms."

"Your mother. She's been gone—?"

"Two years." She felt her smile fade.

"Forgive me. I'm sorry."

"That is all right." She sighed. "I went traveling with my aunt in the spring, as I often do. Our carriage passed a long stand of lilacs in full bloom, and I remembered how much Mother loved their fragrance. But this variety doesn't spread like the more common English lilacs. I ordered this all the way from Limoges."

"That's a very dear gesture."

Charlotte shrugged. "She was very dear to me."

Resuming her work, her shovel clanged against something solid, and Charlotte bent low to pick a large stone out of the hole. As she did, she had the discomfiting realization that William Bentley enjoyed a lingering look down the bodice of her dress.

"Mr. Harris speaks very highly of you, Miss Lamb. I know I said the same of your father, but in all truth I think my uncle holds you in the highest regard of all."

"I'm sure you are mistaken," Charlotte replied, straightening. "Mr. Harris has long been a friend to our entire family. Even Mother was fond of him."

"And you, I think, are not indifferent to him either."

Remembering what Mr. Bentley had said to Bea, Charlotte could not hide her embarrassment. "Of course not. Mr. Harris has always been very kind, the best of neighbors, almost like a son to Father."

"A son? I shouldn't think so. That would make you brother and sister, and I don't think either of you should like that."

"Mr. Bentley, please don't speak so. It isn't fitting."

He appeared genuinely chastised. "You are quite right, Miss Lamb. Forgive me."

"If you are implying what I think you are, you are quite mistaken."

"Am I? Then I confess myself relieved."

"Relieved? Why so?"

"Well, it is just that I should be disappointed were you already spoken for."

"I am not spoken for, Mr. Bentley. I am only seventeen."

"Seventeen. And my uncle is, what? Five and thirty?"

"Not so old as that, I don't think."

He studied her face, and her discomfort grew under his close scrutiny.

"In any case," she hurried on, "I've no thought of marriage. My sister is two years older and has no thought of it either."

William looked up at the vicarage window and Charlotte followed his gaze. She saw Beatrice standing there frowning down at them. When she saw them look up, she spun away.

"I wouldn't be too sure of that, Charlotte," Mr. Bentley said, then lowered his eyes back to her. "May I call you Charlotte?"

"Yes, please do."

"And you must call me Mr. Bentley."

She looked at him dumbly, taken aback.

He smiled, reached out, and rubbed an immaculate gloved finger across her forehead. She allowed him to do so, standing like a submissive schoolgirl. Then he showed her the dirt-stained glove. "Dirt doesn't suit you, Charlotte. You should remain unsullied by the earth you love."

In the manor garden, Charlotte stooped awkwardly over her rounded middle to pick up a stone. She wondered briefly where William Bentley was now and if he truly planned to marry her sister. Had his intentions ever been honorable? Rising gingerly, she hurled the stone into the mossy pond, where it landed with a dull plop.

Unsullied indeed.

⁊

That very afternoon, Charles Harris rode his horse from his estate toward the Doddington vicarage.

A young lad herded a dozen sheep across the pasture path, so he had to slow his horse to allow them to pass. The boy tipped his hat to him, but Charles Harris only gave a terse nod in return. In no mood to be hindered, Charles pulled the reins up short and urged his horse up the embankment and around the walled churchyard. He was irritated to see his nephew's grey gelding in front of the vicarage, old Buxley attempting to hold the jittery horse by its bridle. *What is that boy up to now?*

Here William came in his green coat and cravat and fine hat, his smile decidedly self-satisfied.

"Hello, Uncle. Sorry I cannot stay and chat. Pressing business calls."

The young man was a dandy and a conniver. Charles should have discouraged his visits to the vicarage, but it was too late now.

Astride the horse now, William turned in the saddle and said with seeming innocence, "Miss Charlotte seems to have disappeared utterly. You haven't any idea what that's about, do you?"

Charles stared, dumbfounded at the boy's insolence. He opened his mouth to fashion some feeble reply, but the young man was already spurring his mount down the lane.

Buxley took his horse with a "Good day to you, Mr. Harris." Charles entered the vicarage and Tibbets took his hat and showed him into the drawing room. Gareth Lamb sat on one of the satin settees, staring off into space while his elder daughter, Beatrice, picked at tinny melodies on the pianoforte.

"There you are, Charles," the vicar greeted him gloomily. "We despaired of ever seeing you again."

"Yes . . . Katherine prefers town to country living, I'm afraid. I've just come round to check on the place and visit my mother and all of you."

"Do come and sit down."

But Charles hesitated, looking around the room for some clue that what he had heard was true. Beatrice looked up at him with a brief nod.

"Good day, Beatrice."

"Mr. Harris." She played on, seemingly unconcerned with or unaware of his agitated state or her father's pale stupor.

"And . . . where is Charlotte this fine day?" He attempted a weak smile.

"Who?" Mr. Lamb asked, his expression blank.

"What do you mean, who? Your younger daughter, of course."

"I have only one daughter, and here she sits." The Reverend Mr. Lamb waved vaguely in Bea's direction.

"I am speaking of Charlotte."

"She is lost to me. It pains me to speak of it."

"I beg you forgive me. But if you could only speak a bit more and tell me where she has gone . . . I only want to help."

"I know not."

"You . . . *don't know* where Charlotte is?" he asked in disbelief.

A discordant clang shuddered through the pianoforte, and Bea glared at him over the fading notes. "We do not wish to speak of it, Mr. Harris. I believe Father made that quite clear. And pray do us the kindness of not speaking of her to others either. Charlotte is off"—she waved her hand with dramatic flair—"visiting friends. Gone to Brighton, I believe. Or was it Bath? In any case, we don't expect her anytime soon." She began playing again.

"That young man who was just here," Gareth began, frowning. "I know he is your nephew, but I have to say, I do not trust him."

"Father!" Bea exclaimed.

"I am sorry, my dear, but I cannot help but think he had something to do with the whole infernal affair."

Bea stood quickly. "Mr. Bentley is a perfectly amiable gentleman, and I will not sit by and hear him maligned in my presence." She flounced out of the room, and Charles was relieved to see her go.

"She's pinned her hopes on him." Mr. Lamb shook his head, his eyes still on the open door though Bea was no longer visible. "I know I should encourage it, but something does not sit right with me. You do not think Bentley had anything to do with . . . Charlotte's leaving?"

"I . . . I shouldn't think so. Did you ask him?"

"Not in so many words, but yes, I did inquire of his dealings with her."

"And how did he respond?"

"Perhaps I had better not repeat it. . . ."

"I insist. What did he say?"

"It shames me to speak of it." Still, the older man went on. "He said he was not altogether surprised at Charlotte's 'troubles,' that he saw her being very familiar with more than one man on several occasions."

"He said that?"

"Well, you know how he talks, all hints and innuendo and you didn't hear it from me."

"Insolent fool!"

"You do not think it the truth? The evidence certainly bears him out."

"I am afraid my nephew has motives of his own that no doubt colored his report."

"Have you never seen her cavorting with men?"

Charles hesitated, and the old man set his face bitterly.

"No, my friend," Charles hurried on. "You mustn't think the worst of Charlotte. I have never seen her act in any untoward manner with anyone."

"Then who was it, man? Have you any idea?"

Charles sighed and shook his head. "I am so sorry. If there was anything I could do, I would do it. You know I would."

"Of course, of course. You have your own future to think of. You don't suppose there is any hope of convincing young Bentley to redirect . . ."

"I am afraid not. Not any longer. Has he . . . made any offer that you know of?"

"No. Though Beatrice seems nearly to be holding her breath in hopes of one."

The name of the Milkweed, Asclepias, comes from the
Greek god Aeskulap, the god of healing.

—FLOWER ESSENCE SOCIETY

CHAPTER 7

Through a grated window in the foundling ward door, Daniel Taylor watched Miss Lamb. She was standing alone in the tangled garden behind the manor, and he couldn't help but remember her in a garden far more grand. She had often been there when he'd come with Dr. Webb to call on her mother.

He had spent a few years in Doddington as an apprentice to Dr. Webb before he'd gone off to the University of Edinburgh to complete his studies. He'd enjoyed his time in Kent and had a great deal of respect for Dr. Webb, who seemed never to tire of visiting patients, consoling families, and doling out physic and other remedies as needed.

Mrs. Lillian Lamb was one of the patients he visited most frequently. In truth there seemed little the good man could do for her, though Webb never said as much. Mrs. Lamb was a lovely, serene woman who seemed more concerned with making them welcome and comfortable than with her own prognosis. It was the Reverend Mr. Lamb who insisted on such regular visits. He seemed quite convinced his wife would "be her bonny old self one day soon, now that you're here." Daniel had both admired and feared his optimism.

As was often the case with female patients, Dr. Webb shooed his apprentice from the room soon after the preliminary pleasantries were dispatched and the physical examination commenced. Dismissed and with nothing to occupy him, Daniel would poke through the many books in the vicarage library or wander through the modest grounds or even into the more sprawling expanse of the great estate abutting the churchyard. Fawnwell, he believed the estate was called. But for its more modest size, the Lambs' garden was among the finest he'd seen, and he knew from his pleasantries with Mrs. Lamb that gardening was her dearest pastime. Evidently her younger daughter shared this enthusiasm.

On one of these occasions Charlotte, who must have been fourteen or fifteen at the time, hailed him from where she stood in the garden. Dropping the shears into her basket, she ran toward him, hand atop her bonnet to keep it in place.

"Mr. Taylor," she panted, out of breath, "there you are. And how fares my mother today?"

"Better, I think. And you? I trust you are well?"

"Yes, very, I thank you." Charlotte searched the lawn behind him. "And where is Dr. Webb?"

"Still in with your mother."

"I see." Though from her wrinkled brow it was clear she did not. "Then why are you not with him?"

"It seems Dr. Webb feels that it would be more discreet, more comfortable for your mother, were I absent."

"I am sure Mother said no such thing."

"Of course not. It is assumed, I suppose. I gather the examination was of a delicate nature."

"Delicate?"

Daniel had felt the blood heat his cheeks and silently cursed his tendency to blush.

"Your mother's ailment is of a . . . feminine nature, and being a man . . ."

"Dr. Webb is a man."

"Yes, but I am young."

"Not so young. I understand his last apprentice was much younger."

"Be that as it may, I must bow to Dr. Webb's greater experience."

"But however are you to gain such experience wandering about my mother's garden?"

"An excellent question, Miss Lamb. Most perceptive."

"I can only hope Dr. Webb is not away should I need a physician."

"Yes, well . . ."

"Forgive me. I meant no offense."

"Of course. I understand."

Daniel smiled grimly at the memory. Indeed, Charlotte would soon need a physician and Dr. Webb was nowhere near. He pushed through the foundling ward door and walked out into the garden, in time to see Charlotte bend over and begin pulling on a milkweed with great effort.

"Careful there, Miss Lamb. Do not overtax yourself."

"Dr. Taylor, do please try to remember to call me Miss Smith."

"I shall try, but we are alone here, so I thought it would be all right. May I ask what you are doing?"

"This garden is overrun with milkweeds, as you can well see. I understand gardening is not a priority in such a place, but—"

"You are quite mistaken, Miss Lamb. This garden is one of my priorities indeed."

"There is little evidence of that."

"Ahh . . . that is only because you are looking at it with the wrong eyes."

"Wrong eyes?"

"Yes, the eyes of a formal English gardener who adores box hedges and lilies and other lovely useless things."

She opened her mouth, but he lifted a hand to ward off her rebuttal.

"Wait until you have heard me out. What do you know of milkweeds, Miss Lamb?"

"I read an article about them in one of Mother's journals. It said French people actually plant them in their gardens. But I think most people do their best to eradicate them."

"Yes, you look here and see a patch of pestiferous weeds—is that right?"

"Of course."

"Yet I look here and see a plethora of elixirs and natural healing compounds that aid my work and soothe my patients."

"Really?" Charlotte looked back at the milkweeds with skepticism.

"Really. The down of the seed can be used to dress wounds, and the milky sap creates an instant bandage that can be applied to various skin eruptions. A good root tea serves as a diuretic, expectorant, and a treatment for any number of medical conditions—including respiratory ailments, joint pain, and digestive problems. It serves as an invigorating tonic and helps with stomach problems, headaches, uterine pains, influenza, typhoid fever, and inflammation of the lungs. The sap can even heal warts with topical application."

"You have memorized that entire list?"

He smiled. "You are not the first to question my garden."

"I would imagine not." She smiled back at him.

"Come, I will show you how to harvest the root."

They had dug up only one plant, Dr. Taylor on his haunches to show her where to sever root from stalk, when Sally bolted out the foundling ward door waving her arms.

"Dr. Taylor, do come quick!"

Charlotte noticed he did not question Sally. The urgency in her tone was enough for him to leap to his feet and run toward her. Charlotte followed, though more slowly, the uprooted plant hanging limply in her hand.

Once inside, she heard a woman crying out and shrieking, and old Mrs. Krebs giving orders in her lower-pitched tones.

"What's happened?" Charlotte asked a white-faced Sally.

"Her baby's died."

"Oh no."

They tiptoed forward and saw Mrs. Krebs trying to console a distraught young woman Charlotte had never seen before.

"Who is she?"

"She came to the door last night, asking to be a nurse," Sally began earnestly. "But both Mrs. Krebs and Mrs. Moorling was out for the evening, and Gibbs told her she'd need to come back in the morning. I thought she looked desperate-like, even offered to work without wages, but Gibbs wouldn't hear of it and sent her on her way. Well, this morning she comes back first thing and Mrs. Krebs takes pity on her and lets her start right away. I was helping hand-feed, you know, and I watched her. I seen how she went from crib to crib, looking not at the babes' faces but at their feet! Mrs. Krebs comes and puts a baby in her arms and points to the first rocking chair, and the poor dear sits down and starts to nurse the little one, and I see her work the wee one's foot out of its bundling and look close-like at the heel. That's when I figgered it."

"Figured what?"

Dr. Taylor reappeared and gave the woman a dose of laudanum.

"Just this morning I had to wrap up a babe what died in the night," Sally continued. "And for some reason, I found myself looking at the little angel's perfect wee hands and perfect wee feet. That's when I seen the little black mark on 'er heel. Tar, most like. Marked by its mama, so she could find her own again."

Charlotte watched as Dr. Taylor and Mrs. Krebs ushered the woman, still weeping and moaning, into one of the small sleeping rooms down the passageway.

"I shouldna told her, Charlotte. I should've found some tar or coal and marked some other poor babe's heel. She wouldna known and the both of them be better off now."

"It's not your fault, Sally. You did what you thought best."

Sally swiped at a tear and shook her head, clearly not convinced.

Charlotte had difficulty sleeping that night. She turned slowly and heavily in the swaybacked bed, trying in vain to find a comfortable position and to lure the sweet spiral of sleep.

She heard a muffled call from somewhere in the manor, followed by running footsteps down the corridor. Thinking again of the poor babe who died in the night, Charlotte arose from bed, lit a candle, and made her way to the foundling ward. As soon as she opened the heavy door, the sound of crying reached out to her. She stepped in quickly, shutting the door behind her.

Was this the crying she had heard those other nights? Not likely this far from her room. She moved to the first room of sleeping infants. One was crying, and another awoke to join the first, the cries mingling in an ear-piercing refrain. Charlotte stepped back into the hall and saw a mobcapped Mrs. Krebs struggling to fix a feeding tube with sleep-smeared eyes. "Go and fetch Ruthie for me, will you, Charlotte? It's her turn. Second door on the right."

Charlotte soon returned with the sleepy red-haired woman, who sat down and began nursing the two crying infants. Charlotte walked down the row of cribs and saw another infant lying awake, a boy according to the small card with the child's sex and date of admission pinned to the side of the crib. Occasionally a card contained a name, if the child had been given one, but it was rare. This little boy lay on his back, looking around the room peacefully, taking in the commotion with calm ease. Charlotte paused, looking down at the child, his eyes bright in the candlelight.

Mrs. Krebs sighed. "Fixed the feeder up for nothing, looks like. Usually when one cries a whole choir wake with it. But only two so far, and Ruthie can manage a pair on her own."

"Would you mind if I fed this one?" Charlotte asked quietly.

"Isn't fussing."

"I know, but he's awake and so am I."

"Suit yourself." Mrs. Krebs set the feeding tube on the table and left the room.

Charlotte picked up the swaddled infant, who seemed light as a kitten in her arms. She sat with him in the rocking chair nearest the table, and he immediately turned toward her, molding himself to her body. At first she pulled away, back pressed hard against the chair, feeling embarrassed as the infant rooted against her nightdress. She looked around, feeling guilty, though of what she wasn't sure. But no one was watching. Ruthie was facing the other direction and seemed to have nodded off even while she nursed, and Mrs. Krebs had taken herself back to bed.

Charlotte relaxed and allowed herself to draw the infant close. She felt a sharp longing, and wished she could nurse this little one. She ran a finger along his smooth cheek and he turned toward it, taking its tip between his lips. The force of the suction was surprisingly strong. He took her finger farther in until she felt the wet ridges of the roof of his mouth and his tongue tugging along the underside of her finger. She wondered how it would feel, if it would hurt or be pleasant, when she finally nursed her own child.

"You'll have to settle for goat's milk tonight," Charlotte whispered. She pulled her finger from his mouth with a slick popping noise and picked up the feeding tube from the nearby table. She adjusted it, lowering the open end toward the baby's mouth.

"Here you are," she murmured and smiled when the little one began drinking the milk in earnest.

"If you were my handsome boy, I would not let you out of my sight." She closed her eyes as she fed the baby. *Dear God in heaven,* she silently prayed, *please watch over this dear, helpless child.*

Daniel Taylor stood in the darkness, watching Charlotte. Unable to return to sleep after a trying day and worse evening, he had roamed the manor's corridors. As he passed through the quiet ward, he had been surprised to see her there, especially at this hour. Aware of his hasty dress and need of a wash and shave, he did not make his presence known. He had seen many women hand feed or nurse infants over the years—from beautiful young girls to ancient nuns—why did he feel so oddly transfixed by the sight of Charlotte Lamb feeding a foundling?

Milkweeds are considered field pests, hard to eradicate and a threat to stock. But many people would just as soon have a patch of milkweed. . . . The French, in fact, imported them to their gardens in the 19th century.

—JACK SANDERS, THE SECRETS OF WILDFLOWERS

CHAPTER 8

Daniel Taylor helped his father into his Sunday coat, dusting off, then smoothing the shoulders and sleeves. His hands lingered a moment on his father's upper arms. When had he become so slight? He felt the tremor running through the older man's body and bit his lip. Today was no day for lectures.

"Come now, Father. Wash a bit and then we'll go."

John Taylor appeared far older than his fifty-five years as he hobbled over to the washbasin and bent low to wash his hands and face.

"Give your mouth a rinse as well."

His father paused in his ablutions, then did as he was bid. When he finished he said quietly, "Perhaps I ought to stay in this morning."

"No, Father. You know the service does you good."

"I'm not sure I'm feeling up to it."

Daniel sighed quietly. He was torn between the temptation to feel relieved and go alone, knowing his association with his father would not help him build a thriving practice—at least not among those who could pay—and, of course, guilt at such a thought. He looked at his father, sitting on the edge of his bed now, and felt a combination of feelings too complicated to separate: mild revulsion, pity, anger, protectiveness, love.

"Let's see," Daniel began softly, stepping close to his father and lifting his chin gently, looking into his aging face. His eyes, though tired, were not bloodshot. He then laid his wrist against his father's creased forehead. Warm but not feverish. From this angle above him, he noticed how thin his father's hair was becoming on top and how several white tufts stood in disarray. Carefully, he smoothed down the errant hair, as methodically as if he were performing some important medical procedure.

"There now. The picture of health and decorum."

John Taylor's grin was bleak. "If only that were true, eh, my boy?"

"Come now, Father, we do not wish to be late."

Daniel and his father sat on the high-backed bench in a box near the middle of the church—a box generously shared with them by the widow Mrs. Wilkins, originally with the evident purpose of introducing her grown daughter to an eligible physician. She had been too polite to rescind the invitation once she learned Daniel was already married. An easy mistake to make, he realized, considering no one in that church had ever seen his wife.

As the man in black began his sermon, Daniel's attention wandered, as it usually did. If asked, he would likely acknowledge that he attended church because that was what respectable people did, and what a respectable physician was expected to do. His spirit received little nurture—nor conviction—from the lofty sermons and formal hymns. He did not blame the Church of England. He knew the problem lay within his own soul.

As he sat there, his father listening attentively beside him, the hard bench digging into his spine, the man's deep baritone took him to another church, another time.

How long ago was it? Five years, perhaps. He had just come from seeing Mrs. Lamb. Dr. Webb, eager to return home in time for tea, hurried on but urged him to take his time. He no doubt guessed Daniel was feeling low—first from having been called by a teary-eyed lad to a dismal thatched cottage just that morning, only to find the grandmother already dead, and now the disappointing visit with Mrs. Lamb. Daniel was grateful to the older man and, indeed, felt the need for some solitude.

Walking away from the vicarage, Daniel passed the church and, on impulse, walked inside the empty, echoing old building. The age of the place continued to astound him—sections dated back to the twelfth century. He never tired of gazing upon the unique ornaments of the otherwise humble church—chancel arch, double squint, mullioned windows, wall paintings of St. Francis and Henry the Third outlined in red ochre. He had attended services there the past Sunday and for a moment imagined he could still hear Mr. Lamb's booming baritone reverberating within the stone walls as he delivered his sermon from the raised pulpit. But no, the place was utterly silent but for the crisp turning of a page. He turned his head and there, in a rear pew of the nave, in a spot clearly chosen for its wide swath of sunlight, sat a teenaged Charlotte Lamb.

"Miss Lamb."

"Hello, Mr. Taylor. How fares my mother?"

"A bit weaker than usual, I'm afraid. But she seems in good spirits."

"Mother always is. I only wish her health were as good as her spirits."

Knowing it was not his place to reveal Dr. Webb's prognosis, he changed the subject, nodding to the black book the girl held against her chest. "May I ask what you are reading so intently?"

"Well, it's the Bible, as you see."

"And do you like reading it?"

"Yes, of course. Don't you?"

"I'm afraid I find some of it rather dusty, but there are parts I am quite fond of."

"Which parts?"

"Oh, I like the Gospels, the Proverbs, and some of David's Psalms—the desperate ones. And of course in secret . . ."

"Secret . . . ?"

He felt his face heat and knew he was blushing, "I was going to say the Song of Solomon, but I should not say it to you."

"But you have already said it."

"Forgive me."

She turned to scan the south chapel, then looked back at him and whispered, "You have told me a secret. Now I shall tell you one. Shall I show you what I am truly reading?" She pulled out several folded pages that had been tucked into the Bible. "I am supposed to be reading the book of Numbers, but instead I am reading this letter over and over again."

"It must be a very interesting letter."

"More interesting than Numbers at any rate."

"Is it . . . a love letter?"

"A love letter?" She ducked her head. "No. Not at all."

"But you do . . . receive love letters . . . from time to time?"

"No. I have never."

"I'm sorry."

"Whatever for? I am only fifteen years old."

"Quite right. Those should wait until you are at least . . ."

"Sixteen."

"I quite agree."

"This is only a letter from my dear aunt. I'm to stay with her the month of August, and I long for it. I am reading what she says we shall do and whom we shall likely see . . . all the while pretending to read *this* to please my father. Do you think me very wicked?"

"Never, Miss Lamb."

"Father would. He says if we are all very good, and pray hard, Mother will get better. Do you think it true?"

"It's certainly not fair."

"Fair?"

"For your father to put that responsibility on you. Forgive me, I mean no disrespect, but do you really think God works that way? If we do the things we ought, He'll preserve those we hold dear, but if we forget or neglect our duty, He'll bring down calamity upon us and those we love?"

"I think perhaps you need to read the Old Testament more often."

"Perhaps you are right. But I prefer the New."

"Except for the Proverbs and most desperate of Psalms?"

He smiled, "And that other book, which shall remain nameless."

Now Daniel became aware of the congregation standing around him and quickly joined them, glad to rise from the hard bench. He felt himself smile again at the memory, a smile quite out of place with the serious benediction.

❧

That night, Charlotte dreamt that Dr. Webb was again listening to her mother's heart. And, as she remembered him doing before, he asked her if she would like to listen as well. Smiling, Charlotte climbed up onto the bed, returning her mother's serene smile, and laid her head against her mother's chest. But her mother's smile soon faded. Try as she might, Charlotte could not hear the heartbeat.

"Do you not hear it?" Dr. Webb demanded sternly.

"No," Charlotte cried. "I cannot."

It was her fault. If only she could position her head correctly, find the right spot to listen, if only she could hear it . . . but she could not, and so it beat no longer.

Charlotte awoke, her own heart pounding, a nauseous dread filling her body as the images and cloak of guilt filled her mind. The images soon faded, but that familiar, nauseating guilt remained. It expanded, accompanied now by new pressure in her abdomen, a pressure which soon grew into pain.

Charlotte rose gingerly and removed her nightclothes to dress for the day—and that was when she saw the small, dark red stain.

On shaky legs, she made her way to breakfast, ate little, and was soon sitting at the table with the other women, attempting to finish the blanket she was embroidering for her child. She found it difficult to concentrate. Then a second wave of pain struck.

At the urging of the other women, Charlotte made her way carefully to Mrs. Moorling's office. When she had confided to the matron about the pains and the slight but frightful bleeding, Mrs. Moorling had immediately gone off in search of a physician to see her.

By now, Charlotte had been sitting in the office for a quarter hour or more, shifting on the hard chair, trying to get comfortable, rubbing her abdomen, hoping to somehow ease the tightness, the strange new pains.

Gibbs appeared in the doorway. "Dr. Preston has just arrived. He will see you directly."

"Dr. Preston? Perhaps I could wait . . . see how I feel tomorrow."

"Miss Smith. If you are bleeding, you had better not waste time."

"Is it so serious?"

The woman shrugged. "Can be."

Charlotte felt sick. "Very well."

Gibbs led her down the corridor, through the workroom, and to the examination room. She opened the door and announced without expression, "Miss Smith," before stepping out and letting the door shut Charlotte into the room. Charlotte saw Dr. Preston straightening from a slouched position in the desk chair. He was a very handsome man, she could not deny. His clothes were rumpled, however, as was his hair—even though it was but midmorning. Had he slept in those clothes? She saw him lift the lid of a Smith & Co. tin and pop a "curiously strong" mint into his mouth. Charlotte found it ironic. She, who had grown up in a home that abstained from strong drink, might very well not have identified the odor, but the cure he had taken for it was a telltale sign. He smoothed down each side of his moustache before rising. It was not a dandy's gesture, she judged, merely a very tired-looking man trying to smooth on a professional facade. His next words, however, dispelled the image before it could fully form.

"Remove your frock, if you please."

She felt her mouth drop open. "I beg your pardon."

"Your frock. Remove it. Come, come. I haven't all day."

"But is that really quite necessary?"

"There's no need to feign modesty with me, Miss Smith."

"I am feigning nothing . . ."

"I am a physician, Miss Smith. I assure you the female form holds no mysteries for me."

No mystery she could well believe, but still!

"Perhaps I only imagined the pains. Really. I feel quite, quite well now."

"Do not flatter yourself, Miss Smith. A female body in this distended shape does more to repulse a man than entice him, I assure you."

Now she felt shame heaped atop her embarrassment and irritation. Did he really think she thought he might be interested in her as a woman?

He went on, "I have a beautiful wife at home with blond curls and an eighteen-inch waist." Here he paused. "Of course she also has a tongue to rival King Arthur's sword."

"The two often go together, I find," Charlotte murmured, thinking of Beatrice. She did not move but felt his eyes studying her.

"Do I know you, Miss Smith?"

"I do not believe so."

"You seem familiar somehow. Where do you come from?"

"I . . ." What had she told Mrs. Moorling? She realized he could check her file. "I am lately of Hertfordshire."

"Hertfordshire? Hmm . . . and we have not met before?"

"I do not believe so, no."

"Ah well, it will come to me. Now, do you wish to know if your babe is all right or not?"

She squeezed her eyes shut, swallowing. "Oh, very well." She reached around and began unfastening her buttons. Of all days to wear a frock that buttoned down the back.

"Here, here." He walked up behind her and impatiently began working the buttons. "I'll miss my hunt at this rate."

At that moment, the door burst open and Dr. Taylor strode in. He stopped suddenly, clearly startled to see the room occupied. His bespectacled gaze went from Preston to Charlotte and back again. He frowned.

"What's all this, then?"

"I should ask the same of you, barging in here."

"Mrs. Moorling sent for me. Said you had yet to make it in."

"Well, clearly she was mistaken. For here I am, seeing a patient."

Dr. Taylor opened his mouth, then apparently thought better of what he was going to say. Instead, he tossed his case casually on the desk and said lightly, "I thought you were off hunting grouse today."

"I depart this afternoon."

"Well, why not leave early. Make a day of it."

"But I have women to see. Patients."

"I'll see them for you. My day is already spoiled. No point in both of us being indoors on such a fine day as this."

"Well, I—"

"Off with you, man. I'll see to Miss Smith myself. I saw her when she first arrived."

"I'll wager you did."

"Go on. Before I change my mind."

"I shall. Before I change mine."

Dr. Preston grabbed his bag from the desk, his coat from the back of the chair, and strode from the room without so much as a glance her way. The slamming door punctuated the tension in the room, which didn't fade as quickly as the sound. Charlotte felt unaccountably guilty, awkwardly trying to reach around herself and refasten her frock.

Dr. Taylor stood there, staring at the desk. Then he looked at her, evidently unaware of her struggle.

"Why were you seeing Preston? I saw you only last week."

"Mrs. Moorling insisted. I am having pains."

Instantly his strained demeanor snapped into professional concern. "What sort of pains?"

"Cramping pains, here. And I . . . I am . . ." She could barely make herself say the word aloud to him.

"Any bleeding?"

She nodded, relieved to have it out. "A bit."

"And the babe, when was the last time you felt movement?"

Charlotte felt tears fill her eyes. "Not once all day."

"Do not be alarmed, probably just enjoying a bit of slumber. Still, I ought to give another listen."

He again retrieved the wooden tube from his bag, and Charlotte sat on the table as she had before, but this time she was praying. *Please, God, please, God, please, God. . . .*

He pressed the tube to the center of her abdomen and stared blindly in concentration. Then he repositioned the tube to one side . . . and the other. Charlotte studied his expression with growing trepidation.

"Do you hear anything?"

He moved the tube lower.

"Can you not hear it?" she tried again.

"Not with you talking."

He moved the tube again.

"I suppose some would say I ought to be relieved, but I am not."

"Of course not. Shh."

Charlotte bit her lip. "Do you suppose this is God's punishment?"

"Charlotte, please lie down on the table." He ignored her question. "I need to listen lower, but it's difficult with you sitting up." When she complied, he pressed the tube very low indeed, where the underside of her rounded belly nearly met with her hipbones. He listened intently, his face growing, she concluded, terribly grim. Tears fell down Charlotte's temples and into her hair. He moved the tube above the opposite hip bone and pressed it in deep, nearly painfully so. This time he closed his eyes as if to focus on his sense of hearing alone. Or perhaps he was wincing, realizing the painful truth.

"Well, hello there."

"What?"

"I hear your little lad a'way down here."

"You do?"

He nodded, set his tube down, and lifted his hands above her abdomen. "May I?"

Charlotte appreciated his consideration. She guessed he would not ask permission before examining other patients who came to him. She swallowed but nodded. He put his hands firmly around the lower portion of her belly, feeling and gently pushing.

"Here is his little rump right here."

"You can feel that?"

"He is all curled up down here, bottom side up. No wonder I had difficulty auscultating his heart."

"He is all right, then?"

"Seems so. About the bleeding though."

"It is only a little."

"Yes, and it does not necessarily mean there are any problems. Still, I ought to examine you . . . internally, to see if your body is readying to give birth."

"But it is too soon!" She sat up on the table.

He looked at her quizzically, and Charlotte saw the question in his eyes. *Too soon to examine you or too soon to give birth?* She looked away from his raised-brow gaze.

"Charlotte?"

She squeezed her eyes closed and reached behind herself again, attempting to undo the remaining buttons, unable to look at him as she did so.

Would it be less terrible to disrobe before Dr. Taylor than Dr. Preston—or worse? Eyes still winced shut, she was surprised to hear the door open. She looked and saw him standing at the threshold, his hand on the latch.

"There's no need to remove your gown," he said over his shoulder.

He called for Gibbs and whispered instructions to her in the corridor. In a few minutes she returned, Mrs. Krebs in tow.

Dr. Taylor said, "Mrs. Krebs will have a look at you, Char . . . Miss Smith."

"I will," Mrs. Krebs grumbled, "but I'm no surgeon, mind."

"A finer midwife I have never known."

"That's been a few years now, Dr. Taylor."

"You remember the rudiments, no doubt."

"I suspect so."

To Charlotte he said, "If she sees anything worrisome, I will need to examine you myself, but if not, we shall wait a day or two and see if the bleeding ceases on its own. All right?"

"Yes. Thank you."

He left the room, and Charlotte wondered which of them was more relieved.

Mrs. Krebs found nothing amiss and helped Charlotte refasten the buttons she could not reach earlier. "Dr. Taylor must have taken a shine to you, miss," she said.

"No! Nothing of the kind. It is only that he . . . that he is known to my family. That is, when I was quite young. It is a bit awkward, is all."

She tutted, then said, "As you say, miss." She left the room, leaving Charlotte quite sure the woman didn't believe a word she had said.

Our milkweed is tenacious of life. Its roots lie deep
as if to get away from the plow."

—JOHN BURROUGHS

CHAPTER 9

Charlotte added a few more pieces of coal to the fire, washed her hands and face in the basin, cleaned her teeth, and climbed into bed. She checked to make sure the candlestick was on the night table, within reach. Pulling the rough blanket up under her chin, she waited for sleep—or a scream—to come.

Sleep must have come first, for when the scream came Charlotte awoke with a start, forgetting her plan for a moment. Quietly, so as not to awaken Mae beside her, she crawled out of bed and wrapped her dressing gown around her. Carrying the candlestick to the mantel, she took a match-straw from the tinderbox and lit it in the fire, using this to light the wick. Then she tiptoed to the door. Letting herself out and closing the door quietly behind her, Charlotte listened. Hearing nothing, she lifted her candle high, grateful for the light, hoping it would chase away the fear and ease the raw nerves eating at her heart.

The scream sounded again—and her nerves moved on to her stomach.

Charlotte crept down the dark corridor, her candle flickering against the grey walls and the stone floor beneath her stocking feet. The chill night air seeped through her stockings, through her nightdress and dressing gown. But her shivering had little to do with the cold. It had to do with the scream. Such an unearthly sound. Charlotte had lived in the manor long enough to have heard any number of shouts, cries, and groans of women delivering babes. Those were earthy, striving, determined sounds—awful to hear yet bearable for the sweet relief that followed and, Lord willing, the responding cry of a newborn that rose up to wash away memory of pain and struggle.

This cry was met with no relief, no answering cry of new life. This cry did not rise and fall with the regularity of birthing pains—increasing, building, then abruptly sighing into silence. These cries were clapped off, silenced for hours, days even, only to escape, to rise up in shrill desperation, in anger sometimes, in woeful distress, only to cut off mid-cry a few minutes later. No gradual fading, no sense of the cries having accomplished, nor brought forth, nor delivered anything or anyone. These were the cries Charlotte had come to dread, the ones that brought gooseflesh to Charlotte's skin and darkness to her soul. She longed to banish both.

She continued down the corridor—the opposite direction from the common rooms and foundling ward—to its end. She knew the staircase to the upper floors stood in the center of the building and serviced both wings. So when she reached the far wall and the corridor simply ended, with the cries seeming still quite distant, Charlotte was confused. Had the drafty old house played tricks on her ears, her mind even? The cry rose again, closer yet still muffled. She tried one of the doors, which opened to a small cleaning pantry. Then she tried another door, which opened onto an empty chamber. Why hadn't it been offered her? She extended the candle farther into the room and saw it housed neither hearth nor bed but only a few old chairs and a wardrobe. Without bothering to close that door, she tried the last—a narrow, plain thing, a linen closet, perhaps.

She lifted the latch and the door flew out at her with surprising velocity. Charlotte gasped and nearly dropped her candle. She cupped her hand around the flame and only just managed to keep it alight. She looked inside the door. This was no closet. This was a second set of stairs. And from its narrowness she guessed it had been designed for servants' use in the building's original design. A servant might silently disappear and reappear in the corridor, bearing coal for the upstairs bedrooms or bringing down chamber pots and the like, she supposed.

And that's when she heard it again—the scream, darting down the staircase and piercing her with its nearness, its wildness. What was this? All the girls were on this floor, as far as she knew. The higher floors were more difficult to heat, and the Manor Home had insufficient staff to manage all the available space. She had heard Gibbs complaining of having to haul down a chest of drawers from above stairs, and gathered that some of the upstairs rooms were still furnished while others were used for storage. And Dr. Taylor, she knew, kept rooms up there when he was on duty during the night.

When she heard a door open above her, Charlotte stepped back quickly from the doorway, hand to her heart. Whoever was coming down the stairs was descending rapidly. She knew she would never make it back to her room undetected. She quickly slipped into the empty chamber she had so recently inspected, setting her candlestick on the floor in the corner, hoping her body would block its small light.

Footsteps hit the landing and entered the corridor. Charlotte held her breath. Candlelight preceded the shadowed figure past the open doorway. Charlotte peered out from behind the door and made out the figure of a man. The familiar smell of antiseptic and herbs confirmed the identity of the man more readily than his fleeting figure. Dr. Taylor. Not surprising. He made no secret of sleeping above stairs. Then why was she so frightened?

Charlotte stood there, heart pounding, trying to quiet her breathing as the candlelight and footsteps faded and she was alone again. But for how long? Did she have time to sneak back to her room before he returned from whatever errand or mission took him from his room this late at night? She wasn't sure she wanted to return to her room without knowing who was screaming yet neither was she certain she wanted to know. Did she have the courage to ascend those black stairs alone? Retrieving her candle, she stepped into the corridor and listened once more. Silence. Surprising herself, she took a deep breath, reopened the stairway door, and closed it behind her, allowing it to swallow her whole.

She paused at the top of the stairs, listening. She heard—what was it? Sobbing? Yes, a woman was sobbing now. The same woman who had been screaming? Or another? How many people were up here? And why? Charlotte slowly pushed the door open and held forth her candle to illumine the upper floor. She saw door after door on either side of a long, dim passageway. Midway down its length, one door on the left gaped open, faint light leaking out to blend with the glow of an oil lamp on a small table on the opposite side of the corridor. She could hear the crying more clearly now, but still could distinguish no words.

She had taken two steps down the passageway when she heard the door open and close below. She gasped. Caught. Blowing out her candle, she looked wildly about her, but where could she go? She tried the handle of the door closest her. Locked. She had no time to check every door, and something told her they would all be locked as well. Grateful for stockinged feet, she hurried down the corridor as quickly as her additional girth would allow. Knowing nothing else to do, she bustled through the open doorway and stepped behind the door.

What was she doing? She had stepped into the one lit room, like a moth to a flame. And now she was trapped. Dr. Taylor would come in and find her there in but a few seconds. What would she say? What *could* she say? Foolish girl! She should have stayed in the corridor and simply said she'd heard a scream and came to see if help was needed. She'd done nothing wrong . . . until now. She stole a quick look about the room. Rumpled bedclothes, a coat tossed over a chair. On the chest a leather case, a bulky medical bag, a hat, gloves. A Bible. A miniature portrait of a woman in wedding clothes. She couldn't see it well from this vantage, but she knew it must be Dr. Taylor's wife. Good heavens! What if Mrs. Taylor had been lying there in bed, gaping at this stranger who barged right in and hid behind her door? Then there would be screaming indeed! Relieved, she remembered that Dr. Taylor had mentioned he and his wife had a townhouse some distance away, which they shared with his father.

The footsteps in the corridor were coming closer. Then they paused right outside the door. Did he sense her presence? Had he heard her? She would just step out and tell him the truth. *Forgive me, Dr. Taylor, you gave me a fright. I heard a scream and . . .* She heard the jiggle of a door handle, a key in a lock. She stepped out. Dr. Taylor was unlocking the door across the way. His back to her, he opened it a crack, hesitating, apparently listening. He retrieved an apothecary bottle from his coat pocket and checked the label by light of the table lamp, before tucking the bottle back into his pocket. Then he took hold of the lamp itself. With his free hand, he pushed the door open just enough to allow himself in. In that flash of moment, before the door shut behind him, Charlotte saw a figure fly at Dr. Taylor. Charlotte put her hand over her mouth, stifling a gasp, and stepped into the corridor.

She heard a thud, then a voice—a woman's voice, but strange— crying out a string of syllables. "Nonononon . . . !"

"Stop it!" Dr. Taylor boomed, in a voice so strong and commanding, Charlotte would not have believed it from Daniel Taylor had she not seen him just enter the room. She felt chilled, stunned, as if he were shouting directly at her. Never would she have imagined him speaking to anyone, let alone one of his patients, in that manner. But then the sobbing started again, and she heard the more familiar sound of Dr. Taylor's soothing voice rumble through the closed door.

Charlotte stood there a moment more, too confused to move. Knowing he might come out at any moment, she stepped back into his room and relit her candle off the one burning low on a bedside table. Beside it was the miniature she'd seen from across the room. She picked it up and quickly studied the portrait. The woman was truly beautiful. Thick dark hair, a wide perfect smile, delicate features, white lace and cameo at her throat. The clothing, the pose, were traditional, but there was something unusually appealing, something nearly exotic about the woman. Charlotte supposed it was the broad smile, deemed so unfashionable in formal portraits. The artist had rendered a nearly playful light in Mrs. Taylor's dark eyes, hinting at some secret happiness. Was she at home now, missing her husband terribly?

Remembering herself, Charlotte quickly lowered the portrait. *I've no business poking about.* She hurried from the room and made it back down the stairs and into her own room without incident. With a sigh of relief, she slipped into bed, which had never seemed more comfortable.

❧

At the sewing table the next morning, Charlotte asked in what she hoped was a casual tone, "Have any of you ever seen Dr. Taylor's wife?"

"I never 'ave," Sally said.

Mae shrugged. "Me neither."

"Maybe he isn't really married," Bess said. "Just says so, so's us girls will trust him."

"So you won't fawn all over 'im, more like," teased Sally.

"Well, Dr. Preston has a wife too, by all accounts, and that don't make me trust him none," Mae said.

"Dr. Taylor sure doesn't go about like a married man. Here all hours instead of a'tome," Sally mused.

Bess snorted. "Sounds like most men I know. Gone all hours. Comin' and goin' as they please."

"I still say he hasn't a wife. Looks barely groomed half the time. Needs a wife to dress him I'd say." Mae grinned.

"Don't be foolish, ladies," Gibbs interrupted, stopping at their table. "I have seen Mrs. Taylor with my own eyes I have. More than once."

"Have you, Miss Gibbs?" Charlotte asked.

"Indeed I have. Dr. Taylor once brought her around to see the place. Right fine lady, by the looks of her. Very handsome, with the finest feathered hat I've ever seen. Hair dark as night and eyes twinklin' like stars. Glowed she did. Like she was eating up every word her husband said. Never seen two people so in love."

"Goodness, Miss Gibbs, I've never heard you string together so many words at one time," Charlotte said with an appreciative smile.

The woman frowned and bit her lip. "Well, I could not stand here and not put you to rights. Not about good Dr. Taylor's wife."

"How long ago was this," Charlotte asked, "since you saw Mrs. Taylor?"

"Oh, I don't know. Few months now . . . maybe half a year."

In common milkweed, white juice, which oozes out of

the stems and leaves when broken . . . clots,

like blood, soon after exposure to air.

—JACK SANDERS, *THE SECRETS OF WILDFLOWERS*

CHAPTER 10

After two weeks of caring for the little foundling boy, Charlotte sat on the bench in the manor garden at dusk, tears streaming down her face.

She became aware of Dr. Taylor standing near. When she glanced up at him, his expression grew alarmed.

"What is it?"

"Dr. Taylor! If only you had been here earlier. Dr. Preston said there was nothing he could do, but had you been here, I know you would have at least tried. . . ."

"Slow down, please. What has happened?"

"The little boy—he's gone."

"The one you'd taken to feeding?"

Charlotte nodded, wiping at her eyes with a handkerchief.

"I'm sorry." He sighed in frustration. "I'm afraid it happens more often than I can stand . . . or explain."

"Dr. Preston said, 'Get used to it. I have.' "

"Unfortunately it's a natural response. One must harden oneself or work elsewhere."

"I should never get used to it."

He nodded. After a moment he stepped closer and murmured, "Come, Charlotte." He offered his hand. Her brain mildly noted his use of her Christian name, but at that moment she was beyond caring.

She allowed him to help her to her feet. Her time was drawing near and she would have found it difficult to get to her feet unassisted, even had she not been in so distressed a state.

"Come," he repeated. "I shall help you to your room."

He held her by her arm and guided her inside and down the passage.

"Did I do something wrong?" she asked tearfully. "Is that why . . . ?"

"No, Charlotte, no. I'm sure that little boy lived longer than he would have had you not cared for him so."

"For all the good it did him."

"Of course it did. How much better to leave this world loved and cared for." He opened the door to her new bedchamber. She had gotten her private room at last. "Now, off to bed. You'll have your own little one soon, and you need your rest."

Charlotte was unaware she had sat in the garden so long and that it was evening already. "Very well. Good night."

"Good night."

She went inside and sat down on her bed. She was vaguely aware of him closing her door and the sound of his footsteps fading away, but Charlotte's tear-streaked eyes were filled with another scene, another death. She wrapped her shawled arms tightly around herself and remembered.

"She's gone," young Mr. Taylor had said, looking at her over her mother's still form.

Charlotte gasped. She felt her insides collapse, like a cocoon flattened by a careless boot.

Mr. Taylor stepped forward, as if he might take her in his arms, but at that moment Charles Harris swept into the room, his stride urgent, his handsome face nearly fierce in its grimness.

"Oh, Mr. Harris!" Charlotte cried and turned on her heel, stepping into his arms. He pulled her close against him.

"Dear, Charlotte. Dear, dear, Charlotte . . ." He murmured against her hair. "I am so sorry."

She sobbed against him and felt him stroke her back as he whispered words she knew were meant to comfort her, but no words could diminish the flaming, burning pain inside of her. She was vaguely aware of Mr. Taylor letting himself from the room but was too devastated to care.

🌿

Daniel Taylor did not venture to the club as often as he once had. He went not to drink and play cards, as did the other men, but to further his reputation and, he hoped, his private practice. But tonight, he had no thoughts of business in his weary mind, only a few minutes relaxation before taking himself home.

A group of regulars, gathered tightly around a table, were jesting with two well-dressed newcomers. Daniel looked over and recognized both men immediately, although he knew them from another time and another place.

"So the great Charles Harris is finally married," silver-haired Mr. Milton said, raising his tumbler in salute to the older and darker of the two newcomers.

"Well, yes, for more than half a year now."

"Many are the lasses still crying over it, I can tell you," a second gentleman with a wax-curled moustache agreed cheerfully.

"Miss Lamb is among them, I assure you," a younger voice said.

The young man—perhaps now twenty years old—was another person Daniel had last seen in Kent. William Bentley was sitting beside Mr. Harris—his uncle, if Daniel remembered correctly.

Harris stared at his nephew, clearly astonished. "Miss Lamb?"

"I believe she was brought especially low by your marriage."

"No. I am sure you are mistaken."

"Come, Uncle. You cannot tell me you did not know it."

"Well, then," the mustachioed man interjected wistfully. "This Miss Lamb was not alone in her hopes of catching the most eligible bachelor in Kent. My own Nellie spoke very highly of you."

William ignored the man, keeping his half-lidded gaze on his uncle. "Miss Lamb has had her sights set on you for years," he insisted.

"I do not think so. I have merely been a friend to the family."

William snorted. "Miss Beatrice was hoping for more than friendship, I can tell you."

"Beatrice?"

"You're barking up the wrong tree, young man," Mr. Milton interrupted. "Your uncle here has always been like an older brother to the Lamb girls and feels most protective of them. Do not risk his ire by speaking ill of either of them. Especially now he's married a cousin of theirs."

"A rich one at that," the mustachioed man said, wagging his eyebrows meaningfully.

"And how do you like your wife's townhouse in Manchester Square?" Mr. Milton directed the conversation to more comfortable topics.

"Fine, fine."

"And how do you find life in London?"

"A far cry from Kent, no doubt."

The discussion calmed and continued, but Daniel found himself remembering the first time he had seen Charles Harris—and the way Charlotte had looked at the man. They had been standing in the vicarage garden, as they often did, when the man came riding up on his big black horse, the tails of his greatcoat nearly matching the gleaming ebony flanks. But Daniel's attention was soon pulled from the admirable horse to the equally gleaming look in young

Charlotte Lamb's eyes. And as Daniel looked from girl to horse, from girl to man, he realized she was admiring not the fine animal, as he had been, but rather the man astride it. Her attention was completely captured by him, her eyes, always cheerful, had taken on a glow as though she were gazing on a candlelit Christmas tree, or the first snowfall, or . . . he admitted to himself grudgingly, an exceedingly handsome man.

"Who is that?" he asked her.

She laughed a sudden, surprised laugh, as if amused that someone in the world should not know who this astounding man was. "Why, that is Mr. Harris. Our neighbor."

"And where is Mrs. Harris?" he asked somewhat peevishly.

"Mrs. Harris? There is no Mrs. Harris. Unless you mean his mother."

The man rode close and reigned in his horse in an impressive show of hooves and horsemanship. "Hello, Charlotte. You are looking lovely as usual. Your father about?"

"In the church."

"And Bea?"

"Not in the church."

He grinned a knowing grin, and Daniel wondered at the meaning of that little exchange. Was there something between Charlotte's sister and this dashing neighbor—older though he was?

Harris touched the brim of his hat and quickly spurred his mount off again in the direction of the church. Daniel noticed he barely looked his way.

"He is a bit old for your sister, is he not?"

"Yes, he is much too old for Bea. But not for me."

"But—she is older than you are!"

"Oh, I am only teasing, Mr. Taylor. You will have to forgive me. I have learned that art from Mr. Harris, and I am afraid it is a habit deeply ingrained."

"You spend a great deal of time with him, do you?"

"No. Only small bits of time, but in regular doses over many years."

"Your father approves?"

"Of Mr. Harris? Completely. He rather thinks of him as the son he never had."

"And your sister?"

"Bea has long been smitten with him."

"And you?"

She shrugged. "She would say the same of me."

"And would it be true?"

"Oh, Mr. Taylor," she soothed, touching him lightly on the arm, "we are all smitten with him—every last one of us, from Father to Cook. Who would not be? But we do not expect anything to ever come of it. Well, except perhaps for Bea."

❦

The second time Daniel saw Charles Harris was the day Charlotte's mother died. He remembered that day all too well.

Dr. Webb had been called away that morning to another patient's home, so Daniel alone had attended Mrs. Lamb when she breathed her last. He had felt a heavy mixture of failure and grief, sharpened by the caved-in expression on Charlotte's face. He had stepped forward, intending to take her in his arms, to try in some small way to comfort her, when Mr. Harris swept in. Harris immediately took Charlotte in his own arms, enfolding her in his greatcoat, which looked to Daniel at that moment very much like bats' wings. The man whispered words of familiar comfort, as if it was the most natural thing in the world to hold her in his arms.

Unnoticed and unwanted, Daniel had silently let himself from the room.

A few days later, Daniel found Charlotte alone after her mother's funeral. She was sitting in the garden. Not weeding or cutting

103

anything, just sitting on a little lawn rug. He could remember but few times he had seen her idle. He cleared his throat, clutching his hands behind his back.

"I am terribly sorry, Miss Lamb."

"Thank you."

"We did everything we could for her. But there was so little—"

"Of course you did. We do not blame you."

"I'm afraid your father does."

"Father is wrong. We all knew it was coming. Even Mother knew. Father was nearly cruel with her when she tried to raise the subject. In any case, it is not you he blames."

"What do you mean?"

"How do you think Mother got this ailment? Father told me himself she was never the same after birthing me. She was never able to bring another babe to term—her pain often left her too weak to stand. And here I was, forever tiring her with my questions and tempting her to the garden when she ought to have been indoors resting. She'd been ill so long, I guess I stopped believing just how ill she was. Or was too selfish to care. I should have made her rest. I should have prayed harder. I should have—"

"Charlotte, stop. You did all you could do. You loved her better than any daughter I've known, and it was perfectly obvious she loved you as well. There was nothing more you could do."

"I want so badly to believe this isn't my fault."

"It isn't your fault. Charlotte, it isn't. Don't take guilt upon yourself that isn't yours to take. There's too much of the deserved variety to go around."

He paused long enough to fish out his handkerchief from his pocket and hand it down to her before continuing. "Why does it have to be anybody's fault? I'm no theologian, but I don't suppose it's God's fault either. Allowed it to happen, perhaps. Who's to say? Our medical knowledge and skill is not all it could be—much of it still remains a frustrating mystery. Even if we deduce that some organ has quit functioning, and even if we understand why, that does not mean we have an inkling of how to repair the thing. There was nothing we knew to do for your mother that we did not do. And I don't think God withheld a miracle because you did not read the book of Numbers."

In the early nineteenth century a new term—"puerperal insanity"—
would find its way into medical texts. . . . Women were
believed to be particularly at risk shortly after childbirth . . .
but they could also become mad during pregnancy.

—DR. HILARY MARLAND, *DANGEROUS MOTHERHOOD*

CHAPTER 11

The entry hall was empty as Charlotte walked through it, passing the manor's main staircase. There was normally a chain strung from between the wall and banister, but at the moment it hung limply from the wall. She thought she heard voices above stairs and paused to listen. It was afternoon, and bright sunlight filled the hall from the high, unobstructed windows over the main door. There was nothing sinister about the setting this time, but still, when the cry came, chills coursed through Charlotte's body—accompanied by pity for whatever poor creature had uttered it.

Charlotte put her hand on the banister and took a slow step up and then another.

Suddenly a male voice burst out from above, "Moorling! I'm waiting!" The voice startled her. It was Dr. Preston's voice, angrier than usual. She shouldn't have been surprised, she supposed. She knew Dr. Taylor was not usually on duty during the afternoons— that daytime hours were primarily the reign of Dr. Preston. Still for some reason it perplexed her to hear him up there. She had assumed that it was Dr. Taylor's on-duty residence—and domain—alone.

She heard footsteps clicking across the marble of the ground floor and looked over the railing to see Mrs. Moorling approaching. She was carrying a tray laden with lances and glass vials, iodine and bandages. Charlotte recognized it immediately for what it was. A bloodletting tray. One of Dr. Webb's colleagues had treated her mother with similar instruments over a course of days, and it had weakened her so badly that Dr. Webb forbade its use ever again.

Carefully balancing her tray, Mrs. Moorling had not yet seen Charlotte, but as soon as she reached the foot of the stairs and glanced up, her already drawn expression took on a sharp edge.

"May I ask what you are doing, Miss Smith?"

"I thought . . . I heard voices."

"Of course you did," she snapped. "We have occasional patients on the upper floors as well. Did you not see the sign?"

Charlotte shook her head.

Mrs. Moorling looked over and saw the dangling chain. "Someone's let it down. Put that back up for me after I pass, will you? And please stay on the ground floor."

Mrs. Moorling started up the stairs. Charlotte realized the matron would likely have given her a longer lecture had Dr. Preston not been waiting so impatiently. Charlotte sighed and reached down awkwardly over her bulky middle for the chain. She fingered the small engraved plaque that hung at the chain's midpoint. The plaque read: *Staff Admittance Only.*

Well, there was someone up there who was not on staff and who was not happy about being there.

Why she stood there, she did not know. But she felt oddly rooted to the spot. A few minutes later, she again heard footsteps on the marble—duller male steps. She looked across the hall and saw Dr. Taylor approaching, peering at a document of some sort as he walked. When he looked up and saw her there, he smiled easily. "Good day to you, Miss Smith."

"And to you, Dr. Taylor."

"I say, this place is a tomb. Um, rather, I cannot seem to find anyone about. Have you seen Mrs. Moorling or Preston, by chance?"

"Yes, as a matter of fact. They are both above stairs right now."

He stopped where he was. "Are they indeed?" His expression was both thoughtful and perplexed.

"Mrs. Moorling was taking up some things Dr. Preston must have ordered."

He lowered the document in his hands. "What sort of things?"

"If I am not mistaken, lances and such for bloodletting. I saw that at home on more than one occasion before Dr. Webb forbade it."

His expression transformed from perplexity to alarm and, she thought, anger.

"Thank you," he murmured tensely and jumped over the low chain easily and bounded up the stairs two at a time. He disappeared around the corner hollering, "Preston!" as he ran.

There was something troubling going on above stairs. Quite troubling. She thought to follow Dr. Taylor, but a quick look at that little plaque, still swinging from a flick of Dr. Taylor's shoe, stopped her. That and the thought of Mrs. Moorling's censure.

Charlotte walked quickly back down the corridor, past her room and to the servants' stairs. Looking back and seeing no one, she opened the door and stepped in, closing the door behind her. She climbed the stairs as quickly as her taxed body would allow, and when she reached the top she heard the unmistakable sounds of Dr. Preston and Dr. Taylor shouting at each other, as well as Mrs. Moorling's low, admonishing tones. But then the other voice sounded, the high, plaintive wail Charlotte had heard before. The cry seemed more distressed than ever, and the volume and panicked pitch of it were mounting by the second.

Charlotte cracked the door open and peered down the corridor. The windows up here were unshuttered, so the passage was light enough for her to see clearly. She could also hear clearly as Dr. Taylor exclaimed, "Good heavens, Preston. You have frightened her nearly to death."

"I am only attempting what you hadn't the courage to do."

"Yes, and see how much it has helped her."

"I was not finished."

"Yes, you are."

The fevered wailing rose again, and Dr. Taylor barked a command, "Get out of here, Preston. Now."

"Fine. Moorling, come with me."

Preston marched away down the corridor toward the main stairs, Mrs. Moorling following less assuredly behind him. Charlotte saw the woman glance back.

Dr. Taylor's voice called out, "Mrs. Moorling, please hand me that sponge."

"Mrs. Moorling, you will come with me," Preston insisted. "That room is no place for you."

Charlotte was surprised to see Mrs. Moorling obey the man. The two turned the corner and disappeared, Charlotte knew, down the main staircase.

"Mrs. Moorling!" Dr. Taylor's voice had taken on new urgency. "I need you here!"

The wail broke off into short cries and curses and Charlotte heard the unmistakable sound of struggle.

"I need some help here!"

Dr. Taylor's plea pulled Charlotte into the corridor. She stepped both rapidly and timidly down its length to the open doorway. She peered in and put her hand over her mouth to stifle a gasp. Chills prickled her skin. Dr. Taylor held a wild-haired, half-dressed woman in a wrestling hold against the far wall of the room. In one hand, raised above her head, the woman held a lance like those Charlotte had seen on the tray earlier. Dr. Taylor held her wrist to keep the lance at bay and with the other hand held the woman still as she struggled to free herself. The woman, Charlotte realized, was cursing in French.

Dr. Taylor must have heard her footsteps, because he said, without being able to turn around enough to see her, "The opium sponge on the corridor table. Quick!"

Charlotte turned and found the sponge in a bowl. She picked it up carefully and quickly stepped back into the room, dripping water and who knew what else and swallowing back her fear of recrimination. Dr. Taylor pressed the woman's body with his shoulder and awkwardly stuck out his hand behind himself to receive the sponge.

Charlotte walked closer and laid it in his waiting palm. At that moment she stepped into his peripheral vision and he glanced up at her, and his eyes sparked with—what? Anger? Astonishment? Mortification? She wasn't sure. Charlotte glanced quickly at the woman, and even through the dark hair strewn across her face, there was no missing the fury in her expression.

The woman began yelling at her, lip curled in disdain, obsidian eyes flashing. Charlotte's familiarity with the French language did not extend to whatever vile words the woman was spewing—words that were cut off when Dr. Taylor pressed the sponge against her nose and mouth. Charlotte backed away slowly, watching the woman struggle in vain to turn her face away. Just as Charlotte reached the door, the woman slumped against Dr. Taylor, clearly sedated. He picked her up and laid her on the room's lone bed. Only then did Charlotte realize that the woman was with child.

Dr. Taylor looked over at Charlotte in the doorway. "You are not supposed to be up here, you know."

She nodded. "I know."

She stood there a few seconds longer. He offered no explanation and neither did she.

He covered the woman with a blanket, grumbling as he did so, "Blast that Preston. I have told him never to try that with her. Arrogant fool . . ."

In repose, the woman's face relaxed into lovely lines and features somehow familiar. Recognition flitted within reach and away again.

"There, she will rest quietly now." Rising, he led Charlotte from the room, locking the door behind them.

"I suppose you wonder why I don't have him discharged. What with things like this and those other charges you brought to my attention."

"I was not . . ."

"I cannot release him, though I likely should. He knows too much. And now, so do you. I don't suppose I have any right to ask you to keep silent about what you have seen this day."

"What . . . have I seen?" she asked softly.

He looked at her, then away. He sighed deeply. "A woman who suffers from puerperal insanity."

"What is that?"

"A type of melancholy mania. In her case it commenced with conception. More typically it develops after birth."

"I have never heard of it. Do many suffer from it?"

"More and more it seems. And I have yet to figure out why." He ran a frustrated hand through his hair, then seemed to notice Charlotte's hand pressing against her own chest. "Do not fret, Charlotte. I am sure you will be fine. Mania runs in her family, I discovered, but not in yours, as I remember quite well."

"How can one be sure?"

"There are many early symptoms. Inability to attend to any subject, indifference to one's surroundings, fear, melancholy, suicidal thoughts. . . ."

"Good heavens."

"Yes, good heavens indeed. One might wonder what God is doing up there in those heavens of His when so many could use Him down here."

She stood there watching as he walked away toward the main stairs. Then she made her own retreat down the servants' staircase, pressing a hand to her newly aching back and shaking her head as she relived the details of the startling encounter. So shaken was she that it wasn't until she reached her own room that she fully realized that the wild-haired French woman was the bride in the wedding portrait—Dr. Taylor's wife.

❧

The next morning Charlotte arose from bed and immediately groaned, thrusting her hand into the small of her back. The pain she'd first felt the previous night was now visiting her tenfold. Had she injured herself climbing the stairs? She paced her room, hoping to warm her muscles and ease the ache.

A new belt of painful cramping seized her underbelly. Charlotte stopped her pacing and leaned over the bed, supporting herself with her hands, panting. This was no mere backache. This was something altogether new. Altogether frightening. When the constriction abated, she walked gingerly to the door and opened it. Looking down the passage, she saw Gibbs walking across the entry hall.

"Miss Gibbs!" Charlotte called.

"Yes?" The woman paused, and then quickly strode toward her. Taking one look at her face, Gibbs said, "Your pains have begun?"

Charlotte nodded.

"Very well. I shall alert Dr. Preston."

"Is there no one else who might—?"

Gibbs shook her head, "I am afraid not. Dr. Taylor has gone home."

Charlotte sighed and returned to her room. Why must her babe come now, early in the day, with only Preston on hand to deliver her? Woe filled her at the thought of putting herself in such a vulnerable position in his harsh presence. She would prefer Dr. Taylor to attend her, although she would still be mortified to assume the birthing position—on her side, knees up, facing away from him, according to Sally's whispered description. Was there no one else to help her? Another pain struck. *Lord, please help me,* she breathed.

❧

Hat in place and newspaper tucked under his arm, Daniel locked the door to his private medical office on the street level of his townhouse on Wimpole Street. He had no idea where his father was. He had still been abed when Daniel had left early this morning to pay a house call but was not at home when Daniel returned. He hoped his father hadn't broken down and headed out to a tavern somewhere. Hungry, but with little interest in eating alone, Daniel decided to walk down the street for a quick meal at the Red Hen before his next appointment at two.

He was startled to see Preston rounding the corner and heading toward the Red Hen as well. Wasn't the man supposed to be on duty?

"Hello there, Preston."

"Taylor. Hello. I'm rather surprised to see you here."

Daniel was about to icily tell him the same, and to remind him of the office hours for which the Manor was compensating him, but the man's next words stopped him.

"How fares Miss Smith?"

Daniel pulled a grimace. "Fine last I saw her. Why?"

"She's delivered, has she not?"

"Has she? When?"

"Well, beg me, I am confused. Mrs. Moorling told me to head on home, that Taylor was on duty, helping Miss Smith as we spoke, or some such."

"I haven't been to the manor since last night."

"Something afoul there, then. Shall I go back and sort it out?"

"No. I'll go."

He thrust his paper into Preston's arms and strode quickly down the street, worry pushing aside his hunger. Had there been some misunderstanding? Had Mrs. Moorling sent Preston away, thinking Daniel had spent the night and was still above stairs when Charlotte's time came? Had Charlotte been left alone, to deliver her child unaided? Was she suffering still? Or worse, what if complications had arisen as they had with Charlotte's mother? Fear prodded his heart, and soon he was running down the street, over the manor lawn, and pushing through the doors. It was too quiet, deathly quiet. Was he too late? His shoes slapping against the floor echoed as he ran to Charlotte's room. He knocked but didn't wait for an answer as he pushed the door open and barreled inside. Charlotte looked up at him, clearly surprised at his abrupt entrance. But far from looking distressed, Charlotte smiled a wide, contented smile. Heart pounding in his ears, Daniel bent over, resting his hands on his knees to catch his breath. He looked around the room, trying to deduce the situation. Charlotte was sitting up in bed, fresh nightdress and bedclothes around her, bundled babe asleep in her arms.

"Are you . . ." He panted. "Are you well?"

Charlotte nodded, eyes bright.

"But . . . how? When?"

"About an hour ago. As to the 'how,' I think you should know that better than I." Again she smiled at him, a heavy-lidded, peaceful smile.

"But who delivered you? You were not alone, I trust?"

"No, thank goodness. When Gibbs did not find you at home, your father offered to come in your stead."

"My father? Did he? But was he— That is . . . was his attention . . ."

"He was quite wonderful, Daniel. A godsend."

A quick knock sounded and his father walked in, looking the part of the regimental surgeon he once was—dressed in shirtsleeves, black waistcoat and linen apron, drying clean hands on a white cloth. Only his snowy hair, standing here and there out of place, detracted from his competent appearance.

"Daniel. There you are. Have you ever seen such a stout, healthy lad?"

Daniel looked at Charlotte's babe, which he had yet to examine. "Perhaps I should have a look at him."

"Go on, feast your eyes if you like. But I checked him over myself, I did. A perfect specimen, if I say so myself."

Charlotte grinned up at his father. "I must say I quite agree with you, sir."

"May I?" Daniel asked.

Charlotte nodded, and he began his examination of the plump, pink babe.

His father said mildly, "Miss Charlotte here tells me she knew you when she was a girl."

"Yes, I had the privilege of meeting Charlotte's family during my apprenticeship in Kent."

"And now here you meet again. God looks after His lambs, now doesn't He?"

Charlotte's lips rose in an attempted smile, but Daniel could see she doubted the sentiment. For his part, he did not miss the irony of his father referring to Miss "Smith" as a "lamb."

"You are both correct," Daniel pronounced. "Perfect indeed." He rebundled the infant and returned him to Charlotte's arms.

"And what will you call him?" his father asked.

"I have not decided."

"Well, no great hurry." His father picked up his bag and packed away his last few things. "You rest awhile, miss. You've had quite a day already."

"Thank you. I shall."

Mrs. Moorling knocked at the partially opened door and stepped inside. "I've brought Ruth to nurse your child for you."

"I planned to do that myself."

"In time you shall."

"But—"

Charlotte glanced from Mrs. Moorling to him, clearly embarrassed to discuss such matters in front of two men, but still he didn't feel he could leave without explaining. "Prevailing opinion is that a mother's first milk is not suitable for her child. Most women have nurses for the first few days."

"And you agree with this 'prevailing' opinion?"

"Frankly, I do not. Nor does Father."

"You go right ahead and nurse that bonny boy yourself, if you like, miss," his father soothed. "Won't hurt him a bit. After all, the good Lord knew what He was doing when He designed the whole affair."

"Dr. Taylor?" Mrs. Moorling, clearly disapproving, looked to Daniel.

"I see no problem with it. Perhaps Sally Mitchell would be so good as to instruct Miss Smith on proper positioning."

He noticed Charlotte's face and neck became splotched red with embarrassment.

"We shall leave you for now," he said, wanting to end her discomfort. "Come now, Father."

"I shall return on the morrow to check on you, miss," his father offered. "And I will sign the birth record as soon as you settle on a name."

"Thank you."

Once in the corridor, Daniel took his father's arm and leaned close as they walked away. "What are you doing, Father? You do not really mean to return?"

"I always check on my patients."

"She is not your patient . . ."

"Of course she is. I delivered her son myself."

"Yes, and I appreciate your stepping in to assist when I was not available. But I can check on Miss Smith and the others."

"Daniel, I have not felt this good, this useful, in a long time."

"Yes, I am sure. But remember, I agreed to take your place with the condition that you would stay home and . . . get better."

"Get sober, you mean."

Daniel sighed.

"I am sober, Daniel. Have been for some time. I am ready to return."

"I am glad, Father. I am. But for how long? This institution operates on public funding. We cannot afford any more pocks on its reputation." His father's pained expression lanced his conscience. "Father, I did not mean . . ."

But the older man was already walking past him down the corridor, a bit less steady on his legs than he seemed only moments before.

Lord Clarendon, British foreign secretary, reported that Queen Victoria
was hostile to maternal breastfeeding. "Our Gracious Mistress," Lord
Clarendon wrote, "is still frantic with her two daughters
making cows of themselves."

—JUDITH SCHNEID LEWIS, *IN THE FAMILY WAY*

CHAPTER 12

When Charlotte first attempted to nurse her son, she quickly realized it wasn't as easy as it appeared to be. As Sally helped her position her baby, and herself, she felt awkward and humiliated. When Sally then showed her how to coax the child's small mouth open and compress her flesh to fit more fully inside, she was quite relieved no one else was in the room, that she had her private room at last.

She was just beginning to think she'd been dreadfully wrong in insisting she nurse her babe herself when finally, wonder of wonders, he latched on with a lusty mouthful and began suckling greedily. Seems they'd both figured it out at about the same time. Charlotte giggled with relief and satisfaction, and Sally smiled at her in return.

"There you are now—that's how 'tis done. You shall be an old hand in no time, just like me."

Charlotte opened her mouth to say she had no plans to become an experienced wet nurse as Sally was, but she thought better of it. She smiled at Sally instead.

"You have been such a help to me. To us."

Us . . . the single syllable was an unexpected salve to her soul. She who had lost her family now had her own. The memory of birthing pains began fading more rapidly at the thought.

"Well, I'd better toddle back to the ward. Just you let me know if you 'ave any trouble, Miss Charlotte."

"Thank you."

Sally left, closing the door softly behind her.

Charlotte closed her eyes. "Thank you," she murmured, but she was no longer thanking Sally.

Her son suckled a few minutes more, his pink-fair skin and red lips bowed over her white bosom. His little hands, which had bundled into fists, now relaxed open. Eyes closed, he fell asleep, his mouth popping off in a wet sigh of satisfaction.

"My sentiments exactly," she whispered and held him close. She leaned down and kissed his temple with the fine, downy brown hair. She studied his profile. So like his father. Was it possible for an infant to so resemble a man, or was she imagining it?

"If circumstances were different I should have named you for him. But as it is . . ."

Tears filled her eyes and, though she squeezed them shut, hot wet streaks escaped and seared paths down her cheeks, alongside her nose, rolling under her chin.

Oh, dear God, she silently entreated. *Please, please make a way. I know I do not deserve your mercy, but this little one does. Please watch over him. Please show me how to provide for him—make a life for him. I cannot do it without you. Please, make a way.*

❧

Daniel sat on the periphery of a group of gentlemen. The club was busy this night. He had met with the secretary of the Manor Home for Unwed Mothers earlier about the reduced funding over the last six months and possible ways to cut expenses. One of Daniel's least favorite topics. The man had just bid him good evening and Daniel drank the last of his tea, somehow enjoying the disjointed hum and drone of deep male conversation though not participating himself.

"How is your wife, Harris?" someone asked. The voice was familiar.

Daniel looked up. Charles Harris must have come in during his meeting with the secretary—he had not noticed him there before. Harris was seated with a group of men, speaking with Lester Dawes, a physician who had been a year ahead of Daniel at university and with whom he had a passing acquaintance.

"Katherine is . . . well, how are we putting it delicately these days? Great with child."

"Let's see, you two have been married, what—eight months? Nine?" Dawes said. "Someone did not waste any time."

Harris, perhaps hoping to direct attention away from himself, caught Daniel's eye across the narrow room. "And you, Taylor, how is that lovely French wife I've been hearing about?"

Daniel was dismayed when all those dark and silvery heads turned his direction. He swallowed. "Fine, I thank you."

"I am beginning to believe Mrs. Taylor is just a creation of our dear friend's imagination." Dawes grinned indulgently. "I have not laid eyes on her this half year at least."

Daniel felt compelled to speak. "Mrs. Taylor is also expecting a child."

"Well, well," Harris said.

"Lot of that going 'round these days," a portly man muttered meaningfully.

Then a clearly inebriated dapper gentleman, a Lord Killen, Daniel believed, spoke up. "I say, Taylor, my wife tells me she saw you, em, consulting with that vicar's daughter, Miss Lamb. Is it true?"

"Is what true?" Daniel realized this must be the husband of the ladies-aid volunteer who had seen him talking with Charlotte at the Manor.

"You know, what they are saying about her. Laid up, you know, ruined and all that."

Daniel brought his empty teacup to his lips to buy himself a moment. When he spoke, he feigned a casual tone. "I am not personal physician to the Lambs, but I have, as you say, consulted with Miss Lamb on a few occasions about a simple malady. And when I saw her, she appeared quite the same as ever."

"What?" the portly man asked in disbelief. "When was this?"

"I'd say the occasion in question was about two months ago." He turned to Lord Killen, whose wife had reported the meeting. "Does that seem right to you?"

"About so long ago, yes."

Harris was looking at him closely. "This malady you saw her for. Is she quite recovered?"

Daniel stared at him, no doubt severely, then forced himself to take a deep breath. "Yes. When last I saw her, she was recovered quite nicely. The picture of health."

"And when was that?"

He looked at the man meaningfully. "Six days ago now."

"She is . . . back to her old self?"

"As much as one can be, yes."

"Well, I for one am glad to hear those rumors put abed," Harris pronounced. "I was always so fond of Miss Lamb."

"As am I," Daniel agreed quietly.

"I still say there is something afoot," Killen said. "I have not seen her these many months. And when I asked her father, he was quite rude in not answering me."

"Her father is always rude when not making sermons," Daniel said.

"Even then on occasion," Harris added.

The gentlemen began talking of other things, and Daniel soon left them.

Mr. Harris followed him out into the gallery. "Charlotte told you, then?"

"What do you mean?"

"Do not play me for a fool. You know what I mean. Miss Lamb. She told you."

"Miss Lamb has not uttered your name, Harris. She has told me nothing, but this very evening someone revealed your part in her fall."

"Who?"

"You did. Your words, your looks have said it all."

"It is not as it appears, Taylor."

"And how does it appear? That a supposed gentleman has ruined a young gentlewoman, then left her to fend off the wolves for herself and his child? That not one thing has been done to make amends?"

Harris glared at him, anger beading in his dark eyes. "My hands are tied here, man. If but I could, I would. You force me to say what I would conceal from everybody . . . from every man in that room."

"I force nothing."

"You force me to admit I have no money. Nothing. I am holding on to my family estate by the thinnest thread. The fire, the repairs have brought me to the end of my means. The only cash I have is what my wife sees fit to allow me of her father's money and that is but a pittance, doled out in careful drops to keep me on a short tether."

"Bit late that. Why not tell her? Charlotte is her young cousin. Would she not feel some pity for her sake if not for yours?"

"You do not know my wife. I would lose everything. I would be in even less of a position to help Charlotte than I am now. Perhaps in time . . ."

"You could give the child a name."

"I cannot. As I said, Katherine is expecting her own child any day."

"Congratulations," Daniel said dryly.

"Thank you. Contrary to appearances, I am looking forward to being a father."

"You already are one."

Harris studied the floor for a few moments, then asked quietly, "I have no right, I realize, but could you tell me . . . the babe is healthy?"

"Yes, extremely so."

"A . . . girl?"

"A son."

Harris stared at nothing, shaking his head. "A son," he breathed.

"Yes, a son who will grow up in shame and poverty while you play at cards and live in comfort in a fine house—no, make that two fine houses."

Anger flashed in the man's eyes. "Taylor, you overstep yourself."

"No, sir. It was you who overstepped yourself some nine months ago when you took advantage of a girl half your—"

"Lower your voice! She is not *half* my age, and I will not stand here while you throw out unmitigated charges against me. Has she accused me of anything?"

"No. She refuses even to identify you. That girl has idolized you for as long as I have known her—though I cannot fathom why."

"That's right. You wanted her for yourself, but she refused you."

"Her father refused me, yes, but that is neither here nor there."

"Well, here is your chance, then. Perhaps you ought to set her up somewhere, support her yourself."

"I am a married man, as well you know."

"As am I, but you would have me do the same."

"*I* am not the child's father."

Three older men came out, putting on their coats and eyeing the two of them curiously. Harris glanced at the men, then back at Daniel, saying a bit too loudly, "Well, who can say with women today. One never knows."

Daniel swung at the man's face, but Harris was quicker and stronger and caught Daniel's hand in a grip strengthened with constant horsemanship, no doubt, and rough compared to Daniel's sensitive, skilled hands. Harris squeezed Daniel's hand painfully tight.

"A pity to break a surgeon's hand—do you not think?"

"Physician," Daniel said through gritted teeth and stomped on the man's foot.

Harris howled and reared back. He released Daniel's hand and pulled back his arm, thick hand clenched in a fist.

"Mr. Harris!" A young manservant ran up the salon steps, clearly panicked.

Mr. Harris faltered and swung around to face the newcomer. "What is it, Jones?"

"It's her ladyship, sir. The babe's come early, and she's having a hard time of it. That man-midwife says something isn't right."

Fight forgotten, Harris winced. "I told her to have a physician. But she insisted on Hugh Palmer, some *accoucheur* popular with her friends."

"Please, sir," the servant Jones begged. "He says come at once."

Harris paled. Clasping Daniel's arm he urged, "Taylor, I know you despise me, but please, for my wife's sake . . ."

"Of course."

ℛ

They arrived to screaming. Charles Harris cringed and his expression faded to an ashen mask of panic. "Good heavens." He swiveled to face Daniel. "Please help her."

Daniel took the stairs by threes, his medical bag swinging with each upward lunge. Harris followed close behind.

Hugh Palmer, an elfin-faced beauty of a man, met them at the door, his expression grim. "You are too late."

"Too late!" Harris exploded.

"The child has come," the accoucheur announced, "after much struggle."

Daniel noticed the blood on the man's hands and the fatalism in his voice.

Harris cringed again. "Then, why is she still screaming?"

"The child is . . . I did my best to revive him, but I fear he is not long for this world."

"No." Harris bolted past the accoucheur, through the sitting room and into the lying-in room. Daniel followed. A monthly nurse was trying to keep a wild-faced Lady Katherine from leaping from her delivery cot.

"Where is my baby? Give me my baby! Charles! Oh, thank God you are here. They have taken our baby, Charles. They have taken our baby!"

Harris rushed to his wife's side, and Daniel looked around the room. The nurse nodded toward a table near the door. Daniel jogged over and laid his ear on the chest of the swaddled babe. The skin was warm but he could hear no heartbeat. He struck the soles of the infant's feet to stimulate crying, to no avail. He began blowing small puffs of air into the tiny mouth and lungs. Laying his long hand on the child's abdomen, he applied gentle pressure at regular intervals to mimic exhalation.

"What is he doing? Is that my baby? What is he doing to him?"

"Hush, Katherine. Lie back. That is Dr. Taylor. He's an excellent physician. Everything is going to be fine."

Daniel doubted the words.

The nurse approached and quietly suggested they move the baby to the sitting room, out of view of the missus. Daniel complied.

"The physician is going to examine the babe in the other room, missus," the nurse soothed. "He'll be back soon."

Daniel carried the newborn to the sitting room and took a chair near the fire to keep the babe warm. He continued his attempts to rouse the child. There was little hope of success, but he had to try. For the devastated mother, for Harris even, and for himself.

Daniel bitterly assumed the male midwife had disappeared, far from the wrath of father and misery of mother. He wondered if the man even had any hospital training. Accoucheurs were all the rage with the aristocracy, and Daniel, like most physicians, found them a threat—to their own practices, yes, but also to the medical hierarchy and standards of care.

The nurse paused in the doorway. "Shall I give her some laudanum, sir?"

Daniel paused momentarily in his task and sighed. "Please do. And do not be stingy."

The nurse disappeared into the other room, and a short time later Lady Katherine's heartrending shrieks quieted to pitiful sobs.

Harris joined him. "Well?"

Daniel shook his head. "Only the faintest of heartbeats. I am afraid we are losing him."

Harris stared blindly at him. "Dear God, no."

The accoucheur reappeared in the doorway, leather bag in hand. "Do not blame providence. I find women who live in affluence and luxury often endure prolonged suffering and more difficult births than the lower orders of women."

"How dare you . . ."

Harris lurched forward, raising his arm to strike the man, but Daniel called out, "Harris, don't."

Slowly, Harris lowered his fist and his voice. "Get out of my house this instant," he growled.

The young man inclined his nose, turned on his heel, and left the room.

Daniel continued his ministrations on the child. "If we were at the lying-in hospital with my warming crib and stimulants, maybe, but in any case, there is so little I can do."

"Go then, in my carriage. Or send my man for whatever you need. Spare no expense."

When Daniel did not move, Harris exclaimed, "Good heavens, man, why do you sit there?"

The nurse reappeared. "Her ladyship will sleep 'til morning I'd wager. I gave her a hefty dose. Poor lamb."

Charles Harris swung his gaze to Daniel, steely resolve and desperation flinting in the candlelight. "Take my son to that hospital of yours, Taylor. Take us both."

After the copulation concludes, butterflies fly away

[to] areas with an abundance of milkweed....

—MORGAN COFFEY, CORONADO BUTTERFLY PRESERVE

CHAPTER 13

Charlotte sat up in bed. She'd heard a sound, a moan. This was not the wail from the French woman above stairs; this was a male cry. The sound vibrated with anguish. It struck her deeply somehow, as though she'd heard the sound before. But how could that be? She didn't think it was Dr. Taylor. And she barely knew the other men about the place.

She looked down at her little son, asleep beside her, a feather pillow keeping him close. She'd retrieved him from the little crib at the foot of her bed for his last feeding and they had fallen asleep together. She had awakened only long enough to secure the spare pillow on his other side to make sure he would not fall from bed. He slept peacefully still, undisturbed by the sound. She stroked his head lightly, needing to touch him but hoping not to wake him.

When the sound didn't come again, she settled back against her pillow. What was it the cry had reminded her of?

Then she remembered. And that memory she had so often pushed away reasserted itself. Lying there, looking down at the profile of her newborn child in the moonlight, she let the memory come.

That night Charlotte had also awakened to a sudden sound. Someone had called out in pain, she was sure, and her mind quickly identified the familiar voice. *Mr. Harris.* Lightning flashed in her bedchamber, and for a moment she hesitated. Perhaps she had imagined it or it had only been the wind. She should stay in bed. Safe. But she couldn't sleep, wondering if Mr. Harris was ill.

He had come to stay at the vicarage two weeks before, after the Christmas Eve fire at Fawnwell. What a night that had been. Fire brigades and people from all over Doddington had come to help. Charlotte herself had run over and was soon put to work hauling pitchers of tea and water for the volunteers. There was little they could do to stop the fire tearing at the south wing with fiery claws. In a matter of hours, the south wing was a black, smoking heap of rubble and skeletal ribs. At least they had managed to keep the fire from spreading to the north.

Still in her bed, Charlotte heard Mr. Harris moan once more. Rising, she quickly wrapped her white dressing gown over her nightdress, quietly opened her door, and stepped out. The upstairs rooms were arranged around a square court, open to the ground floor. She stepped to the balcony railing. A faint light from below drew her eye and compelled her toward the stairs.

She found him slumped in a chair before a dying fire in the drawing room, staring at a sheet of paper.

"Mr. Harris?" she whispered.

But at that moment, a loud clap of thunder shook the vicarage and he didn't hear her. He crumpled the letter in his hand, dropped the tumbler he'd been holding in his other, and held his face instead.

"Mr. Harris!" She flew to his side, kneeling before his chair, reaching for the spilled glass and turning it aright on the floor.

Her hands were tentative on his knee, entreating him to notice her presence. "Are you ill?"

He looked at her with strange wonderment. "Charlotte? Did I wake you? Pray forgive me."

"There is nothing to forgive. Has something else happened? Mr. Harris, you look very ill. Should I send Buxley for Dr. Webb?"

"No. There is nothing he can do for me."

"What, then?" She spied the crumpled letter. "Have you received bad news?"

"Yes. Bitter news."

"Your mother?"

"No. Mother is fine—still staying with friends in Newnham. Doing as well as can be expected for a woman forced from her home." He rubbed both hands over his face, clearly distressed.

"Is there nothing I can do? Is there something you might take for your present comfort?"

"If you mean brandy, I have had plenty . . . with little relief to show for it."

"Shall I call Father?"

"No. Let him sleep."

"Shall I leave you alone, then?"

"Stay, Charlotte, if you will."

"Of course."

"You are a comfort to me," he said idly, still staring at the embers in the grate. "Always have been."

Lightning flashed, filling the room with light, then leaving it more shadowed than before. Wind howled, holding the curtains aloft on the breath of its wail.

"You must be freezing!" She rose and rushed to the window, wondering why on earth it had been opened on such a cold January night.

"I had not noticed . . ."

She closed the window firmly, pausing to look out at the swaying tree limbs and swirling snow. "Thunder and lightning in January."

She shook her head in wonder. "This is going to be an incredible storm."

She walked to the hearth and tossed a few scoops of coal onto the fire, then turned to him. Seeing him shiver, she pulled her father's wool lap robe from the back of the chair and laid it across his shoulders.

"Is it Fawnwell?" she asked, straightening the robe over his arms.

He didn't answer, so she continued. "You shall rebuild—"

"In time." He straightened in his chair. "Though it is not Fawnwell alone which weighs on my mind this night."

She again knelt before him. "It is not the wind, is it?" She attempted a mild tease. "I have never known you afraid of a coming storm."

But his answer was contemplative, serious. "Afraid? Why be afraid when there is nothing I can do. This I know, but still—I detest my utter helplessness to stay its hand. I dread its power over me. I dread the . . . damage . . . it will certainly havoc."

She squeezed his hand and he looked down at her, as if suddenly realizing she was there.

"Good heavens, you look beautiful like that."

"Like . . . what?"

"Your hair down around you, the firelight . . ."

His eyes fell from her face to her neck, and Charlotte for the first time was aware of her own state of dress. But rather than the rush of embarrassment she would have expected, a strange feeling of power filled her instead. She had come into this room a little girl, to comfort her dear Mr. Harris, with no care for her dress or decorum, only to soothe the man she loved most in the world. It was as if, as she knelt there before him, she grew from little girl to desirable woman in a space of a few aching heartbeats. And, if she was reading his expression rightly, he was witnessing the same startling transformation as well. But perhaps it was only her view of herself that had changed, because she had indeed seen that look in his eyes before—that admiration, that desire—but had been blind to its meaning.

He leaned nearer, inspecting her closely. He lifted his hand to touch her face, tenderly outlining her jaw, her chin, with his fingers.

"I always knew you would be beautiful, Charlotte. But you always were to me. Promise me you will forget all my foolishness in the morning—chalk it up to lightning and brandy—but now I feel I must say what I very soon will no longer be able to speak of."

She opened her mouth to speak, but she feared whatever she might say would break this pleasurable spell. He ran a thumb over her silent, parted lips and her heart throbbed within her.

"I have loved you since you were a little girl, Charlotte—I suppose you know that—and I love you still. To me, you are the dearest creature God ever made. You have always been so kind, so affectionate to me—more than I deserved. When I see myself in your eyes, I am the best man on earth. Or at least in Kent."

His mouth lifted in the crooked half grin she'd always admired, and in thoughtless response to his warm words, she leaned close and placed a quick kiss on his mouth, and instantly his grin fell away.

He stood suddenly, awkwardly, and since her hand was still clutching his, pulled her to her feet with him. He looked down at her, then away. "You had better go back to bed."

He stood rock still, but made no move to turn from her nor to turn her out. She stood before him, wishing she might kiss him again, to wipe that bleak look from his face, to see him smile once more. But he was too tall for her to reach, her head reaching only to his shoulders.

"Go on," he repeated in a rough whisper, and for a moment she wasn't sure if he wanted her to leave or to continue with her unspoken desire. Rather than feeling dismissed or rejected, she felt instead emboldened, sure at last of his attachment to her and feeling the pleasure, the intoxicating sweetness of it. How could she not, after a lifetime of thinking him the most handsome and cleverest of men? After endless years of loving him, of dreaming of him, of believing him out of reach, here he was, right here now, loving her.

She lifted his hand, caressed it in both of hers and kissed it. He winced as though she were hurting him.

"Leave me."

She looked at him, wild emotions coursing through her. "How can I?" She pressed his hand over her heart. "When I love you as well?"

"But"—his eyes fell to the discarded letter—"I cannot love you."

"You already do."

Slowly his hand slid lower and she could barely breathe. She leaned closer to him.

He whispered, "Charlotte. You are killing me. I am only a man."

She lifted her face toward his, and he pulled her into his arms, lowering his lips to hers, kissing her deeply. He half sat, half fell into the chair behind him, lifting her onto his lap, holding her close, still kissing her.

Then once again he pushed her aside, standing and twisting away, leaving her sprawled in the chair alone. He ran his hand over his face. "Charlotte, go. We cannot be together like this."

Though his back was to her, she reached around and took his clenched hand in hers and turned him back around to face her. Gently, she pulled him down to his knees before her and, for the second time in their long relationship, their positions were reversed. His eyes were wide, desperate, full of desire. She felt the cold night air on her neck, her limbs, her shoulders, she felt his hand in hers and wanted to feel more. She did not truly think, made no conscious decision to cross the threshold; she was not versed in such things. She knew a woman could comfort a man, though she knew not how. And she knew she loved this man. She thought only of lengthening this time together, of holding him close as she had

133

never been allowed before. When she pulled him toward her, he peered at her closely.

"This is your last chance, Charlotte."

But she pulled him into her arms and kissed him, feeling, foolishly, as if she, too, were helpless to stop the coming storm.

She knew little of the rudiments of physical love. She had been told only that some men were not trustworthy and that is why she must never be alone with a man without a proper chaperone. But she had always trusted Mr. Harris implicitly and knew her father did as well. Mr. Harris was not "some man"—he was looked upon practically as relation. She had not known a moment's fear in his presence, even alone with him, until this moment. Only when he leaned against her and she felt her nightdress begin to slide up did the warning bells finally go off in her desire-drunk mind. She tried to pull her mouth from his, to pull herself away, but the back of the chair pinned her in. She finally wrenched her mouth free and entreated, "Wait, I—"

He halted immediately, staring down at her in growing apprehension, suspended. Frozen.

But somehow, though she felt no pain, the damage was done.

In the morning, Charlotte awoke with the dreadful hope that she had somehow mistaken the events of the previous night. She was not completely certain that what she feared transpired actually had. But in the cold, dark hours she had lain alone in bed since, she knew without doubt that she had left behind all modesty, all rules of polite society, and, she feared, lost all virtue as well. Worse yet, she felt she had lost Mr. Harris, his esteem and his love. She sat up in bed and in so doing, spied the letter, which had apparently been slid under her door. She knew better than to hope for a love letter now. So this was how it was to be—worse than she thought.

With fatalistic numbness she arose and picked up the folded stationery. She climbed back into bed and cocooned herself beneath the featherbed, shielding herself from the cold reality she knew awaited her. She opened the letter and read the single line:

Somehow, someday, please forgive me.

It bore neither salutation nor signature. *Cold indeed.* But at least, it seemed, it bore no blame either.

A mere fortnight later, Charlotte had been shocked, sickened, and scared to death when another letter came. Her father read it aloud during breakfast.

"Well, well, a letter from your cousin Katherine."

"What does she say, Father?" Bea asked, spearing a sausage. "Do read it to us. She is ever so amusing."

Father's face looked anything but amused as he scanned the inked script. "I fear you will not enjoy it, my dear."

"What is it?"

"An announcement of her upcoming wedding."

"Wedding? You are joking! Katherine has long proclaimed herself a determined spinster."

"Well, she has clearly changed her mind."

"Who is the brave soul who finally convinced her?"

He didn't immediately answer.

"Do we know him?" Bea persisted, sausage forgotten.

"Yes. We know him quite well. Or at least I thought we did."

Charlotte clenched her hands together beneath the table. Bea's face began to grow concerned.

"Not Bentley," Bea breathed. "He's too young."

"No, not Bentley. Charles Harris himself."

Bea's expression barely had time to clear before it blanched, her mouth falling open, slack.

Charlotte was stunned but kept her expression as blank as possible, seeing her own feelings mirrored in her sister's face. She knew her own desolation, her humiliation, must be deeper, more complete, than Bea's, but she willed herself not to show it.

"But . . ." Bea protested. "There was no reading of the banns in church. . . ."

"Applied for a license no doubt. Never one for public displays, your cousin."

"I cannot believe it."

"I have never approved of these licenses," their father began. "The banns are not merely tradition, they serve a purpose, allowing anyone with a preexisting marriage contract or other cause to object, to 'speak or forever hold their peace.'" He sighed. "Now a few pounds to a bishop and one may forgo the banns altogether."

"But it isn't right!" The words burst from Charlotte, surprising them all.

"Why not?" Bea glared at her. "Would you have stood up in church and spoken against it had you the chance? Have you some reason to object to Mr. Harris marrying our cousin?"

The bile rose in Charlotte's throat and she stood on shaking legs. "Please excuse me," she mumbled, putting her hand over her mouth and walking quickly from the room.

Bea called after her, "You never seriously thought he would marry you, did you?"

Charlotte threw open her bedroom door and made it to the chamber pot just in time to lose her breakfast.

A few hours later, Charlotte was in the garden when the man she was trying not to think about came thundering across the grounds on his horse. She turned and ran.

"Charlotte, wait!" Charles Harris leapt from his horse, not bothering to tether it, and ran after her. Charlotte hurried through the garden gate and across the lane to the churchyard, hoping to hide herself there. She did not think this rationally—her core instinct simply told her to flee this man. To be close to him was to invite another mortal wound.

She had made it through the church doors when he grabbed her shoulders, swinging her around to face him.

"Let go of me," she commanded.

Panting from his run, his face was stricken, his hair disheveled.

"Only if you will listen to me."

She pulled out of his grasp and stepped back, but didn't run. A foolish part of her still hoped he would tell her it was all a mistake, that he had no intention of marrying Katherine.

"I had no idea she would send the announcements so soon," he began. "My mother received one as well, and I rushed over here the minute I realized. I had hoped to tell you myself, to explain. . . ."

She only stared at him, offering him no encouragement.

"Charlotte. I realize that, considering what happened between us, you might have expected . . ." He pushed his hair off his forehead with a stab of his hand. "That is, under normal circumstances, I would have behaved differently. . . ."

"Do you mean that night, or afterwards?" she asked, her tone pointed.

He sighed heavily. "Both actually. I was stupid and selfish that night. I had just gotten a letter from the bankers, you see, and I was so desperate . . ."

"Yes, I remember."

"I should have tried harder to put a stop to it."

"It was all my fault, then, was it?"

"Of course not. I am to blame. I knew better."

"Yet you accept no responsibility."

He studied her sharply, clearly worried. "Is there . . . something for which I need bear responsibility?"

Mouth open, she shook her head, stunned at the stupidity of the question. Did he not realize she was forever changed? Her future like a candle without a wick?

But clearly he took her shake of head as a longed for answer and blew out a rush of air, relieved. "Good."

Good? "Tell me this. That night—were you already engaged to her?"

He lowered his head. "Not . . . exactly. She had proposed an alliance . . . a marriage of sorts, prior, but I had put her off. But then the fire occurred. . . . Charlotte, you have no idea what it's like, the responsibility I bear for Fawnwell. I was hanging on by a thread before the fire. After it . . . it was all but lost. That letter from the bank confirmed it. I had neither the funds to repair nor rebuild. My mother had no idea. She assumed we would simply rebuild, maybe even improve on the original structure. I hadn't the heart to tell her the truth. I promised my father I would keep the place going, make it prosper. . . ."

"So you are marrying Katherine for her money."

"I am sorry. Truly I am. But there is nothing else to be done."

Now, lying there in the manor, his child in her arms, Charlotte remembered what her parting words to him had been: *"Your house has been destroyed . . . but I must pay the price."*

Because of the deep roots, successful transplantation
of mature plants is difficult. Attempt it only with
small offspring of the mother....

—JACK SANDERS, *THE SECRETS OF WILDFLOWERS*

CHAPTER 14

I n his office in the manor, Daniel rested his palm on the infant's small chest in silent benediction. "I am sorry," he said quietly to the child's father. "There is nothing else to be done."

Harris stared up at him, clearly not able or not willing to comprehend.

"He is gone," Daniel added gently.

"Give him to me," Harris ordered tersely, and for a moment Daniel feared the man might continue with vain attempts to breathe life into his son's small body. Daniel wrapped the child securely in a donated blanket and reverently handed him over to Charles Harris, who reached both hands out to receive the bundle.

When the weight of the infant's body filled his hands and arms, it seemed the child became real to the man all at once. He stared down at the little face and buckled over as if struck hard. He cried out in anguish. A cry that must certainly be echoing throughout the manor. The man sank to the nearest chair and held the bundled child to his chest, face contorted, tears streaking from his eyes. A different man indeed from the smug man Daniel had sparred with only a short time before. His heart tore for the man, his loss. He could not help but imagine himself in the same situation, if his own wife or soon-to-arrive child should die during childbirth. His answering tears were for himself as well as for Charles Harris.

"Katherine will not bear it," Harris whispered.

"Of course the loss is terrible, but in time . . ."

"No, you don't understand. Katherine feared this might happen. She insisted I should plan to have her locked away immediately should the child die. That she would go insane with grief—want to die herself. I promised her everything would be all right. Nothing would happen to our child. . . ." The man's grief rendered him unable to continue.

"It is not your fault, man. You did everything you could."

"I did nothing."

"Your wife will want her time to say good-bye to him. We should take him back to her before—"

"No! Did you not notice her state? I have never seen her like that. I cannot bring home a . . . lifeless . . . child. . . ."

"It will be painful, yes, but in the end it will help her overcome her grief."

"No." He spoke the word with less vehemence, shaking his head thoughtfully, staring at nothing. Suddenly he looked up, startled, his face alight with manic purpose.

"Where is Charlotte?"

Instantly, panic, dread, and profound fear struck Daniel Taylor with full force. He could see what was coming, should have foreseen it an hour before. "Mr. Harris, whatever you are thinking, I beg you to put it from your mind."

"What am I thinking?"

"I forbid you to approach Miss Lamb on this. You are grieving, I realize, but—"

"You cannot keep me from seeing Charlotte."

"Actually I can. I am her physician and she is still in recovery."

"She will want to see me."

"Will she? Even when she discovers your purpose? I cannot believe you are thinking to . . . I cannot conceive of a more cruel offer."

"Cruel? What is cruel about offering my son—my other son—a decent life? You said it yourself, if I do nothing, he will grow up with nothing—no advantages, no opportunities, let alone the basic necessities of life."

"I never said . . ."

"How many other fatherless children could hope for such as I, as *we*, could provide?"

"But your wife . . ."

"Need never know!"

"You offer only because your own son is dead. Had he lived . . ."

"Then you and I would not be having this conversation, I grant you. But he did not live, did he? And here I stand, not—what?—a few steps from my own flesh-and-blood living, breathing son? I say it's providence."

"I say it's heartless and selfish."

"But it does not really matter what you say. It only matters what Charlotte says, does it not?"

Daniel shook his head, arms crossed, head pounding.

"Please, man, I beg of you. Let me at least see her!"

Daniel stared at the man, but instead saw a younger Charlotte, smile beaming, looking up into the face of this man before him. *Would she want to see him? Consider his wretched offer?* Daniel longed to protect her, but who was he to make such a colossal decision?

Daniel insisted on entering Charlotte's room first, on having a few moments alone with her. To prepare her, somehow—as if such a thing were possible.

He sternly waved Harris back, waiting until he was hidden in the shadows several steps down the corridor, before knocking softly on Charlotte's door.

"Yes?" she answered after only a moment's hesitation.

Pinning Harris with a "stay there" stare, he opened the door a few inches. "Charlotte? It's Daniel Taylor. May I come in a moment?"

"Of course."

He stepped into the room, closing the door behind him, his lamp held low at his side, hopefully providing her some modesty should she need it.

"Good evening," he said, striving for normalcy. "Please forgive the lateness of the hour."

"I was still awake, watching him."

He noticed that a candle burned on her bedside table. He set his small oil lamp atop the chest near the door, causing large shadows to quiver on the room's walls.

She sat up on the bed, facing him. "Is everything all right?"

He stood awkwardly clenching his hands, then realizing he was, stuffed them into his pockets. In the bed beside Charlotte the babe awakened, fussing a bit. Charlotte leaned over and picked him up. She leaned back against the headboard, bouncing him gently in her arms.

"There, there. You cannot be hungry yet, little one."

When the infant relaxed back to sleep, Charlotte smiled up at Daniel, her tired eyes alight with a look of maternal wonder at, perhaps, her unexpected skill with her child. Her smile held a touch of pride; her face, glowing in the golden light of the candle, beamed with deep contentment. What a lovely portrait she and her babe made at this moment. He smiled at her in return, and felt another pricking at the back of his eyes and a tightness in his throat. He feared that this was the last time she would ever look this happy again.

"Have you decided what to call him?" he asked, putting off the inevitable.

"I believe I have. I found the task much more difficult than I would have imagined." She laid the child on the far side of the bed beside her, securing him with a pillow.

"Why is that?" The moment the question left his mouth, he knew it was a stupid one and wished it back.

"Well, because normally I should name him for . . . his father. At least that is customary. But there is little customary about this situation." She straightened a blanket over the babe. "Or I should name him for my own father. But given the circumstances. . . ."

"Yes, I see what you mean."

He cleared his throat.

She turned to him. "Is something the matter?" she asked gently.

"Yes, I am afraid there is something. Something that might—potentially—trouble you."

"What is it?"

"There is someone here who wishes to see you."

"Now? Who is it?"

"It's, um . . ."

"My father?" she asked, surprise and, he could not miss, a note of hope in her voice. His heart ached dully at disappointing her.

"No, I'm sorry. Not your father."

She stared at him but didn't reply. He took a deep breath and continued.

"It's Charles Harris."

"Mr. Harris?"

"Yes, you see, his own child . . . that is, his wife Katherine's child was born this night."

He saw Charlotte's face harden at his words, and for a moment he was relieved. He hoped she might rebuke the man without a second thought.

"But he lived for only a short time," Daniel continued. "I revived him but was not successful in keeping him alive."

"Poor Katherine."

"Yes, though Mr. Harris is distraught as well."

"Is he?"

The door creaked slowly open and both turned to look.

"Charlotte?" Harris's voice was both plaintive and determined. "Sorry, Taylor, I could not wait any longer." He stepped into the room, closing the door quietly behind him. "Charlotte, I had to see you."

He approached the bed, hat in hand. "What has Taylor told you?"

Charlotte stared up at him. "That your . . . that Katherine's newborn child died this night."

"Oh, Charlotte. I am laid low indeed." Charles dropped to his knees beside the bed and grasped her arm, his hat falling unnoticed to the floor. Now he looked up at her with tear-streaked eyes.

"A little son—did he tell you?"

Charlotte nodded mutely.

"I held him in my hands as he died. . . ." A sob broke through his throat, and Daniel looked away from the painful scene. Still, Harris must have suddenly remembered that he was standing there. "Taylor. Give us a moment, will you?"

Daniel wanted nothing more than to flee from this room, filled with one man's pain and likely to soon flood with another's. But he feared the older man might pressure Charlotte, who was clearly susceptible to his persuasion. And given her fragile emotional condition as a new mother . . . No, he couldn't leave her to face this alone.

"I am staying."

Charlotte looked over at him, clearly surprised. She opened her mouth as if to argue but then closed it, saying nothing. She returned her gaze to Charles Harris.

"Katherine will be insane with grief as you might imagine."

"Any woman would be."

"She does not yet know. The nurse sedated her while Taylor here tried to revive him."

She stared at the man, clearly perplexed. "I am sorry for your loss."

"Thank you. That means a great deal to me. I know I made an immense mistake where you are concerned. That you could still say that, well, I thank you."

Her brow wrinkled as she listened to him, perhaps trying in vain to follow his line of thought.

"And you, Charlotte? How do you fare?"

Harris was evidently avoiding the issue—that is, the baby—a mere arm's length from his nose. Waiting, most likely, for Charlotte to bring him into the conversation.

"Quite well, actually. Everyone here has been very kind to me, and my son and I are in good health."

"Your son, yes. Taylor mentioned him."

She looked up sharply at Daniel, eyebrows high. "Did he?"

"Well, I asked him about you. How you were . . . and everything. He deduced the rest himself."

"I see."

"And your son. What do you call him?"

"Dr. Taylor and I were just discussing that very topic. I have decided to call him Edmund, after my grandfather."

"That was my father's name as well."

She looked away from both men's gazes. "Yes," she murmured.

Charles Harris smiled through fresh tears. "You honor me."

Charlotte's gaze shifted to her sleeping son. "It was not my intention."

"May I . . . see him?" he asked.

She looked at Harris, clearly confused by his attention, but she complied, shifting the little bundle to her other side. Harris laid out both forearms on the bed to receive him. In the lamplight, Harris studied the small face, the tiny hands, and a new wave of sorrow stole over his features.

"He is beautiful . . . perfect . . ." He forced words over his tears. "Like his mother."

Charlotte's eyes filled with tears of her own at the man's obvious awe layered over raw grief.

She smiled, causing a tear to run down each of her cheeks. She whispered, "Actually, he looks a great deal like you."

Charles nodded, tears coursing down his face too.

Daniel stood there feeling the worst of interlopers and had just decided to leave the sad pair to themselves when Charles changed tactics.

"I cannot help wondering . . . how will the two of you get along? I would help you if I could, but you know I haven't any money of my own at present. Perhaps in time, but for now . . . how will you live?"

"I do not know exactly, but we will manage."

"Will you? Charlotte, forgive me, but I must ask. You are young, you might yet marry and have more children. Katherine, as you know, is much older. The pregnancy was very difficult for her and she has vowed never to bear another child should anything happen to this one."

Charlotte stared at him. "What are you saying?"

"Charlotte . . . think about it before answering."

"Before answering what?" Her voice rose.

"Charlotte. Think. You could go back to your old life. Reenter society. I would raise him as my own."

"He is your own! And that has never tempted you to any duty before now."

"I do not deny I have treated you ill. But I would treat Edmund very well. You know I would be a good father to him. And Katherine . . . You would be saving your cousin from a broken heart, from the brink of insanity."

"It is you who is insane. Do you think I would just give my child to you? How dare you ask such a thing? He is my son!"

"He is mine as well."

"He is yours no longer. You gave him up when you married my cousin." She gathered her infant back into her arms and held him close.

"I had no choice."

"You had a choice. And you made it. Now leave us alone. Leave, this instant."

Daniel took a step forward, ready to escort Harris from the room, feeling none of the satisfaction he had anticipated now that Charlotte had refused him. There was no happy ending for such a situation as this.

Harris rose to his feet, clearly shaken and chagrined. "I am sorry, Charlotte. I had no right to ask."

She shook her head, wonderingly, despairingly. "Again you would choose your own happiness—and Katherine's—over mine. *Again.*" Her voice shook as she spoke. "You would have me take on Katherine's heartbreak, to suffer in her stead. I cannot have her place in your life, but I can have her intolerable grief?"

Mr. Harris looked at the floor. "You are right, Charlotte," he said quietly. "It is too much. Forgive my asking."

Harris turned toward the door, Daniel a few paces behind him. He opened it and gestured Daniel through. As Harris was about to shut the door behind him, Charlotte called out, "Wait."

Charlotte swallowed as Mr. Harris stepped cautiously back into the room.

Dr. Taylor stood near the door, searching her face. "I shall wait just outside the door," he said. "If you need me, you need only call."

Charlotte nodded mutely, and Dr. Taylor closed the door behind him. Mr. Harris took a tentative step back toward the bed, arms behind his back, head bowed.

Charlotte looked away from him, away from her son. She stared toward the window, its shutters folded back. From across the room, the light of the moon outside drew her gaze. She was silent for several minutes. Unable to think. Only to feel.

"You know I want what is best for him," she began, her throat tight and burning. "But this . . . this is too much, too sudden."

From the corner of her eye, she glimpsed his nod, but he said nothing. She turned from the moonlight to look at him.

"Do you have any idea what you are asking of me? He is my son—my heart! I love him more than my own life. Have you ever felt that way about anyone? Or do you love only yourself . . . and that estate of yours?"

"That might have been true once. But no longer."

"You really do love her, then—Katherine?"

"Yes. Not at first, perhaps. But now . . ."

"And would she . . . love my son?" Sobs racked her entire body.

He did not answer immediately. When he did, it wasn't the answer she expected. "Charlotte, you know my wife. Katherine is very loving, but she is also very proud, very jealous, and very possessive."

"Yes, I know her well."

"If we act now, and give Edmund to her, she will believe him her own and he will grow up with every advantage, free from scandal, with both a father's and a mother's love. But if she knows he is not her own flesh and blood, I fear she will reject him, or at best be bitter toward him—and me—all his life. While Katherine has her failings, she is capable of great love, great loyalty and devotion, and I can promise you Edmund will have all these things from her."

"She will not mistreat him?"

"Of course not. He is my own son! And she will believe him hers as well."

"*If* I were to consent to this, would you be willing to promise me something?"

He nodded cautiously.

"If she does realize Edmund is not her own, if she cannot love him utterly, I beg you please, return him to me. Promise me you would not let him suffer."

"I give you my word."

"Would you give me some time to think about it?"

"We haven't much time, Charlotte. If I take Edmund home now, or at the very least in the next few hours, when Katherine is just waking from the sedatives, I can easily persuade her that this little boy is her own, home safe and well from his trip to the hospital. If we wait and she suspects, not only is her devotion in question, but my ability to bequeath my land and holdings to him as my legal heir would also be at risk. If we are to do this, it must be now. Tonight."

"But how . . . ?"

"Taylor!" He startled her by shouting.

Dr. Taylor opened the door, behind which he had been standing at the ready as promised.

"Come in, man, and close the door."

When Dr. Taylor had complied, Mr. Harris said in a low, conspiratorial voice, "Is there any reason—should Miss Lamb agree, of course—if I left here tonight with this child, that anyone would know he is not my own? The one I arrived bearing?"

Daniel Taylor's face looked ashen and angry behind his grim mask. "For that to work, Miss Lamb would need to falsely claim your, pardon me, deceased son, as her own. And I should also have to lie to verify that somehow a perfectly healthy infant in my care has died during the night. The death certificate would need to be forged and the birth certificate falsified. And then there is the problem of the accoucheur and the monthly nurse who witnessed your son's struggle. But beyond these minor inconveniences"—his tone was acid—"I see no reason whatever."

Mr. Harris ignored his sarcasm. "The accoucheur will be so relieved his patient has a living child—that his own reputation will not suffer—he will raise no alarm. And I am quite certain he completed neither birth nor death certificate. Remember, my poor child was still alive, though just barely, when we left the house."

"And why would I lie for you and risk my own reputation and career?"

"You would not for me," Mr. Harris said, "but you would for Charlotte. You'd do anything you could to help her."

Dr. Taylor paused but did not deny the man's words. "If it was what she truly wanted." He looked at her, and the panic and nausea that rose in her while they discussed details of an act that would surely kill her now made her whole body tremble.

"How can I? How can I part with him?"

Mr. Harris searched her face earnestly. "I shall appeal to you only once more, Charlotte, and then torment you no further. But think on this. You do not know how you would provide for Edmund, though I've no doubt you would try admirably. With Katherine's wealth and, God willing, a return to prosperity for Fawnwell, Edmund will have the best of everything—the best doctors, the best tutors, the best schools. When Katherine and I die he will be our heir. He will know no want and want for nothing."

"And he will never know me."

"A terrible loss to be sure, but he will not know what he is missing."

"But I shall know what I am missing."

"Yes, dear Charlotte. You will know."

They stayed as they were for several moments, none of them speaking. Charlotte thought not so much on Mr. Harris's promises of abundance for her child but rather on the alternatives. What flashed before her mind were not idyllic images of Edmund romping about the croquet lawn in a fine suit of clothes, but rather the things she had seen at this place. She saw the perfect brown-haired boy she had fed die for no apparent reason. She saw the desperate young woman who put her infant on the turn beg for a wet-nursing post hoping to be reunited with her baby—only to find her heel-marked daughter dead by morning. She thought of women like Becky's mother, who couldn't afford to feed her children, of Becky herself, who would likely have to give up her baby and go back to work or starve.

But surely she had more options. Wouldn't Aunt Tilney help her? She'd already offered her a place to live, and she could nurse Edmund herself for at least a year, if her milk held out. But what then? How would she buy him food, let alone all the other things he'd need? Would her uncle allow her aunt to help further against her father's directives? Not likely. What sort of post could she get with an infant to nurse every few hours? The words she had so naïvely spoken to Mae echoed back at her, *"I would never give my child to someone else to feed . . ."* And here she was, considering doing just that. *I must be insane.* She shuddered.

Dr. Taylor cleared his throat. "Perhaps, Miss Lamb, there might be something I can do. I haven't a large income, but I am sure I could find a way to help you out of this predicament."

Dr. Taylor clearly had no idea how inappropriate his offer was, but she knew he offered with the best intentions.

"I thank you anyway, Dr. Taylor, but you have a wife and your own child to think of."

Charlotte looked down at Edmund's small face, which had instantly become so precious to her. Sobs overtook her again. "Must I decide right now? I cannot. I cannot."

She held her tiny son close and glared up at the men. "Can you both please excuse me? I need a few moments alone. I cannot think with the two of you staring at me."

Charles looked at his pocket watch. "But—"

"Of course," Daniel overrode him, leading the other man from the room. "We shall return directly."

When the door closed behind them, Charlotte got up, one hand on Edmund to keep him safe, and fell to her knees beside the bed. Tears dripped from her face onto the blanket she'd embroidered as she looked down at her bundled son. *I cannot do it, Lord, I cannot. When I prayed for you to provide a way for him, this is not what I meant! This is too hard. Too cruel. Is it truly the right course? Your way out of this muddle? If so, you will have to help me. I cannot do this alone. . . .*

Her prayers turned to thoughts of her son, and she whispered through her tears, "Oh, my little one, you will never remember me. But I will always remember you. Always love you. Never think I did not love you . . . or want you. Oh, God, it is too hard. . . ."

Charlotte Lamb laid her head down on the bed beside her son and cried, knowing she must somehow do an impossible thing.

The milkweed pods are breaking,
And the bits of silken down
Float off upon the autumn breeze
Across the meadows brown.

—CECIL CAVENDISH, *THE MILKWEED*

CHAPTER 15

Daniel left his carriage in the lane and walked across the Doddington churchyard just as dusk was falling the next eve. Two men were digging a grave beneath a yew tree near the cemetery wall.

He called out as he approached, "I am looking for a Ben Higgins."

The younger of the two men looked his way without ceasing his labors.

"You found him. Though folks call me Digger."

Not very original, Daniel thought grimly. "Might I speak with you?"

Digger straightened. "Well, I am a bit busy, man. What's on yer mind?"

Daniel didn't answer, but still the young man laid his shovel aside and climbed from the hole. He walked forward, removing his floppy hat as he came, revealing a mop of chestnut hair in need of cutting.

"You're that doctor's boy," Digger said. "Apprentice, rather."

"Yes, I was." Daniel walked back toward the carriage, where the horse was tied to a post. Digger followed.

"Haven't seen you 'ere since I was a lad."

"I am relieved you remember me."

"And why is that?"

Daniel turned toward the wooden box on the carriage floor, and Digger followed his gaze. The young man's eyes became wary and his mouth pursed.

"Oy, if that's what I'm thinkin' it is, you best move along. I'd be losin' me job if I was caught doin' any buryin' not approved by the vicar."

"I am not asking for myself." Daniel pulled the sealed note from his pocket and handed it to the young man. He took it reluctantly.

"I am told you can read."

"And who told you that?"

Daniel didn't answer.

The young man read and his eyes widened. "Miss Charlotte . . . merciful heavens. Miss Charlotte's own wee one. We did wonder what become of her. The vicar won't even speak her name."

"Which is why no one must ever hear of this."

"I'll take it to the grave with me. . . . Oh, sorry. Fault of the trade."

Daniel reached over with a wad of folded bank notes. But Digger waved it away, then swiped at his eyes with the same hand.

"You tell Miss Charlotte for me. You tell her rest easy. Ben Higgins will take care of her wee one. A boy was it?"

He nodded.

"You tell her Ben Higgins will watch over her little lad. Never fear. You tell Miss Charlotte that for me, will you?"

"Yes, thank you. I certainly shall."

❧

My dear Aunt,

I know I should not write to you, but I feel I must. You have long been my most trusted confidante. As you have been asked not to correspond with me, I will not expect an answer. But still, I must tell you. Must share this awful weight or I fear I shall go mad.

My child is gone . . . lost to me. But it is I who feels lost. The pain, the self-recrimination presses on me until I cannot breathe. I cannot bear it. I must away. I feel the loss too keenly in this dreadful place. The milkweed pods have all broken, the soft white down flown away. Only empty wombs and dry stalks remain.

I feel I must soon depart for the place you offered me. Might I prevail upon you to see me one more time before I go? I so desperately need the comfort and counsel only you can give.

But no, I do not want you to risk condemnation from my father. Did he not threaten to prune you from the family tree along with me? One of us cut off is more than sufficient . . . .

Seeing Charlotte's door ajar, Daniel looked in and saw her writing furiously at the little desk in the corner. She laid down the quill only long enough to swipe at the tears on her cheeks, then picked up the pen and dipped it again. In truth, he was surprised to see her out of bed. When he had last seen her the day before, she had seemed almost incapable of movement, of thought beyond her grief. It reminded him pitiably of his own dear Lizette, and the thought of Charlotte sinking in similar fashion made him feel physically ill. He wondered to whom she was writing. Had Charlotte already changed her mind—was she writing to Mr. Harris?

Suddenly, Charlotte dropped her quill and sat very still. He was just about to make his presence known and step in to speak with her when she picked up the single sheet and crumpled it into a small ball. Her expression was bleak. She laid her head on her arms on the desk and gave way to great shoulder-shaking sobs. He longed to rush to her, to comfort her, but he knew that such an action would be not only inappropriate but also futile. No man could ease a pain as tormenting as this. Only time and only God. Still, he wished there was something he might do.

At that moment, the tall nurse, Sally Mitchell, walked into the passage and he gestured her over. He nodded his head toward the room and Sally followed his gaze. Pausing only long enough to give him a grim nod, she hurried into the room.

"There, there, love . . ." he heard her murmur.

Daniel decided then and there, if ever he could do some good for Sally Mitchell, he would.

After Charlotte had finally cried herself into a grief-exhausted slumber that night, she was awakened by screaming from down the corridor. The screams were familiar and yet different. Dr. Taylor's French wife, yes, but this time crying out with the regularity of labour pains. Charlotte turned over in bed, feeling aware but dulled in her senses. She couldn't bear to give too much thought to another baby at the moment.

Then she heard the matron barking orders and people rushing about in the corridor. Feeling a sudden pull, Charlotte rolled back over and climbed out of bed. She put on her dressing gown and stockings and opened her door, peering out. Lamps were lit and shadows and echoes danced off the walls as people ran past on their way above stairs.

Gibbs marched past, clean linens in her arms.

"Gibbs, what is happening?"

The normally aloof, efficient assistant had been unusually warm and consolatory toward Charlotte since the news of Charlotte's loss.

"The doctor's got hisself a little girl," Gibbs said matter-of-factly. "But the missus . . . Oh, Miss Smith, she is utterly changed. I wouldn't have known her! I best get back up there. Go to sleep, Miss Smith. Nothing you can do."

Of course there was nothing she could do. Even so, and not knowing why she did, Charlotte made her way to the servants' stairway at the end of the corridor, as she had on those other nights that now seemed so long ago. She walked as one sleeping, without aid or need of a light, knowing the way well enough by now. She felt her way up the stairs and cautiously pushed the top door open.

From here, the screaming was even louder. And now came the clamor of things being thrown and smashed as well.

Charlotte winced.

"Take eet away from me!" the woman cried in her accented English.

Charlotte took a few tentative steps down the corridor. Mrs. Moorling suddenly emerged from Mrs. Taylor's room, a bundle in her arms. Someone inside the room slammed the door shut behind her.

Charlotte walked closer and, by the light of the oil lamp, saw a long angry scratch on the matron's cheek. Her brown hair had come all but loosed from its knot.

"Mrs. Moorling?"

"Oh, Charlotte!"

"Are you all right?"

"I will be."

From behind the closed door, Dr. Taylor barked out, "Bring the restraining device—hurry!"

Mrs. Moorling's flushed face grew even more strained. She took a step closer to Charlotte and thrust the baby toward her. Charlotte shrank back and opened her mouth to protest. Then she caught a glimpse of the little face, clearly resembling Daniel, just as her own son resembled his father. Had God planned it thusly—designed to garner paternal support? She accepted the baby into her arms and Mrs. Moorling ran toward the main stairs.

Charlotte stood there, staring down at the tiny infant whose eyes were wide open, looking at her. Then the babe began nuzzling her, instinctively looking to nurse. Charlotte's pent-up milk let down in response. She looked down at the front of her wet dressing gown in growing horror. Then another voice startled her. Mobcapped

Mrs. Krebs had come up the stairs and was striding toward her in the same militant style of Mrs. Moorling.

"The babe, is she all right?"

"Yes. Mrs. Moorling gave her to me. Here." Charlotte started to hand the baby over to Mrs. Krebs but then pulled the infant back against herself to cover the mortifying stains.

"I am . . . forgive me. I did not mean to . . ." Charlotte stammered. "She cried and it just happened."

"Perfectly natural. Do nurse her for me. There's a love. I've got me hands full now."

"But . . . I cannot. I should not."

"Come now, you know how it's done."

"Yes, but this is Dr. Taylor's baby. His wife might . . ."

"His wife's a raving loony at the moment, dearie. Best thing for that wee one is to be as far away from her as possible for now. Go on, nurse the wee one. Nurse your own grievin' heart as well."

Charlotte saw the compassion, the understanding in the older woman's eyes, and her own eyes filled with tears.

"If you think it would help her," she whispered.

Mrs. Krebs smiled a sad smile and squeezed Charlotte's arm. "It will help, Charlotte."

Using the better-lit main stairs, Charlotte returned carefully to her room. She sat in her chair and loosened her gown and offered her heavy breast to the baby. After a few awkward tries, the little girl latched on and began nursing. Charlotte wept the whole while. Blood and tears and milk were flowing out of her at such a rapid rate that Charlotte felt as though her very life were being drained from her . . . yet returned to her at the same time.

❧

Daniel Taylor shuffled through the corridor, exhausted and defeated. His wife was worse than ever. The delivery had sent the puerperal mania to new heights. Or was it depths? His poor little daughter! Would she ever know the bright, loving woman he'd married?

Mrs. Krebs came out of the infant ward, closing the door behind her.

"Mrs. Krebs. Have you found someone to nurse the baby?"

"Aye."

He headed toward the foundling ward.

"She isn't in there. I asked Miss Smith to nurse 'er."

"Miss Smith? Why on earth?"

"I have me reasons."

"And she agreed?"

"That she did."

"Where is she?"

"Told her she could take the wee one back to her room. Poor lamb—never seen a girl so modest-like."

He walked quietly back through the manor to Charlotte's room. The door was closed. Through it, he could hear Charlotte Lamb singing to his infant daughter in a tear-cracked voice. It was not a lullaby she was singing. He recognized the tremulous melody of a hymn:

> "...To thee in my distress, to thee,
> A worm of earth, I cry;
> A half-awakened child of man,
> An heir of endless bliss or pain,
> A sinner born to die. ..."

He leaned his forehead against the smooth wooden door, to absorb the sound, the sadness . . . if he could.

PART II

It has long been customary to provide facilities for ladies requiring wet nurses to obtain them at the Hospital on payment of a small fee. Many ladies are accommodated with wet nurses in the course of the year, and the Hospital is, in this way, a great convenience.

—T. RYAN, *QUEEN CHARLOTTE'S LYING-IN HOSPITAL FROM ITS FOUNDATION IN 1752 TO THE PRESENT TIME* (LONDON 1885)

No object, however beautiful or interesting, gives pleasure to their eye, no music charms their ear, no taste gratifies their appetite, no sleep refreshes their wearied limbs or wretched imaginations; nor can they be comforted by the conversation or kindest attention of their friends. With the loss of every sentiment which might at present make life tolerable, they are destitute of hope which might render the future desirable.

—THOMAS DENMAN, CELEBRATED MAN-MIDWIFE, DESCRIBING MELANCHOLIA FOLLOWING CHILDBIRTH, 1810

Now, in chusing of a Nurse, there are sixe things to be considered:
Her birth and Parentage: her person: her behavior:
her mind: her milke: and her child.

—James Guillemeau, *Childbirth or*
The Happy Deliverie of Women

Chapter 16

A few days after the birth of little Anne Taylor, a knock sounded on the door of Charlotte's bedchamber. She rose gingerly from bed and opened it.

"Hello, Dr. Taylor."

"You needn't have gotten up."

"I do not mind."

"Most physicians insist on a full month's recovery. But I see it as a good sign that you are up and about already."

She nodded, briefly attempting a smile. "I suppose you are wanting your daughter?" Charlotte retreated back into the room toward the cradle. "Let me bring her to you. Mrs. Krebs asked me to nurse her or I should never have presumed . . ."

"Nonsense. I am most grateful."

"Your wife. She is . . . ?"

"No better, I'm afraid. I regret you had to see her in that state. But that is not why I am here."

Charlotte lifted wide eyes and waited.

"I thought you would like to know. Mrs. Harris wants a wet nurse for your . . . for the newborn child."

A swell of hope rose within Charlotte, which she immediately realized was vain and foolish. She could not apply to nurse her own son. Katherine would know the truth at once.

"Mr. Harris has asked me to recommend someone," Dr. Taylor continued. "Have you a preference?"

She smiled gratefully. "Indeed I do."

There was comfort, at least, in choosing someone to care for Edmund.

❧

"Oh, no, Miss Charlotte," Sally protested. "I'd never get hired in such a great house, not the likes of me."

"But you have the kindest heart of anyone I know, Sally. If I were choosing a nurse, you would be my very first choice."

"Thank you, miss. But them likes the pretty, genteel girls, not some big baggage like me."

"Nonsense. I shall help you. I shall show you exactly what to say and how to act. Please, you must at least try! It would mean the world to me to know you were there, looking out for him."

"Are they family to you, miss?"

Charlotte swallowed. "Only distantly . . . but if I could help them, I would."

"I don't know . . ."

"Dr. Taylor has a list of qualifications for a wet nurse. He will let us borrow the pamphlet and we shall have you ready in no time."

"Oh, very well, Miss Charlotte." Sally smiled, her front teeth protruding as always. "I'm afraid I'm a beetle-headed burdock, but I shall give it me best try."

❧

Charlotte stood outside the door to Mrs. Moorling's office, waiting while the matron made the introductions inside.

"Well, I shall leave you to it," she heard Mrs. Moorling conclude. Then she exited the room. Seeing Charlotte there, Mrs. Moorling left the door ajar. She knew Charlotte had helped Sally prepare for this interview but not the reason why. Charlotte smiled her gratitude and took up sentry at the narrow opening, watching the proceedings with nervous hope.

Katherine Harris sat with perfect posture, her back to the door. Charlotte could see her profile as she turned to whisper something to her husband seated beside her. Charles Harris nodded stiffly and shifted in his chair, clearly uncomfortable. Before them stood Sally, petrified into stony stillness. She was dressed in one of Charlotte's gowns, its hem lengthened with six inches of material taken from forgotten curtains in the unused room at the end of the corridor. Hugh Palmer, the man-midwife, stood beside Sally, facing the Harrises. In his hand, he carried a small booklet, which he held open, referring to it as he spoke.

"First, concerning lineage," Hugh Palmer began, in his somewhat nasally voice. "Have any of your kindred, whether it be parents, grandfather, or grandmother, ever been stained, or spotted, either in body or mind?"

Sally silently shook her head no.

"And what is your age?"

"Five and twenty."

He glanced at Katherine. "Between five and twenty and five and thirty is the best age, wherein women are most temperate, healthful, and strong."

Katherine nodded her understanding and he continued. "And your child's age?"

"A half year."

"Good. If her child be above seven or eight months old, then her milk will be too stale. It would also call into question whether she would have milk enough to nurse your son."

Katherine again nodded, and Hugh Palmer continued, walking around Sally and eyeing her as one would a gown in a dress shop.

"She is a little tall perhaps. Not too fat nor too lean, however. Arms good and fleshly . . ." He suddenly reached out and pinched Sally's arm, and she gasped.

". . . and firm."

He returned his gaze to the book. "'She must have a pleasing countenance, a bright and clear eye, a well-formed nose, a ruddy mouth, and very white teeth.'" He paused before Sally. "Open your mouth, if you please. Now smile. White, yes, but not very straight."

He read on. "'Her hair should be between yellow and black, ideally a chestnut color. But she especially should not have red hair.'"

Sally self-consciously touched her golden hair, pinned up in a classic twist by Charlotte herself.

"'She must deliver her words well, and distinctly, without stammering.' Please tell us something about yourself."

Taking a breath and swallowing hard, Sally began in careful, practiced tones, "My name is Miss Sally Mitchell. I am five and twenty years of age . . ."

From behind the door, Charlotte held her breath. Sally had already told her age. Charlotte hoped they wouldn't find it odd that she was repeating it.

"I have one child. His name is Dickie. He's a rascal but I loves him."

Oh dear. She was extemporizing now.

Sally, apparently seeing the fine lady frown, returned to the rote speech Charlotte had prepared for her.

"My son is a half-year old and is in the care of my dear sister . . ."

"Thank you. Moving on . . ."

But Sally wasn't finished yet. "Leaving me free to seek employment as a nurse."

"As we see. Thank you." The haughty man returned his focus to the book. "'She must have a strong and big neck, for thereby, as Hippocrates said, may one judge the strength of the body.'"

Sally swallowed as three pairs of eyes studied her neck. She lifted her chin higher as though to accommodate them.

"'She must have a broad and large breast. . . .'"

His gaze lowered and Sally's strong neck turned bright red.

Katherine dipped her head, touching gloved fingers to her temple, her lowered hat brim no doubt concealing her face. Charlotte noticed that Mr. Harris had the good grace to turn his face away. He cleared his throat. Mr. Palmer looked up, oblivious to their discomfiture.

Mr. Harris said, "We shall leave it to you to examine, um, that aspect of her nature. We need not hear those particulars."

"Ah . . . yes. Very well." Palmer moved on to the next page.

"'She ought to be of a good behavior, sober, and not given to drinking, or gluttony, mild, without being angry or fretful: for there is nothing that sooner corrupts the blood, of which the milk is made, than choler or sadness.'"

"Yes, well, we have letters from a physician and the matron testifying to her character on those accounts," Mr. Harris said dismissively.

"Indeed. 'She must likewise be chaste.' Miss Mitchell, are you married?"

"No, sir."

"'She must not desire the company of her husband or strange men, because carnal copulation troubleth the blood, and so by consequence the milk.'"

Sally blushed once more, and again Katherine's hand went to her temple.

"Yes, yes." Mr. Harris rose, agitated. "Mr. Palmer, do try and remember there is a lady in the room."

"I am only trying to determine if this woman is a suitable choice."

"I understand that. And what is your conclusion?"

"Well, I have yet to examine her breasts or her milk for the correct color and consistency . . ."

Charles Harris lowered his head and bit out, "And how long does that require?"

"Not long. For the milk, I shall have the nurse express a small quantity onto a looking glass. It should be pure white, have a sweet smell, and be neither too thick nor too thin."

"Then get on with it, man." Mr. Harris sat back down.

The accoucheur and Sally disappeared behind a curtained partition, placed there for this use.

Even from her position of modest safety, Charlotte felt her heart pound, her face and neck heat at the thought of what poor Sally must be enduring on the other side of that partition. The only sounds were the rustling of fabric and an occasional murmur of "Mmm-hmm . . ." from Mr. Palmer.

Five minutes later the man reappeared, a square of glass in his hand. He tilted it gently from side to side. "The milk flows in a leisurely fashion, not too watery, nor too thick."

"So?"

"She will do," Hugh Palmer announced. "The height and crooked teeth are not ideal, but overall an acceptable specimen."

Stepping back into view, Sally beamed at the words, as though they were the finest compliment a woman could receive.

❧

Charlotte sat on the garden bench, a swaddled Anne Taylor asleep in her arms. She remembered how her mother believed fresh air and sunshine were as important as mother's milk for a child. Dr. Taylor came out the side door and waved to her. She tucked the child into the handled basket beside her and rose as he approached.

"Miss Lamb, may I say you look like a woman who has borne many a child."

She looked at him quickly, then away, her hand moving self-consciously to her midriff, still somewhat rounded.

Dr. Taylor's pale cheeks turned pink beneath the sandy stubble.

"What I mean to say is . . . you look quite the experienced. . . . That is, quite . . . as if you know what you are doing." He rubbed his eyebrows with thumb and forefinger. "Though I obviously do not."

Charlotte wondered why he seemed so nervous.

"Do you still plan to depart for Crawley soon?" he asked.

"Yes. Unless I hear otherwise from my aunt."

Hands behind his back, he studied the earth. "Miss Lamb, I wonder if you might consider another course." He cleared his throat. "That is, I do not suppose you would do me the honor of, um . . ."

He left off and began again. "You see, I'm afraid I know not when my wife will be sufficiently recovered to return home. I should only hope it will be soon. But, as my wife must, I fear, reside here longer, I would be eternally obliged . . . Of course I shall understand completely if you refuse. I know it is terribly presumptuous, that you no doubt would rather be rid of this whole business forever, but . . ."

Charlotte furrowed her brow, trying to follow his rambling. Then she understood. He was asking her to continue on as his daughter's nurse. She recalled Sally's examination and interview with humiliating clarity. She swallowed.

"But any of the women here would be happy to oblige. I do not . . . That is, why would you ask me?"

Dr. Taylor seemed to calm at the question. "Common wisdom dictates that a nurse passes on not only nutrition but her very character, her qualities, her good and vice through her milk. I do not believe science bears this out, but if there is any truth in it at all, I certainly believe that the care of a kind, loving, and honorable woman can only be to my daughter's benefit."

"How can you say such things of me. After everything . . . ?"

He took a step closer to her and looked directly into her eyes. "There's not one of us who passes through this life without making a mistake, Miss Lamb," he said gently, "but it's a rare soul who redeems one so utterly. I have never known a more noble, more honorable, more worthy woman . . . and if my daughter can glean any of those qualities, well, I should be exceedingly grateful."

She stared up at him, seeing the sincerity shining in his blue-green eyes.

She opened her mouth to give an answer, but at that moment she heard a familiar voice call out her name.

"Charlotte?"

She turned and saw a finely dressed and wonderfully familiar woman at the garden gate. She excused herself from Dr. Taylor and strode quickly up the garden path, hardly noticing that Dr. Taylor quickly stepped back inside the manor.

"Aunt Tilney! How I've longed for you to come!"

The two women embraced, and then Charlotte led her aunt to the garden bench. Amelia Tilney's eyes widened as she looked into the basket at the sleeping infant.

"Is this *your* child?"

"No."

"I thought not."

Charlotte looked at her aunt, brows raised.

"The tone of the letter suggested something was amiss here."

"But I did not send a letter."

"A letter from a physician, a Dr. Taylor."

"Dr. Taylor wrote to you?"

"Yes." Her aunt sat beside her, withdrew a folded note from her reticule, and handed it to her. "Very wise, really. Your uncle would have recognized your hand and chastised me. He might have read *this* directly and not known it pertained to you."

Charlotte read the brief note quickly.

To Mrs. Amelia Tilney,

Madam, I thank you for your interest and support of our work at the Manor Home in the past. I am writing to inform you of a new development here which will be of particular interest to you. In fact, we are in need of the wise counsel that your past association uniquely equips you to offer. We understand you are a person with innumerable commitments and restraints upon your leisure, but do urgently hope you will find the time. Our facilities are open to you at any hour. Please do call on us as at your earliest convenience.

Most sincerely,
Dr. Daniel Taylor
Physician, The Manor Home for Unwed Mothers

"I never asked him to write," Charlotte said, still staring at the letter. "I do not see how you understand anything from these few lines."

"I read between them, as they say. What has happened?"

Charlotte handed back the note. "I had a child. A son. But he is gone. Lost to me."

The tears that sprang immediately to her aunt's large brown eyes were salve to Charlotte's soul. Her mother's sister sat next to her on the bench and laid gloved fingertips on Charlotte's hand. "My dear girl. How long ago?"

"He was born ten days ago. I had him for six days. Six very short days."

"I am so sorry, my dear. So very sorry. How this loss must pain you."

"Indeed it does. At times I can barely breathe for it."

"I understand. And yet, who can question God's will? Perhaps He allowed this so you might return to your family."

"I do not see how this changes anything."

"But it does! The evidence is—"

"Evidence! He was not evidence—he was my son. My precious little boy, my heart."

"My dear, forgive me. I do understand." Her aunt wrapped her other arm about her shoulders.

"I am so glad you are here."

"May I ask, then . . . whose child this is?" She nodded toward the basket.

"Dr. Taylor's daughter."

"And why are you . . . ?"

"His wife is ill. He has asked me to be the child's nurse."

Amelia Tilney lifted her gloved hand from Charlotte's and laid it across her lace-covered chest.

"Can you seriously be thinking of accepting this offer?"

Charlotte nodded.

"You know what disgrace such a thing would bring to your family were it known?"

"More disgrace than I have already brought?"

"Substantially. My dear, if you must have a post, be it that of a governess."

"And who, pray, would hire me to teach and mold their children?"

"Many families would. Many fine families."

"Now that I haven't a babe with me, you mean. I shall not lie about it."

"I understand your scruples, my dear—though some might wonder where they were in other matters."

"Aunt—"

"Forgive me. You know I only want the best for you."

"I do know that."

The older woman squeezed her hand again, and the two sat quietly for a moment. Then her aunt continued, "I think your secret is still safe, my dear. Your father and sister know, of course, and the people here, but they are not likely to be in contact with the type of family with whom you would seek a situation."

"Surely others have guessed . . . or at least suspect."

"Suspicions do not allegations make. Of course there is the . . . father. Does he know?"

"Yes."

"And is he trustworthy?"

"Evidently not. If you mean, will he keep my secret, then, yes, I believe he will. Now more than ever."

"Are you absolutely certain there is nothing that can be done in that regard?"

"No, Aunt. Nothing."

"But certainly a gentleman. . . . He is a gentleman?"

"Aunt, I told you. I will not reveal his identity, so please do not fish about for hints."

"I only want . . . Please tell me it wasn't that young gravedigger who ogles you so rudely."

"Ben Higgins? He doesn't ogle me. Heavens no, Aunt. You can rest on that score."

"But someone, at least, of your station in life?"

"Aunt, please. I will tell you this, and then let it be the end of the matter. Our family would suffer no further from either the man's name or connections, were they known. All right?"

"A gentleman. I knew it. Then why . . . ? Forgive me. We will speak of it no more."

"Thank you." Baby Anne began to fuss, and Charlotte drew her forth and cuddled her close. "I am sorry you disapprove of my course, although I am surprised by the vehemence of your objections."

"My dear, wet nurses are infamously ill-bred, uneducated, immoral creatures . . ."

"Thank you."

"I mean, in general, of course. You will be little higher than a scullery maid. The mistress of the house will treat you with ill-concealed contempt so long as her infant needs you. If you vex her, there is nothing to stop her from putting you out on the street as soon as another nurse might be found."

"The mistress will not be in residence, at least not for some time."

"What? But that is worse yet. Really, my dear Charlotte, I must put my foot down here. You cannot live in a house with a man if his wife is not living there with him."

"Servants do so all the time."

"But Charlotte Lamb does not."

"His father lives there as well."

"Two men, Charlotte?"

"But his wife is in hospital. She is indisposed and may be for some months. Dr. Taylor hopes for less, but he cannot be sure."

"Why can he not care for his wife in his own home? He is a physician, is he not?"

"Yes, but she . . . Well, it is not for us to question. Dr. Taylor wants only what is best for his wife, I am sure."

"What's best for her . . . or for him?"

"Aunt. I am certain he is completely selfless in this situation."

"But what is best for you? Certainly not this. My dear, I beg you reconsider. If it becomes known, you will not be able to secure a position as governess, I am quite sure. Your father and sister would be mortified, and I confess, I should not be far behind. But think, Charlotte, even if it is not known, could you really bear another parting? And you will be parted from this child—make no mistake."

"I know this," Charlotte said dully.

"Can you really bear it? Would it not be better to leave this place now, to make a new start?"

"I do not know. All I know is . . . I need this. I feel as though I am standing on a ribbon's edge over a black pit, and this is the only way I can keep my balance. Why should I not use this God-given sustenance to nurture this child?"

"It is not your child."

"I am very aware of that Aunt. Painfully aware. I know this will not bring my son back, if you fear I am suffering from that misapprehension. But this little girl needs me."

"No. She does not. Any of a dozen women in this place could care for her needs."

"But who will care for mine?"

"God will."

"I believe that, Aunt, I do—or I would be in that pit already. But I cannot hold God, smell or caress God. His cries do not drown out my own as hers do. She gives me a reason to get out of bed, to keep living, for today, for a little while longer."

"There are other ways to cope."

"How do you know? Forgive me, but you are not a mother. You have no children of your own."

"I did." She stared off, a sudden sheen of tears brightening her eyes. "I had a little girl many years ago, long after your uncle and I had given up hope of children. She lived but a few days."

"Oh, Aunt. I am sorry. I had no idea."

"She had dark curls, just like you. I suppose that is one reason I have always felt close to you."

Charlotte gazed at her aunt's profile, but instead saw bits of memory like pieces of colored glass, a beautiful jumble of special moments and little kindnesses collected over a lifetime. "How did you get past it?" she asked quietly.

"I am still getting past it. Every day. The pain is dimmer now, but still there. The first days, weeks, were torture—like being skinned alive. But it is not something we talked about. Infants die all the time. Women are supposed to be strong and try again as soon as possible. But there was no trying again for me. I lost my womb along with my babe."

"Dear Aunt. How dreadful for you."

"Yes. And for you."

"But . . . you always seemed so cheerful. So happy when you visited us."

"I was happy. In many ways. Especially when your mother was alive. Although visiting your family was a joy with a slice of pain all its own. My sister with her two beautiful daughters. And you, with your dark hair and eyes . . . I could never look at you without thinking of my own daughter. How old she would be, what she would be like, how similar and how different from you."

"I never knew."

"I did not wish to spread my sorrow."

"Yes, but we might have shared the burden with you."

"Yes, well. That is why I am biting my puritanical tongue and having this conversation with you. I would share this sorrow with you, if you would allow me."

"Of course. You have done so much for me already."

"Tosh. I have done nothing. Would that I could take you into my own home had your father not forbidden me. But do you not see how this situation in a man's home could open your family to more talk and scandal?"

"Dr. Taylor is not much out in society. He certainly does not entertain in his home, where people might see me. But I do see your point."

"Do you? Then you do feel some . . . unease about the man?"

"No. Not about Dr. Taylor. I believe his intentions are honorable. But still there is something . . . a discomfort at the thought of living in his house."

"You fear he would not treat you well?"

"No. I think he would treat me very well. As he does here. But you see, Dr. Taylor is some acquainted with our family. He attended Mother during her illness."

"Did he?"

"Yes. Dr. Webb was mother's physician, but Dr. Taylor was one of his apprentices before he went to university."

"So he is a young man, then?"

"I suppose he is but five or six years older than myself."

"All the more reason."

"Dr. Taylor holds nothing but respect for me—even after everything he has learned about me. Do not look at me so. I mean only that he treats me like a gentleman's daughter—a lady—even after I have proven otherwise. Still, I see the wisdom in what you say. . . . Do you think your old aunt would still welcome me if I brought a baby not my own?"

"Oh yes, I am sure of it! She wrote back directly to assure me of her pleasure in having you and the babe come, and I do not think this will sway her, once I explain . . . I know you will not wish to lie to her. Nor do I, but perhaps the villagers need not be told that the babe is not your own."

"Better for them to think me an unmarried mother than a wet nurse?"

"Yes. I am afraid so. Others might insist you pass yourself off as a recent widow, but I will not suggest such a ruse. We shall hope the distance from Doddington and my aunt's solitary life will provide all the shield you require. I shall write to her directly and apprise her of the situation."

"Thank you."

"Still, I must beseech you one last time. Let me call for the matron. She will find another fine woman to suckle this child, and I shall take you to Crawley in my own carriage."

"Aunt, I appreciate your concern. And I am sorry to disappoint you. But I could no more give up this child than my own, had I to do it over again."

"But you did not give him up—the good Lord took that situation out of your hands. He has something else in store for your future. He knows what is best."

"I do feel Him, somehow. A bit of comfort amid this . . . broken glass slicing at my heart. I am clinging to the hope that He is in this. That He will redeem this, me, my son."

"Of course He will. Your son is with his loving father right now."

"Yes." Charlotte nodded. "Yes, he is."

After Aunt Tilney left, Charlotte found Dr. Taylor in the foundling ward. Together they walked to the far end of the entry hall—out of earshot of the other nurses.

Charlotte began quietly, "It would not be appropriate for me to live in your house without your wife present."

Dr. Taylor lowered his head. "Of course you are right. I had not considered that. My father does live with us, but still . . . I understand." He nodded, resigned.

"I could take Anne with me to Crawley," Charlotte continued, knowing she sounded too eager, "and nurse her there for as long as you need. My aunt assures me we would both be welcome."

Daniel's face brightened. "You know, it was very common until recent times for infants to be sent to the country for a year or so. It was believed the fresh air away from London would benefit the children, and some families still hold to this practice. Would you really be willing to take her with you? To care for her?"

Charlotte nodded. "Unless, of course, you cannot bear to be apart from her. . . ."

"Crawley is not so far off, you know," he said. "If I might visit Anne from time to time, I should think it an excellent plan. I wonder I did not think of it." He tapped his thumb against his lip as he thought. "I would ask that you postpone departure for a fortnight. Give both you and Anne time to gain strength for the journey. The roads can be treacherous at times."

"Very well."

"You are quite certain you are willing?"

"Yes. I will care for her as if she were my own. Until your wife is recovered, of course."

"You do not know what this means to me, Miss Lamb. You will be recompensed well and have my eternal gratitude."

Charlotte smiled weakly. *Now if only I shall be able to bear another parting. . . .*

The Hospital Foundling came out of they Brains
To encourage the Progress of vulgar Amours,
The breeding of Rogues and the increasing of Whores,
While the Children of honest good Husbands and Wives
Stand expos'd to Oppression and Want all their lives.

—Porcupinus Pelagious, *The Scandalizade*, 1750

Chapter 17

"Miss Lamb." Dr. Taylor stopped her in the corridor the following week. "May I ask how Anne is faring?"

"Fine. I have just come from her. She is sated and sleeping peacefully."

"I am glad of it." He hesitated. "I don't suppose . . ."

"What is it?"

"It's just that I am in a bit of a bind. I need to make a brief call on a patient, one who is quite adamant about needing a female chaperone, and neither Gibbs nor Mrs. Krebs can get away at present. I have just come from Mrs. Moorling's office, though it would have been quite presumptuous to ask her such a thing, but she is out for the evening."

"You need me to accompany you?"

"I know it is difficult for you to get away . ."

"Anne will most likely sleep for another two or three hours. I am sure Mae would be happy to listen and tend her should she awaken. How long would we be?"

"Only an hour or so. But I don't want to impose on you. And while we are both aware of how insensitive I can be on points of propriety, I realize it would not be proper to ask you to ride alone with me in the carriage."

"Is it urgent?"

"Not really. Some stitches I need to attend to, make sure no infection sets in. I promised I would be by tonight and the night is nearly gone. It really should not wait until tomorrow. But perhaps she will forgive me arriving on my own this once. When I explain."

"She lives alone, then?"

"Well, not alone exactly. She has three children in her care. Two are her own, one she wet-nurses for hire."

"I see."

"Well, I must away. Pardon me for speaking before I thought through the notion."

He bowed and walked past her, setting his hat upon his head and lacing his arms through the sleeves of his coat.

Charlotte turned and watched him go.

"Might I have a moment to collect my wrap and speak to Mae?" she called after him.

He turned and looked at her, his face weary. "Of course. If you are certain you do not mind."

She shrugged and smiled blithely. "I shall wear my most concealing bonnet."

And she did.

They rode through the cobbled streets of London in relative silence.

"Do you often make calls at this late hour?" Charlotte asked lightly. She was unprepared for the thick silence which answered her question. She glanced over and saw Dr. Taylor's eyes narrow. He took a corner rather more sharply than needed and urged the horse forward with a click of his tongue.

"No," he answered dully.

She nodded but kept her eyes forward. His tone invited no further inquiry. She did wonder, though, what was special about this particular patient to bring him out for a call this late in the evening—and having to bring someone with him too. The patient was a wet nurse, was she not? No genteel nor wealthy lady that she should have such influence over a physician.

When they halted in front of a worn three-story tenement and Dr. Taylor did not even offer his hand in helping her descend, Charlotte knew his mind was preoccupied and the task ahead an unpleasant one. She lifted her skirts a bit more than she would have liked, but managed to step down to the filthy street without mishap.

"Dr. Taylor!" She was obliged to call, for he was already inside the doorway without her, as if he had forgotten she was behind him.

He looked back, winced, and then held the door open for her as she stepped through. He stopped at the first door on the left.

"You needn't say anything," he whispered. "Just stay near the door."

She nodded in feigned understanding. She was dumbfounded when he extracted a key from his breast pocket and, after but a slight knock on the door, unlocked and opened it. He stepped in and indicated that she ought to follow and stand in the small cramped entry.

"That you, Taylor?" a husky female voice called.

"It is," he answered, setting his hat on a cluttered bench.

"Mrs. Krebs with you?" the voice called again.

"A nurse tonight."

"Pity, that."

With a nod to Charlotte, Dr. Taylor disappeared into a room a few feet away.

"Let's check those stitches, then," she heard him say.

"Let me get a look at her you brought first," the woman said.

After a pause, Daniel called, "Miss Smith, would you mind stepping in here a moment? Miss Marsden would like to meet you."

Charlotte stepped forward and paused in the doorway. An attractive though fleshy woman of thirty or so years lay in bed, propped up with pillows and a mobcap over her blond curls. An infant suckled each breast and a toddler lay asleep, curled up peacefully at her side. The woman somehow managed a free hand, from which she was feeding herself a biscuit.

Mouth full, the woman said, "Hoy . . . a pretty one. And young."

"That will be all, Miss Smith."

Charlotte took a step back, but the woman's voice stopped her. "Wait on. What's your hurry." She turned a calculated gaze on him. "Does she know?"

He began to form what must certainly be the word "no," for what other answer could he utter, but instead he closed his mouth, then tried again. "Miss Smith has... She knows my father, yes."

Charlotte felt a smile touch her face at the thought of Daniel's gentle father. "Yes, he delivered my own babe."

But instead of the answering smile and empathetic chat she expected, the woman's face fell into a coarse scowl.

"Oh, did he? And just when was that?"

Before Charlotte could reply, Daniel cut her off. "Only because Miss Smith is a family friend. I have known her since she was a girl. Is that not so, Miss Smith?"

"Oh yes!" she said, grasping the plea in his voice, though not entirely sure how to answer. "Since I was quite young. Dr. Taylor has long been a friend of the family."

"Just so," he said, clearly relieved. "His sole patient. Now, then, please let us proceed. I want to make sure all is healing nicely."

"'Course you do." the woman said superciliously. And Charlotte wondered at the sarcasm in her tone.

Back in the carriage a quarter of an hour later, Charlotte could not keep herself from asking, "Has that woman some sort of hold on you?"

Daniel stared straight ahead, his face bleak. "Yes."

This was all he said, but his grim expression, and what she had seen this night, told her much more.

She nodded, and the two fell into silence.

Several minutes later, Charlotte realized they were taking a different route on the return trip. Suddenly Dr. Taylor pulled the reins up sharply.

"Dear me," he said. "I turned on the very street I meant to avoid. Or my horse took the way she knows best without consulting me."

"What is the matter?"

"Carriages ahead. We've just crossed into Pentonville." He leaned over to try to see past the fine tall carriage in front of them. "There are a couple of grand manor houses ahead. One of them must have something going on tonight."

"Awfully late in the season for a ball," Charlotte mused. "Must be someone's birthday."

The carriage ahead of them pulled forward. "There we go." They rode alongside the broad stone manse just in time to see a finely clad couple allowed entrance by a black-suited butler.

"Just the one carriage holding up traffic. Good. Latecomers by the looks of it."

"Could we stop for a moment?"

She knew he looked at her in surprise, but Charlotte's gaze was focused on the manor and the golden light streaming from the windows.

"I have been here before."

He reined the horse to the right and halted the rig along the side of the street.

"Yes, I was here with my cousin Katherine during my first season. I cannot recall the family name. But I remember something she said, about the place being 'on the very edge of decent society.'" Charlotte began parroting an upper-crust accent. "'If the building were one street over, we should have declined the invitation. But since the family throws the most lavish balls in town—perhaps to make up for their lack of pristine location—we shall condescend to taste their fine meal and dance with their handsome guests.'" Charlotte chuckled dryly. "I had no real idea where I was at the time, or how true her words."

She stared off, remembering. "Please. I'd like to get closer. Just for a moment."

"But—"

She half rose from her seat, giving Dr. Taylor little choice but to step down from the carriage, pausing only to tie down the reins. Before he could step around to her side to help her down, she was already lowering herself from his side. He offered his hand and she accepted it.

She preceded him across the street, quiet now. She was aware of his footsteps behind her. Then he caught up and walked by her side.

She did not go up the steps to the door but instead daintily lifted her skirts and stepped up over the brick gutter and onto the lawn. She took a few steps closer to the facade, then paused. She looked up, and side to side. The windows were like moving paintings in gold-leaf frames. The light spilling from the windows pooled close to where she had paused, but she did not step into that light. Instead she stood at a distance and watched. Across one window passed couples dancing, swirling gowns of every color flowing by, men in black-and-white smiling solicitously to partners pink-cheeked with pleasure. In another window, people mingled, drinking tea and punch, talking and laughing with one another as though they hadn't a care in the world beyond the quality of the musicians, the strength of the tea, or the quantity of sugar buns.

Though her view was limited, Charlotte was relieved to see no one she knew. No sign of Bea or William, Charles or Katherine—though Katherine, no doubt adhering to the prescribed month of bed rest, would surely not be in attendance. Charlotte's breath caught at the sight of Theo Bolger and Kitty Wells. Kitty had always been an attentive friend, and Theo had never failed to seek out Charlotte for a dance. Now, the two danced on without her. She was on the outside, separated forever by glass, by choices.

"Charlotte . . . ?" Daniel began.

"Let us leave," she said, turning abruptly and brushing past him without meeting his eyes.

A couple was coming up the street, arm in arm. The man hailed her. "I say, is that Charlotte Lamb?"

Charlotte glanced over and was chagrined to see William Bentley with a girl she did not recognize. Mr. Bentley's smile was wide in obvious surprise and inebriation.

"It *is* Charlotte Lamb, and looking . . . well, quite herself. But I thought—"

"You thought wrong," Dr. Taylor said brusquely and gently took Charlotte's arm, leading her across the street. She stole a glance back over her shoulder.

"Not going so soon, I hope? I hadn't even one dance with you . . ." He tripped and the girl caught his arm. "'Course I am a bit unstable on my feet at present."

Behind them, the girl laughed. "You'll be a danger on the dance floor tonight, that's for certain."

He must be drunk indeed to not notice neither Charlotte nor her companion was dressed for dinner, let alone dancing.

As he helped Charlotte back into the carriage and urged the horse down the dim street, Daniel recalled the last time he had seen William Bentley.

It was at a ball held at Sharsted Court in Doddington more than three years ago now. Daniel had been standing awkwardly in an archway, drinking tea, when two young ladies passed and he thought he heard his name. He stepped back into the shadows, hoping to avoid blatant humiliation.

"I do not see why he's here," Beatrice Lamb was saying, her lip curled. "A bone and blood man at a ball—it's revolting. What were our hosts thinking?"

"The man is not a surgeon, Beatrice," the friend consoled, "he's a physician, or plans to be."

"Still, it turns one's thoughts in a most gloomy direction, seeing him."

"He's treated their little nephew, I believe, to most satisfactory results."

"Well, send him home with an extra guinea, then, but don't dress him in tails and expect me to dance with him. Just imagine what those hands have touched."

The two girls passed out of earshot, and Daniel stepped forward, embarrassed and contemplating the quickest route to claim his coat and make his exit when a more pleasing voice called to him.

"Mr. Taylor. I am surprised to see you here."

He turned and saw the welcome face of Charlotte Lamb. "Yes. I am not often invited to such as this."

"And why not, I wonder?"

"It seems people do not like reminders of illness and death—and I'm afraid that's what people think of when they see me. Do you?"

"Well, I don't know. I—"

"Forgive me, Miss Lamb. I had no intention of raining on your pleasure this evening."

"Now I see why many a wise hostess has left you off her guest list." She smiled at him, clearly teasing, hoping to put him at ease.

"If you wonder if seeing you brings my mother to mind," she continued, "I suppose it does. But you needn't worry that you have ruined my evening. My mother is never very far from my thoughts."

"You miss her a great deal, do you, Miss Lamb?"

"I do. But it is not a morbid missing, I hope. I think of her often and strive to remember her. I plan to tell my children all about her someday."

"I have little memory of my own mother—she died when I was quite young."

"I am sorry, Mr. Taylor. Why have you never told me this before?"

He shrugged.

"And worse, why have I never asked?"

"Do not make yourself uneasy. You have had your own worries."

"You must think me a terribly self-interested person."

"Caring for your mother is not selfish, Miss Lamb. Or if it is, it is the best kind of selfishness, I think."

"You know, my mother was the least selfish person I think I've ever known. She would do anything for anybody, especially her children. I should like to be a mother like that someday."

"I am certain you shall be, Miss Lamb."

The music started, and after a glance at the musicians, Mr. Taylor looked back at Charlotte, clearly unsure of himself.

"I am a terrible dancer, Miss Lamb, but if you would care to . . . ?"

"I would, Mr. Taylor. Very much. It's only that . . . I'm afraid I have promised the first two dances to another gentleman."

At that moment, emerging from a sea of feathered hats and swishing gowns, young William Bentley appeared, looking dapper in a fine tailcoat, striped waistcoat, and extravagant cravat that had no doubt cost ten times what his own had. At least Daniel had the pleasure of looking down at the boy, whose height barely surpassed Charlotte's.

"There you are, Miss Lamb," Bentley said with a bow. "I've come to claim you."

"Mr. Taylor," Charlotte said, turning to him, "may I present Mr. William Bentley, Mr. Harris's nephew. Mr. Bentley, this is Mr. Daniel Taylor, physician's apprentice and long-time family friend."

"Physician, eh? And you have known Miss Lamb for some time?"

"A few years now, yes."

"So you are uniquely qualified to give me your professional opinion about her."

"How so?"

"Is it just me, or is she not absolutely perfect?"

"Mr. Bentley, please," Charlotte protested. "I am not perfect, as Mr. Taylor knows very well."

"Do you, man? Has she some hidden flaw, some malady I've yet to discover?"

"Mr. Bentley, you are speaking utter foolishness. Come, the other couples are starting."

"Very well. Excuse us, Taylor."

While Charlotte danced with William Bentley, Daniel went to retrieve his coat, then sought out the host and hostess to say his thank-yous and farewells. He felt the coward, running off with his coat tails between his legs, but he had used up his courage for one evening. He was just making for the door when the music paused. He glanced over and saw Bentley escort Charlotte from the dance floor and bow, excusing himself to claim his next partner. He noticed Charlotte's head swivel as she looked about the room. She must have seen him and guessed his route of departure, for she crossed the room at a diagonal and met him at the foot of the stairs.

"Mr. Taylor, you are not leaving, I hope?"

"I am afraid so." He lifted slightly the coat over his arm.

"Oh dear. I was hoping to see if you are as terrible a dancer as you claim."

He laughed. "I can assure you on that point, madam."

She looked at him steadily. "I would rather judge that for myself."

At the time he was unaware that her words had been rather forward, nearly a breach of etiquette. But clearly she was aware, for her face turned a pretty shade of pink. "Though I realize it is bad form, begging a partner this way."

He laid his coat and hat on a nearby chair and offered his arm. "Very well. But you have been forewarned."

Daniel soon proved that his assessment of his dancing skill was honest indeed. He was painfully aware that his steps were ungainly, his form inelegant. He did not pretend to enjoy the sneers from the other couples he inadvertently jostled, nor the dance movements themselves. What he did enjoy, however, was being with Charlotte Lamb, holding her lightly in his arms and gazing into her lovely face. When she smiled up at him, he felt as though he was not *such* a poor dancer after all.

When the music ended, Daniel escorted Charlotte from the dance floor. "You know," he said, "when you said you had promised your dance to another gentleman, I immediately assumed you meant Mr. Harris."

"Did you? I wonder why. Mr. Harris rarely dances, and when he does, it is only with the finest, most handsome lady in the room."

"Charlotte, there you are." Charles Harris appeared, looking elegant and confident in black-and-white evening attire. "Would you do me the honor of dancing with me?"

Charlotte swallowed, clearly stunned.

Smiling at her hesitancy, Mr. Harris slanted a glance at him and said, "Unless you are otherwise engaged?"

"Mr. Taylor and I have just been dancing."

"Taylor, is it? Oh, yes, Webb's apprentice. How do you do."

Daniel opened his mouth to reply, but Harris had already returned his attention to Charlotte. "Come, Charlotte, we have not danced since you were a girl."

"I was just telling Mr. Taylor that you dance but rarely."

"Not so rarely." He held out his hand to her, and she looked at the hand, the slight bow, the wry grin. She placed her white-gloved hand in his.

"If you will excuse us," Harris said to him.

Charlotte looked back at Daniel, lips parted, clearly wanting to say something to him, even as she was being drawn away by the charming Charles Harris.

"*Mr. Harris rarely dances, and when he does, it's only with the finest, most handsome lady in the room,*" Charlotte had said.

Well, his record is unchanged, Daniel thought, wondering at the leaden disappointment in his stomach. What had he expected, for her to refuse Harris? And why should she?

❧

A week after that long ago ball at Sharsted Court, Daniel had walked briskly from the study and presence of the Reverend Mr. Gareth Lamb, hat in hand, disappointment in his chest.

He had made it out the vicarage door, past the garden, and onto the road toward the village when he heard rapid footfalls behind him. He knew who it was, of course. He had hoped to take his leave without this encounter. He did not wish to share his humiliation with anyone. Nor could he forget the triumph on the vicar's face as he assured him that his daughter shared his views. Daniel took a deep breath before turning around.

She looked more like the girl-Charlotte again, rather than the poised young woman he'd danced with last week. Cheeks flushed, eyes wide, hair loose from her run, falling around her face, more concerned for the feelings of others than proper appearances. The girl he'd fallen in love with in the first place.

"You're leaving?" she asked between breaths. "For keeps, I mean?"

"Yes."

"Without saying good-bye?"

"I thought it best, under the circumstances."

"Oh . . . I suppose I should apologize for spoiling your dignified parting by chasing after you in a most undignified manner."

He smiled at this in spite of himself. "Your father would not approve."

She looked at him meaningfully, her earnest eyes sad. "No, he would not."

He looked away from her, toward Doddington, grasping his hands behind his back. He felt her gaze on his profile.

After an awkward moment, she asked, "Are you sure you must go?"

"Charlotte, I am sure of very little. Except that I need to improve myself. I am determined to complete my studies at the University of Edinburgh and become a licensed physician."

"But Oxford or Cambridge would be so much closer."

"I am afraid I haven't the status nor means for either of those institutions. Dr. Webb recommends Edinburgh—it is where he studied."

"You admire Dr. Webb."

"Yes. My own father is a surgeon, but I want to do more than set bones and cut out offending bits . . ." He paused. "Forgive me. That was terribly unfeeling of me."

She gave him a tiny smile. "You certainly do not have Dr. Webb's discretion."

"Quite right. Another thing I shall have to improve upon."

"My mother was quite fond of you—just as you are."

"Thank you. I am honored."

"Father, however . . ."

"Yes, Miss Lamb. I quite understand. Your father himself has made his opinion of me quite clear."

She opened her mouth as if to say more, to apologize, perhaps, but instead she pressed her lips primly together and said no more.

Knowing there was little more he could say on that subject, or any other, Daniel Taylor bid farewell to Miss Charlotte Lamb and to Doddington, determined to rarely think of either of them again.

Since they may be hindered by sickness,
or for that they are too weake and tender,
or else because their Husbands will not suffer them,
it will be very necessary to seeke out another Nurse.

— JAMES GUILLEMEAU, *CHILDBIRTH OR*
THE HAPPY DELIVERIE OF WOMEN

CHAPTER 18

In the London townhouse of Lady Katherine and Mr. Harris, Sally sat in a rocking chair in the third-floor nursery, holding the small boy in her arms, enjoying the warm weight of his compact body against her bosom. Holding him both comforted and pricked her heart. She missed her own dear boy, a few miles away with her sister. She had only seen him once since coming here the previous month. *'Tis for you I'm doin' this,* she thought. *I'm savin' every shilling. We'll have us a better life, Dickie. You see if we don't.*

The lady of the house entered without knocking, and Sally sat up straighter in the rocking chair, quickly making sure her frock was properly done up.

"Good evening, m'lady," Sally said quickly.

"And how is my son this evening?" Lady Katherine asked, eyes only for her boy.

"His belly is full and his dreams sweet."

Lady Katherine slanted a wry glance at Sally. "And how would you know the content of his dreams?"

"Oh, just look at him, m'lady. He's got the look of peace about him. He sleeps the sleep of one with no worries. No twitchin', no moanin'."

"Well, let us hope he is this quiet during the churching tomorrow."

Sally lifted the boy gently from her lap, offering him up to his mother. "Would you like to hold him?"

"Not tonight, I fear. We're off to a small dinner party and I haven't time to clean spittle—or worse—from my gown. You understand."

"O' course."

Katherine turned and stepped back to the door, then paused. "Just listen to that wind. It will ruin my hair. Do find Edmund an extra blanket for the night. This house is so drafty when the wind blows."

"Yes, m'lady."

The townhouse *was* drafty, especially up on the higher floors. It was tall and narrow, like those adjoining it. Sally guessed their interiors were similar too, though she had little to base this on, as she had barely been out of the house since hiring on as Edmund's nurse.

The warmest room in the house was the kitchen below stairs. Its high windows looked out onto a small herb garden, ruined this late in autumn. The dining room was on the main level, with large windows facing the street. On the first floor up were the drawing room, sitting room, and library; and on the second, the master and mistress's bedchambers and dressing rooms. Above that were the nursery and two other bedrooms, and on the top level, the servant's quarters. It had taken Sally weeks to get used to all the climbing of stairs. Her appetite since coming here had grown, and she'd overheard the cook grumbling more than once about how much she ate. *'Tisn't my fault*, Sally thought, *what with the milk I must give and all this added exercise.*

Sally laid the sleeping child in his cradle and went searching for another blanket as her mistress had bid. This child already had more belongings than Sally herself had owned in her entire life. She dug through the wardrobe, then lifted the cover of the cedar chest behind the settee. She soon discovered a thick wool tartan and a small satin quilt. She ran her hands over each for the sheer pleasure of feeling the fine materials and textures. The silky ivory quilt felt cool to her touch, the wool scratchy but substantial. Surely the poor thing would sweat under either of those.

She dug farther. Near the bottom, she found a small blanket rolled up like a sausage. Curious, she pulled it from beneath the layers and unrolled it. The material was coarse—ordinary unbleached cotton. Just like the material the girls at Milkweed Manor used to stitch up blankets and nappies. She was surprised to see such a homely article in this chest of treasures. Had some poor relative given it as a gift, only for the thing to be stuffed to the bottom of the heap, with no hope of touching Edmund Harris's delicate skin? She felt embarrassed for the foolish pauper, whoever she was.

But then the lamplight fell on the corner of the blanket and Sally's fingers flew to trace the unusual stitching. She lifted the corner and inspected it closely. Why, she recognized this embroidery, this flower and pod. This was Charlotte's work, surely. Wasn't that the faintest hint of her initial C in the leaf of the flower? But how had Charlotte's blanket . . . the one she had stitched for her very own child . . . ended up here, at the bottom of Lady Katherine's cedar chest?

The door creaked open and Sally jerked awake. She had fallen asleep rocking Edmund. Lady Katherine and Mr. Harris stepped into the nursery, no doubt to check on their son after their evening out.

"What is that?" Censure obvious in her tone, Katherine stood beside the chair, looking down her nose at Sally.

"What?" Sally looked down at herself, then at Edmund, asleep in her arms.

"That filthy thing you've wrapped him in?"

"'Tisn't filthy, m'lady. Only plain."

"Wherever did it come from?"

Mr. Harris stepped closer, quickly looking from the blanket, to Sally, to his wife, and then back to Sally. His face was somber.

"Perhaps Nurse brought it with her," he suggested.

"No, sir, I found it in the chest."

The father shrugged. "It might be from the hospital. It was cold that night, and I believe the physician might have sent Edmund home bundled up in an extra blanket or two."

"The hospital? Well, get it off him, then. Who knows how filthy the thing is."

"I'm sure it's been laundered," Mr. Harris assured her. "During your recovery."

"Still . . . we have all these fine lovely blankets," Katherine walked to the cedar chest herself and lifted its lid. "Please use these."

"Yes, m'lady." Sally bobbed her head.

Lady Katherine selected the ivory satin quilt, and realizing her mistress meant *now*, Sally quickly unwound the hospital blanket from the infant. Lady Katherine handed her the quilt and took the embroidered blanket from her with two fingers held far from her body. She furrowed her brow and brought it closer to her face. "That's odd . . ."

"What is?" Mr. Harris asked.

"This stitching. I have seen something very like it before."

"All stitching's alike to me. It's late—come to bed."

"Very well. Dispose of this for me, please."

"Yes, m'lady."

Sally folded up the offending blanket but could not bring herself to discard it. After her employers left the room, she shoved it back down into the bottom of the chest.

Charlotte hired a hansom using the few bank notes her aunt had slipped into her hand prior to her recent departure. She knew she should not go. But she couldn't seem to stop herself. Once more leaving Anne in Mae's capable hands and donning her large brimmed bonnet, she stepped into the hansom and gave the driver the simple directions.

She had received her aunt's note just yesterday. Knowing now that her niece had an ally in Dr. Taylor, Amelia Tilney had sent him a brief letter of gratitude, thanking him for alerting her to Charlotte's situation and within that note, enclosed another addressed to Charlotte herself. Her aunt had thought to cheer her, Charlotte supposed, with her news. But she had not.

> *My Dear Charlotte,*
>
> *I thought it might please you to know that two you have long held dear are celebrating the joyful occasion of the birth of a son. We all feared how your cousin Katherine would do, considering her somewhat advanced age and the discomfort she experienced late in her lying-in. But I know you will be happy to hear that all is well and Charles and Katherine have a little son they have named Edmund. I understand Katherine is to be churched this Wednesday at St. George's Hanover Square. They have even graciously included your uncle and I in their plans for a christening dinner in honor of the occasion. Our old friend Lord Elton will also attend, so it will no doubt be a grand celebration. I am sure if things were different, you would have been invited as well. But let us think only on the joy of such news, in hopes that you will glean hope that life indeed goes on. It was a difficult lesson for me, but I hope to ease your way a little if I might. So please take this news with the happiness intended. . . .*

The letter went on to explain that after her recent visit to the manor, Aunt Tilney had instructed her driver to take her directly to Crawley to speak with her aunt personally, and yes, Margaret Dunweedy was still perfectly happy and willing to receive Charlotte and the child. But Charlotte's mind was focused on the news of the churching to be held not so very far from the manor.

Charlotte arrived at St. George's early, passed between the columns of the portico, and entered the grand church through a side door as discreetly as possible. She tiptoed through the entry hall, hoping to diminish the echo of her boots on the stone paving, and climbed the curved rear staircase to the upper gallery. Selecting a box to the rear, where she could see but hopefully remain unseen, she quietly opened its latch and sat on the bench. Below her, she saw a portly cleric lighting candles near the front altar, but otherwise there seemed to be no one about.

A quarter of an hour later, the center doors opened and a small group of gaily-dressed women entered, chattering and laughing like a clutch of hens. Charlotte recognized one of Katherine's friends but none of the other regal ladies. There was Katherine in the center of them, wearing a pale blue walking dress and a fur-trimmed cape. A blue hat ornamented with feathers crowned her head. In her arms, she held a babe . . . Charlotte's babe, gowned even more lavishly than his attendants, in flowing white satin. As the women chatted amongst themselves, Charlotte heard bits of their plans to visit an elegant tearoom after the churching.

An Anglican priest in flowing robes entered and the women hushed. He directed them to a small chapel beside the chancel, its size conducive to the intimate gathering. There Katherine kneeled, as directed by the *Book of Common Prayer*, and the service began. Having grown up a vicar's daughter, Charlotte knew the service was formally named the "Thanksgiving of Women after Childbirth."

"'For as much as it hath pleased Almighty God of His goodness to give you safe deliverance, and hath preserved you in the great danger of childbirth: you shall therefore give hearty thanks unto God,'" the priest intoned.

Katherine responded, "'I am well pleased that the Lord hath heard the voice of my prayer. The snares of death compassed me round: and the pains of hell got hold upon me.'"

Charlotte unconsciously mouthed the familiar words along with her cousin. She was touched by the unexpected humility of

Katherine's audible response. She had long known Katherine to be cynical of religion, but her declaration seemed wholly sincere.

"'Oh, Almighty God,'" the priest continued, "'which hast delivered this woman thy servant from the great pain and peril of childbirth: Grant, we beseech thee, most merciful Father, that she through thy help, may both faithfully live and walk in her vocation, according to thy will in this life present . . .'"

This part of the service did not apply to her, Charlotte realized with a dull ache. Katherine was being exhorted to remain faithful to her husband and to bear other heirs for him. Charlotte swallowed back remaining dregs of bitterness.

"'. . . and also may be partaker of everlasting glory in the life to come: through Jesus Christ our Lord. Amen.'"

Would Katherine bear more children? Even though she was older and had experienced such a difficult childbirth? Katherine believed a healthy child had resulted from the ordeal . . . so would Edmund yet have a brother or sister? Or would he grow up an only child?

"'Children,'" continued the priest as he delivered the liturgy, "'are an heritage and gift that cometh of the Lord. Happy is the man that hath his quiver full of them.'"

Charlotte sat and waited as Katherine's friends filed cheerfully from the church, their heels and laughter echoing in the lofty space. Katherine paused to thank the cleric, then turned and followed after the others. Charlotte watched until Katherine and Edmund disappeared from view beneath the gallery railing.

Then her tear-filled gaze fled to a carving of Mary holding the infant Jesus and, above, the magnificent painting of Jesus at the Last Supper. She stared at the images as Katherine's footsteps faded away below. Charlotte felt her lips part and her chest tighten. She had spent her life in a church not unlike this one, but this was the first time she had been so deeply struck by the immensity of what God had done in giving up His only Son. *How did you do it?* she breathed, tears running down her cheeks. Of course she knew the situations were beyond compare. God's sacrifice had saved count-less multitudes. Hers, only one precious child.

A few days after the churching, Katherine pulled the long-forgotten handkerchief from beneath the sachet in her drawer. How long had it lain there, concealed? The smell of musty lilac was heavy on the material, its folds now permanent creases. She turned it over and there it was. The unusual flower, the pod, the curve of the leaf resembling the letter C. Yes . . . this was a C and now she remembered. This was Charlotte's signature. Cousin Charlotte, who detested needlework but had nevertheless made a pretty handkerchief for Katherine as a gift for some birthday or Christmas many years ago now.

Clutching the handkerchief, Katherine marched up the stairs to the nursery.

Sally jumped when she entered.

"Where is that blanket? The embroidered one?"

"I . . . I'm not . . ."

"Did you dispose of it as I asked?"

"Well, I . . . I meant to put it out with the children's aid dona-tion. But let me see . . ."

Sally lifted the lid of the chest and flipped through the linens. "There 'tis."

"I knew it." Katherine snatched the blanket from her and walked to the window, comparing the two items in the light.

"Do forgive me, m'lady."

"Look. They are so similar, are they not?"

Sally approached cautiously and leaned close. "Seems so."

"Do you know who made this?"

The nurse hesitated. "Well, I . . ."

"My cousin Charlotte, that's who."

"Charlotte?"

"Yes, Charlotte Lamb, my young cousin. I've been wondering where's she gone to."

"Charlotte Lamb?"

"Yes, yes."

Katherine strode from the nursery, both pieces in hand. She found Charles in the library.

"I knew it. Look."

"What am I looking at? Not the confounded blanket again."

"Yes . . . and the handkerchief. See—they were made by the same person."

"I do not see that they are so alike."

"I asked and asked, and no one would tell me. I detest secrets! I have had my suspicions, but I did not want to believe—"

"Katherine," he said sternly. "What are you talking about?"

"Charlotte Lamb, of course."

"What of her?"

"She made this blanket, just as she made this for me years ago. That could only mean one thing."

"What are you suggesting?"

"You said you got this from a hospital. Which hospital?"

"What does it matter?"

"Was it a lying-in hospital? The Manor Home? Queen Charlotte's?"

"I had my mind on other things. The physician directed the driver to the nearest facility . . ."

"Yes, yes. Which was it?"

"Why do you need to know?"

"Because Charlotte is there . . . or was. And I have the proof of it." She lifted the blanket.

"You have nothing of the kind. All sorts of ladies aid societies make blankets for hospitals and foundling wards and other worthy charities. If, and I repeat *if*, Charlotte Lamb stitched that blanket, that by no means proves anything other than her stitching hasn't improved."

"Can you imagine Charlotte sitting around stitching with some ladies aid society? And with such cheap material? I for one cannot."

"For a good cause . . ."

"Yes, for a very good cause—her own. I tell you she has disappeared, and my uncle will not speak her name nor hint at her whereabouts. Neither will her trying sister."

She suddenly looked at him, staring baldly at him, daring him to lie. "You do not know where she is, do you, Charles? Tell me honestly."

He replied levelly. "I do not know where she is."

"I should ask Amelia Tilney. She would know if anyone would."

"Why do you want to know?"

"Why do you think? So we can help her."

"Even if what you are suggesting is true . . . that she's had a child out of wedlock?"

"Yes. Not publicly, of course. But if she's been left to fend for herself, there must be something we can do."

"That is very kind of you, Katherine."

"Do look into it for me, won't you, Charles?"

"Very well. If it's important to you, I shall."

✥

Daniel's father, John Taylor, looked at him sadly from across the table. "But to send your child away . . . ?"

"What would you have me do?" Daniel asked.

"I could help care for her. Have the nurse stay here."

"What sort of woman would live alone with two men?"

"Plenty would."

"Not the sort I want nursing my daughter."

"Anne is my grandchild."

"And my daughter. Do you not think I shall miss her as well?"

"But Lizette will want her near . . . once she is sufficiently recovered."

"I pray that will be so."

"May I ask what—" his father hesitated—"what course of treatment you will try next?"

"I do not know."

"Allow me to help you, Daniel."

"You are not to practice, if you'll remember."

"It was one mistake. And even then both child and mother survived."

"Yes, I thank God I happened by."

"She was not expected to deliver for a fortnight at least. If I'd had any indication her time might come sooner, that I might be called into duty, I should never have allowed myself to . . . to . . ."

"Get drunk?"

His father winced.

"Forgive me," Daniel said. "That was uncalled for."

"I have not taken a drink since," his father said quietly. "But if I'm not allowed to work, to help people . . . I do not know . . ."

"Perhaps in time, Father. Once that episode is forgotten. Do not forget Miss Marsden threatened to go to the courts with her charges if she caught wind of you practicing."

"I have not forgotten. Still, I might be of use to my own granddaughter or daughter-in-law. . . ."

"You saw how Lizette was while she was still here with us. You would barely know her now. The mania is completely out of control. If you have some idea . . ."

"I confess I have never treated a case so severe."

"Nor I, Father. Nor I."

❧

The following week, Katherine again raised the topic of Charlotte's whereabouts. "I was speaking with my accoucheur and he remembers a physician by the name of Taylor being on hand the night of Edmund's birth."

"Yes, that's right."

"Well, where does he practice? Have you contacted him?"

"What do you plan to do once you know?"

"To inquire after Charlotte, of course."

"I'm sure such information is confidential. For obvious reasons."

"Oh, I have my ways—as you well know." She smiled at him.

"Have you considered for a moment, my dear, that if Charlotte were in such a place, she might not like the fact to be discovered?"

"Bah. I am sure it is only that preening vicar-father of hers that sent her into exile. Charlotte has always been very fond of me. I am sure she would be happy to see me, once she knows where my sympathies lie."

❧

"I am sorry, Mrs. Harris." The matron, a Mrs. Moorling, was either ignorant or refused to address her properly. "But I cannot divulge the name of any of our girls—neither current nor past residents. Surely you understand."

"Normally, yes. But I assure you this instance is different. I only want to help my cousin."

"Very noble, I'm sure."

Katherine sighed. "Very well, I shall leave my card." Katherine handed one across the desk. "Perhaps you might deliver it to her and ask her to contact me, if that would be more suitable."

"I told you, there is nothing I can do." Mrs. Moorling rose. "I trust Sally Mitchell has proven herself a suitable nurse?"

Katherine had little choice but to rise as well. "Yes. Quite suitable, thank you."

Unaccustomed as she was to being refused anything, Lady Katherine's departing smile was quite false.

As she left Mrs. Moorling's office, she saw a thin, plain, officious woman with a sheaf of papers in hand.

Katherine smiled at her. "You look a very knowledgeable, helpful sort."

"I do?" The plain woman curtsied. "Thank you, mum."

"I would be ever so obliged if you could help me. I am looking for my dearest cousin, sent here by her tyrant of a father. Poor dear thinks she hasn't a friend in the world, when here I am ready to offer hearth and home."

"'Tis good of you."

"So. If you could just direct me to Charlotte's room . . ." She took a tentative step toward the stairs.

"Charlotte?" the young woman asked.

"Yes, Miss Charlotte Lamb." Katherine paused on the first step.

"Oh . . . I'm afraid we haven't anyone by that name. We did have a Charlotte not so long ago by another surname. But I'm afraid she's left and I know not where. Poor soul."

Katherine arched a brow.

"Lost her wee babe, she did."

"How dreadful."

"Yes, mum. A finer young woman I've never known."

"But not . . . a Miss Lamb?"

"No. I'm afraid not."

Discouraged, Katherine was just leaving the manor when she heard a voice call out a familiar name. "Afternoon, Taylor. Any new patients I should know of?"

Katherine whirled around. Two men stood talking in low tones on the other side of the hall. Both looked up as she approached, her shoes clicking on the marble floor. One was handsome—dark hair brushed back from his forehead with a touch of silver in his sideburns. The other man was taller, but thin and pale.

"Dr. Taylor?" she asked.

The thin one inclined his chin and answered, "Yes?"

She introduced herself. "Lady Katherine Harris."

Before Taylor could respond, the handsome man bowed. "Lady Katherine . . . a pleasure. Allow me to introduce myself. Jeffrey Preston, esteemed physician. May I be of service?"

"Actually I'd like to speak to Dr. Taylor." She turned to him. "That is, if you have a moment?"

"Of course. Excuse us, Preston."

Dr. Preston bowed curtly before turning on his heel and stalking away.

"You must forgive me," Katherine began once they were alone. "I am told you were on hand the night my son was born, but I am afraid I don't remember meeting you . . . or little else for that matter. I was not myself that night."

"Perfectly understandable. It is a pleasure to see you looking so well."

"Thank you."

"And how does young Edmund fare?"

"Very well." She beamed. "I am surprised you remember my little son's name." Then her pleasure transformed into a question. "But how do you know his name, I wonder? We had not yet decided what to call him."

"Oh. I don't know. Someone told me. Your husband, perhaps. I've seen him by chance a time or two since."

Her eyebrows rose. "Have you really?"

"Only in passing."

She looked at him closely, opened her mouth as if to say more, then closed it again. She smiled. "I have not thanked you for everything you did for my son that night."

"You needn't thank me."

"Of course I do. You saved his life."

"Well . . ." Dr. Taylor looked down at the floor, clearly uncomfortable.

"Let me tell you why I'm here," she began. She told him of her quest and the man's discomfiture only seemed to increase.

"I am afraid I cannot help you. The Manor Home has strict policies—"

"Yes, yes, your Mrs. Moorling has explained all that already. But I thought, perhaps since you are some acquainted with my family . . ."

"I'm sorry."

She pulled a small paper-wrapped bundle from her reticule. "I have funds here I was hoping would help my cousin. Shall I be forced to roam the corridors, calling her name?"

"No. That will not be necessary. You have my word that Char . . . that no one by that name is in residence."

"But she was here."

"I cannot say."

Katherine sighed in frustration, then forced a smile. "Very well." She returned the bundle to her bag and turned to leave.

Dr. Taylor called after her. "If I were to . . ."

Katherine turned around.

". . . to somehow come into contact with this person. Can you tell me, what exactly is the money for? Is it . . . in payment for . . . something?"

"Payment? Goodness, it isn't payment for anything. I simply want to help her and never imagined I would have so much trouble doing so."

Dr. Taylor again studied the floor. Katherine closed the distance between them.

"It is clear you know more than you let on. I know—I will give you a . . . donation. If you can get it to Charlotte, wonderful. If you cannot, use it for the worthiest cause . . . or woman . . . you know. Surely you cannot reject such an offer."

"It is indeed generous and there are many needs."

She pressed the money into his hand.

"I trust you to help her, if you can."

Wanted, a child to wet nurse.

A healthy young English woman having abundance of milk,

wishes to take a child to wet nurse at her own house—every attention will

be paid to the comfort of the child, as she is living

in a quiet and healthy house. . . .

—Philadelphia Public Ledger, 1837

Chapter 19

Charlotte and young Anne were established in Margaret Dunweedy's snug cottage in the village of Crawley, not far from The George Inn—a midway stop on the coach route between London and Brighton.

Margaret Dunweedy, Charlotte's great-aunt, was a small, wiry woman with surprising vitality for one of her advanced years. Her hair was white and twisted around the crown of her head in a long plait. Her eyes were the color of cornflowers, as were many of the veins around her eyes, making her irises appear even bluer. She was rarely still. She received Charlotte and the baby with great warmth and enthusiasm, bustling about, making tea, bringing extra blankets, exclaiming over the joys of having someone sharing the old place again. Her husband had been gone twenty years, and her son, Roger, was living in Manchester and too busy with his post to visit very often.

Margaret Dunweedy's sole fault, Charlotte soon surmised, was her inability to cease speaking. The cheerful woman seemed never to run out of things to say. For the first few weeks, this was quite a pleasant relief, for Mrs. Dunweedy felt no need to question Charlotte, happy to simply relay countless tales of her own life. But as the long months of winter wore on, Charlotte began to grow weary of the constant chatter.

Otherwise, the winter passed in relative ease and comfort. Dr. Taylor visited his daughter every fortnight or so, as his schedule and road conditions allowed. His wife was somewhat improved, he'd reported, but was still suffering.

Anne began sleeping through the night, and so did Charlotte. She was amazed at how much better she felt, how much lighter the anguish, the pressing weight of her grief. It was still there, of course, like a hooded cloak about her head and shoulders. The cloak had at first been fashioned of barbed chain mail that threatened to knock her to her knees. Over the winter months, it had become a cloak of heavy grey wool, its hood falling over her eyes and blocking out the light, encasing her in darkness, suffocating her. But as winter gave way to spring, so too the cloak lightened as if to a dense velvet or thick damask. She could still feel it with every fiber of her skin, her being, but now it let in the light and allowed her, finally, to breathe. Even so, there was not a waking hour in which she didn't think of Edmund. And rare was the night when she did not dream of trying to find him, or of him about to fall from some dangerous precipice. How she tried to get to him, but he was always out of reach.

As soon as the weather allowed, she took to bundling up Anne and taking the baby outside with her in the untidy remains of last year's garden and beyond, to the damp fallow field behind the cottage, parroting her mother's wisdom about the benefits of "fresh air and exercise." She closed her eyes and breathed in the loam, the wilted sage, the rare silence.

On one such day in March, she noticed a carriage coming to a halt on the road on the far side of the meadow. Something about the horse and rig seemed familiar, but at such a distance she could not see the driver. As the carriage sat there on the open road, Charlotte saw a glint of light, as off glass. *Strange*, Charlotte thought. Was someone watching her?

❦

On the first day of April, Gareth Lamb, her brother-in-law, stared at her incredulously over his teacup. "Are you suggesting she might yet be recovered?"

Amelia Tilney nodded, taken aback by his sharp tone.

Across from Amelia, her eldest niece said between clenched teeth, "I suggest we discuss this no further."

"Beatrice, please," Amelia began. "I have reason to believe she's lost the child."

"Must we speak of it! The indecency . . ."

"The babe lives," Gareth Lamb said flatly.

"What?" Amelia asked, stunned.

"I saw them with my own eyes."

Amelia's heart began to beat painfully within her. "You did? When?"

"I was in Crawley for a clerical meeting Monday last. Drove by your aunt's cottage, and there she was in the back garden, babe in arms."

"Will my mortification never end!" Bea flopped herself down on the settee in a most unladylike manner.

Amelia realized her hand was over her heart. "I confess I am speechless . . ."

Gareth gave her a knowing look. "I am sure you are."

"Did Charlotte see you?"

"No. I was too far off. I—" He shifted uncomfortably. "I happened to have an opera glass with me."

"Well, she cannot return here," Bea stressed. "Really, Father, it is too much."

"If only the man would do his duty," Mr. Lamb shook his head somberly. "Plenty of other children have come into the world in such a manner. Many have been granted educations and gone on to marry well. Some have even been given titles . . ."

"Father. I doubt *this* father has any title to bestow beyond that of assistant gravedigger."

"Beatrice!" Amelia gasped.

"Have you another theory, Aunt? Another explanation?"

"She assures me the man in question is a gentleman of good repute."

"How can that be?"

"She declines to blame him, but it seems clear that he must have chosen to marry another."

"She said so?"

"Not directly, but I gathered this from her certainty that there was no way to bring him around."

"I have another theory," Gareth Lamb said with a frown. "Perhaps the bounder has intentions for her sister and refuses to yield."

It was Bea's turn to gasp. "Father! I forbid you to speak so of Mr. Bentley! It's slanderous!"

"Well, the young man has yet to ask for your hand. Has all but disappeared. Have *you* another explanation?"

Bea raised her chin. "If it has anything to do with Charlotte, it is that our family's disgrace has somehow come to his attention."

Bea flounced out of the room, more for escape than out of any true emotion. She was off to meet her friend Althea. They were to attend a reading together in the bustling market town of Faversham. Buxley was already waiting for her outside with the carriage as she had requested.

Arriving in Faversham a quarter hour ahead of schedule, Bea asked Buxley to let her down near the town center. She would walk to the library from there. It was a market day and vendors filled the streets surrounding the old guildhall, their carts, baskets, and makeshift tables overflowing with sausages, cheeses, bread, fish, and fruit. Taking her time, she strolled past the booths, then paused to look at the hats displayed in the milliner's window, noting with disdain that they were terribly out of fashion. She sighed. It was too bad they did not live closer to London town.

Ahead she saw a tearoom. Outside its doors, several tables stood beneath a striped awning. She noticed two couples enjoying refreshment *al fresco*, taking advantage of the unseasonably warm spring day.

"Mr. Bentley!" Bea called before the scene fully registered. Then her breath caught and she nearly stumbled. There was no mistaking the smile William was giving the young lady across the table from him, how close he was leaning . . . that light in his eyes. Bea had seen all these before. She knew. It was either slink away, ashamed, and hope he had not heard nor seen her, or mount an offensive. Beatrice Lamb had never slunk away from anything in her life, and she decided not to start now. She wouldn't give him—or her—that satisfaction. She squared her shoulders and waved a handkerchief. His handkerchief.

He saw her and quickly excused himself from the redhead. Squire Litchfield's daughter, if she was not mistaken. Pretty, yes. Dumb as a mule. That her father had more money than hers, there was no doubt.

Did she imagine the slight sheepish expression, the flush of his fair cheeks? The awkward smile now as he approached? Surely she had, for the man clearly had no shame.

She summoned her most confident smile and stood tall. "How fortuitous to happen upon you, Mr. Bentley."

"Yes. Miss Lamb, um, how good to see you again. How do you fare?"

"Wonderfully well, I thank you. And so relieved to see you out enjoying yourself on such a fine afternoon."

"Yes?"

"I have been hoping for an appropriate time to return this to you. Trite thing, this, but how glad I am to happen upon you in a public place. There you are. Now I am relieved of that obligation. I do thank you, sir. And wish you well."

She turned to leave, smile stiff but resilient. If only she could manage not to trip and disgrace herself on her departure.

"Bea!"

She started, which she hoped he did not notice, and forced herself to turn around slowly at his unexpected call.

"Yes, Mr. Bentley?" she began, but fearing she sounded too hopeful, added breezily, "Did I forget something? Oh, forgive me, please do give my regards to your companion. I must hurry to a reading with a friend or I would adore meeting her."

"You must know her. It is Amanda Litchfield."

"Oh, one of the Litchfields. Do say hello for me."

"Bea . . . Miss Lamb. Are you certain you are all right?"

"Of course I am."

"And . . . your family?"

"Better than ever, I thank you. Now I really must fly."

He looked at her, clearly perplexed. There was a speculative look in his eyes that told her he might suspect her act but wasn't quite sure what to believe. It would have to be enough.

❦

Amelia Tilney studied the stern face of her brother-in-law. He had moved on from tea to port, though she knew he was not given to drink. She felt only mildly guilty for driving him to its solace this day. "Gareth, I must say your coldness surprises me most unhappily."

"Madam. There are consequences to be reckoned with, and certainly we are all aware that there is no happy outcome in such a situation."

Amelia leaned forward and adjusted the framed miniature of her sister on the table. She said softly, "You are a man of God, Gareth. You of all men should know that God is forgiving, a God of mercy—"

"He is also a God of wrath. And of consequences."

"But must Charlotte pay such a dear price—the loss of her entire family? She has already suffered greatly. She was a mere shadow of herself when last I saw her."

"Was she?" He seemed to contemplate this. "Is she repentant? Sorry?"

"Oh, a sorrier girl I have never seen."

"And is she being well provided for by your aunt?"

"Well, there is not much money for coal or meat, but she has a nice kitchen garden and preserves all she can for winter. I am afraid Margaret's son is a mean sort who provides little for her upkeep. My husband and I send what we can. If you would but allow us, we would do more, now that Charlotte is there."

"No. You have done enough. I must ask you to do nothing further. And to speak no more of this."

"You may depend upon my discretion. I only speak now because I feel Charlotte's plight so keenly—"

He halted the rest of her sentence with a dismissive wave of his hand. "Yes, yes." He rose. "Now I really must bid you good day."

Amelia rose as well. Though stung by her brother-in-law's rudeness, she believed him not quite as unmoved as he appeared.

❧

A week later, the bell jingled as Margaret Dunweedy pushed open the butcher shop door. The gust of wind that accompanied her sent the hanging fowl and sides of meat to swaying on their hooks. The smells of sausages, strong English cheeses, and meat-pie pastries greeted her, as did the cheery butcher with his ready smile and crisp apron. "A good day to you, Missus Dunweedy."

"And to you, Mr. Doughty. What have you today for sixpence per pound?"

"No need for soup bones today, ma'am. Not with your account bulging with a good two pounds to spend."

"Two pounds—you are surely mistaken, Mr. Doughty. On my account?"

"No, ma'am. No mistakin' it." He winked at her. "You've got yourself a secret admirer, I'd say."

"Don't talk foolishness, man. At my age."

"Not foolishness at all. Well, then, what will it be. A fine leg of lamb? Or perhaps a stuffed goose? A roast of beef?"

"You are quite sure?"

"Sure I'm sure."

Margaret Dunweedy would have liked to believe the gift from her son, Roger. But she knew better. She guessed the two pounds had more to do with her lodger than with her, but she was grateful to be able to provide the sweet lass something finer than the stews and soups she'd been preparing.

"I haven't had a roast of beef since I don't know when," she admitted.

"Roasted with potatoes and onions . . ." The butcher closed his eyes, savoring the thought.

"The roast it is, Mr. Doughty."

"Excellent choice, ma'am. Excellent choice." He wrote himself a note.

She raised a brow at the paper he scribbled upon.

"I'm to account for how the pounds is spent, ma'am. Seems your admirer has more generosity than trust in an old scuff like me. Afraid I might take your two quid and leave you none the wiser."

"Then he doesn't know you, Mr. Doughty. A more trustworthy butcher I've never known."

"Thank you, ma'am. And here you are. You enjoy that, now." He handed her the wrapped package.

"Indeed we shall."

"You've company, then?"

"Oh, just my niece come to call."

"Ah, that explains it."

It didn't. Not fully, Margaret knew. But she was wise enough to know the village butcher didn't need to know her great-niece's troubles. He might not cheat on the fair weight of meat, but he wasn't above handing out juicy gossip along with his chops.

Tibbets announced Lady Katherine's arrival and her father stood. Bea merely laid aside the book she had been reading. Her cousin strode into the room, looking—Bea noted begrudgingly—elegant in a feathered hat and a full pelisse that did not quite conceal her figure, still somewhat rounded from her confinement last autumn.

"Lady Katherine. Niece!" Father boomed.

"Good day, Uncle. You're looking . . . well, rather tired, actually. Are you not well?"

"I am not getting any younger. But I cannot complain."

"And Beatrice. How nice to see you again."

Beatrice merely nodded.

Her father smiled in her stead. "What an unexpected pleasure."

"Is it unexpected? Surely you heard that we were returning to Fawnwell."

"We did hear that the repairs were nearing completion, but not that you—"

"Yes. I've shut up my London home for the season. We're doing everything quite the wrong way round this year. Now that most of our friends have left their country homes and are returned to London, we have quit town to stay here for the spring and summer. I detest the thought of missing the London season, but Charles believes the country air will be so much better for Edmund. Oh! You must meet him." She turned to the servant. "Do ask the nurse in as soon as she's done changing the child."

"Yes, m'lady." Tibbets curtsied and left the room.

"Won't you sit down?" Beatrice offered coolly.

"Thank you. That gown . . . Rather severe, is it not? Yet it fits you somehow."

"I think so." Bea liked the high-necked frock in a color she thought of as storm grey.

"I would have called sooner," Katherine chatted on, filling the silence. "But first I had my recovery, of course, and then this dreadful winter. Did you not find it so? I do detest traveling in inclement weather. The roads get so rough and rutted. How glad I am that spring is here at last and I can be out calling again."

Tibbets returned a moment later with a tall horse-faced woman holding a chubby baby in a satin gown. The nurse bobbed a curtsy, then carried the child to his mother and placed him in her outstretched arms.

Katherine, smile bright, turned the baby around to face them.

"This is our Edmund. Is he not the image of Mr. Harris?"

Bea stared. For a fleeting moment, she saw Charlotte in the child's features, his upturned nose and fine brows above large brown eyes. Was she really feeling so guilty about her? Or missing her so keenly? The little boy smiled a toothless grin in Bea's direction. She did not return the gesture.

"He looks like Charlotte," her father said dully, staring too. He'd said her name, as he'd vowed not to.

"You mean Charles, Father, surely," Bea rushed to correct.

"Oh, yes, yes. Charles. The names are so very similar. I meant to name my son Charles if I'd had one."

Katherine's brows were furrowed as she looked from one to the other.

From the corner of her eye, Bea noticed the ungainly nurse staring at her from across the room, where she stood in wait behind her mistress. *Why had Katherine even brought the sorry creature?*

"Speaking of Charlotte . . ." Katherine began.

"We were not," Bea said. "In fact we prefer other subjects."

"Yes, do tell us about Fawnwell," Father added. "Is all as it once was? Before the fire, I mean."

Katherine stilled, only her eyes moving between them, scrutinizing. She opened her mouth, closed it, and changed tack.

"Beatrice, Charles and I are thinking of hosting a house party this summer to celebrate the restoration of Fawnwell, and of course, to introduce Edmund. We are considering inviting many of our London friends down, many eligible . . . persons you might enjoy meeting. Has that any appeal for you?"

Beatrice shrugged. "Perhaps." *Why is that nurse still staring at me?*

"And you, Uncle, certainly you would not mind a little variety in society? A chance to debate theology with like-minded men of rank?"

Bea did not miss the patronizing choice of words, but Father did, and beamed.

"I should not mind at all. Sounds grand. When is it to be?"

"Why, just as soon as you tell me what I wish to know."

Wet nurses are unfortunately a necessary evil. Without them the children
of the better classes . . . would suffer very materially.

—T. C. HADEN, ON THE MANAGEMENT AND DISEASES
OF CHILDREN, 1827

CHAPTER 20

She had no warning.

Charlotte was pacing Mrs. Dunweedy's small parlor with Anne in her arms, hoping to lull the child to sleep, when she heard the familiar sound of a carriage on the street outside. It was pulled by a team of at least four horses, she judged, by the thunderous beating of hooves. Being this close to the High Street, that sound did not alarm her—in fact it barely registered. It was the sound of the hooves slowing, the coachman shouting "Whoa" to his horses that caused Charlotte to walk to the window. She shifted Anne to her left arm and parted the curtains with her right hand. Her heart began pounding, faster and faster even as the pounding hooves slowed, then ceased. A fine carriage indeed. Tall and enclosed. A carriage made for traveling some distance in speed and comfort. Lady Katherine's carriage.

Oh, God, help me. . . . The breathed prayer was automatic. What else could she do? She couldn't flee. How had her cousin found out where she was? Had Aunt Tilney told her? No, she would never do such a thing, loathe as she was for anyone in the family, or in their general acquaintance, to discover Charlotte's position as a wet nurse. Then who? And how was she to honor her aunt's fervent plea and keep that fact hidden?

The coachman helped her cousin alight. There she was in fine, full-length cape and plumed hat. Had she—*Oh, dear Lord*—had Katherine brought her son? *Her* Edmund? How would she hide her feelings?

Behind Katherine, a second woman alighted on the coachman's hand. This one far taller and more simply attired. Sally! Sally—here, now? Charlotte was elated and dread-filled all at once.

Sally will know Anne is not mine.

That thought pushed Charlotte into action. Hurrying, she gently laid Anne in her little cradle in the guest room, wincing in anticipation but breathing deeply when the child did not cry. She then quickly opened the front door and stepped out onto the path, not waiting for her visitors to knock.

"Lady Katherine! What a lovely surprise!"

Both women, still standing beside the tall carriage, turned to look at her. But it was Sally who sprung into movement first, handing her bundle to Katherine and hurrying over to Charlotte, arms outstretched, her thin face overwhelmed by her crooked, toothy smile.

"Bless me, Charlotte! I didn't know it was you we was visiting!"

Sally threw her arms around her and held her tight.

Charlotte took the opportunity to whisper urgently. "Sally. Please. Don't say a word about . . . my son. I've a baby here, a girl. Please don't say anything. They all think she is mine."

"But . . . I don't understand . . ."

"Please. I'll explain when I can."

"Well, I gather you two have never met," Katherine said wryly. Charlotte and Sally pulled apart. Katherine was looking at them with a speculative grin.

"Sally and I met in London."

"Oh?"

Charlotte took a deep breath. "Yes. She worked at the lying-in hospital where I . . . spent my confinement."

Katherine shook her head, lips pursed. Charlotte lowered her focus to the ground.

"That father of yours . . ." Katherine grumbled. Charlotte looked up at this unexpected response. "Well, cousin"—Katherine raised a brow—"are we to be invited in for tea or not? I am dying to show off my son."

Charlotte glanced quickly at the bundled child in Katherine's arms, where she had been trying to avoid settling her gaze.

"Yes! Forgive me. Please do come in."

Once they were all inside, Charlotte began the introductions. "This is Margaret Dunweedy, my great-aunt on my mother's side. And this is Lady Katherine, my cousin on my father's side."

"And this is my son," Katherine added. "Little Edmund Harris."

"Oh, he's lovely," said Mrs. Dunweedy appreciatively. "How old is he?"

"He was born October . . ." Katherine thought for a moment.

Staring at him, Charlotte whispered, "The second . . ."

Katherine looked at her, puzzled. "The seventh."

"So, six months old," Margaret went on quickly, smiling and glancing at one, then the other of them.

"And this . . . ?" Margaret nodded toward Sally.

"Oh." Katherine waved her hand dismissively. "This is Edmund's nurse."

"Sally Mitchell," Sally supplied with a friendly smile.

Katherine sat on the worn, stuffed chair, holding Edmund on her lap. She turned sideways a bit in her seat to show her child off to the fullest vantage. "What say you, Charlotte? Is he not absolutely perfect?"

Charlotte swallowed, her eyes drinking in the still-familiar face—the prominent, upturned nose, the crease between the faint eyebrows. Yet how changed he was! He was able to sit up now, with a bit of support. His cheeks were rounder, his close-set, serious eyes more alert. Her heart ached. Her arms ached to hold him.

"Yes, perfect," she mumbled, then forced a smile. Edmund gave a toothless grin in response, and Charlotte had to bite her lip to hold back tears.

"I think he looks just like Charles. Do you not agree, Charlotte?"

"I could not say . . ."

"Of course you could, for you've known my husband longer than I have."

Charlotte's mouth went dry, and she studied the child's face again, glad for the excuse to savor the sight of him.

"Yes, I see the resemblance," Charlotte said quietly. "Indeed."

Charlotte excused herself and she and her great-aunt went into the kitchen to prepare tea. Charlotte helped her hostess bring out the tray of tea things and served their guests, trying in vain to keep her hand from shaking as she poured tea and passed the plate of scones. She was relieved Margaret had decided to purchase an un-accustomed sweet from the baker in addition to their usual sparse fare.

Katherine handed Edmund over to Sally and placed one of the damask napkins in her lap in his place. Katherine took a sip of tea, barely covering a grimace—Margaret made their tea weak to conserve—and began filling the awkward silence with her articulate speech, telling how they had closed up their London home for a few months and returned to Charles' estate.

"Charles feels the country air will be so much better for Edmund. I am not so sure how I shall fare, so isolated from the rest of the world. How I shall miss the season in town. But you know how it is—maternal sacrifice and all that. Whatever is best for my Edmund."

Charlotte's stiff smile began to waver, and she brought her teacup to her mouth just in time to cover the quiver of her lips.

Katherine took a bite of her scone, with a somewhat more approving expression, leaving the room silent again. Even Margaret was not her talkative self for once. Perhaps she found having a titled lady in her home somewhat intimidating.

Then, above the dainty clink of china cups on saucers and the clicking of the mantel clock, a baby's single cry pierced the silence. For a moment it seemed everyone froze, or didn't appear to have heard. Charlotte kept her eyes on her teacup, praying Anne would fall right back to sleep. Another cry arose. Margaret looked over at her first. Sally looked down at Edmund—sitting happily on her lap—then glanced up at her, questioningly. Katherine looked around the room at them all.

Charlotte got to her feet and said brightly, "Well! That was a short nap." She walked to the guest room and looked down into the cradle at Daniel Taylor's daughter. Anne's face was a wrinkled peach of need, which relaxed into contentment as soon as Charlotte lifted her into her arms.

"Forgive me. I don't know what else to do," she whispered and returned to the parlor.

"And this is Anne," she said, returning to her seat on the settee and holding the child close to her. She attempted to move the conversation along. "We were all so dreadfully sorry about the fire. Have the repairs been completed?"

"Yes, for the most part," Katherine said, eyes on Anne.

"And Mrs. Harris. That is . . . Mr. Harris's mother. She is well, I trust?"

"Yes. Quite well. Pleased to be back in her beloved home and delighted with her new grandson."

"Of course she is."

"You are familiar with her other grandson, are you not?" Katherine asked.

"Yes. Mr. Bentley visited the vicarage on occasion."

Katherine looked at Charlotte closely, then her gaze dropped again to the child in her arms. She set down her plate.

"Here, let us see her. Anne, was it?" Katherine held out her hands, leaving Charlotte little choice but to rise and place the child in her arms for inspection.

"Hello there, Miss Anne," Katherine began, situating the girl on her lap. "Was that you making all that fuss? Not very ladylike, are you? Oh, that is better. I believe she has fixed her eyes upon my feather." No conventional platitudes about the child's beauty nor perfection from Katherine Harris. "She is so different from Edmund. They look nothing at all alike."

Was that relief in her voice? Had she suspected, somehow, her own husband?

"Well, that is not surprising," Charlotte said. "You and I are not so closely related. And though they were born only a week or so apart, boys and girls are often so different—"

"She is a bit on the small side, is she not?" Katherine interrupted.

"Perhaps a bit," Charlotte allowed.

Katherine seemed to study the child more closely. She looked from the babe to Charlotte, then back again.

"We have not seen William for quite some time," she said quietly, not lifting her eyes from Anne's face.

Charlotte did not answer immediately, for she had not seen him nor anyone from home these many months, save Aunt Tilney and Charles. Neither of whom she could mention.

Just when Charlotte decided Katherine expected no response, that she had merely mentioned William idly, Katherine looked up at her, eyebrow raised in question.

Charlotte shrugged. "Nor I."

Only belatedly did she remember that she *had* seen Mr. Bentley, though only in passing—and him very drunk on his way to a ball with another woman. But, considering, well, everything, she thought it not worth reporting.

Katherine looked back at the infant. "Yes, I see the resemblance," she announced finally.

Charlotte's stomach lurched. Was she really suggesting the child resembled William Bentley?

"Resemblance?" Charlotte asked weakly.

Katherine smiled at her. "She looks a great deal like her mother."

Charlotte smiled stiffly, steeling herself as Katherine went on.

"You forget—and some days I should like to—that I had already seen my first season when you were born. She reminds me very much of you as a baby. The big eyes and something about the mouth . . ." Katherine waved vaguely about the child's face in a circular motion.

Charlotte swallowed. "Thank you."

She could feel Sally's eyes, wide and questioning, on her profile, but she kept her own gaze straight ahead.

Charlotte refilled teacups, although Katherine refused with another wave of her hand. When Charlotte had set the pot back down, Katherine handed Anne back to her.

"I went through no small ordeal to find you, Charlotte. I trust you do not mind the invasion?"

"Of course not," Charlotte said halfheartedly, returning to her seat.

"I even asked after you at that lying-in hospital back before Christmas. But neither the matron there nor Edmund's own physician would acknowledge you had been there, nor give me a clue to your whereabouts. All very private."

Charlotte's mind was whirling. *Edmund's own physician?*

Suddenly Charlotte remembered, and her palms began to perspire and her breathing escalated. She had to get Katherine out of here!

"It was your own father who finally tipped me off," Katherine continued. "And I had to all but threaten him with social ostracism before he would."

Father knows where I am?

"Why?" Charlotte asked with a half smile and a broken laugh.

"Why indeed! To help you, of course."

"Thank you, but . . . how?"

"Well, for starters, I shall be sending over more tea."

Anne began to fuss in earnest. Charlotte had put her off as long as she could, bouncing her and offering her little finger to suck on, but the child would have no more of that and was burrowing her face into Charlotte's bosom in a most humiliating manner.

"Please excuse me. Anne needs to be fed."

"Sally, do nurse Edmund as well. Then we really must be going."

"Yes, m'lady." Sally nodded.

"Why not join me in my room, Sally?" Charlotte offered. "That way these ladies may remain where they are."

Sally nodded again and, when Katherine didn't object, followed Charlotte to the guest room down the short passageway.

Both women busied themselves with their gowns and helping their charges latch on and begin nursing. When Anne was settled against her, Charlotte looked up. Sally, already nursing Edmund, was watching her, her eyes moving from Charlotte to the child and back again.

"Who is she?" Sally whispered.

Charlotte, sitting on the small chair near the door, cocked her head, listening, before responding. Hearing Katherine's voice as she regaled Margaret Dunweedy with an enthusiastic description of Edmund's christening—"The finest London has seen in many a year, I can tell you"—Charlotte reached over and pulled the door nearly closed. "Sally . . . I . . ."

"Is she a foundling?"

"Well, in a manner—"

"Bless your heart, Charlotte, I guessed it! You're motherin' a wee one from the foundling ward in place of your own poor lad gone to heaven. What a saint you are."

"I'm no saint, Sally. Far from it."

"Well, I think you are."

She opened her mouth to tell Sally the truth. But how could she admit she had lied to avoid the immense shame it would bring her family if it were known she was a wet nurse—Sally's own chosen profession?

"Well, all I can say is that this little girl needed a mother's care. So I'm caring for her—at least for a time. But, please, Sally, don't say a word to Katherine or anyone about my son. Please. I cannot tell you why, but it's very important. Promise?"

"But if she knew, she could—"

"No, Sally. No one must know. Ever."

Sally looked at her, eyes wide, searching. Finally she said, "Very well, Charlotte. If that's what you want."

"It is. It is what I need."

Charlotte looked down at Anne, who had nursed for only a few minutes before falling into a deep sleep. "Oh, Anne . . ." Charlotte mumbled, gently trying to rouse the baby.

"No use." Charlotte sighed. "She's hardly nursed all day. Too tired, I suppose." Charlotte rose and laid the sleeping child in the cradle. "She didn't sleep well last night. I think the poor thing had an earache."

"Would you mind, then?" Sally looked at her, then away, almost too casually.

"Hmm?"

"Well, you're needin' to nurse and I'm needin' a rest. This lad is never satisfied, and I want to have enough milk fer the long ride home."

Charlotte was stunned. A warm ache of need pooled within her as she stared at Edmund. Sally pulled him gently from her breast and stood, child in arms. Charlotte sat down, speechless, and Sally handed him to her.

"Mind if I take a lie on your bed?"

"No, of course not," Charlotte whispered, still staring down at Edmund.

Sally left her peripheral vision, but Charlotte didn't pay attention. Her mind barely registered the creak of the bed ropes as Sally reclined—her eyes were focused on her son. She guided him to her breast and cuddled him close. She felt his wet little mouth, the tug of his tongue, the sweet sting of milk coursing through her, the bittersweet flow of tears on her cheeks. She glanced up and saw Sally lying on her side on the bed, watching her all too closely.

Daniel Taylor alighted the horse drawn London-Brighton coach at The George, then began the walk down Crawley's High Street. As he strolled, he pulled out the schedule pamphlet and double-checked the return departure times. Looking up with the barest glance, he made the turn through Mrs. Dunweedy's gate and nearly walked straight into Katherine Harris.

"Well, Dr. Taylor, imagine meeting you here."

He dropped the schedule.

"Lady Katherine!" He gulped a deep breath. Then he bent over to pick up the pamphlet, and as he raised back up, took in her traveling clothes and just then saw the large carriage in the lane. He silently berated himself for his inattention. "I am surprised to find you here."

"I imagine you are. And here I thought you said you had no idea where Charlotte was."

"Well, I . . . I am not here to see Charlotte. I am here to see my—"

"Dr. Taylor!" Mrs. Dunweedy interrupted with a great burst of voice and smile as she hurried from the cottage and took his arm. "How good you are to come all this way to see me. My poor back has been hurting dreadfully. So good of you to come."

Katherine looked from Mrs. Dunweedy to Dr. Taylor, skeptical brow rising.

"You are here to see Mrs. Dunweedy?"

"Oh yes, Dr. Taylor has offered to come look in on me," Margaret Dunweedy said. "He's a good friend of my son. School chums, they were."

"An awfully long way for a house call, is it not?" Katherine asked.

Dr. Taylor looked at the cottage and saw Charlotte in the window, her face pale and somber, eyes pleading.

"Not so great a distance," he said. "I come this way now and again on business."

Katherine Harris followed his gaze and no doubt caught a glimpse of Charlotte before she stepped away from the window. "What sort of business, I wonder."

"Dr. Taylor, I should tell you," Mrs. Dunweedy interjected, "I've taken a boarder since you were here last."

"Oh?"

"Yes, her name is Charlotte Lamb, but I believe you knew her in hospital as Charlotte Smith. She has her daughter with her. Poor fatherless angel . . ."

Lady Katherine appeared incredulous. "You mean to tell me you are not here to deliver . . . to act on my behest of last autumn?"

"But of course I will," Daniel said. "Now that I am here."

As soon as Lady Katherine's carriage disappeared down the road, Charlotte turned away from the window and faced him, her expression downcast.

"Dr. Taylor, please forgive me." Charlotte all but pressed young Anne into his arms and took three long steps back. "I had no right to presume . . . to claim your child as my own. How awful that must have made you feel."

"And you would know," he said softly.

She glanced up at him quickly, as though fearing censure. He smiled grimly, hoping to put her at ease.

He looked down at Anne for a moment before saying, "I had no idea, until this moment, just what an awkward predicament I placed you in, asking you to do this."

"It is not your fault."

"Still, I am not sure if what I am about to tell you will be a relief or a greater trial."

Her gaze flew to his face. "What is it?"

He chewed on his lower lip. "Lizette is better."

"That is wonderful. You—" she began, but he cut her off soberly.

"She wants Anne home with her."

Charlotte's mouth opened, but for three full ticks of the clock no words followed.

Then she said quickly, "Of course. How wonderful. I am happy for you. And for your wife. And, Anne—Anne should be with her mother."

"Thank you," he said with a single nod, then studied the floor. "Considering . . . what just happened here—how difficult this is for you—and the fact that it will become, I'm supposing, only more difficult, I won't ask you to come with us," he said. "I will find another nurse and release you to find a more appropriate post . . . or to return home."

"I shall not be returning home," she said.

"What will you do, then?"

"I do not know. I imagined I would be occupied with Anne for the foreseeable future. I should have been better prepared."

"I'm sorry."

"Don't be." She smiled admirably, then asked, "Are you returning to London?"

"Yes, for a time. Though I've been offered a seaside cottage for a few months and am considering taking it. I think a change of scenery might do Lizette good."

"Where is the cottage?"

"Not far from Shoreham on the south coast. Nothing very fashionable, I'm afraid."

"I don't know a soul there . . ."

"Of course it is not that we do not wish you to come. If you wanted to continue on, we—"

"I would. I would like to continue on as Anne's nurse."

"Really? Well, wonderful."

"I do not like to leave my great-aunt so suddenly, but I am sure she will understand."

"Yes. She seems a loyal friend." He smiled, thinking of the old woman's enthusiastic falsehoods, as though she were playing a part in some Shakespearean farce.

"Now that Katherine knows I am here . . . well, should she return and find Anne gone, I would have to explain. I am not prepared to go through another false mourning. Although neither would be truly false."

He nodded.

"And seeing Edmund like that," she continued, "with her. I don't know. It is both nourishment and deprivation. Pleasure and pain."

He bit his lip. "But if you stay here . . . you would be more likely to see him now and again."

"Yes. No doubt you are quite right. And yet, I know myself. I would both hope—and fear—that someone would see a resemblance, or some inexplicable quality in my manner of looking on him. I know I should give myself away. Give him away." She expelled a puff of dry laughter. "Poor choice of words, that."

"You hope still to amend your arrangement?"

"Only every other moment. Most of the time I remain convinced I have done the right thing."

He ran his long hand over his face. "I feel so responsible—"

"Dr. Taylor," she said almost sternly. "We have been through this before. You are not to blame. Not for any of it. Not even for this." She nodded toward Anne as a new thought struck her. "Perhaps it is I who should be releasing you to go home without me, back to your former, trouble-free life. As long as you must see *me* you will always be reminded of how I came to be in your employ, will always feel responsible somehow."

"A *trouble-free* life." It was his turn to laugh dryly. "I am afraid my former life is as far from me as yours is from you. Though there are days when I am tempted to hope. Like now, when Lizette seems almost herself."

"Well, then, let us not tarry." Charlotte smiled bravely. "Let us get this dear one back to her mama. One cannot help but be cheered by her sweet presence."

"I quite agree. And I am pleased you will meet my wife now that she is recovered." He hesitated, then continued awkwardly, "It might be better if we did not mention her . . . time . . . in the manor."

"Of course. I understand."

Soon, farewells said and bags packed, Charlotte sat across from Daniel Taylor in the London-bound coach, Anne asleep in her arms. Two other passengers rode with them, an elderly couple with expressions as worn as their faded traveling clothes and drooping hats. The old woman smiled politely.

"How old is she?" she asked.

"Five-and-a-half months."

The woman glanced at Dr. Taylor, who was already reading a medical journal. "She looks a great deal like your husband."

Charlotte felt her cheeks warm. "We are not . . ."

But Dr. Taylor looked up from his book and interrupted her, saying kindly, "Thank you, madam. Though I dearly hope my daughter shall grow more handsome in time."

He smiled at the woman, and she smiled in return, not seeming to notice anything amiss.

Later, when both the man and the woman had nodded off, Charlotte leaned across the aisle and asked quietly, "Do you think my cousin suspected anything . . . about your coming to my aunt's as you did and, well, everything?"

"I cannot say," Daniel whispered back. "I fear I am not the thespian your great-aunt is. It's quite possible my expression gave something away. What do you think? You know her better than I."

"I think the questions are even now parading through her mind."

WANTED

A NURSE with a good Breast of Milk,

of a healthy Constitution and good Character,

that is willing to go into a Gentleman's Family.

—MARYLAND GAZETTE, 1750

CHAPTER 21

Charles Harris attempted to read while his wife paced the length of Fawnwell's newly restored sitting room.

"Really, Charles. A journey of that length to pay a house call? On a widow who cannot have more than a hundred pounds a year?"

"What did the woman say?"

"Something about her son and Dr. Taylor having been at school together."

"Well, then." Charles flipped over his newspaper.

"I do not believe it. I cannot imagine the Dunweedys affording Oxford or Cambridge. Which did Taylor attend, do you know?"

"I do not."

"I think I shall find out."

"To what purpose?"

"Clearly something is amiss with the entire situation."

Charles looked at her over his paper. "Of course there is. Did you not find your unmarried cousin with a child?"

"Yes, yes. I do not mean that. I mean with Taylor showing up there."

"Did you not ask him to get the money to her?"

"Yes, but I had the distinct impression he was there as a course of habit."

Charles shrugged, resuming his reading. "Even if he was there to check on Charlotte, a former patient, I don't see that as so unusual."

"Do you not?"

Keeping his tone casual and his eyes on his paper, Charles said, "You said Charlotte has a girl . . . a daughter?"

"Yes. Calls her Anne. Little thing. Not at all as robust as our Edmund."

"And what did Charlotte have to say about Edmund?"

"The usual niceties, I suppose. Though without the enthusiasm I might have expected. She did agree he looks like you."

Charles nodded but said no more.

"I also admit, I studied her child quite closely, thinking to see a resemblance to someone we both know quite well."

He looked up at her, feeling suddenly anxious. Had Katherine suspected the child would resemble *him*? He shifted uncomfortably in his seat.

"Of course she admitted nothing about William. Still I wondered. But then this Taylor showed up, all the way from London. You don't suppose . . . ?"

"Taylor is a married man."

"We both know that is no guarantee of anything. He traveled alone."

"Common enough. Besides, I heard his own wife was expecting a child. Taylor is likely a father already."

"Indeed?"

"Indeed."

Katherine shrugged, her pretty lips screwed up in thought. She seemed satisfied. For the time being.

❧

The Taylors' London townhouse was a tall narrow building sandwiched between a dozen others just like it. The medical offices were housed on street level, above the kitchen and beneath three floors of living quarters above. When they arrived, Daniel preceded Charlotte into his offices, where he dropped his medical case and picked up a few pieces of correspondence. He gave her a reassuring smile. "This way."

Holding Anne, while he carried her heavier bag, she followed him up the stairs. Up on the first floor, he stepped into an adjoining room, the sitting room most likely. Charlotte hesitated on the landing.

She heard the happy, accented voice of Mrs. Taylor call out, "Daniel! *Mon amour. Tu m'as manqué!*"

Charlotte stepped forward tentatively. From where she stood in the doorway, she could see Dr. Taylor's back, his arms wide, and a brief view of Mrs. Taylor's dark hair and bright smile before she disappeared into her husband's embrace. Charlotte averted her gaze and stepped back into the corridor.

"I've missed you too. More than you know."

"Have you brought her? *Notre fille?*"

"Of course, my love."

Charlotte stepped forward just as Daniel reached the doorway. She handed Anne to him carefully but swiftly and again stepped back.

She heard Lizette Taylor's gasp, followed by a moan that was at once joyful and mournful.

"Annette! *Ma petite. Ma fille. Chair de ma chair.*" The words were a warm litany of love and loss. *"Tu es très grand."* Charlotte heard laughter mixed with unseen tears. *"Quel bébé dodu!"*

"Yes, she has been well fed," Daniel said.

"La nourrice?"

"Yes, my dear, I should like you to meet her."

Again, Charlotte stepped forward, hands clammy, stomach churning. Her eyes were downcast as she entered the sitting room.

"May I introduce Miss Charlotte Lamb. Miss Lamb, my wife, Lizette."

Charlotte glanced up quickly at Daniel's wife. His beautiful wife.

"*Madame Taylor*," the woman corrected pleasantly, slanting a look at her husband.

Charlotte looked back at the floor and bobbed a quick curtsy.

"*Enchantée*," Charlotte mumbled, unsure whether her use of French would please her new employer or not.

When Charlotte darted another look, Mrs. Taylor smiled graciously at her. And with her smile she was even more beautiful. Charlotte could hardly reconcile this poised, exquisite woman with the howling, pitiful creature she had seen at the Manor Home.

Lizette Taylor's eyes narrowed. "Have we met?" she asked.

Charlotte swallowed, instantly knowing the correct answer. "No, madame. We have not been introduced."

Mrs. Taylor scrutinized her a moment longer, then turned her head.

"Marie!" she called out.

A maid with red-chapped cheeks entered, greying hair fringing out from her mobcap, "*Oui, madame?*"

"Please show Nurse to her chamber, would you?"

"*Bien sûr, madame.*"

"Welcome, Miss Lamb," Mrs. Taylor said. "I hope you will be happy with us."

As do I, Charlotte thought.

❧

Charlotte did not see Mr. John Taylor, Daniel's father, that first evening. But the next morning, while she breakfasted alone, he joined her in the dining room and greeted her with a warm smile.

"Miss Smith! How good to see you again. Oh, forgive me—it's Miss Lamb now, if I understand correctly."

"That's right. And a pleasure to see you again, Mr. Taylor."

He poured himself a cup of tea from the sideboard and sat across from her at the table.

"I was so sorry to hear of your loss."

"I thank you, sir."

Keeping his gaze on his teacup, he asked timidly, "It wasn't anything I did, or failed to do, was it . . . ?"

"Oh no, of course not, Mr. Taylor. I could not have asked for a kinder, more skilled surgeon."

"Thank you, Miss Lamb. You are most kind to say so. What a blessing for Anne to have been in your care. Where is the little mite this morning?"

"Still asleep. Tired from the journey, I suppose."

"Yes, and what a boon to have you here with us. With three beautiful ladies under our roof, well, I don't see how Daniel or I could be happier."

She smiled at him. "And you, sir, how do you fare?"

"I miss the work, I must say. I take great pleasure in feeling useful, helping people, you know. I miss it."

"Of course you do. Is there no hope of returning?"

"Daniel says not." He looked about the room, as if to reassure himself they were alone. "That Miss Marsden has quite a hold on me, I'm afraid. Says if I ever practice again, she'll bring me up on charges."

"But certainly your word, sir, against such a woman's . . ."

"That's right, Daniel mentioned you met her." He sighed. "It's not her alone who holds power over me. It's her patron, the father of her child, or so she says. Some rich and revengeful lord, to hear her tell it."

"May I ask who the man is?"

"A Lord Phillip Elton."

"Lord Elton . . ."

"You know him?"

"The name is familiar. I think he might be known to my uncle."

John Taylor shook his head sadly. "Well-known and well-connected, I'm afraid. There's naught I can do. For myself I might risk it, but I would not endanger Daniel's career any more than I have done already."

"Would you mind, sir, if I made a few inquiries on your behalf?"

"I would not *mind*, but do not trouble yourself, my dear. I shall be happy again now that I have my granddaughter here at home."

Charlotte and Anne were to share the nursery on the third floor. It wasn't a large room, but it would do nicely. John Taylor hauled up an old screen from one of the exam rooms in the office downstairs. With her permission, he set it up between the door and Charlotte's bed, to give her some semblance of privacy should one of the family wish to come in and pick up Anne, whose cradle was on the other side of the room.

During those first days they were all in London, Lizette Taylor seemed happy indeed. Happy, especially, to have her daughter back in her life. She held Anne for hours on end, bouncing her on her lap, speaking to her in French, singing French ditties and lullabies. Anne, for all her unfamiliarity with her own mother, was delighted with this enthusiastic attention and went happily from Charlotte's arms to Lizette's with little fuss. Charlotte was relieved for Mrs. Taylor's sake.

Anne was slower to take to her grandfather, unaccustomed as she was to male attention beyond the occasional visits her father had made over their months in Crawley. But still, after the first few days, her lower lip no longer quivered when he spoke to her—though she watched him carefully whenever he came near.

Sensitive to how Daniel's wife must be feeling, having missed those first precious months of her daughter's life, Charlotte was careful to stay in the background as much as possible, only offering to take Anne when she began to fuss or it was clearly time for another feeding.

So she was not sure of the cause of Lizette Taylor's growing moodiness.

"You take her, Miss Lamb, I feel a headache coming on," she began to say nearly once a day. Or, "There you are, back to Nurse. *Ta mère* must lie down and rest."

The spring that year was gloomier than usual, and during the last half of April it rained five out of every seven days. *Such weather could make the cheeriest person morose,* Charlotte thought.

Mrs. Taylor began spending hours in the sitting room alone, reclining on the settee, staring off into nothingness. Often she would neglect to raise the shades in the morning, or to light a lamp when darkness fell. With only one servant about the place, there was often no one to do it for her. Charlotte helped as much and as quietly as she could. She prayed as well.

❧

"I am worried about Lizette," Daniel's father said quietly as the two men sat in the dining room over lukewarm tea. Gone were the days of after-dinner port for this household.

"As am I," Daniel confided. "I have been wondering if a change of scenery might do her good. I've been offered a seaside cottage for a few months."

"Where?"

"The south coast. In France she lived by the sea."

"But . . . the Manor Home—what of your work there?"

"I don't know. Perhaps I can find someone to take my place for a time. I know how important the Manor is to you, but I can only do so much."

"It is important, Daniel. It is my life's work."

"It *was* your life's work, Father."

Daniel saw the light dim in his father's eyes and immediately regretted his words. "Again, I ask your forgiveness, Father. I have no right to take my exhaustion out on you."

"You are distraught, son. I understand. I know I have disappointed you. Truth is, I have disappointed myself. I have been weak—not the brother I should have been, not the father I should have been, and not the surgeon I should have been. . . ."

"Father . . ."

"But I have done some good. I have. Mothers who would have died, lived. Children too. That is why the Manor Home is so important. Promise me—keep the place going if you can. If not for me, for your poor aunt Audrey—God rest her soul."

Daniel squeezed his eyes shut, the guilt pouring over him as it always did when his father mentioned Aunt Audrey—a woman Daniel had never known. His father's sister had died as a young woman in a disreputable lying-in hospital. Until recent years the standards of care and cleanliness at such facilities meant fatalities were all too common. It was in his sister's honor that John Taylor had joined forces with other surgeons, physicians, and charity groups to establish the Manor Home for Unwed Mothers in the first place. Of course that was before he fell into disrepute.

"The Manor is not going to close if I take a leave."

"We cannot be sure. Did you not mention donations were down?"

"Yes, and expenses rising." Daniel ran a weary hand over his face. "I shall see what I can do. Perhaps I can carry on at the Manor during the week and travel to the coast at the weekend."

"Thank you, Daniel." John Taylor's hand trembled as he brought his teacup to his lips, then returned it to its saucer, untasted. "When my time comes, I can go thinking of the Manor Home and the lives saved there. May the good Lord forgive the rest. And you, Daniel. I pray you forgive me as well."

A few days later, Daniel was disconcerted to find his father and Miss Lamb waiting for him in his study. "What is it?" he asked.

His father glanced at Charlotte. "Miss Lamb has some news she wishes to share."

Daniel took in her anxious expression. *She's not leaving, I hope.*

"I fear you will mind," Charlotte began. "But I took the liberty of writing to my uncle—who is a solicitor—about the situation with Miss Marsden."

"What?" Daniel's relief that she wasn't announcing her resignation was quickly replaced by anger.

"Forgive me, I know it was presumptuous."

"Father, you were not to divulge—"

"Please," Charlotte interrupted. "Allow me to explain."

His father studied his hands, folded together in his lap as he sat. Daniel lifted his own hand, gesturing in irritated compliance for her to continue.

"Your father did not offer the information, Dr. Taylor. I asked for the man's name, this Phillip Elton."

Daniel groaned and shook his head.

"I thought the name was familiar but not for the reasons I guessed. In any case this man's father, Lord Elton himself, has long been a friend to my aunt and uncle. It was his name I had heard spoken with fondness over the years. I have even dined with him at my uncle's home on one or two occasions. However, this Phillip Elton is Lord Elton's son, and my uncle has had to wrest him from trouble more than once.

"I wrote to my uncle to inquire—do not fret, I did not mention your names nor the details of the situation but only asked whether this Miss Marsden was known to him. My uncle has written back." She lifted a letter she held in her hand. "In all truth, I wondered if he would, what with my father asking my aunt to cut off communications with me. But since I wrote with a 'professional' question, he thought it within his rights to reply. In any case, he assures me that not only is this woman no longer connected in any way to Phillip Elton nor Lord Elton himself, but that the Elton family has disowned the child she claims is his. They have severed all relationship with her. Beyond that, Phillip himself has had his privileges reduced and hasn't the money to pay his club tab, let alone take anyone to court. So you see, the woman has no hold on either of you any longer."

She smiled triumphantly—first at his father, who, Daniel noticed, did not meet her gaze, and then at him. Clearly, theirs was not the reaction she had expected.

"Perhaps my father forgot to mention that the woman's allegations were not unfounded. He *was* guilty of negligence during the delivery of her child."

Charlotte's smile faded, but she did not answer.

"Yes. Father is very skilled in garnering sympathy but less so in staying sober. Had I not happened along when I did, the child might have died."

"Daniel, I told you. I have not taken a drink since. It has been over a year. Will you never trust me again?"

Hands on hips, Daniel shook his head. "I don't know, Father. I want to, but I just don't know."

❧

Dr. Taylor arranged to take Lloyd Lodge for the months of May, June, and July. His wife and the servant Marie, a maid-of-all-work, journeyed to Shoreham a week earlier than the rest of the family to set up housekeeping.

Charlotte enjoyed those days, alone in the house much of the time with Anne and John Taylor. Aunt Tilney would not have approved had she known, but Charlotte felt not a moment's unease in the kind man's company. He treated her more like a daughter than a servant. And his gentle fondness was a warm salve that filled in the injured places, the jagged cracks in her heart, left there by her own father's cold indifference.

And to his delight—and Charlotte's—Anne grew quite attached to her grandfather during that time. His son, however, remained cool.

"I am sorry, Mr. Taylor," she said to Daniel's father one afternoon as they sat together in the sitting room during Anne's nap. "It seems I have succeeded only in making things worse between you and your son."

"Do not fret, my dear. I was touched by your efforts to help me. I know you acted with the best intentions. Daniel knows it, too, but is struggling to admit it. You see, he takes my failure quite personally. He resents that my disgrace has cast a pall on his reputation. I fear my son has always been overly sensitive to the criticism of others—real or perceived. I am sure he believes more censure has befallen him due to my failings than actually has. He has not the confidence some men do. I do not know why. Perhaps it has to do with his mother dying so young. Finding out his sole-remaining parent was fallible was a blow to him. I suppose it is always difficult for a child to realize his father's flaws do not reflect on him. That he—or she—must make the best of the life God gave him."

Charlotte felt tears sting her eyes but smiled at John Taylor nonetheless, knowing he could have little idea why his words affected her so.

"You will join us at the coast, will you not?" she asked.

"I do not believe I will. Daniel needs some time alone with his wife without his father hanging about. And I think I shall see what needs doing about the foundling ward. Mrs. Krebs will put me to work washing nappies if nothing else. Daniel cannot object to that." He smiled warmly at her. "Especially not now, after what you have found out for us."

When the week passed, they all stood in the entry hall, Charlotte holding Anne on her hip.

"I cannot change your mind, Father?" Daniel asked, picking up the last of the baggage to carry down to the waiting hansom.

"And who would water your gardens if I leave?" John Taylor bent his head to Anne's eye level and rubbed her cheek. "*Someone* has to work around here." He winked at Charlotte.

"Very well. I shall see you Monday week. Write or send a messenger if you need anything before. You have the directions?"

"Yes, I have everything I need. Do not worry about me, my boy. Just go and have a grand holiday—rest and rejuvenation for everyone, that's what I prescribe. And I shall be praying for you all as well."

"Thank you, Father." Daniel walked out the door.

Charlotte stepped forward and offered the dear man her hand. "We shall miss you, Anne and I."

He took her hand in both of his. "And I shall miss you. But the summer will fly quickly, as it always does in soggy ol' England, and we shall all be together again soon."

If only his words could be true.

Wet nurses earned twelve dollars a month, paid five dollars

for the care of their children, and netted an impressive seven dollars.

This was top dollar in the New York City servant market.

—HARPER'S WEEKLY, 1857

CHAPTER 22

The seaside cottage Dr. Taylor had taken for the summer was a boxy Georgian of blond stone. From the village, where they had alighted the coach, they hired a boy with a pony cart to take them the rest of the way, across the Adur River bridge and west along the coast. It would have been a taxing walk with Anne and all their things. The road approached the cottage from the rear, and Charlotte could see neither beach nor sea as they walked up the cobbled path. The boy carried their baggage to the back porch, where Daniel paid him and waved him on his way. As Charlotte held Anne and waited quietly, she thought she heard the distant cry of gulls.

"We're a hundred yards or so from the sea. You cannot see it from the cottage, but I understand it's an easy walk down the hill."

Daniel preceded her inside, dropping his medical case in the entry porch as he went. Taking a deep breath, Charlotte followed.

Mrs. Taylor seemed in good spirits and received Daniel and Anne warmly, taking the child and kissing her repeatedly. She offered a reserved but cordial greeting to Charlotte.

The French servant, Marie, led her upstairs, pointing out the rooms where the master and mistress would sleep, then preceded Charlotte up another set of stairs. Huffing and puffing, the woman pointed to two doors close to each other.

"For you and for ze nursery."

Charlotte opened the first door and saw it led to a small but pleasant room with a narrow, canopied bed, dresser, and walls of white planking. *A child's room,* she thought. Then she opened the nursery door and stepped inside, instantly noticing that it was much larger than her bedchamber. It was a lovely room with a white cradle made up with cheery pink bedding, two chests of drawers and two chairs, one of which was occupied by a doll and a stuffed rabbit.

"We are not to share, then?" Charlotte asked, wondering what to make of it. This room was certainly large enough to accommodate another bed.

"*Non,*" Marie answered haughtily. "Madame does not wish to bother you every time she wants to see her own baby."

Charlotte raised her eyebrows. Perhaps it was only her accent, but the maid's tone made Charlotte wonder if what she really meant was Madame did not wish to *bother with* her.

But Charlotte said only, "I see," and forced herself to smile at the woman, who, had she been young or pretty, might have found easier, higher-paying work as a ladies' maid—a post for which French women were in much demand. But Marie was neither. Charlotte wondered if this explained her sour and resentful disposition.

In short order, Charlotte established a daily routine. She nursed, bathed, and dressed Anne. Then, when the weather allowed, she bundled her up and took her for walks along the sea. Charlotte ate her meals with the servants: Marie and Mr. and Mrs. Beebe, who maintained the place for its absentee owners and were the doting grandparents to six children who lived nearby. Elderly Mr. Beebe took care of the simple grounds and what repairs he could, though judging by the worn condition of the place, he was no longer equal to the task. Mrs. Beebe, a few years his junior, was a decent, no-nonsense woman who cooked and did basic cleaning, though she made it clear she expected Marie to help with the housework and laundry while they lodged there.

On her first Sunday in Shoreham, Charlotte nursed Anne and handed her off to the Taylors as they prepared to leave for church, dressed in their finest clothes. The Taylors would drive together in the gig kept at Lloyd Lodge for tenants' use. Charlotte also planned to attend services, but she would go on foot. Together with Mr. and Mrs. Beebe, she walked across the bridge to the Old Shoreham Church.

When they arrived, she saw the Taylors already seated near the front of the church. Charlotte sat near the back, next to Mrs. Beebe, whose head kept lolling against Charlotte's shoulder during the long sermon. At one such moment, she noticed a broad-shouldered young man across the aisle, looking her way. He was a head taller than anyone else in the building and had a strong, square face and long nose. His light brown hair was short and tousled. He was not handsome, Charlotte decided, but was a very pleasant-looking young man. He looked from Charlotte to Mrs. Beebe in repose, and then back at Charlotte, smiling at her in amused empathy. It was a boyish, friendly expression, and Charlotte smiled in return.

After the service, when they had shaken the curate's hand and walked out of the church a dozen paces behind the tall man, Charlotte asked Mrs. Beebe, "Do you know that young man?"

Mrs. Beebe followed her gaze. "Can't say I'm surprised you'd notice him, Miss Charlotte. He does stand out in a crowd."

"Indeed."

"His name's Thomas Cox. His family lives up coast from us a bit. One of his younger sisters is at school with our granddaughters."

"Are his sisters tall as well?"

"No. He's the biggest of the lot. But a gentler soul you'll never find. Shall I introduce you, Miss Charlotte?"

"Oh, no. I only wondered." Charlotte changed the subject, lest Mrs. Beebe misinterpret her interest as something it was not. "And what will you and Mr. Beebe do on your Sabbath day of rest?"

"We're to dine with my daughter and her husband. They're the ones with the four little girls. It's my son in Worthing what's got the two older boys. We'll see them Sunday week."

"How blessed you are to have your family so close at hand."

"Indeed, Miss Charlotte. And close in heart." The woman surprised Charlotte by reaching out and squeezing her hand. "Someday you will as well, my dear."

A few days later, Charlotte borrowed Mr. Beebe's pride and joy— the baby carriage he had built for his own grandchildren. It was much lighter and simplier than the large, ornamental conveyances afforded by only the very rich. His was fashioned after the invalid chairs he had once seen in the spa town of Bath, with a hood and push-handle. Promising to be careful, Charlotte put Anne securely inside, and together they strolled along the sea. The large wheels of the carriage turned more easily on the water-worn pebbles of the shingle beach than they likely would have on sand. Enjoying the breeze and the rhythmic roar of the waves, Charlotte walked for nearly a mile, she reckoned, passing the rooftops of several houses on the ridge as she did. In the sky ahead, she saw a kite flying. The sight cheered her somehow, the colorful diamond, soaring on a wind. She picked up her pace, hoping to catch sight of the child flyer.

She soon realized the flyer was not on the beach but up on the ridge, hidden from view. As she passed a path leading up to the nearest house, the kite came crashing down beside her. So startled was Charlotte that she shoved the carriage to the side too quickly and it struck a large stone. She heard something snap.

Oh no . . .

Charlotte sunk to her haunches between the injured carriage and the fallen kite and almost immediately heard feet crunching over the pebbles toward her.

Looking up, she saw a boy of nine or ten years, spool of thread in hand, brown curls flopping up and down on his head as he ran.

"I didn't brain you, did I?" the child called, worried.

"No. Not quite." Charlotte smiled, and as the child stepped closer she realized it was not a boy after all, but a girl with hair cropped short around her face and dressed in boys' trousers.

"When I saw you down on the ground like that, I thought I must have."

"I was just examining this wheel. I seem to have knocked it from its, em, rod there."

"Axle."

"Right."

The girl peeked beneath the carriage hood to look at Anne. "What's your baby's name?"

"Her name is Anne. But she isn't mine. I'm her nurse."

"She's lovely."

"As are you. I like your hair." Charlotte looked at the loose, springy curls, much like her own hair would be, she guessed, if she cut it that length. "Must be less fuss short."

"That's what Mother says. Keeps all our hair short."

"All?"

"My sisters and brothers. I have three of each."

"I see. Shall I help get your kite back up?"

"Do you know how to fly a kite?"

"No. My mother and I tried once, but there was insufficient wind."

"Plenty today."

"What shall I do?"

"Well, if you'll hold the kite while I take out the slack and start running . . ."

Charlotte was already picking up the kite and flicked a piece of lichen from it.

Over her shoulder, the girl called, "Just let it go when I say."

Charlotte saluted. "Aye, aye."

The girl ran, the string grew taut, the girl shouted, and Charlotte released the kite. It struggled low to the ground for several seconds, then wavered. Just when she feared it would crash to the rocks, it caught the wind and leapt up. It rose higher and higher in the sky, level with the ridge, then beyond. It danced in the currents and reached higher still, straining at its tether. Watching the bright thing fly, Charlotte felt unexpected tears prick her eyes.

"Woo-hoo, Lizzy, that's the way!" A man stood high on the ridge, his fist and face raised to the sky. The girl's father, she assumed.

A few moments later, there came the man bounding down the steep hill, a broad smile on his face. He was younger than she would have expected. Wait, she recognized the man—the very tall man.

"Hallo there," he called.

She waited until he jogged closer. "Hello. I was just admiring your little flyer there."

"That's Lizzy, my sister. I'm Thomas Cox."

"Charlotte Lamb. I believe I saw you at church Sunday last."

His eyes widened in recognition. "That's right. And has your shoulder recovered from serving as Mrs. Beebe's pillow?" He smiled his boyish smile.

"Indeed, there was little recovery needed."

"I am surprised to hear it. But don't let on I suggested Mrs. Beebe has a large head or I shall never hear the end of it. Nor enjoy those apple tarts of hers anytime soon."

"Thomas! Thomas, look how high!" Lizzy Cox called from her position up the beach. Her brother turned to look her way. Again he whooped and raised a triumphant hand in the air.

Charlotte bent to reexamine the wheel. She really should be getting back. Mrs. Taylor might worry.

"Broke, did it?" With one large step, Thomas drew near and hunched beside her, hands on his knees.

"I'm afraid so. I feel terrible—it belongs to Mr. and Mrs. Beebe."

"Never fear. I helped Mr. Beebe build the wee gig. We'll have 'er fixed up sharp." Thomas loped back up the hill, as if the incline were no effort for his long legs.

A few minutes later, Lizzy jogged over, winding the twine back around its spool. "Thomas can fix anything," she confided.

"Did your kite fall again?"

She shrugged. "No, I reeled it in. I need to finish my work in the garden."

"That's your home there?" Charlotte asked, looking up the ridge.

"Goodness no. That's Shore Hill House. Thomas works there."

"He's their gardener?" Charlotte asked, watching Thomas return across the pebbled shore.

Again Lizzy shrugged. "Gardener, carter, cooper, surgeon, and all around repair boy."

"Surgeon?"

Thomas clearly overheard at least part of their conversation. "Lizzy, don't abuse Miss Charlotte's ear so—and you know I'm not a surgeon." He bent to the task of repairing the baby carriage.

"Did you not set Johnny's arm and put a cast on it? And make those poultices for Mother that set her to rights last winter?"

"Yes, but you're family."

"You stitched up the McKinleys' dog when it got into a fight last week. And Mrs. Moody says you're better at getting her boy's shoulder back in place than that surgeon in town."

Thomas looked at Charlotte apologetically. "Not everyone can afford to call a surgeon for every ache and injury." He shrugged, the gesture charmingly similar to his sister's. "I just do what I can."

"How do you know what to do?"

"I read a great deal. One of the families I work for—and have for some eight years now—the grandfather was a physician. When he died they gave me a few of his books."

Charlotte nodded her understanding, wondering though, what Dr. Taylor would think of an uneducated man setting bones and stitching wounds. Of course she knew there were plenty of men who worked as surgeons or apothecaries who had never read a single book on the subject.

"The family I work for—the father is a physician."

"The family letting Lloyd Lodge?"

Charlotte nodded.

"Is he planning to practice here?"

"I do not believe so. We're only to be here for a few months."

He looked oddly disappointed.

"But if you wanted to see him for something . . ."

"I should not like to trouble him on his holiday."

She wanted to say more, but Thomas abruptly rose to his feet, and to his full impressive height.

"There you are, good as new."

"Thank you so much. I shall tell the Beebes of your noble service."

"Please do—perhaps I shall earn an extra tart from the telling." He smiled.

"I should like to pay you something for your time, but I haven't my purse. . . ."

He waved her offer away. "Don't give it a second thought, Miss Charlotte. It's what neighbors do."

"So you do live nearby?"

"Yes, a modest cottage further inland. About midway between here and Lloyd Lodge, I'd say. Wouldn't you, Lizzy?"

"About that, yes."

Charlotte began pushing the carriage. "Well, then, perhaps I shall have the pleasure of seeing you again sometime, Lizzy. And Thomas."

He smiled again. "The pleasure, Miss Charlotte, would be ours."

Mrs. Beebe looked up from the buns she was brushing with egg-water. "There you are, Miss Charlotte. The missus was looking for you."

Regret filled her. "I feared as much. Where is she?"

"She and her maid went into the village to do some shopping, though I don't suppose she'll find much there to her fancy. She wanted to take Anne along, but I told her, I did, 'Mrs. Taylor, I have six grandbabies. So believe me when I tell you, you shall have a much more pleasant outing without a babe in arms.'"

Mrs. Beebe winked at Charlotte.

"Thank you." Charlotte smiled, relieved. She could ill afford to anger Mrs. Taylor. "I happened upon Thomas Cox and his sister Lizzy on my walk."

"Did you now?"

"Yes, I understand Thomas works for several families in the area."

"That he does. Does an odd job for Mr. Beebe now and again as well. That boy can fix anything he puts his hand to, whether it be an object or growing things, animals, even people."

"Lizzy said he set her brother's broken arm."

"That'd be Johnny, the rascal. Always gettin' into some mischief or other."

"And I'm afraid I broke a wheel of Mr. Beebe's carriage—but Thomas repaired it."

"That's a mercy. No one likes to see the old man cry." Mrs. Beebe grinned. "Thomas has the touch, he does. What a blessing he is, especially to his mother—what with the mister out to sea fishing for days on end."

"I wonder he's so much older than his sister."

"Than all the others, aye." Mrs. Beebe looked as though she might say more but seemed to think better of it.

"Do pass me that sugarloaf, will you? There's a love."

On a fine afternoon the following week, Charlotte again took Anne for a walk on the shore. She looked up hopefully but saw no kites in the sky. She enjoyed the wind—though the arrangement of her hair did not—and she relished the freedom of being out of the cottage and the atmosphere of malaise that seemed to indwell it. So, too, the relief of being out from under the watchful eye of Mrs. Taylor. Her mistress was certainly not cruel, but she was exacting in her expectations of how Anne should be cared for—how she should be dressed, upon which side of her head the bow should be fastened in her small tufts of hair, and so on. It was tiresome to always be on one's guard against a misstep. And unsettling to realize one's livelihood and lodgings depended on a mistress who was both particular and changeable.

"Miss Charlotte!" a voice called down to her from the ridge above. There was Lizzy Cox, in those same trousers, waving down to her. "Come and see!" she called excitedly. "Come and see!"

Charlotte did not relish the prospect of pushing the baby carriage up the steep incline, so she maneuvered it off the side of the path, picked up Anne, and carried her up the slope. Lizzy met her halfway. "You're just in time!"

"For what?"

"Lambs!"

She followed Lizzy around a fine house and to a timbered outbuilding. Inside, the smell of hay and grain and animals was strong, but not unpleasantly so. In the straw bed of a stall, Thomas sat cross-legged beside a ewe, on her side breathing rapidly. Thomas held one lamb in his arms, a second draped over his leg. "That's it, then. Hello, Miss Charlotte."

"Hello, Thomas."

"Always best to be on hand during lambing. Tend to have trouble, they do. This girl is late—and see how big her lambs are." He held up the one in his arms for her inspection.

"She was having trouble at first," Lizzy said, "bellowing something awful. But Thomas helped her along."

"Old Bob is a friend of mine. Had to go to town for his daughter's wedding, so I said I'd watch this ewe for him."

He stuck a piece of straw into the lamb's nostrils. The lamb sneezed. Thomas wiped at its nose with a rag, then wiped down the rest of the lamb as well. "Sneezing helps them breathe."

He offered the lamb in his hands to Lizzy. "Would you like to hold this little lad?"

"Yes, please."

She took the lamb into her arms and held him gently against her chest. "How soft he is."

"Would you like a turn, Miss Charlotte?" Thomas asked. "I'd offer to hold Anne for you, but my hands are soiled."

"Here, I shall hold her, Miss Charlotte." Lizzy handed her lamb back to Thomas, wiped her hands on her trousers and held out her hands to receive Anne. Anne, one fist in her mouth, opened her mouth even wider, forming a smile around her hand. Drool leaked out, but Lizzy didn't seem to mind. She held Anne as if she had held many babies before. And likely had.

Thomas handed Charlotte the lamb and she held it and stroked it.

"You're right, Lizzy. He is soft indeed."

Little Anne's eyes lit up as she watched the baby animal. She babbled happily and reached both hands toward the lamb.

"Not this time, moppet," Charlotte said gently. "He's not to put into your mouth."

She handed the lamb back to Thomas, who set it on the floor near its mother, followed by its sibling. The ewe scrambled to her feet and began licking first one lamb, then the other. Stretching their necks eagerly, the lambs began to nurse.

"They'll be all right on their own now," Thomas said, and rose to his feet. Charlotte took Anne from Lizzy, and they all stepped outside into the sunshine. Thomas washed his hands in a bucket and wiped them with a clean rag.

"I'm off to finish picking the beans," Lizzy announced, running off.

"Care to see the garden, Miss Charlotte?" Thomas asked.

"Very much. I love a garden."

They strolled through the gardens inland from the house. In the vegetable garden, Charlotte grinned at the sight of Lizzy, tongue between her lips in concentration, carefully plucking bean pods from the vine. They also toured a kitchen herb garden and several flower gardens, all very well kept.

She was surprised to spy several milkweeds along the garden wall, near the hollyhocks. "Do you mind if I take some milkweed back with me?"

He looked at her, an amused grin on his face. "Have a wart, do you?"

Embarrassed by this, she laughed. "No! But my employer is quite fond of milkweeds—uses them to treat a whole list of ailments."

"Does he now? I should like to know the contents of that list."

"You shall have to come by the cottage. I know he would be happy to tell you."

From the garden, Charlotte and Thomas walked to the top of the ridge, overlooking the sea. "Care to sit for a moment and enjoy the view?" Thomas asked.

"Thank you."

He reached out his hands to take Anne, and Charlotte was surprised when the child went to the big man willingly. Charlotte sat on the edge of the lawn and straightened her skirts around her. Thomas plopped down not far from her, easily holding Anne in the crook of one arm as he did so.

She lifted her arms to take Anne back, but Thomas shrugged. "I'll hold her, if neither of you mind."

Lizzy bounded up and sat beside Charlotte. "Cook gave me a sixpence," she said proudly.

"My goodness. For picking beans?"

"Well, there were the peas and lettuces this morning too."

"What a hard worker you are. So, Lizzy, tell me about your brothers and sisters—three of each, I believe you said?"

"Right. There's my sisters: Hannah, Hester, and Kitty. They don't like the out-of-doors as I do. Then my brothers: Thomas here, of course. And Johnny and Edmund."

"Edmund? That is my very favorite name. How old is he?"

Thomas leaned closer to Charlotte and said in a low voice, "We lost Edmund as an infant, but Lizzy still counts him."

Charlotte looked at Lizzy, who was staring down at her lap. Feeling tears spring to her eyes, Charlotte put her arm around the girl's shoulder and gave her a squeeze. "Of course she does."

Lizzy looked up, and Charlotte smiled gently at her. "And so do I."

Lizzy smiled shyly in return.

A few minutes later, Lizzy ran off to find a litter of kittens a mother cat was reported to have hidden somewhere about the place.

"She's a lovely girl," Charlotte said, craning her neck to watch her go.

"Yes."

"Is she the youngest?"

"No, Edmund would be nearly five now, had he lived. Kitty is seven. Lizzy there is ten. Johnny's twelve. Hannah and Hester are twins at fourteen.

"It's a wonder there are so many years between you and the others."

"Not such a wonder, really." Thomas tossed a twig out over the ridge. "Our mum took me in when I was already a lad of nine. Adopted me as one of her own. Hannah and Hester were but a year old at the time."

"Were you relations?"

"No. My first mother was only a neighbor. Died in childbirth, the baby girl with her."

"I am sorry."

"Do not make yourself unhappy. I feel blessed to have Rachel Cox as my mother. And these children to call brothers and sisters."

"How well do you remember your first mother, as you called her?"

Thomas's eyes stayed on the distant sea as he thought. "Quite well, though I cannot recall her features as clearly as I once did." He picked up a pebble and tossed it as well.

Charlotte swallowed the lump in her throat. She asked quietly, "Do you miss her?"

He looked at her, clearly surprised by the question, or her shaking voice. No doubt he saw the tears in her eyes as well. He returned his gaze to the sea. He was silent for some time, picking at the pebbles near his legs, gathering them into his large hands. Finally he said, "I have all I could wish for with my family here. But . . . yes, there is a . . . a quiet longing for her. I am a man of two and twenty but still I sometimes dream of her. In the dreams, I cannot see her face, but I can feel her arms about me."

Charlotte nodded, biting her lip. Tears rolled down her cheeks. Thomas looked at her, his expression serious and aware. He said nothing but simply waited.

She opened her mouth then closed it again. Finally, voice quivering, she whispered, "My son . . . is being raised by another."

Slowly, he nodded his understanding. "Edmund?" he asked quietly.

She nodded, and neither said more.

❧

As soon as Charlotte stepped into the parlor, Mrs. Taylor rose from the settee. "You have been gone a long while, Miss Lamb. I was beginning to fear I would never see you—or my daughter—again."

She smiled as she spoke, but an understandable mixture of relief and displeasure strained her features.

"Please pardon me, madame. I took Anne for a walk and lost track of time."

Only then did Charlotte notice the older woman seated across from Mrs. Taylor, half hidden by the wings of the tall arm chair. The lady appeared to be in her fifties and had a beautiful coif of silver grey hair under an elegant black hat.

"Mrs. Dillard has been waiting for nearly an hour to meet Annette."

"Forgive me. I did not realize you were expecting guests." Charlotte handed the little girl to her mother.

"Here she is, Mrs. Dillard. Is she not beautiful?"

The older woman rose and Charlotte saw that her attire, though practical, was finely made. Mrs. Dillard stepped across the carpet with dignified ease. "Yes, lovely." She patted the child's head with jeweled fingers. "Very like you."

"Thank you. Please, do sit down again, Mrs. Dillard. I shall call for more tea."

But the woman remained standing. "Now that I have met your charming daughter, I really must be going. Ladies' Charity meeting begins—" she lifted the watch pendant hanging from a chain at her waist—"dear me, half an hour ago."

"I am so sorry to have kept you waiting, Mrs. Dillard."

"No need to apologize. I understand how difficult it is to find a dependable nurse." The woman spoke as though Charlotte were not standing there in the doorway. "My daughter has been through two in the last four months. The first one nearly ate the larder down to the walls." She pulled on her gloves. "Thank you for the kind invitation, Mrs. Taylor. I do so hope you enjoy your holiday here."

Mrs. Taylor's smile was forced. "You are very kind. Thank you."

The woman bid her good-day and Charlotte held her breath, preparing for the worst.

The door closed, but Lizette Taylor still stared after the woman. "There will be no answering invitation, I can promise you."

"I am sorry, madame."

"Yes—you did not help me impress the ladies." She sat down heavily on the settee, jostling Anne, and waved her hand in a fatalistic gesture. "But they would not be impressed in any case. The other two ladies left before tea was even served. They remembered some church meeting they 'simply must attend.' I am surprised Mrs. Dillard stayed as long as she did."

Before Charlotte could form some consoling response, Mrs. Taylor continued, "They were eager enough to respond to my written invitation. And how they smiled when they first arrived— surprised to find a doctor's wife so finely dressed, I think. But then I began to speak and how their smiles fell from their faces. When they realized I was French, they could not leave quickly enough."

"Perhaps they really did have obligations."

Again the dismissive wave.

"Mrs. Taylor, I cannot tell you how sorry I am. I never considered how it must be for you to—"

Lizette Taylor held up her palm, ceasing Charlotte's words midsentence. "I may be a French woman living apart from my country and my family . . . but you are in no position to pity me, *Nourrice*."

Charlotte looked down and Mrs. Taylor followed her gaze, until her eyes widened.

"Your hands . . . what has happened?"

Charlotte looked down at her dirt-streaked gloves.

"I stumbled upon a patch of milkweed and wanted to bring some back, but I fear they proved too stubborn."

"Why?"

"Well, the roots as you may know are very strong and run very deep, so I settled on bringing back the one."

"No. I meant why would you want to bring this back. This weed?"

"The milkweed has medicinal qualities, as you are no doubt aware. I thought Dr. Taylor might find it useful, having none in the garden here."

Mrs. Taylor continued to look at her, her gaze scrutinizing. So Charlotte continued, "I have always loved a garden, but I confess I thought milkweed a mere nuisance. But then I saw your husband's garden in London—all the varieties of plants for this medicinal purpose and that." The more Charlotte prattled on, the less she recognized her own voice. She realized too late that Mrs. Taylor knew how to use silence to her advantage. That by saying nothing, Charlotte felt compelled to blather on, chipping away at her own dignity with each word. "Quite the man of science, your husband."

"Indeed? Well, here is the man of science now."

"Hmm?" Daniel looked up from the post in his hand to smile amiably at his wife and then at Charlotte. "What have I missed?"

"My dear, tell me, where did we find such a nurse?" Her voice sounded pleasant enough, but Charlotte detected suspicion in Mrs. Taylor's tone.

"From the Manor, as I believe I told you. But I knew Miss Lamb's family a long time ago as well."

Her rather thick eyebrows rose. "And how were you acquainted with this woman's family?"

"It was during my apprenticeship in Kent. I called often on her mother with Dr. Webb."

Mrs. Taylor turned again to Charlotte. "And your mother, how is she now?"

"I'm afraid she died. Many years ago now."

"And how is it you came to be a nurse? I don't mean . . . the particulars. I mean, where is your own child?"

Charlotte swallowed. "I'm afraid he . . . he is gone as well. I had him but a few days."

Mrs. Taylor looked at her husband, eyes wide under tented brows. "And *this* is the fit woman you would have nurse my child?"

"Lizette. You have no cause for concern. I can attest to Miss Lamb's character and her health. She has cared for Anne these many months while you were . . . indisposed."

"If madame prefers, I can leave on the morrow," Charlotte quietly interjected.

She could feel the woman's stare on the top of her bowed head. Charlotte was mortified, but if she wasn't wanted, she would leave. Even if it meant saying good-bye to Anne.

"No, do not be foolish. I meant no offense, Miss Lamb. I am simply a mother concerned for her child. You understand, *non?*" Suddenly the woman's face brightened. "Of course you must stay. Clearly my daughter needs you, and who knows how long it would take to find another suitable nurse? Please. Consider this your home. For as long as Annette needs you."

She said it graciously, but Charlotte did not miss the message. Accented or not, her English was skilled . . . and pointed.

And every one knowes how hard a thing it is,
to finde a good [nurse], because they have been
so often beguiled, and deceived therein.

—James Guillemeau, *Childbirth or*
The Happy Deliverie of Women

Chapter 23

Sitting in the nursery at Fawnwell, Sally held little Edmund close, studying the shape of his nose, his brows, his mouth. "The image of yer mum, you are," she cooed, running a finger over his smooth cheek.

"What did you say?"

Sally looked up, startled. She hadn't heard the mistress, but there she stood, looking sternly down at her.

"Nothing, m'lady," Sally said, panicked. Had she broken her promise so quickly? What would become of her little charge . . . of herself?

"I heard you. Repeat what you said," Lady Katherine demanded imperiously.

"I . . . I only meant . . ." Sally stammered.

"You said he looked like his mother," Lady Katherine supplied.

Sally lowered her head, waiting for the hot words to rain down.

Instead the mistress took a step closer. "Between you and me, I quite agree."

Sally looked up at her, trying to discern the meaning, the mood behind Lady Katherine's pensive expression.

"Do you?" she asked weakly.

"Yes. I always make a point to say how much he resembles his father—I think it wise to offer such comments to build a man's esteem, his bond with his offspring."

"Oh . . ." Sally whispered, still not at all sure what the woman was saying.

"Still, I do see hints of myself in his features. The arch of his brows, the coloring of his fair skin . . ."

"Aye . . ." Sally murmured, slipping back to a word Charlotte had advised her not to use. Still, she thought Charlotte would not mind, considering her secret, it appeared, was still safe.

⁘

Sally looked with wide eyes around Chequers, Doddington's crowded, noisy inn. Through the haze of smoke from many pipes and the inn's fireplace, she took in the tables ringed by men drinking ale and laughing. She felt out of place, sitting there with her new friend, the two of them the only women in the place, save for the innkeeper's wife.

She'd met Mary Poole when she'd been out walking with Edmund. Mary worked as a nurse for the Whiteman family down the road, in a house that lay between her master's estate and the village itself.

"Your first night out?" Mary said, aghast. "Sally girl, you must make your conditions known."

"Conditions?"

"Conditions of employment. 'Tisn't right they shouldn't give you a night out each week."

"But I need to be on hand to nurse the child. 'Tisn't anyone else to do it."

"Aw, he's not going to starve in a few hours, now, is he?"

"I suppose not."

From over her cup, Mary slanted a look across the room. "My, my—two gents are looking this way."

Sally followed her gaze and saw two men near their own ages standing at the bar.

"Sit up straight," Mary whispered sternly, "and do close your mouth."

Sally only then realized she was staring at the men, mouth drooping open. She hurried to close it and sat up straighter on the bench.

"The fair one's mine," Mary whispered through smiling lips.

But it soon became obvious that the fair one had set his sights on Sally.

The slight, wiry man with light hair and dark eyes was handsome indeed. He smiled boldly at Sally as he walked over, and she felt her face, already warm from the ale, burn red.

"Name's Davey. And my mate here is George. Mind if we sit with you lovelies?"

Mary giggled coyly and scooted over on her bench. Sally still stared dumbly at the man named Davey.

"I'm Mary and this is Sally," Mary said and kicked her under the table. Sally again closed her mouth and followed Mary's lead in making room on her bench. Davey sat down right next to her.

"Evenin', Miss Sally. Yer a sight for these weary eyes, I can tell ye."

Sally looked away from his admiring stare, biting on her lip to keep from smiling too broadly.

As the evening wore on, Sally's cheeks glowed warmly from Davey's many compliments and the second glass of ale he bought for her. Not since Dickie's father had a man given her such admiring attention. And Sally drank it in.

Sighing, Mary gave up and turned her focus to the bearded, dark-haired man named George.

A week later, Sally and Mary met out in the lane as planned, each with their respective charges.

"You're coming out again tonight, I trust," Mary said, bouncing little Colin Whiteman in her arms.

"I cannot. They only gave me the night out last week because it was my birthday."

"I'm surprised the new missus gave you that much."

"Well, it was the master who did it. I let the day slip in his hearing."

"Very clever."

"I suppose I was desperate for some time away."

"'Course you were. And the way Georgie tells it, Davey is very desperate indeed to see you again."

Sally tried to close her lips around her teeth, but she could not help the smile that overtook her.

"Is he?"

"Yes. Says you are the handsomest girl he's ever seen."

"He didn't."

"He did."

"Must have had too much ale that night, then."

"Don't be foolish, Sally. You have very pretty . . . hair. Just—well, try to keep your mouth closed. And don't stand up quite so . . . tall."

Sally bit her lip. "I shall try."

"Well, then, meet me here tonight at nine o'clock and we'll walk into the village together."

"I don't know. The master and missus are going out for the evening. I don't know who could look in on Edmund for me."

"One of the other servants?"

"Perhaps."

"Listen, love. You're not the first nurse to find herself in this fix. But if your charge sleeps till you get back, who's to be the wiser?"

"Oh, but Edmund will want his eleven o'clock feeding. If he wakes the whole house, I shall have the devil to pay by morning."

"Well, what if you could make sure he sleeps quiet as a mouse right through the night?"

Sally laughed dryly. "By what magic?"

Her new friend's eye lit up with a mischievous gleam. "By this." She pulled from her skirt pocket a small corked bottle.

Sally felt her eyes widen. "What is it?"

"Just a bit of laudanum."

"Where did you get it?"

"Never you mind."

"Does it make babes sleep?"

"Aye. Surgeons use it all the time—it's quite safe."

"Is it?"

"Yes, I've used it several times myself."

"Really?" Sally's eyes seemed fixed on the small vial.

Mary held it out to her. "Go on, then."

"But—how do I . . . ?

"Just put a bit into his mouth before you nurse him."

"How do I know how much to give him?"

"Oh, I'd say half a teaspoon ought to do it."

"You sure it shan't harm him?"

"'Course I'm sure. When did sleep ever harm anybody?"

Sally looked at her friend's earnest face and back to the bottle.

"Here, take it." Mary pressed the vial into her hand.

Sally gingerly took hold of it.

"Go on, then, and meet me back here at nine. Wear that pretty blue frock of yours."

"You're certain?"

"Yes, your eyes look so blue when you wear it. I am quite sure Davey shan't be able to look away from you."

Sally had not been asking about the dress but did not correct her. "I did so like Davey."

"'Course you did. Any girl would be a fool not to. Quite a looker, he is."

"Aye . . ."

"Well, then, see you back here tonight."

"All right."

Sally turned to go, then turned back. "Wait. Won't you be needing some o' this yourself?" She held the vial aloft.

"I have another in my room." She grinned archly. "My last employer was a surgeon."

For some reason, the face of Dr. Taylor appeared in her mind. Unsmiling, soft-spoken Dr. Taylor. He was a physician. She had often assisted him in the ward. Had he ever used the stuff? Yes, she believed he had on one or two occasions, when an infant had been inconsolable in pain or had arrived in the turn injured.

Would it be all right, even though Edmund was quite healthy?

❧

Mrs. Taylor requested a morning alone with her daughter, and Charlotte gladly obliged, offering to go into the village to do a bit of shopping and pick up a spool of wicking Mrs. Beebe wanted from the chandler's. Daniel said he was going in, as well, and would give her a lift in the carriage.

"Thank you, but actually, I long for a walk," Charlotte said.

"As you like."

But instead of harnessing the horse, Mr. Taylor caught up with Charlotte on the road, medical bag in hand. "I've decided to walk in as well. Exercise is good medicine, and I have taken too little of late. Do you mind?"

She shook her head, supposing it was appropriate to share a public road with her employer but still hoping neither Marie nor Mrs. Taylor was looking out a rear window.

They walked more than the proper distance apart, she with her hands behind her back and he switching his bag from hand to hand as his arm tired.

After walking in silence for several minutes, he asked, "And how do you like the coast?"

"Very well indeed."

"Glad to hear it." He cleared his throat. "I hope things are not too . . . strained . . . between you and Mrs. Taylor?"

She faltered, "Umm, no. Not really."

"She is still not quite herself. I wish you could know her as I do, happy and loving and full of life—"

"But how improved she is!" Charlotte interrupted. "That is something to be thankful for."

"I am. Still, I had hoped the two of you might become friends."

"Dr. Taylor, you and she are my employers. I do not expect friendship." Charlotte hurried to change the subject. "Are you leaving for London again this week?"

"Yes. I shall put in a few days at the Manor and visit my father."

"Do greet him for me."

"I shall."

They had just crossed the wooden bridge over the river and were on the path leading into Old Shoreham when a well-dressed man approached from the opposite direction. His head was tilted down as he walked, evidently preoccupied. Blond curls shown from beneath his hat. Charlotte fell behind Dr. Taylor to make way for the other man to pass.

Ahead of her on the path, Dr. Taylor stopped short.

"Kendall? Richard Kendall?"

The man with the golden hair looked up. His heart-shaped boyish face broke into a wide smile.

"Taylor! Is it really you?" The two men strode toward one another, shook hands vigorously and slapped one another's shoulders. Charlotte stood to the side, off the path, where she could observe without intruding.

She had rarely seen Daniel Taylor smile so warmly, with such genuine delight. She felt unexpected tears prick her eyes at the happy sight of good friends reunited. And perhaps the slightest twinge of envy.

Two workmen were walking toward the bridge now, crates of fish on their shoulders. One looked at her boldly. Unconsciously, she took a step closer to Dr. Taylor.

"I thought you were practicing in London," Dr. Kendall said.

"I am."

"What brings you to our fair village, then?"

"My wife and I let a seaside cottage not far from here."

"Well, do introduce me."

Following his friend's gaze, Dr. Taylor looked over his shoulder in her direction. "Oh, no this isn't my . . . That is, Mrs. Taylor is at the cottage with our daughter. This is Miss Charlotte Lamb. Our . . . friend of the family."

"Miss Lamb." The man's smile was guileless, which Charlotte found both relieving and charming. He bowed, then looked up at Daniel, brows raised.

"Oh!" Daniel started. "Forgive me. Miss Lamb, may I present Dr. Richard Kendall, physician and friend."

"How do you do, sir." Charlotte curtsied.

"Very well indeed. Pleased beyond reason to run into old Taylor here. We were at university together, did you know?"

Charlotte shook her head.

"Miss Lamb, you never saw poorer, sorrier excuses for candidates, I can tell you."

"None poorer, I assure you," Daniel agreed.

"Miss Lamb . . ." Kendall eyes lighted as he repeated her name. "Not *the* Miss Lamb, surely."

Charlotte cocked her head to one side, uncertain. "I am not sure . . ."

"Of Kent. Doddington, was it?" He looked at Daniel, whose face began to redden.

"Yes," Charlotte said, uneasy.

"Taylor here spoke quite highly of you at Edinburgh, I can tell you."

Daniel cleared his throat. "You have quite the memory, Kendall."

"Yes. Helps me sort out my many patients and their various complaints."

"I'm sure you do so admirably."

"I try. Now do tell me exactly where you are staying. I probably know the place. Probably set a bone there or bled somebody nearby." He smiled teasingly at Charlotte.

"It's an old stone cottage west of here. Owned by the Lloyds."

"Lloyd Lodge? On a cliff overlooking the sea? Yes, I know it! Well, Taylor, you must be doing well for yourself."

"I am afraid not. I treated the Lloyd's granddaughter, and in lieu of payment they let us have the cottage for the season."

"Generous."

"I suppose. Though by the looks of the place, it is evident they don't use it much anymore. It has seen better days."

"Haven't we all? Still, when my patients are low on quid, I get mutton and codfish. I would say a seaside cottage is not too shabby—even if it is."

Dr. Taylor smiled. "Well, come see for yourself, then. Yes, come for dinner, Kendall. You must."

"I should be delighted. Just name the date."

"Would Saturday week suit? That should give Lizette time to prepare."

"Lizette . . . ?"

"Yes. I hope you are not opposed to French cuisine, nor French wives."

"If she is your wife, I have no doubt she is all a lady should be."

"Indeed, she is very lovely," Charlotte felt compelled to say.

"And will you be there, Miss Lamb? Or will your holiday conclude by then?"

"I . . . that is . . . I shall be there . . ." *But not at a formal dinner!* She looked at Daniel for help, but he was still smiling at his old friend.

"Then, I shall look forward to seeing you again as well," Kendall said gallantly, offering another brief bow.

When they had bid Richard Kendall farewell and were walking alone again, Charlotte asked quietly, "Why did you not tell him I was your daughter's nurse?"

"I did not think you would want me to. Did you?"

"No, but he will find out for himself when he comes for dinner. Then I shall feel doubly foolish."

"I am not sure I follow. . . . But I am awfully sorry to have upset you."

"I should not have minded otherwise."

"Otherwise?"

"Do you not see? He knows of the other Charlotte. Charlotte of Kent. The vicar's daughter. The young lady you once spoke highly of . . ."

"But I still—"

"But I am not that person anymore," Charlotte interrupted him. "And now I shall have to see your friend's opinion of me undergo that awful transformation." Charlotte sighed. "I shall have to fall all over again."

❧

Sally could not rouse the child. She removed his blanket, tickled his bare feet, stroked his cheek. No response. She picked him up gently, hoping the movement would wake him. He lay limp, his little arms drooping down and swaying as she swayed, bouncing as she bounced. She went to the pitcher and basin on the dressing table and dipped her fingers in, rubbing the cool water on his forehead and neck. Nothing.

Sally groaned. "And I haven't even given you the stuff yet." She had planned to give him one last feeding, with the laudanum, before she left, but the groggy biter couldn't be bothered to wake up. She thought of getting dressed first, putting on the blue frock as Mary suggested, but she feared Edmund would spit up on it, or worse, that his nappy would leak and spoil it. Could she somehow get the stuff into his mouth without waking him? Then he could just go on sleeping. Shifting him into the crook of her left arm, she picked up the vial on the dressing table. She'd need both hands to uncork it. Setting the vial down, she went to return the child to his crib, then walked back to retrieve the vial. She uncorked it and peered down its narrow shaft. She pulled the silver teaspoon from her pocket—she had snatched it from the tea service on her way upstairs—and poured a bit of the liquid onto the spoon, until she reckoned it was halfway full. Should she try to get the spoon into his mouth? Small though the delicate utensil was, it seemed too large for Edmund's little buttonhole mouth. Should she put the little vial itself into his mouth? But how, then, would she measure the amount? It would surely spill all over and she'd have to clean that up too before she could sneak out again.

She stood there with the teaspoon in her hand, debating. The image of Davey's bonny brown eyes flashed in her memory. Such a handsome man, Davey was. And to think, he admired *her*! *Just do it and be done,* she bolstered herself.

But she hated the thought of letting the baby go hungry for so long. She looked at the mantel clock. She had only a half hour more before she should be on her way. She walked purposely to the cradle, spoon in hand. She looked down at the babe and was surprised to see the child's eyes open, watching her. *Charlotte's eyes,* she thought.

❧

Daniel watched Lizette's reflection in the dressing table mirror as she brushed the thick dark hair that fell past her shoulders.

"And how are you feeling tonight, my dear?"

"Do you ask as my husband or my physician?"

"Take your pick. Both are very happy to see you in such good health and spirits."

"You seem happy as well, I would say. Happier than I have seen you in some time."

He unfastened his collar, grinning. "Why should I not be? I have a beautiful wife I adore, a healthy daughter, a rent-free home by the sea . . ." He leaned down and kissed her cheek.

"Do not forget the nurse."

"Hmm?" he asked, wrinkling his brow.

"I mean that Annette is so well looked after . . . all through the night." She smiled, a suggestive lift to her eyebrows. Then she stood and leaned against him. She kissed his cheek, his chin, his mouth.

He kissed her back. He knew he should be thrilled. Physically, emotionally, he was thrilled. It had been so long. But his mind leapt to the potential consequences, the terrifying possibility of another pregnancy. Another nightmare.

He pulled gently away and cupped her exquisite face in his hands. He looked at her, relishing, delighting in her contented, loving expression. Before him was the woman he had fallen in love with.

"Come." He sat on the bed and took her hand, slowly pulling her to lie next to him. He wrapped one arm around her, holding her tight to his side. With his free hand, he brushed the long dark hair from her face. When her hand began to caress his chest and then move lower, he clasped his hand over hers, stilling its path. He knew from painful experience that speaking of her condition directly would only stir up in his wife a cauldron of defensiveness, denial, and anger.

"I just want to hold you," he murmured, bending his neck to kiss the top of her head.

The truth was much more complicated.

The practice of dosing young infants with proprietary
medicines, usually containing opiates,
increased during the nineteenth century. . . .

—VALERIE FILDES, *WET NURSING: A HISTORY*
FROM ANTIQUITY TO THE PRESENT

CHAPTER 24

Sally picked up little Edmund, his eyes now open, his drooling little mouth working, showing his pink gums, his soft fair cheeks plump with health. Going a few extra hours without a nursing wouldn't harm a stout boy like him. She took him to the dressing table and changed him into a dry nappy. Back in her arms, his pleasant expression wrinkled in restlessness as he began rooting against her. *Put a bit in his mouth,* Mary had said, something like it anyway. Then follow with his feeding. He was definitely ready to nurse now.

Her thought should have been, *finally the little biter's awake. Now I can give him the stuff, nurse him, and be off for a night o' fun with Davey.* But it wasn't. Instead she thought of her own Dickie. Had her sister ever done the likes to keep him quiet? She supposed it was possible, but she believed her sister had genuine feeling for the boy. They were relation after all. This boy was no relation to her, so why did she feel such a strong urge to protect him? She thought

271

again of the embroidered blanket she'd stubbornly refused to toss on the rubbish heap. She knew why.

Sally sighed.

Still, she hated the thought of disappointing Davey. She longed to see him again. Perhaps if she hurried she could still catch Mary.

Sally ran down the lane as fast as she could, pressing her arm over her heavy bosom to protect herself from the jarring pace. Mary would be put out with her indeed, for she was a quarter hour late. Ahead, she saw her friend's shape in the shadows of the moonlit hornbeam tree.

Mary must have heard her approaching and no wonder, she must sound like a big mule thundering down the hard packed road, eager to win some race.

"I'd about given up on you," Mary called. "I was just now heading in without you."

"Sorry, Mary." Sally panted, hands on her knees to catch her breath.

"I thought I told you to wear the blue," she said peevishly. "You're still in that same soiled dress?"

"I'm not goin'."

"What?"

"I'm not goin'. Here." She thrust the vial into Mary's hand, making her take it.

"Whyever not?"

"I couldn't do it."

Mary expelled a loud humph, clearly vexed. "But I told you how."

"I know." Sally shook her head, already backing away. "Please tell Davey I am sorry and maybe we can meet up another time."

"I shall tell him no such thing. If you don't come with me right now, Sally, all bets are off. A man like that doesn't stay unattached for long, and I'll be hanged if I don't take a try at him myself."

Sally paused, then nodded sadly. "Good-bye then, Mary." She turned and began trotting back toward the house.

"You're a bigger fool than I thought," Mary called after her. "Giving up your own chance at happiness to wet-nurse the brat of some stranger what don't give a farthing about you."

The words burned at her ears and heart like stove irons. *I am a fool*, Sally thought. But still she ran up the lane, as fast as her large feet would carry her, as though wild dogs were on her heels.

❧

In the morning, Sally awoke to fierce pounding on the nursery door. She'd already given Edmund his early feeding and had fallen back to sleep, his warm form still beside her. The little biter had woken up three times in the night, fussing and crying. She'd barely gotten two hours of sleep put together. She'd nearly come to regret not giving him the sleeping stuff. When the child had seemed to stare at her, eyes wide, she'd murmured, "Oh, don't pay me any mind. I just gets cranky when I don't gets me sleep." And clearly, she thought wryly, she also forgot how to speak properly when she was overtired.

"Hang on—I'm coming," she called now, quickly pulling her dressing gown around her. But the door banged open before she could get to it. She jerked the tie into a rushed knot and stared, shocked as first the missus and then the master rushed into the room and to Edmund's cradle.

"Where is he?" he asked.

"What have you done with him?" she accused.

"Edmund's right here. In my bed." She pointed to where Edmund lay propped between a pillow and a rolled-up blanket.

"Is he all right?" the lady asked, breathless.

"Seems to be," her husband said, bent over to peer at him.

"Oh, thank God," Lady Katherine exclaimed and picked him up, cuddling him close. She gave Sally a sharp look. "Why isn't he in his cradle? You might have suffocated him!"

"I fell asleep after his last feedin'. The little thing kept me up half the night."

"Did he indeed?" she asked pointedly.

"Yes, m'lady."

Lady Katherine lifted her chin toward the open door. "Search the room," she ordered.

"What is it?" Sally asked as men from the place—the butler, the groom, the manservant—strode into the room. "What's happening?"

"As if you don't know!" Katherine snapped.

"I don't."

"The Whitemans' baby was found dead early this morning," Mr. Harris said. "The nurse was apprehended, clearly intoxicated, with laudanum on her person. It is assumed that she drugged the infant."

"It is more than assumed—she killed him!"

"My dear, allow me," he soothed, and then turned a hard gaze on Sally. "You are familiar with this nurse, this . . . What was her name?" he asked the groom searching through her drawers.

"A Mary Poole, I believe, sir."

He turned back to Sally.

"Yes, I know 'er." Sally swallowed. "A little."

"Did you not, in fact, see her yesterday?" he demanded.

"Only for a moment . . . I'm sure she did not mean for it to happen. She told me it was quite harmless."

"Did she? She claims the laudanum found on her person belongs to you."

"'Tisn't true!"

"Was it not in your possession?"

"Well, she did give it to me, but I gave it right back."

"Did you bring it into this house?" Lady Katherine interjected.

She swallowed again, dread filling her, and nodded.

"Into the nursery?"

Sally nodded again, eyes downcast. "She told me it wouldn't hurt him. Surgeons use it, you know. Well, I believed her."

"I shall give you one chance to answer this question truthfully," Mr. Harris said. "Did you or did you not give any to Edmund?"

She looked at him then, meeting his eyes directly. "No, sir, I did not. Not one drop."

"How can we believe her?" his wife asked. "She had it with her. In this very room."

"Aye, but then I ran down to the road and gave it back."

Katherine turned toward the butler. "Call for the physician. He must come at once and examine poor Edmund."

"Why did you?" Harris asked Sally.

"I don't know. It's a hard life sometimes, never getting an hour to yourself, never seeing people your own age . . ."

"I meant, why did you not give it to him? You certainly intended to. You no doubt had plans to meet up with this Mary, to go to the inn with her, as she clearly had from the state of her, I gather. You brought it up here with the intention of drugging my child so you could have this 'hour to yourself.' But you want me to believe you didn't follow through with it. And if you expect me to believe you, to not have the police come and haul you off straightaway, I need to know why."

She looked at the man, the child's father, obviously shaken and angry, yet trying so hard to control his emotions. Oddly, she thought fleetingly of other occasions when he had shown some kindness to her, and understood what a certain young lady had once seen in him.

She stared directly at him and said quietly, "For the sake of his mother."

❧

As dusk fell, Charlotte sat on a bench overlooking the sea. She held Anne on her lap, for the two had fled the cottage and the frenzy of preparations for company and Lizette Taylor's shrill orders. Charlotte was sure Daniel's wife did not mean to be demanding nor difficult. But it was clear she was tense and determined that everything about the place and the meal should be perfect. Anne's fussing had only added strain to the woman's agitated nerves, and Charlotte had been relieved when asked to "take the child away somewhere."

The walk and the cool evening air had quickly calmed Anne, and now the two sat in peaceful silence, listening to the tumbling of the sea and the call of gulls.

She was surprised when Richard Kendall walked briskly up the slope from the sea path. She had not expected to see him—nor anyone—on this side of the cottage and felt disquieted to meet him again. She rose to greet him.

"Miss Charlotte Lamb," he called. "How pleased I am to see you again."

"And I you, Dr. Kendall." The two bowed politely to one another.

"And this is Taylor's daughter, I take it? I'd recognize that bit of strawberry hair anywhere."

Charlotte smiled. "You have a keen eye, Dr. Kendall. Yes, this is Anne Taylor."

"Hello, little lady. Let's hope your father's hair is all you've inherited." He put his face close to the child's and wrinkled up his nose. The baby smiled, releasing a stream of drool down her cheek. "That's very like her father as well," he joked. Then he smiled warmly at Charlotte. "Nice of you to look after her. Mrs. Taylor busy overseeing preparations, I suppose?"

"Well, yes, and well, you see . . ."

"Does Mrs. Taylor care for the baby herself or do they have a nurse for her?"

"They have a nurse. In fact, I—"

"Kendall!" Dr. Taylor called out from the back stoop. "You found us! Do come and meet Mrs. Taylor."

"On my way, old boy."

Daniel waved and stepped back inside.

Kendall turned back to Charlotte. "You're coming in as well, I hope."

"No . . ."

"Joining us for dinner later, then?"

"No, I'm going to watch over Anne here. You go on ahead."

"Better let the nurse do that. It's what she's paid for, isn't it?" He began to walk toward the cottage, smiling at her over his shoulder.

"I am the nurse, Dr. Kendall."

"What?" He paused, turning back to face her.

"I am Anne's nurse. It is why I am here."

"I don't . . ."

"Your friend Dr. Taylor was a great help to me when my own child . . . was lost to me. And since Mrs. Taylor . . . needed someone, well, here I am."

"I see."

"I am sorry for the deception the other day."

"No need to apologize." He nodded thoughtfully, then cleared his throat. "Well. I best be getting in."

Yes, yes, hurry away. "Please do."

Daniel led Kendall into the parlor, where Lizette waited.

"My dear, allow me to present my old friend Richard Kendall. Kendall, this is my wife. Madame Lizette Taylor."

Kendall's eyes widened at the sight of Lizette, resplendent in her ivory gown, her hair piled high on her head, her black eyes shining. It was a reaction Daniel was used to, even enjoyed. He still sometimes found it difficult to believe he had such a lovely wife.

"*Enchantée,*" Lizette said, smiling coyly before dipping her head.

"I am delighted to make your acquaintance, Mrs. Taylor." Kendall bowed. "You are even more beautiful than your husband described."

"You are very kind, Dr. Kendall. Now, please come and sit down. Dinner will soon be served."

Both men instinctively offered their arms. She laughed, her smile brilliant, and she crooked her arm first through Kendall's, then Daniel's. The three walked slowly together to the dining room, arm in arm.

After dinner, the two men sipped their port in Daniel's study.

"Why did you not tell me?" Kendall asked.

"Hmm?"

"About Miss Lamb. Your *nurse*?"

"Oh. How did you . . . ?"

"She told me herself. Outside, before I came in."

"Well, I saw no need to humiliate her—you are a stranger to her. I was not thinking ahead."

"You might have sent a note and saved us both the embarrassment."

"I am sorry. She berated me as well for not telling you. I only meant to spare her feelings."

Kendall looked at him closely. "Were you and she . . . ?"

"What?"

"She mentioned a child."

"Heavens no. I had not seen her in several years when I came upon her in hospital, quite far along in her lying-in."

"I must say I find this situation highly unusual."

Daniel shrugged. "My daughter needed a nurse. Miss Lamb needed a post."

"Does Mrs. Taylor know?"

"She knows I am acquainted with Miss Lamb and her family from my time in Kent."

"But not how you felt about her?"

"I saw no need. It's years ago now."

"Is it?"

"Yes. Kendall, I am devoted to my wife."

"Of course you are. I did not mean to imply anything untoward. It is the irony of this situation—do you not recognize it? You have Charlotte Lamb in your service, living under your roof,

278

nursing your child, looking as lovely as ever I imagined from your descriptions—"

"And what is your point?" Daniel asked in growing irritation.

"I am only pondering. I take it the bloke responsible has offered no marriage, no arrangement?"

"No. He is married." Daniel took a sip. "As am I."

"Yes, yes. And Mrs. Taylor is very beautiful, I grant you." Kendall shook his head. "Here I am a year your elder with no woman in my life and you have two."

"I do not have two women!" Daniel heard the anger mounting in his own voice.

"Look, I know you to be a man of honor and all that. Always have been. But you know, Daniel, these things *are* done. It is nearly respectable these days to support a beautiful lady in such a situation. Though I suppose the word *lady* must now be applied rather loosely."

"Richard. You know not of what you speak. I have been and shall remain faithful to Lizette. I took vows. Sacred vows. And, well even if I had not. I am devoted to my wife!"

"Yes, so you have said."

Daniel turned away, on the verge of ordering this man from the house. He forced himself to relax his fisted hands flat against his trouser legs and take several deep breaths.

"Forgive me," Kendall said. "I have clearly overstepped and misspoken. You are not the only one who disgraces himself socially, you see." Kendall sighed. "I shall see myself out. Do thank Mrs. Taylor again for the excellent meal."

Daniel nodded stiffly without turning.

Later, when they were preparing to retire, Lizette smiled at herself in the dressing mirror as she let down her hair.

"Your friend could barely keep his eyes from me all evening."

"I noticed."

She glanced at him. "You do not seem afflicted with such difficulties."

"My dear. You know I consider you absolutely beautiful."

"So you say."

"You do not believe me?"

"You do not prove your words. I do not *feel* that you find me desirable or irresistible. Nor understand why you should want to resist."

"It is only out of consideration for your . . . health."

"Unless," she went on as if she had not heard, "some other woman has captured your attention?"

"Of course not, Lizette. You know better. You have been my only lover."

She stepped close to him. "But we do not live as lovers. I need to *feel* that you desire me. I need to feel you . . ."

She pressed herself against him, her breath hot on his neck, and he found he could resist no longer.

❧

Daniel sat in the study in the cottage, refolded the letter, and laid it on the desk. He removed his spectacles and rubbed his eyes. Replacing them again, he saw Charlotte walking past his door.

"Miss Lamb? Might I have a word?"

"Of course." She stepped into the study and stood before his desk. "What is it?"

"I've had a letter from Charles Harris."

"Yes?" Worry stretched itself across her features.

"Your . . . the family is all well. He wrote to tell us that he's had to let Sally Mitchell go."

"Go? Why?"

"It seems she was given laudanum by a neighboring nurse— meant to drug the child—"

"Dear God, no . . ."

"Put yourself at ease. Edmund is fine. There is every indication that she did not give him any, but it appears the neighboring nurse administered a fatal dose to the infant in her care."

"Merciful heavens."

"He says, given that I personally recommended Sally, and considering the continuing health of his child, he is prepared to believe her innocent of all but considering the act. But that is enough that his wife cannot bear the thought of keeping the child in Sally's care. She has hired a—" he briefly consulted the letter again—"a Mrs. Mead from the village to replace her."

"I know her. A kind, honest woman from what I remember. But still, poor Sally—what must she have been thinking?"

"That is at least one purpose for Harris's letter. To alert me to the fact that the nurses coming from the Manor may be under the misapprehension that the drug is suitable for such purposes. It is clear that I have some reeducating to do when I return. I can rest, at least, in the knowledge that the neighboring nurse was not a resident of our institution."

"What will become of Sally?"

"They are not pursuing legal redress. Though I'm afraid the other nurse will not be as fortunate. I suppose Sally will be free to return to her own home, her own child."

"But how will she support herself and her son?"

He sighed. "I do not know. That continues to be a problem for many."

The moral character of the future man may be influenced by the treat-
ment he receives at the breast and in the cradle.

—Almira Phelps, *Godey's Lady's Book*, 1839

Chapter 25

After Sunday services a few weeks later, Thomas Cox caught up with Charlotte as she stepped through the churchyard gates into a fine summer's day.

"Good morning."

Charlotte smiled up at him. "Hello. How fare the lambs?"

"Very well, and how fares Miss Lamb?"

"Very well, I thank you."

"I noticed Mrs. Beebe took pity on your poor shoulder this morning."

"Yes. I was careful to refill her teacup twice at breakfast."

He chuckled and they walked on.

"Miss Lamb!"

She was surprised to hear Mrs. Taylor call out to her. Lizette Taylor gestured for her to stay where she was and, taking her husband's arm, all but pulled the man over to where Charlotte and Thomas waited.

When they drew near, Mrs. Taylor smiled brightly from Charlotte to Thomas. "Miss Lamb, you must introduce us to your new friend."

"Of course. This is Thomas Cox. My employers, Dr. and Madame Taylor. And you know Anne."

"Yes, of course. How do you do?" Thomas gave an awkward bow and a charming smile.

"Dr. Taylor is a physician, as I mentioned," Charlotte said to him, then turned to Dr. Taylor. "Mr. Cox is very interested in your uses of milkweed."

Thomas quickly added, "Oh, that and other plants as well, sir."

"Mr. Cox is known as quite the local healer," Charlotte explained.

"No, no," he demurred, "purely amateur. I do what I can for my family. But I am interested in learning more."

She noticed Dr. Taylor look from her to Thomas, then back again.

"Well, then, you must come by the cottage this afternoon and take tea with us. I shall tell you all I know, and you shall be left with the better part of that hour to enjoy Mrs. Beebe's cakes."

"Thank you, sir. But I should not like to intrude on your holiday."

"No bother at all, Mr. Cox," Dr. Taylor said.

"Of course you must come," Mrs. Taylor added cheerfully.

Charlotte had hoped to arrange such a meeting but was a bit bewildered at how it had all come about so quickly. And with so much enthusiasm on the part of Mrs. Taylor.

Since Marie took her half-day on Sunday, Charlotte sat at the work table with Mrs. Beebe that afternoon, helping her arrange buns, biscuits, and small cakes on a silver plate. Thomas, still wearing his Sunday suit, knocked on the kitchen door, hat in hand. Rising, Mrs. Beebe wiped her hands on her apron and opened the door for him.

"Hello there, Thomas."

"Mrs. Beebe."

"I half expected you to come 'round to the front door."

"And when have I ever?"

She returned to her work, *tsking* her tongue against the roof of her mouth. "Taking tea with the tenants. My, aren't we rising in the world."

"Now, now, Mrs. Beebe, you know I am only here for your apple tart."

Mr. Beebe, drinking tea at the three-legged chop block, winked at him. "I figgered that was the way of it. Any time to help me with the hedges this week?"

"Would Tuesday suit?"

"That it would. Any time before two or after three."

Mrs. Beebe shook her head. "Heaven forbid you should interrupt the old man's nap." She smiled begrudgingly at her husband, then nodded to Thomas. "Well, then, off with you into the parlor. But don't expect me to call you 'sir.' "

"I wouldn't know who you were addressin' if you did."

Mrs. Beebe took his hat from him, then swatted his backside with it as he passed through the kitchen door.

Mrs. Taylor insisted that Charlotte join them for tea, which was a first. In many ways, Charlotte would have preferred to stay in the kitchen with the Beebes. But Anne was still napping and she had no excuse to decline. Besides, she would enjoy the time with Thomas and looked forward to witnessing his discussion with Dr. Taylor firsthand.

As she had imagined, the two had a great deal to talk about. Dr. Taylor gladly told him all about the medical uses for milkweed—as well as costmary, foxglove, wood sorrel, comfrey, candytuft, and several other plants.

Thomas asked question after question, and Dr. Taylor never seemed to tire of answering. Mrs. Taylor, however, tired of the conversation and soon rose and excused herself, saying not to get up, she would just go check on Anne.

Charlotte relaxed in Mrs. Taylor's absence, knowing how closely the woman had been observing her and Thomas during the afternoon.

At one point, Charlotte interjected, "Tell Dr. Taylor about the poultices you made for your mother."

Thomas reddened, embarrassed, but described the herbs and method he had used.

"Very well done," Dr. Taylor said. "I could not have prescribed better."

Thomas beamed with pleasure.

Two hours later, the men parted, shaking hands. Under his arm, Thomas carried two books that Dr. Taylor insisted he borrow.

"That's quite a young man," he said to Charlotte as the two stood near one another, watching from the window as Thomas walked away down the path.

"Yes," Charlotte agreed.

Feeling his gaze on her profile, she added, "Though not so young, really. Only four years or so younger than you yourself."

"Really? Feels like more. Some days I feel quite ancient."

✺

At week's end, Lizette Taylor insisted Charlotte take the morning off—walk into the village or visit that "*très grand* friend of yours." She smiled meaningfully and Charlotte felt the need to correct her.

"He is not my particular friend."

"*Non? Tant pis.*"

Too bad, she had said, though Charlotte had the distinct impression it was Mrs. Taylor herself who was disappointed. Charlotte admired Thomas and enjoyed his friendship, his easy acceptance, and their shared love of growing things—but friendship was all she felt for him. Wasn't it?

"Are you certain you want me to go? You will be all right?"

"I do know how to care for my own child."

"Of course you do. I only meant . . . Well, she has been fed, so you should be fine."

Thomas had mentioned he would be visiting cousins this day, so Charlotte didn't take the sea path but instead walked into the village. There, she walked from shop to shop, idly taking in the displays in the windows. She planned to stay away from the end of the street where Dr. Kendall kept his offices.

Turning, she walked right into the man.

"Oh! Dr. Kendall, you startled me."

"Miss Lamb." He bowed. "Do forgive me."

She dipped her head. "Good day, Dr. Kendall." She turned her face back toward the milliner's window, effectively dismissing him, allowing him to walk on without appearing rude. She felt his gaze on her, but feigned interest in the bonnets, hats, and hair ornaments on display. He stepped past her. After their last awkward encounter, he was no doubt relieved to have this unexpected meeting done with as quickly as possible.

His footsteps halted. "I say, Miss Lamb?"

Surprised, she turned toward him as he retraced his steps to stand before her.

"I am on my way to take tea at the little shop on the corner. I do not suppose you would care to join me?"

She pursed her lips, but her brain didn't know quite what words to form. Finally, she managed, "Why?"

"I know things may be a bit awkward between us at present, but I see no need for us to continue so. Your current . . . station . . . in life might be somewhat of a shock to a proper Londoner, I suppose. But here, in this small village, well, such things are quite ordinary and need not form a barrier between us."

She looked down at her hands, clasped before her.

"Come now, Miss Lamb. Have we not a dear friend in common? Are we not two educated gentlepeople, free to take tea together in a public place?"

"I wonder you did not miss your calling, Dr. Kendall. Politics would have suited you." She could not keep a hint of a smile from softening her words.

"Is that a yes?"

"Very well."

He grinned.

But before they had taken four steps, a young voice called out, "Dr. Kendall! Dr. Kendall!"

They turned and watched a young boy running toward them at full speed, panic evident in his features. "Mrs. Henning says come quick! She needs you something awful."

Kendall's expression grew grim. He turned briefly. "The midwife. Forgive me, Miss Lamb—perhaps another time."

"Of course you must go."

"Would you mind coming with me? I may need an extra pair of hands."

"Of course."

"Mrs. Collins, is it?" Dr. Kendall called out to the boy, who was already turning back.

"Yes, sir."

"Bring this lady along, if you please." And to Charlotte he said, "I'll run on ahead."

She nodded, but he was already jogging up the street.

"This way, miss," the boy said.

They arrived at a small tidy cottage with thatched roof. The boy went in first, leaving the door open for her. When she stepped in, she was stunned to see Thomas there, holding a swaddled infant in his large hands. She thought instantly of the lambs.

"Bring another blanket, Freddie," he said. "We've got to get your sister here warmed up."

Thomas looked at the boy—her escort—then his gaze rose to her. "Miss Charlotte?"

"Dr. Kendall asked me to come along."

"He's in there with her now." He shook his head, clearly worried. "She's strugglin', I'm afraid."

"The mother?"

He nodded. "Twins. Seems they're having a terrible time with the second one. Mrs. Henning handed this one to me and told me to keep her warm."

Freddie jogged back into the room holding a wool blanket.

"Here, let me help." Charlotte took it from the boy and helped Thomas wrap the blanket around the tiny baby.

She said, "I thought you were off visiting cousins today."

"Betsy is my cousin."

"Miss Lamb?" Dr. Kendall appeared in the doorway, rolling up his sleeves. "Please, if you will."

She gave Thomas a look of empathy before following Dr. Kendall into the bedroom. In the bed, Betsy Collins looked exhausted. The midwife standing nearby did as well.

"Mrs. Henning. Do rest yourself," Dr. Kendall admonished.

"But—" The grey-haired woman paused in her mopping of the patient's brow and shoulders.

"You cannot help if you faint on me." He turned to Charlotte. "Miss Lamb, please."

Charlotte gently took the bowl and rag from the elderly midwife and began wiping Betsy's forehead. She was sweat-soaked and clearly weak. Charlotte smiled at the woman, who was close to her own age. "I saw your new daughter in the parlor. What a beauty she is."

"Is she?"

"Oh, yes."

Betsy smiled faintly.

"I shall have to attempt to reposition the baby," Dr. Kendall announced sternly.

Betsy grimaced and squeezed her eyes shut.

"Take her hand, there, Miss Lamb," he instructed.

Mrs. Henning had already risen from her stool to take the other.

He pushed and strained against the woman's abdomen, sweat pouring off his forehead. "I cannot . . . quite . . ."

"Thomas can help," Charlotte said. "Thomas!" she called without thinking.

Thomas strode into the room, babe in arms.

"Give her to me," she ordered. "The doctor needs your help."

When Dr. Kendall looked at Thomas and hesitated, Mrs. Henning said, "He's good, he is. He can help."

"Just tell me what to do," Thomas said.

"You push on her abdomen, here, when I tell you."

Together the two men struggled and Betsy cried out and moaned.

"Hang on, Betsy," Thomas said, looking pale as he glanced at his cousin's contorted face.

Dr. Kendall looked again beneath the sheets. He swore beneath his breath. "I shall have to use the forceps."

"No! Please, no . . ." Betsy moaned and began sobbing. They all knew the dangers for both mother and child with the dreaded instrument.

"Mrs. Henning . . . ?" Betsy beseeched.

The older woman shook her head grimly. "Nothing else I can do, love."

Betsy turned her head toward her cousin. "Thomas, please. Do something," she begged.

Thomas nodded and said to Dr. Kendall, "May I try?"

Before Dr. Kendall could answer, Thomas was already moving into position at the foot of the bed, leaving Kendall little choice but to step aside.

"There now, Betsy, relax. Everything's going to be all right. Just relax now—ease those muscles."

Hunching low, one hand propped on the bed and the other reaching under the sheet, Thomas's face was gripped in concentration.

"Sorry, Betsy, won't be long. Try to relax."

"All right, Thomas, all right," Betsy panted.

"There's the little one. I feel his head and neck. Come on, little one, come on . . ."

His expression tightened with the effort of tempered strength. Betsy cried out.

"Not yet, not yet. Now push!"

Betsy gritted her teeth and pushed.

"Here he comes. Here he comes."

Thinking swiftly, Charlotte pulled out the bottom drawer of Betsy's dresser and laid the first baby into it. Then she leapt forward to hand Thomas a clean sheet left there for this purpose.

"That's it—get ready to catch him, Miss Charlotte."

With a final cry, Betsy pushed and Thomas retracted his arm and together he and Charlotte guided the slick infant into the sheet.

Relieved and revived, Mrs. Henning hurried over and helped Charlotte rub the infant dry and clean out her mouth and nose before handing her to Dr. Kendall.

"It's another girl, Betsy," Mrs. Henning announced.

"Is she all right? I don't hear anything—is she breathing?"

Dr. Kendall carefully turned the child upside down. When she didn't respond, he swatted her gently on her bottom, then once again more smartly. The baby whined, then broke out in an angry cry. Dr. Kendall handed the child to Betsy, and her tears became those of joy.

"Oh, thank you. Thank you, all."

Charlotte turned to look at Thomas. Dr. Kendall was staring at him too, clearly impressed. "How did you know to do that?" he asked.

Thomas shrugged. "Works with sheep."

"Indeed?"

"I'll go brew some yarrow tea for Betsy," Thomas said quickly and left the room.

Dr. Kendall watched him go, amazement on his face.

"Who *is* that young man?"

"His name is Thomas Cox."

"Ah yes . . . I've heard of him. Friend of yours?"

"Yes."

"Has he ever considered the medical profession?"

"I believe he has."

"I wonder if he would be interested in an apprenticeship."

"I believe Dr. Taylor wonders that as well."

Charlotte returned to Lloyd Lodge two hours later, only to hear the baby's piercing cries before she had reached the door. Charlotte hurried inside. Mrs. Taylor was pacing the parlor, bouncing the child in an attempt to soothe her. Lizette's face was flushed red, and it was clear both mother and daughter had been crying for quite some time.

"*Ici.* Take her." Mrs. Taylor thrust the child toward Charlotte. "I cannot make her stop crying. It seems only you have such power."

"No power, madame," she said gently, taking the child in her arms. "Only milk."

"*Non.* It is clear my daughter prefers you. My husband as well . . ."

"No, madame. Anne only wants me when she's hungry." She sat down and skillfully unfastened the hidden front flap of her nursing frock, discreetly allowing the child to nurse with minimum exposure of her person. "There you are." She looked back up at Mrs. Taylor, hoping to assure her. "As for Dr. Taylor, he was a friend to my family long ago, and I appreciate his offer of employment. I am grateful to have a position with such a respectable family as you are."

New tears filled the woman's eyes. "You say the right words. I know I should believe you. I should be thankful that you are here, taking care of my child. But I am not. I want to nurse her myself. But I cannot."

"I am sorry."

"My body, my mind, betray me. My husband . . ."

"No, madame. Never your husband."

"*Non?* Then, why am I so angry? *Je pleure de rage.*"

Lizette Taylor turned and strode from the room, the echo of her words capped with a sob. *I am so angry I weep.*

After laying Anne down for her nap, Charlotte knocked softly on Dr. Taylor's study door, her heart pounding painfully.

"Yes?"

She stepped inside, leaving the door ajar.

"Good afternoon, Miss Lamb."

"Good afternoon." She cleared her throat. "Dr. Taylor, I am afraid the time has come for me to leave your employ."

"Pardon me?"

"Do not think me ungrateful. I do appreciate all you have done for me. But it is time I moved on. I wonder if you might consider sending a messenger to find Sally? If you find her quickly, before she takes another position or her milk fades, she would serve you well, I have no doubt. Or if that does not suit, perhaps another nurse from the Manor."

"But why? Has Lizette said something?"

"No. But I am certain Mrs. Taylor will understand my decision."

"Charlotte. You have done nothing wrong."

"Thank you. But I want you—both of you—to be happy, and I do not wish to be a hindrance to the peace of your family."

"You are not—"

She lifted her hand to stop him. "Dr. Taylor, I know how your wife feels about me. In many ways, I understand her fears, her jealousy . . ."

He looked at her, eyes wide. "You do?"

But she was not referring to him. Tears shimmered in her eyes as she whispered, "I know what it feels like to have my child look at another woman as his mother."

He swallowed. "But this will be the case with any nurse."

"Dr. Taylor . . ."

"Forgive me. Of course that is not entirely true. She has no doubt seen my . . . regard for you. Careful as I have been to conceal it. Have I not treated you with the utmost propriety?"

"Utmost."

"I'm afraid Lizette is, by nature, a jealous person. I cannot deny I am concerned for your well-being, but of course, other aspects of our relationship are long over."

"Of course," she echoed. "Still. I feel it would be best if I leave. As soon as possible."

He rubbed his hand over his eyebrows. "Do you think Sally would come?"

"I do. And it would put my mind greatly at ease if she did."

"Very well. I shall do my best to find her."

"Thank you."

Charlotte walked from the room, still in control of her emotions. She walked quickly from the cottage to the seashore, where the waves could swallow her cries and a bit more salt water would not be noticed.

She was melancholy and . . . dissatisfied with herself constantly,
incapable of attending to anything, and entirely indifferent to things
around her. She felt at times as if she were nobody, and would rather
be dead than have that feeling.

—L. SHAFER, M.D., CASE OF PUERPERAL INSANITY, 1877

CHAPTER 26

As soon as Dr. Taylor sent out his messenger, Charlotte began to regret her decision. She almost hoped he would not reach Sally or that she would be unable or unwilling to come. Charlotte doubted Dr. Taylor would strive to find another unknown nurse, though Mrs. Taylor might wish it, especially while they were in temporary lodgings. But even as Charlotte entertained such thoughts, she knew it was foolish to think staying would make her—or anyone—happy. She supposed it was the dark unknown future that caused her to long for things to remain as they were.

When the return message arrived, Charlotte held her breath. She tried to find some small satisfaction in being right—as she had predicted, Sally would come. In fact her letter reached them just ahead of Sally herself, who wrote to say she would be arriving in Old Shoreham on the late afternoon coach.

From Sally's few hastily written lines, Dr. Taylor ascertained that he had located her the first place he tried—with the Harrises in Doddington. Mrs. Mead, it seemed, had needed a few more days to wean her own child and had arrived at Fawnwell the same day as Dr. Taylor's messenger. Sally had secured passage on the next morning's coach.

Now that it was settled, Charlotte felt the block of sadness begin to break up and sift out through all the broken places in her heart, replaced with a numb pragmatism. There was nothing she could do about it now. It was the right thing, whether it felt like it or not.

That afternoon, Charlotte took a basket of clean laundry to hang on the line outside. She had offered to help Marie, reasoning that keeping busy might take her mind off her impending departure. But as she began hanging little nappies and sweet little bed gowns, she realized she ought to have volunteered for some different task.

Suddenly Thomas was there beside her, bending low and coming up with a pair of knitted socks barely large enough to cover his thumbs. She was immediately relieved the basket held none of her own undergarments.

Charlotte watched as he hung the tiny socks in mock concentration. "Hello, Thomas. Here to help Mr. Beebe again?"

"Why—are these his?"

She shook her head, amused.

"Actually, Miss Charlotte, I am here to ask you to take supper with us at the week end. Mother wants to meet you."

"She does?"

"Well, Lizzy has been going on about you. And, I confess, I have as well."

She smiled quickly, then bit her lip. "Thank you, but I am afraid I will be gone by then."

"Gone?"

"Yes. I am leaving my post here. There's to be a new nurse. In fact, she arrives today."

"But—" He stared down at her in dismay. "This is a blow. Is . . . is this what you want, Miss Charlotte, or . . . ?"

Mrs. Taylor appeared on the lawn, looking from Thomas to Charlotte and back again. "Good day, Mr. Cox. You have heard the news—Miss Lamb is leaving us?"

"I have just."

"But you will still come to visit us, will you not?"

"I—"

"Of course you must. Now, I shall leave you to your farewells." She returned to the cottage, humming a seaman's tune.

Thomas looked back at Charlotte, his eyes sparking with uncharacteristic emotion. Was it anger?

Charlotte answered his question as though they had not been interrupted. "I am learning, Thomas, that what I *want* is not always the wisest course."

"Miss Charlotte . . ."

She forced a bright smile. "Actually, it is quite a happy turn of events, for the new nurse is a friend of mine. I know you will like her. She was raised on a farm and will so enjoy all the things Lizzy enjoys. I am certain you will all get on famously."

Thomas had been looking down at the ground while she spoke but now glanced up at her earnestly. "You cannot be so easily replaced, Miss Charlotte."

Again she bit her lip. "Thank you. You are most kind."

"Might I at least accompany you into the village to meet the coach?"

She hesitated. "I should not like to trouble you—haven't you work waiting?"

"The work will always be here, Miss Charlotte. You will not."

Mrs. Beebe insisted they take the gig to the inn. Leaving Anne with Marie, Charlotte and Thomas rode into Old Shoreham, halting only long enough to pay the shilling-per-horse toll to the boy at the bridge. When they arrived, Thomas helped her down in front of the Red Lion.

"I'll tie up Old Ned. You go on and greet your friend. I'll be waiting when you're ready."

"Thank you."

When the coach arrived, Charlotte stood back while the dust and horses settled and the innkeeper ran out to meet prospective guests. When she saw Sally's fair head duck low to descend the carriage on the coachman's hand, she stepped forward to meet her.

"Miss Charlotte!" Sally cried as soon as she saw her, but she did not offer her usual toothy grin. Instead her long face looked forlorn and she clearly had difficulty meeting Charlotte's gaze. "Please believe me, Miss Charlotte. I didn't do it—I swear I didn't. I would never even have thought of it if I'd known it might harm him."

"I believe you, Sally."

"Oh, thank you, Miss Charlotte. God bless you." The two women embraced. Then Sally stood back, her hands on Charlotte's shoulders, regarding her. "Now, tell me you haven't gone and gotten yourself sacked too."

"Not exactly. But it is time for me to leave."

"A fussy one is she?"

"No. Anne's an angel."

Sally stuck her elbow into Charlotte's side. "I meant the missus." Sally's smile was back, her front teeth protruding over her bottom lip.

"Let us just say it might be best if she did not know you and I are so fond of one another."

Sally nodded her understanding.

"I've told Mrs. Taylor I knew *of* you at the Manor and that she would be very pleased with you."

Thomas appeared, already bending low to pick up Sally's two carpetbags before standing to his full height beside her. Sally's gaze followed his upward movement with a slight opening of her mouth.

"Sally, this is my friend Thomas Cox. Thomas, this is Miss Sally Mitchell."

Thomas gave an awkward bow, then looked at the newcomer. "A pleasure it is to meet you, Miss Sally."

Charlotte did not miss the admiration in his expression.

Sally shook her head in wonder. "I'll be bobbed, but you're tall," she said, then giggled, teeth splayed as she did so.

Thomas smiled in return. "Yes, we have that in common." He looked back at Charlotte beside him. "As well as a dear friend."

Charlotte pretended not to notice his blush nor the question in Sally's eyes as she looked at them both.

When they arrived back at Lloyd Lodge, Mrs. Taylor welcomed Sally warmly. As Charlotte had predicted, the mistress seemed very pleased with her replacement. There was something about the large, simple woman that seemed to put people, perhaps especially jealous wives, at ease.

Charlotte helped Sally carry her carpetbags up to the room Charlotte had used. She moved her own packed bags off the dressing table to make room for Sally's things.

"You're not leaving already, Charlotte, surely?"

"Not today. Dr. Taylor said I might stay as long as I like."

"Stay, then. I don't mind sharing."

"I shall stay just long enough to see you settled with the Beebes and the Taylors, and with little Anne, of course."

"Won't it be difficult for you, Charlotte?"

Charlotte chose to ignore the deeper implications of the question. "You have just arrived. Of course I want to spend a day or two with you before I go."

"Will you see Thomas again . . . after you leave, I mean."

"I shouldn't think so. Why?"

"You don't, that is, the two of you are not . . . ?"

"No, Sally, we are not."

"You don't . . . love him, then?"

Charlotte took a deep breath and exhaled slowly. She heard Anne, who had been napping, gurgling happily to herself in the next room.

"She's awake," Charlotte said. "Please excuse me." She walked to the nursery and picked up Anne.

Sally followed her. "It's all right if you do. I just want to know how things are between you."

Charlotte lifted Anne into her arms. "There is someone here for you to meet, Miss Anne."

"Isn't she a gorgeous thing. And so much grown since I seen her last."

"Yes." Charlotte stroked Anne's cheek. Then she sighed and placed Anne into Sally's arms. "I will miss Thomas and he will miss me, but that is the end of it."

"But I saw the way he looked at you."

Charlotte smiled gently at her friend. "And I saw the way he looked at you. Something tells me he will not be missing me for long."

Unlike Mrs. Taylor, young Anne was slower to hand over her loyalties. She wouldn't nurse from Sally that first night and cried and reached for Charlotte. Charlotte sat in the rocking chair with her, nursing her and soothing her—and herself. She knew she ought to refuse and let off nursing all at once, but she felt unable to do so, unable to withstand Anne's pitiful tears.

Finally, when Anne awoke at dawn, crying to be fed, Charlotte laid her in bed at Sally's side. While nurse and child were both only half awake, hunger won over and Anne nursed. Sally's sleepy eyes filled with tears as she looked at Charlotte in silent understanding.

❧

Richard Kendall stood before the writing desk in the study that served as Daniel's office.

"Have you no objections, then, were I to offer her some . . . situation?"

Daniel stared at the man, wanting very much to throttle him. Instead he said in controlled tones, "You will offend her."

"Quite possibly. Beyond that risk, have you no objections?" When Daniel made no answer, Richard continued. "You said yourself she has few options. That the man who should have made some recompense, should be providing for her, has failed to do so. You are not in a position to do so, but I am."

"Yet you do not offer marriage."

Kendall frowned and sighed. "No. I am afraid not. Not at this point. We are not so well acquainted."

"But acquainted enough to ask her to become your mistress?"

"Well." He cleared his throat. "The particulars are yet to be agreed upon, of course, and will be strictly between Miss Lamb and myself. You can be assured of my discretion."

"She will refuse you."

"I am aware of that possibility."

"I would ask that you dispense with this line of thinking altogether. But I have no authority to stop you."

"No, being merely her former employer . . ." He nodded thoughtfully. "Though I am beginning to understand why you chose not to tell Mrs. Taylor about your *past* regard for Miss Lamb."

Richard Kendall found Charlotte Lamb strolling along the path parallel to the sea, swinging a stick of driftwood in her hand. He fell into step beside her.

"Where will you go now, Miss Lamb?"

"To Crawley. I have a great-aunt there."

He nodded. "A pleasant prospect, then?"

She shrugged. "Pleasant enough."

She seemed pensive, her eyes far away on the grey water, the distant gulls and beyond. "If I could go anywhere I liked, I suppose I would return to Doddington. Though I am no longer welcome in my own home. Still, I would steal back to that dear place if I could. I was just imagining that very thing: strolling through the village and up the lane, past the churchyard and into my mother's garden."

"Your family would not approve of such a visit?"

She shook her head. "My father would not likely see me, spending so much time in his library as he does. Beatrice, my sister, is so often at her pianoforte, or lost in the pages of a book, that the world outside the vicarage windows holds little appeal and she would not likely see me either."

"What would you do there?"

"I would walk along the garden paths, pausing at every flower bed and ornamental tree, taking in which have flourished, which are languishing, and which have died. I should no doubt cry foolish tears over their loss. And feel just the slightest satisfaction that my absence has left some small mark on the place. Then, when no one was about I would find dear Buxley, our gardener, and see if he could, with every kindness and attention, save those suffering from neglect. And perhaps even coax the lost to return once again."

She paused to toss the stick of driftwood into the sea. "But, as that is not a real possibility, I suppose my second choice would be to return to the home of my aunt and uncle in Hertfordshire. I have spent many happy hours in their company and would find much solace in doing so again. Of course, I doubt my uncle would see fit to have me out in society, but even confined to their home, I believe I should be happy. My aunt has the most comforting way about her. Everyone who meets her says so."

Charlotte stopped and turned toward him, hand over her mouth. "Do forgive me! I have used a week's worth of words on your poor ears."

He grinned. "Think nothing of it."

"I suppose it's due to spending so little time in adult company."

"I am happy to oblige." They continued walking. "So—why not away to Hertfordshire, then?"

She sighed. "My father has forbidden my aunt and uncle to shelter me. So"—she straightened her shoulders—"I shall return to Crawley. I am sure I shall enjoy it."

"You did enjoy your time *here*—before recent conflicts, that is?"

"Yes indeed. I am sorry to leave such a beautiful place and such fine company."

"I am happy to hear you say so. I had thought of a possible solution to your dilemma, if I may be so bold as to make a suggestion?"

"Of course."

"I had thought that I might offer another alternative."

"Yes?" She turned to look at him and they stopped walking.

"Yes. That is . . . Please forgive my presumption. I realize we are not so well acquainted, but it did occur to me that you and I enjoy one another's company."

"Yes," she agreed, but her brow began to wrinkle in growing confusion.

"As a physician, I have some means—not an overly grand income but sufficient, I believe, to offer you a comfortable living here."

Her eyes lit, as if with pleasure, but, just as quickly, the hint of a smile evaporated and her mouth opened, then closed, then opened again.

"For a moment I thought you were offering me a post." Her chuckle held no mirth.

He shifted on his feet and cleared his throat. "Well, in a manner of speaking . . ."

"As a midwife. Or monthly nurse . . ."

"Oh . . ."

"I suppose I should be flattered. Or offended."

He laughed nervously. "So, which is it to be?"

"Both, actually. I'm afraid you have rather stunned me."

He found the blush in her cheeks charming. He asked timidly, "But you do not find the idea . . . totally repugnant?"

She swallowed, looked at him and then away. "I do not find *you* repugnant, Dr. Kendall. But the nature of the offer . . . yes, I'm afraid I do."

"Well," he said, and looked down at his boots. He forced himself to swallow the sting of her rejection, relieved for her manner of delivering it, the concession to his person. "Then, do forgive me. It was not my intention to offend you, though I cannot say I am overly surprised at your response."

An awkward silence ensued.

"I do not suppose there is any hope of your forgetting the former portion of this conversation and allowing me to begin anew?"

She smiled tentatively. "If you like."

He returned her smile and straightened. They began walking back toward the cottage. "I am sorry I had not thought to offer you a more, shall we say, traditional post. In all truth, the midwives and nurses I know are older, work-hardened women with little education—very different from my perception of you. Still, I have no doubt you are more than capable, should such a position truly appeal to you."

"I should never have guessed so until recently. Though I suppose a position of governess or lady's companion is more in keeping with my upbringing."

"I'm afraid I have no need of either at present." He smiled wryly. "I also have a quite competent monthly nurse at the moment. And there is a local midwife as well—Mrs. Henning, whom you met—though she is getting up in years. Perhaps I might call on you in the future, should the need arise?"

"Indeed you may. Though I would have much to learn."

"As do we all, Miss Lamb. But I have no doubt you would be a most able student. Have we an understanding, then?"

She nodded. "We do."

"And may we . . . part as friends?"

She smiled. "We may."

Daniel watched the discussion from afar. The exchange took longer than he would have thought and she did not strike Kendall nor stalk off as he'd guessed she would—hoped she would. And now there was no mistaking the nod of her head, the slight bow the two exchanged, the smile on his friend's face. She had agreed. Daniel did not wish to think about what it would mean . . . or to ponder why his chest felt like it might cave in on itself.

You will suckle your infant your self if you can;
be not such an ostrich as to decline it, merely because
you would be one of the careless women, living at ease.

—COTTON MATHER, ORNAMENTS FOR THE DAUGHTERS OF ZION, 1692
(NOTE: MATHER'S OWN CHILDREN WERE WET-NURSED.)

CHAPTER 27

Before the assembled family and staff, Charlotte bid Mr. and Mrs. Taylor a formal, somewhat stiff farewell. She was careful to only glance briefly in Sally and Anne's direction, lest she give too much away. She had sat up rocking the little girl half the night, so those farewells had already been endured. Ignoring Marie's smirk, she smiled at Mrs. Beebe, who had earlier that morning embraced her in the kitchen and stuffed a bundle of food and jingling coin into her reticule, brooking no objection. Now Charlotte bit her lip to keep it from trembling, turned, and left the cottage, reticule in hand and heart in her throat.

Thomas walked with her into Old Shoreham this time, carrying her bags as though they weighed nothing.

As they crested the bridge, a family approached from the other side—father with child in arms, mother holding a little boy's hand—and she and Thomas stepped close to the rail to allow them to pass. When they had, Charlotte walked on but quickly noticed Thomas stayed where he was.

Retracing her steps, she looked at him questioningly. "What is it?"

He stood stiffly, and in a voice nearly petulant said, "I wish there was something I could do."

She studied his face, so unusually somber. "Thomas," she soothed, "there are some things even you cannot fix." She smiled gently. "It's all right."

He turned and gripped the bridge rail, still refusing to go farther.

She stood at the rail beside him, an arm's length away. Staring at the river below, she sensed his agitation, his deliberation.

But what could he do? She knew any money he made went to help his mother provide for his many siblings. Even if he began working as an apprentice, he would have little money of his own for several years. He was surely not yet thinking of taking a wife—not her, in any case. Was he?

Charlotte squeezed her eyes shut, realizing that if she did not speak, he would. Without turning to face him she said cheerfully, "I told Sally how it was, between us."

She heard him move a step closer to her. His voice was uncertain. "Did you?"

She stole a glance at him before returning her gaze to the water. "Yes, I told her that you could never think of me the way I do you."

"Charlotte—"

She went on quickly, "For you already have four sisters, but I have never had a brother."

Turning toward him, she self-consciously lifted her gaze to his. "And I have always longed for one."

His eyes glimmered. He lowered his head, bringing his face close to hers. "I should be honored to be yours."

They stood that way for a moment, in a silence heavy with unspoken things.

Charlotte took a deep breath. "Sally is dear to me, as you know. I hope you . . . and Lizzy . . . will be kind to her." She put her fist to her heart. "It will please me if you show her every attention."

Quietly, he asked, "Will it?"

She nodded. "Yes."

He straightened but continued to peer down at her for a long moment without speaking. He reached out his hand toward her. It was not customary, to·say the least, but Charlotte understood the impulse behind it. Some culmination of feeling must occur. It was either shake hands or embrace. But that, of course, would be inappropriate and foolish and unfair to them all. So instead, she gripped his hand with her smaller one and felt his answering squeeze. She held tight a moment longer, then let go.

Charlotte sipped her tea in the dining room of the inn, waiting for her coach to be announced. She had insisted that Thomas return to his work, that he need not wait with her. He had gone, though reluctantly.

Dr. Kendall came in, hat in hand and out of breath. "Miss Lamb. I am so glad I found you before you left. I wonder if I might trespass on your kindness for some time longer?"

"Of course. Please, do have a seat, Dr. Kendall."

"Thank you." He sat down and leaned across the table to speak in confidential tones. "A couple has come to me in dire need of a nurse for their infant son. The young mother is unable to nurse him properly, and the father fears his son will suffer."

"What is the problem?"

"Well, that is rather delicate to discuss here. But if you could come to my offices and meet them . . ."

"But my coach—"

"They pass through for London with stops in Crawley twice each day, Miss Lamb. If you could postpone at least until the afternoon's coach, or tomorrow's, I am sure the couple would pay for your lodgings. Or I shall, if you would allow me."

"I had not thought to continue on as a nurse."

"This would only be a temporary position. I am certain the mother will, in time, be able to nurse her son herself as she desires to do."

He leaned closer yet. "You are still . . . able, do you think?"

She looked at the table, self-consciously slouching a bit to diminish her swollen breasts. She nodded.

"If you could relieve the child's distress and hunger even for a few hours, I am sure the couple would be most grateful."

Charlotte had no real desire to wet-nurse another child. But neither could she stand the thought of an infant suffering hunger when she could help. "I shall come."

"Thank you. I have already told them about you. In fact, they are waiting on us as we speak. If you would not mind . . . ?"

"My bags . . ."

"I shall ask the innkeeper to stow them for you. Until you decide?"

"Thank you."

They walked quickly through town to Dr. Kendall's offices, where he lost no time in making introductions. "Mr. and Mrs. Henshaw, may I present Miss Charlotte Lamb."

Charlotte curtsied.

Mr. Henshaw was older than she would have imagined, in his early fifties, perhaps. He was well dressed with craggy features and light brown hair combed to one side. He remained seated, legs crossed, impatiently bouncing his knee. His wife was young indeed. No more than seventeen or eighteen, Charlotte guessed. She was a lovely, dainty girl, with fair hair pulled into a fashionable coil and wide, pale blue eyes—eyes which looked terribly concerned. In her arms, she held a baby, wriggling and red-faced. Yet he made no loud cry, merely whined in high-pitched bursts of protest every half minute or so.

"Poor dear. How old is he?" Charlotte asked.

"A week tomorrow," Mrs. Henshaw answered quietly.

"If he lives that long," Mr. Henshaw snapped. "Now, let's not waste time, Kendall. You've found us this nurse in haste. How do we know she even has sufficient milk to nurse my son?"

"I can attest to the robust health of her last charge."

"She might have dried up since then."

Charlotte recoiled at the man's bald words.

"No, sir. She left my friend's employ only this morning."

"Why was she sacked?"

"It was nothing of the kind. I can vouch for her character and dependability, sir. Rest assured."

"Well, have you examined her yourself?"

"Examined? Not in so many words."

"Then do your job, man, and let's be done. If she's fit, I want her to nurse little Crispin here before he starves."

Charlotte felt the blood rushing to her face and neck.

"Miss Lamb is a naturally modest girl," Kendall muttered, biting his lip.

"Then use that screen there. I don't know a thing about this girl. Is it not reasonable to want some proof of her health, that she isn't ill or infected with some foul sores that would harm my boy?"

Dr. Kendall opened his mouth and closed it again. He looked at Charlotte soberly.

"Miss Lamb, would you mind stepping behind the screen? It won't take but a moment."

Charlotte opened her mouth to protest further, but the infant's whines grew into pitiful squeals that tore at Charlotte's heart—and threatened to cause her milk to let down on its own.

She stepped behind the screen and waited as Dr. Kendall adjusted it to enclose them more fully. He looked at her and mouthed the words *Forgive me.*

He looked from her face down to the neckline of her gown meaningfully. Heart pounding, face burning, she looked away from him and worked her bodice down until it pooled at her waist. Then she lowered one strap of her chemise from her shoulder, then the other. She had forgotten she had bound her breasts with muslin, to alleviate the pain and swelling since she was still full of milk. She swallowed, then unpinned the cloth where she had fastened its end. As she began to unwind the long strip, she glanced surreptitiously at the doctor and saw that he endeavored to maintain a detached, officious expression.

"Make sure her milk is still flowing," the dreadful man called from the other side of the screen.

Wincing, Charlotte paused. Would Dr. Kendall expect her to express milk in front of him? How mortifying.

At that moment the infant began crying in earnest. As she had feared, her milk let down in response, wetting through the remaining layers of muslin before she could wrap her arms over herself. Dr. Kendall lifted a hand, silently motioning for her to cease unwinding.

"Milk flow is excellent," he called over his shoulder. "The . . . everything . . . looks quite perfect."

He returned his gaze to her face. Although Charlotte was relieved beyond words not to have to expose herself fully, she was still too embarrassed to meet his eyes.

"You may redo your things, Miss Lamb. I apologize for the inconvenience."

Charlotte quickly repositioned her gown. "Why do I not nurse him right now?" she said, attempting to regain her composure. "Have you another room I might use?"

"Yes, of course."

Charlotte sat in a chair in a small examination room, nursing the babe who suckled with desperate voracity. The sensation was both relieving and slightly painful. She hoped he would be gentler in subsequent feedings.

The young wife watched with eyes wide, not averted as politeness might have dictated. "You *are* perfect," she breathed.

Charlotte did not know how to respond to such a shocking remark. The young woman clearly realized what she had said, for her face flushed pink. "I only meant, compared to me . . ."

"I'm sure you are fine."

"No. I am not."

When Charlotte next glanced up from Crispin's fuzz-covered head, she was stunned to see that Mrs. Henshaw had unfastened the nursing panel of her gown. Charlotte glimpsed dark purple bruises before the young woman closed the panel again. Charlotte's shock was replaced by compassion.

"Oh, you poor dear! No wonder you cannot nurse Crispin. How painful that must be!"

"The physician thinks I may have some infection. All I know is that I cry out in pain when I try to nurse my son. Crispin starts crying then, too, and Mr. Henshaw starts shouting."

Charlotte shook her head in pity.

"I do not blame him," Mrs. Henshaw said. "What kind of woman cannot nurse her own child? He says his own mother nursed him, and he would not have his son farmed out to some crude, greedy peasant. Oh! Forgive me, I did not mean you—"

"It's all right. I have heard such opinions before. You know, you are not the only woman to have trouble, Mrs. Henshaw."

"Please. Call me Georgiana."

"Very well, Georgiana. And you may call me Charlotte."

"Thank you."

"I have seen that once before. At the lying-in hospital."

"You have? Is it curable?"

"Of course it is. I shall nurse Crispin for you for a few days while you heal. It appears that he has not been latching on properly." Georgiana lowered her head and Charlotte hastened to add, "But how would you know if no one showed you? I realize women have been doing this since creation, but it does not always come as naturally as one might think."

Georgiana attempted a smile. What a lovely, gentle expression she had. Charlotte liked Georgiana Henshaw very much, felt nearly as maternal toward her as she did toward little Crispin. Her husband, however—she'd prefer to have as few dealings with him as possible.

"My own mother is gone, I'm afraid," Georgiana said wistfully.

"As is mine."

"I have one sister. But she is far off in Newcastle. Have you a sister?"

"Yes. But she is far away from me as well."

[Milkweed] has also been used in ancient times
to poison arrows. It also induces vomiting in birds
that eat the Monarch butterfly.

—JACK SANDERS, *THE SECRETS OF WILDFLOWERS*

CHAPTER 28

His wife vomited daintily into the basin, then wiped her mouth with a lace handkerchief. It was a graceful act, nearly ladylike. At least until she swore.

"What is wrong?" Daniel asked.

"Nothing. I am only sick of this foul English food."

"Are you all right now?"

"*Oui—maintenant.* Why will Mrs. Beebe not allow Marie to cook our meals? If I must eat that wretched cabbage fried in mutton fat one more time, I shall spew out my soul."

He chuckled and helped her to her feet.

"This is not funny. *C'est terrible.*"

"It isn't that bad."

"Not for you. You are here only at the week end. She saves the tripe mash and greasy cabbage until you are gone to London."

He smiled. "Why do we not go to the inn in the village tomorrow. Kendall said the food there is fine."

"I doubt they have anything that resembles cuisine in that little fishing village."

"Well, let us venture there and find out, shall we?"

"I do not know if I shall feel up to it, Daniel. Let us see what tomorrow brings."

❧

"Dr. Taylor?"

He opened his eyes. Mrs. Beebe stood in the parlor doorway.

"Hmm?" He had fallen asleep in a chair, tired from the coach trip and the long nights at the Manor before. He glanced at the mantel clock. He'd been asleep for nearly an hour.

"I thought you should know—the missus has gone out in the rain."

"What?" He looked toward the window. The rain that had been pouring down all afternoon had slowed to a steady drizzle. "When?"

"A quarter hour or more."

"Did she say—?"

Mrs. Beebe shook her head. "Didn't say a word. I thought of sending Mr. Beebe, but after the way your missus chewed my ears after supper, he isn't feeling too charitable toward her—if you know what I mean."

"I understand. And I am sorry for it. I will go. Do not trouble yourself further. Mrs. Taylor has always liked the rain."

This was not true, and he felt guilty for the lie as well as the motive behind it. He didn't want others to realize—didn't want to realize it himself. *It is happening again. . . .*

He found his wife sitting on the bench overlooking the sea.

She sat perfectly still, her hair, dress, and face thoroughly soaked.

"Lizette, my love, what are you doing?"

"Trying to see France. Smell France. And, after that wretched supper, *taste* France. I cannot see it by day with this country's ever-present fog and rain . . ."

"The channel is too wide here. I wish I could take you, but things are still too volatile—"

"But tonight I saw a light," she said urgently, as if he hadn't spoken. "On the horizon. I thought, *voilà! Bien sûr!* At night I can see France. I watched the light for a long time. It did not move. Just winked at me, called to me. I felt so happy. But then the light moved. Sailed closer and away down the coast. Just another stinking fishing boat. Bringing more stinking cod for your Mrs. Beebe to fry in her mutton fat."

"You might have spoken more kindly to her."

"I should repay with kindness the poison she feeds me? I can feel it, Daniel, filling my bowels and flowing through my veins. Poisoning me. Changing me. I used to be so . . . so different. So alive, so lovely."

He knelt beside her. "You are still."

"I used to be so happy too—remember?"

Tears filled his eyes. "I remember," he said quietly. He laid his hands on her knees. The hot tears trailed down his cheeks, mingling with the cool raindrops on his face. "You will be happy again, my love. *We* will be happy again."

※

The following afternoon, Marie brought in a tray of tea things, but Lizette waved the servant away. She picked up the book, glanced at a single line, and tossed it down again. She rose from the settee and stalked about the room, as restless as a creature caged.

Daniel lowered his own book. "Shall we go for a walk, my dear? Some exercise might do us both good."

"What is the use?"

"We'll take Anne. She always seems to enjoy a stroll in Mr. Beebe's carriage."

"Sally and Thomas Cox have already taken her for a walk."

"Well, have you thought any more about having the neighbors over for tea?"

She expelled a dry laugh and rolled her eyes.

"Kendall assures me Mrs. Dillard and her lot are the worst of the village snobs. Our neighbors would be far kinder."

"Why would they accept an invitation from me? I am nobody."

"That is not true. You are a fine woman—you are my wife."

"You are nobody as well."

"Granted."

"And you leave for London tomorrow, again, leaving me caged up in this strange house."

"I shall stay if you prefer." He paused. "One of my patients is expecting twins and I fear it shall be a difficult birth, but I am sure Preston can manage it."

"That man is not fit to deliver goats. No, go. Go and do what you must."

❧

Five days later, the front door of Richard Kendall's offices opened and in strode Lizette Taylor, beautifully turned out in crimson gown and feathered hat.

"*Bonjour*, Dr. Kendall."

"Mrs. Taylor. This is a pleasant surprise. What brings you by?"

"Are we not well enough acquainted that I might visit without an appointment?"

"But of course we are. Is there something I might help you with?"

She looked at him, opened her mouth, hesitated, and then said, "Yes, there is. It is silly, really, a trifling complaint, but if you would not mind . . . ?"

"Of course not."

She glanced toward the old man sitting near the door. "Should we not step into your private office?"

He followed her gaze. "Of course." Then more loudly, to the man, he said, "I shall be with you shortly, Mr. Dumfries."

He showed her into his office. "Now, what seems to be the problem? Are you not feeling well?"

"Do I not look well?"

"You look very well indeed. As usual."

"You are very gallant to say so." She lowered her dress from one shoulder. "There. Do you see?"

"Ah . . . what am I looking at?"

"I am usually more modest, but I suppose, being a physician, you are unmoved by the sight of the female form?"

He swallowed. "Usually, yes."

She stroked the exposed skin below her clavicle. "This patch of skin—does it not look red to you?"

He stepped closer, peering down at the spot. He cleared his throat. "What has Daniel said about it?"

"I have not asked him. He is away in London again at that precious lying-in hovel of his."

"I hear the old Manor Home is quite well run."

"Manor indeed."

"How would you describe the irritation? Does the area itch? Burn?"

"Yes, I burn . . ."

He looked from the mild rash up to her face, into her smoldering eyes.

"Do I not feel warm to you?" She let her dress fall farther down her shoulder, exposing a hint of cleavage.

He hesitated, feeling beguiled and perplexed. He forced his gaze away and focused again on her face. This time he saw that, indeed, her complexion looked flushed, her eyes nearly fevered. He looked once more at her lovely neck and shoulders. He reached out and pressed his fingers to the side of her throat. Then he lowered his hand across her bodice, to her abdomen, resting there, kneading, exploring. She shivered.

Again he cleared his throat and stepped back. "Yes, well, I believe I have all the information I need. You may do up your frock now."

He turned his back to her and picked up a pen and prescription booklet.

"That is all?" Her tone was bitter.

"Yes. I shall write up a prescription for some salve that should help." He ripped the script from its binding and turned to hand it to her. "I am sure the chemist will have this in supply."

"That is all you great physicians are good for. You write your orders like a housekeeper with a list for the greengrocer." She held up the paper and crumpled it into a ball. "But you *do* nothing." She let the wad fall to the floor.

Stepping nearer, she grabbed a handful of his coat in one fist and pushed her face close to his. "You do not help us. You do not give us what we need."

Swallowing hard, he stepped back, pulling his coat loose from her grasp. "You must excuse me, Mrs. Taylor. I have another patient waiting."

He turned, opened the door, and stopped abruptly. Daniel Taylor stood waiting, hat in hand.

"Taylor! How good to see you," Kendall enthused rather falsely, though his relief at his friend's sudden appearance was genuine enough. "We thought you were in London. That is, Mrs. Taylor here was just telling me that you were. But how could you be, for here you are."

Daniel's pleasant expression faded and his brow furrowed. Kendall self-consciously smoothed down his coat. Glancing over his shoulder, he noted that Mrs. Taylor had shrugged her gown up higher on her shoulder, but it was still not properly done up.

"I've only just returned by the afternoon coach," Daniel said flatly.

"How fortuitous. You are just in time to offer a second opinion on my diagnosis. Mrs. Taylor has a skin irritation she was just pointing out to me."

Daniel looked at him a moment longer, than swung his gaze to his wife, to her exposed shoulder.

"You have not mentioned this to me," he said, stepping into the office. "Is this a new affliction?"

She looked at him pointedly. "I have suffered for some time."

"You knew I was on my way. Could you not wait?"

Lizette Taylor narrowed her eyes. "You have shown little interest in my skin of late, Dr. Taylor."

Daniel glanced up and Kendall shook his head slightly, forcing himself to meet his friend's stare. He had done nothing wrong, whatever fleeting thoughts had flitted across his mind. He hoped Daniel would believe him.

Dr. Kendall asked Lizette to wait in his office while he spoke to Daniel in the other room. Mr. Dumfries took himself home, saying he would return on the morrow.

Once they were alone, Kendall began somberly, "I believe it is as you feared."

Daniel stared at the man without seeing him, dread filling his gut. "Are you sure?"

"No. But she has symptoms—accelerated pulse, itching, and, um, certain uncharacteristic behaviors. . . ."

"It's true she has not been herself—demonstrated again this afternoon by the looks of it."

"Daniel, I hope you do not think—"

"I don't know what to think. Why now? Our child is more than seven months old. Lizette seemed so recovered from the postnatal mania. Yes, she's been melancholy, but not nearly as out of control as she was before."

"You don't know?"

"Know what?"

"Well, I did only a preliminary examination, but I do believe your wife is pregnant."

Daniel squeezed his eyes shut as if to block out the truth. He had been so determined to avoid intimacy with Lizette that he had barely allowed himself to look at her nor touch her for months, save that one time. The signs he had noticed, he had tried to ignore or explain away. *Not morning sickness, surely—merely Mrs. Beebe's greasy food....*

His friend must think him an idiot.

"The symptoms of puerperal insanity often start with conception," Kendall said. "Whereas for other women, it doesn't make itself known until after delivery. Did it strike her during her first lying-in?"

Daniel nodded, the fear beginning to grow.

"Good heavens, man, how bad was it?"

He looked at Richard, too devastated to lie. "Very."

"Did she try to harm herself?"

Daniel nodded.

"How did you treat her?"

"Herbs, purgatives, blisters.... Nothing worked. When she became violent I resorted to laudanum for a time and finally had to institutionalize her."

Richard stared at him, horror and pity a terrible pall on his face. "I am sorry, Daniel."

"As am I."

"What will you do?"

"The best I can. For now, she is melancholy and restless but has yet to become violent. I will find someone to cover for me in London. I will stay with her and keep her here as long as I can."

"If I hear of anything . . . any new developments or treatments . . ."

"Thank you, Kendall."

Women turned against their husbands, neglected themselves and the household, bullied their servants, broke the china . . . displayed an overt sexuality, making vulgar and suggestive comments to complete strangers. Yet so common was this disorder . . . that it came to be seen as an almost anticipated accompaniment of the process of giving birth.

—DR. HILARY MARLAND, *DANGEROUS MOTHERHOOD*

CHAPTER 29

After dinner, Lizette began scratching her arm, then her neck. He watched calmly at first, but when she began scratching with great vigor, he rose to his feet and took her by the arms to still her. Already she bore long streaks of red down her white neck. "Come, I shall give you something for that."

"Nothing helps."

"I shall find something. Come."

Pausing to pick up his medical bag, he led her upstairs to their bedroom and closed the door. She flounced down on the bed while he set the bag on the dresser and began looking through its contents. "Here we are."

He sat on the bed beside her and began applying the ointment to her neck, lowering her gown from one shoulder to avoid getting the sticky medicine on the fine material. He smoothed the ointment onto her throat, then bent to kiss her bare shoulder. She had been trying to seduce him for weeks. Now, the damage done, why not enjoy his wife while he could? He kissed her clavicle and slid the gown off her other shoulder, his hand moving lower to stroke her exposed skin. His lips moved lower as well.

"*Non.*"

She shoved him with startling strength and he fell away from her. Stunned, he looked up at her, surprised to see tears streaming down her face.

"Can you not see how I suffer? And yet you force yourself on me!"

"I . . . I thought you wanted . . . I am sorry."

"Yes, you are sorry indeed."

❧

The next night, Daniel found Lizette sitting alone in the dark parlor, weeping. He lit a lamp, forcing optimism into his voice. "Dr. Kendall sent this tea for you. He thinks it might help."

"There is no use in doing anything, as I shall die soon."

"Please do not say that. Think of Anne."

"Why? Is it not she who ruined my body and my mind?"

"Lizette. It isn't her fault."

"Nor is it mine! You behave as though it is all in my mind. As though I am insane!"

"Shh . . . calm yourself. I know what ails you is real. And you are not the only woman to suffer from it."

"Do you think that helps me? Do you think that makes me want to live?"

"No, you live for us, for Anne and for me and for the babe to come."

"I do not care about any of you." She rubbed her forehead roughly. "I just want this to end."

"My dear. I think it's time we thought about returning to London."

"*Non!* I will not go back to that place. That hospital, that dark little room."

"Only until the baby comes."

"*Non!* Please, Daniel, I beg you. I shall be fine. I will get better. I like it here by the sea. I can breathe here. I can smell France."

Daniel looked at her beautiful, pleading face. "Very well. For now. But you must try to calm down, to control yourself."

"*Oui, mon amour.* I shall."

But a few days later, Daniel heard Lizette and Marie shouting and swearing in French. He leapt up from his desk and sprinted into the parlor.

His wife held a large brass candelabra in her hand and was about to strike the windowpane. Marie tried to wrest it from her.

"Lizette! Put that down!" he shouted.

"It will not open. I need air."

"Then ask me to help you."

"I can help myself."

"Allow me." He took the candelabra from her and placed it on the table, then tried pulling and shoving at the old window. "It is painted shut."

Marie nodded, "*Oui, monsieur.* Zat is what I tell madame."

"I am trapped in this old ruin of a place," Lizette cried. "I need air!"

"Take hold of yourself! Calm down."

"I am so sick of those words—that patronizing way you speak to me! You are not my father. Do not speak to me as if I were a child."

"You are acting like one."

"*Non.* Having a child is making me this way. I cannot stand it. I want out of this body . . . this skin!"

He gave up on the window and took hold of his wife's elbows, motioning the maid out of the room with a lift of his chin. "Lizette."

"It is my life, *non?*"

"No," he said gently, shaking his head. "You are not God."

"Well, neither are you. Some great physician you are, *Doctor* Taylor. You cannot even heal your own wife."

"I am trying. I am doing all I know to do."

"It is not enough!" She pulled away, grabbed the candelabra and threw it across the room, shattering the gilt mirror over the fireplace mantel.

He froze.

Marie reappeared in the doorway and hesitated there, frowning at the broken mirror and then at him.

"Stay with her, please," he instructed. Then he dashed from the room, leapt the stairs three at a time, and knocked on the nursery door. Sally opened it, white faced. She had obviously heard the commotion from below.

"Sally, please collect Anne and whatever things you need. I am taking you into the village. I want you to stay at the Red Lion. Here—" He pulled several bank notes from his wallet and handed them to her. "That should do for a night or two."

"Yes, sir."

After seeing Sally and Anne safely to the inn, he drove the carriage to Kendall's office.

"Richard," he began, hat in hand before his friend's desk, "I do not know what to do. I am at my wits' end. Lizette has begged me not to take her back to the Manor Home, but now with Anne to think of . . . I may even have to find a more equipped asylum."

"There are one or two I might recommend."

"Please. Come one more time. See if there is anything I have left undone."

"Of course." Richard rose and followed him outside.

But the scene that greeted them was not at all what either gentleman expected. The cottage had been restored to rights. Although the mirror was missing, the glass shards had been taken down and discarded, and the late afternoon sun lit the room in a peaceful, golden glow. Lizette looked up at them from a pristine table laid with a full tea service, as well as plates of sandwiches and cakes. Lizette herself looked serene and lovely, dressed in a pink silk gown, her hair done up properly, her face powdered. She even had the strand of pearls around her neck that Daniel had long ago given her but she seldom wore.

She greeted them warmly. "Welcome, gentlemen." Dumbly, Daniel stepped forward, Kendall close behind.

"Hello, darling." She rose and smiled at him as he approached, eyes glowing, then reached up and kissed his cheek.

"Dr. Kendall, how pleased I am to see you again. Do sit down."

Both men were speechless. They laid their hats aside and sat as they were bade, watching in awe as Lizette poured tea with practiced precision and grace.

"Dr. Kendall, how do you take your tea?"

"Uh . . . milk will do nicely, thank you."

She complied and handed him the cup and saucer with a steady hand.

"And I know my husband likes sugar in his. There you are, my dear."

"Thank you."

Daniel stared at her, and then he and Kendall exchanged a look, brows raised. Hopes too.

"It does happen," Kendall said to him later, behind the closed doors of the study. "Some remedy creates a delayed effect or a woman's balance somehow restores itself on its own."

"But will it last?"

"I don't know. But it seems quite possible."

"Thank God."

"Indeed."

"Will you do me a favor and stop by the inn and let Sally Mitchell know she may return?"

Kendall paused, then nodded. "Of course. I shall tell her she may return . . . in the morning." Kendall smiled at him and turned on his heel, donning his hat.

For an unmarried man, Kendall was quite astute.

"When puerperal mania does take place, the patient swears,
bellows, recites poetry, talks bawdy, and kicks up a row. . . .
Every precaution must be taken to prevent her doing
injury to herself, to the infant, or her friends."

—ROBERT GOOCH, EARLY 19TH CENTURY PHYSICIAN

CHAPTER 30

The next morning, Daniel came down the stairs whistling, knowing all the while how cliché it was to do so. Still, he could barely keep the smile from his face. The day was sunny and so were their prospects for the future.

In the kitchen, he found Sally Mitchell eating a biscuit.

"You're returned early. How is Anne?"

"She fell asleep on the way home. Already laid her down for an early nap. 'Fraid the inn was awful noisy last night. Neither of us got much sleep."

I know how you feel. "Sorry to hear it," Daniel said, though the cheerful tone did not match his words.

"The missus really has turned the corner, then?"

"Yes, it seems she has, thank God. Though we must still monitor her progress."

"That is good news, sir. Your friend said as much, but I was afraid to believe it."

"I understand."

"I told Charlotte as well. She was most relieved, I can tell you."

"Charlotte?"

"Yes, she stopped by the inn this morning."

"Oh? She did not return to Crawley?"

"Nay. She's staying on in Shoreham for a time."

"Is she?"

She nodded. "Something to do with your Dr. Kendall, but I didn't hear the particulars. Place was too loud to hear much of anything."

Daniel swallowed. "I see."

Taking a deep breath, he changed the topic. "Mrs. Taylor is still asleep. Peacefully at last. Do your best to keep Anne quiet so as not to disturb her. I am just going to ride into town and send a message to my father. I shan't be long."

"Yes, sir."

When Daniel returned an hour later, he opened the door gingerly and was relieved at the peace and quiet that greeted him. He laid aside his hat and went in search of his wife. No one was in the parlor or dining room. She wasn't still sleeping, surely—although they had lain awake together until the early morning hours.

Upstairs, he found their bedroom empty, the bed neatly made. Peeking into the third-floor nursery, he saw it, too, was empty. Stepping down the passage, he tapped lightly on Sally's door, thinking to check on Anne. Sally answered the door, sleep etched plainly on her features, her mouth stretched wide in a yawn. "Must have fallen asleep," she said.

"Is Anne awake?"

"I believe so."

"She isn't here with you?"

"Mrs. Taylor wanted to have her to herself. Poor dear said it felt like a month of Sundays since she'd held her little girl."

Daniel smiled. Had Lizette's maternal feeling been restored, along with her affection—and desire—for her husband? Nearly as quickly, his smile faded.

"Where are they? I saw no one downstairs."

"Off to get some fresh air, I believe she said. Oh dear, have I done wrong?" Sally's expression grew pained. "She told me to go on and have a rest. And after last night, I was happy to oblige."

"I'm sure all is well," Daniel muttered, already heading for the stairs. But he wasn't sure at all.

"Should I start packing, sir?" Sally called after him.

"Packing? Why?" He paused midway down the staircase.

"Mrs. Taylor said something about going home."

He froze. "Home?" But he had assured her he would not yet take her back to the Manor.

"Aye. Are we returning to London soon?"

"I . . . I don't know," he called over his shoulder as he rushed down the stairs.

He found Mrs. Beebe in the kitchen.

"Have you seen Mrs. Taylor?"

"Yes, sir. She went outside with the little one."

"When was this?"

"Oh, about a quarter of an hour ago."

"Where were they headed?"

"Toward the sea, I suspect. And a lovely day for a stroll it is."

The sea? Panic gripped him. *Oh, dear God . . .*

Daniel ran outside, across the wide lawn, down the rocky decline and onto the pebbled shore. He looked wildly about, up and down the coast. Then, out on the channel, he glimpsed a lone, dark-haired figure swimming with clumsy strokes, then disappear below the surface.

"Lizette!" he cried. *God, help me!*

He ran across the rocks and splashed into the water, pausing only long enough to haul off his boots and throw them back on shore, then he swam out after her. He tried to gauge where he'd seen her go under. At least he thought—feared—it was her.

When he reached the spot, he dove down. He searched frantically through the cold, dark water. When his lungs forced him, he lurched up and sucked in air. He searched the surface, desperate to see her.

Hearing a shout, he spun around. There were Thomas and Kendall on the shore. Remembering Kendall had never learned to swim, Daniel dove back down, scarcely giving thought to the men. He swam deeper, deeper, his long arms stretching, his fingers combing the water. There! He caught a handful of fabric. He held on and kicked closer, wrapping one arm around the figure and trying to drag her to the surface. At first he could hardly lift her, but then she began to rise. He kicked and pawed at the water with all his might. He felt her moving, kicking beside him, and rejoiced. She was alive!

He broke through the surface and filled his burning lungs with air. Only then did he realize that Thomas was there, had swum out and helped him pull up Lizette. His gratitude was quickly suffocated by the realization that it had been Thomas's movements, not his wife's, he had felt beside him.

The long, full gown Lizette wore, sodden with water, had become a weighted anchor dragging all three of them back down. Slowly and painfully, the two men kicked, paddled, and pulled themselves back to land. Together they hauled Lizette carefully toward shore. Richard Kendall waded into the surf to help them, and together they laid her carefully down onto the pebbled beach.

Richard leaned close, listening for breath. He turned her on her side and began compressing her abdomen, releasing a stream of water from her mouth.

"I've got to find Anne!" Daniel ran over the surf and dove back into the water. Thomas followed after him.

Back and forth they swam, pawing the dark water, coming up with only handfuls of shale and debris. After seemingly endless, exhausting dives, Daniel fell back on shore, panting. Thomas crawled out after him.

"She's gone," Richard said.

"I know. We could not find her."

"I mean your wife. She's gone. I could not revive her."

Daniel fisted his hands and pressed them to his forehead and down into his eye sockets. Then he forced himself onto his hands and knees and crawled over the wet pebbles to the prone body of his wife.

He laid his head on her chest, then looked up at her face and stroked her damp cheek.

"I am sorry, Daniel," Kendall said quietly.

"She was going home. To France. She was trying to swim there." Daniel's voice broke.

Richard laid a hand on his shoulder.

Daniel moaned and sat down, pulling Lizette onto his lap, into his arms. "I could not find Anne. I know you did not mean to lose her. I tried, I did . . ."

Kendall sent Thomas to the cottage to fetch some blankets. One to warm him, Daniel supposed. Another to cover his wife's body. His own body was wracked with shivering, his muscles tight and convulsing. The waters of the channel were cold, even this time of year. Had the cold stolen her consciousness, even before she drowned?

For a moment, he was struck with the desire to walk back into the sea that had claimed his wife, daughter, and unborn child. Let it claim him too. Anything to stop this crushing pain.

But even as he entertained the thought, his own words to Lizette echoed in his mind, *"You are not God."*

"Oh, God . . ." He moaned and began sobbing. How could he go on? It was all his fault. How could he ever forgive himself?

"Daniel," a voice spoke softly behind him. Or maybe he had imagined it.

"Merciful heavens!" Kendall exclaimed beside him. "Is that Anne?"

Daniel turned. There was Charlotte, the sun at her back, casting a golden glow around her. He winced. His mind must be numb, or hallucinatory.

"Yes," the Charlotte-image said. "I found her asleep up the shore. Surrounded by rocks and driftwood."

"Thank God," Kendall said. "Daniel! Anne's all right. She's alive. Do you hear me?"

Daniel sat mutely as Charlotte walked toward him, tears streaming down her face as her eyes darted to, then away from Lizette's still form.

She knelt beside him and gently handed Anne to him. Then she rose and stepped back.

Daniel stared down at Anne, who was awake now and seemed pleased to see him. She wriggled and babbled, her little fists moving from her mouth to clasp his nose.

"Yes . . . I seem to have lost my spectacles. Do you still recognize me?"

The little girl opened her mouth in a toothless grin.

"Your *maman* is gone. I am so sorry, dear one. She loved you—never think she didn't. She just . . . could not stay. I tried to help her, but I could not. . . ."

Thomas and Sally returned with blankets, and Kendall wrapped one around Daniel's shoulders. Then he laid the other one carefully over Lizette. Sally took Anne and headed back toward the cottage.

"Come, my friend," Kendall urged gently. "Let's get you into the house and out of those wet clothes."

Daniel looked over at his wife's shrouded form. "I cannot leave her."

"I shall see to her," Kendall assured.

Together Charlotte and Thomas helped Daniel up and into the cottage.

❧

The day after the funeral, Charlotte found Daniel sitting on the bench, staring out at the sea. Wordlessly, she sat down as well, careful to leave a proper amount of space between them. He acknowledged her presence with the slightest nod before returning his gaze to the sea.

"You never really knew her, Miss Lamb. Not really. Not the woman she once was."

She asked softly, "How did the two of you meet?"

"She was working as a governess in Edinburgh when I was at university there. I first saw her in the park, swinging her little charge around and around until the sound of their laughter filled the square. I can still see her in her green-striped dress, her dark hair escaping her straw bonnet, her smile so bright—the only brightness to be seen on that grey Scottish day. She told me she had left her home in Normandy, looking for adventure.

"Only later did I find out she was looking for escape, that her mother was afflicted in much the way Lizette was, at the end." He leaned over, elbows on his knees. "I don't think she meant to deceive me. I think she truly believed, or at least desperately hoped, that she'd left all of that far behind her, that she could avoid the same fate. We traveled to Caen only once to meet her family. I suspected how it was with her mother, but by then it was too late. I was in love with Lizette. I could not have stopped myself from marrying her, even had I known what was to be."

After a few minutes of silence, Daniel sighed. "Still, I should have seen it coming. Should have prevented it somehow."

She glanced over at him, saw him shake his head dolefully.

"I wanted to move her someplace safe, but she begged to stay. She said she loved it here—felt closer to home. Too close, it turns out."

"How could you know? She was much improved."

"So we thought. Or so she wanted us to believe. But I should have known better."

"Mr. Taylor . . ." Without intending to, she had slipped back to his former address.

"If only I had found a more effective treatment. Or insisted we return to London a fortnight ago."

"Mr. Taylor . . . do you not remember what you said to me when my mother died?"

"No."

"I was sure that if only I had been a better daughter, or prayed harder, or insisted she not tire herself in the garden, then she would have lived."

He shrugged.

"But you told me God does not work that way. Remember?"

"And I believe you told me I needed to read the Old Testament."

"*That* you choose to remember." She smiled gently. "It is not your fault."

It had taken a long time for Charlotte to believe this herself. She feared Daniel Taylor would prove no quicker a student.

He took a deep breath, then straightened. "Thank you again for finding Anne. I don't know that I could have gone on if—"

"Shh . . . Someone else would have found her had I not happened along."

"I can only hope so. How did you happen to be here that day?"

She took a deep breath. "I awoke with the darkest foreboding that morning. Even though Sally assured me at the inn that all was well, I had to come. I should have walked, but Dr. Kendall and Thomas passed by on their way here and offered me a ride."

"And what were they about? I never asked, and after, well, everything, I quite forgot."

"Dr. Kendall brought Thomas out with the intention of convincing the both of you that Thomas should remain here as *his* apprentice. But after he saw Thomas's loyalty to you that day, I believe he quite gave it up."

"Yes. That boy has a place with me for as long as he wants one."

The two sat for several more minutes without speaking before Daniel said, "I shall be returning to London soon. Letting go of this place early. You are welcome to stay on here until I do. That is, unless Kendall . . . unless you have made other arrangements."

"I have made other arrangements."

"I see." He rose abruptly. "Of course that is none of my affair."

"My arrangements are not with Dr. Kendall, however," she said.

"No?"

"I have taken a post with a family in Old Shoreham."

"May I ask in what capacity?"

"As their nurse."

"Oh . . . I had not realized you planned to continue in that vocation."

"I had not planned to do so. But they were in need and, well, there I was. It is only temporary."

In fact, Georgiana Henshaw was well on her way to nursing her son herself. She had begun nursing him once or twice a day as her recovery allowed while Charlotte kept up with the other feedings. But the young mother was quickly assuming the majority of nursing. Mrs. Henshaw had assured Charlotte she would be welcome to stay on as long as she liked, but Charlotte doubted Mr. Henshaw would agree to such generous terms.

"And after?"

She shrugged. "Return to Crawley, I suppose. As I intended to do before."

❧

But the next morning, Sally received a letter that changed Charlotte's plans once again.

Charlotte had returned to take breakfast with Sally and, privately, to assure herself that Mr. Taylor was all right. As they sat visiting, Mrs. Beebe came into the kitchen with the morning post. "Letter for you, Sally."

Sally took the letter and studied the direction with surprise but none of the happiness Charlotte might have expected.

"'Tis from my sister."

Dr. Taylor came in for a cup of tea while Sally opened the missive and read as quickly as her skill allowed. After a moment, she propped a hand on the table as if to support herself.

Alarmed, Charlotte asked, "Sally, what is it?"

"'Tis Dickie. She says he's very ill. Oh! I must go to him at once."

"Steady on," Dr. Taylor said. "What else does she say?"

"He's weak, high fever, won't eat. . . . She fears the worst. And this was written days ago now! Dr. Taylor, please help him. You will come, won't you? Please."

He hesitated a moment, in which time Charlotte feared he was offended by Sally's presumption that he should drop everything to help a child he barely knew, or that, in his morose state, he felt ill-equipped to save anyone.

Instead, he set his cup down. "We shall go directly."

In a flurry of plans and instructions, Charlotte agreed to remain at Lloyd Lodge for a few days to nurse Anne and give notice to the Henshaws. Marie would return with Sally and Dr. Taylor to prepare the London house, which had no doubt gathered dust during their absence with only John Taylor to care for it. Charlotte would stay behind long enough to see to the packing and help the Beebes set the place to rights. Then she would escort Anne back to London, to the home Dr. Taylor shared with his father. After that . . . she did not know.

It wasn't within her to refuse any help Anne Taylor—or her father—needed. Still it chafed her a bit to realize she was allowing her course to be set by the winds of circumstance. Yet again.

Forcing thoughts off herself, she set to work and prayed fervently for the recovery of Sally's son.

What will you think when I tell you she is not yet weaned?

How to set about it is more than I know . . .

—1765 LETTER BETWEEN FRIENDS, FROM
THE GENTLEMAN'S DAUGHTER BY AMANDA VICKERY

CHAPTER 31

Mr. John Taylor met her coach with broad smiles for both Anne and herself.

"How good to see you again, Miss Charlotte. And little Anne! How much you have grown!"

Anne's little lip trembled as her grandfather put his face close to hers. "Forgot me already, did you? We shall soon put that to rights."

"I am sure you shall—if you can catch her. She has just learned to creep about."

"Has she indeed. Well, there'll be no rest for any of us now. All those tempting staircases."

He gestured to the hackney driver he had hired to take them the rest of the way to the Taylor residence. The bulky man came and gathered her baggage and carried the load to his carriage. They followed and Mr. Taylor held Anne while Charlotte climbed in. The child looked at him warily but did not cry.

Once they were all settled and Anne back in Charlotte's arms, Mr. Taylor looked across at them and said, "You look as well fed as a stuffed goose at Christmas. I mean Anne, of course. I must say you look far too thin. You are in good health, I hope."

"I am. Thank you."

"What a trying time this has been for all of you, no doubt. Daniel looked positively dreadful upon his return."

"And little Dickie?"

Mr. Taylor shook his head gravely. "I'm afraid the lad is very ill indeed. Still, Daniel hasn't given up hope."

Coming to a halt at the Taylors' offices and residence on Wimpole Street, Mr. Taylor paid the driver and asked him to bring the baggage to the living quarters above.

Marie, looking worn and apathetic as usual, met them on the first floor up. "You and ze child will be in ze same chamber as before." She turned her back without offering to help carry up their things.

"I must say that having you back with us is the one bright spot in the whole dismal affair," John Taylor added kindly. "Though I would not have chosen the circumstances for the world."

"No, of course not."

"I'm afraid we won't see much of Daniel for some time, between his work at the Manor, his own practice, and seeing the Mitchell boy. But we'll do quite nicely on our own, I trust. Do let me know if there is anything you need."

"Thank you. You are very kind." Tears filled Charlotte eyes as she spoke the words, and she didn't stop to wonder why.

❧

"You are certain you do not wish your post back?" Charlotte asked Sally over tea in the Taylors' sitting room a few weeks later.

"No. My place is with Dickie now."

"How does he fare?"

"He's fully recovered, I am happy to say. Thanks to your Dr. Taylor."

"He is not my Dr. Taylor."

The look Sally gave her said she begged to differ.

"And how is your Thomas?"

"'Tisn't mine." She hid a toothy grin behind her hand. "Yet . . ."

Charlotte smiled. Soon after her return to London, Thomas had arrived to begin his apprenticeship to Dr. Taylor. The young man slept either in one of the manor's upstairs chambers or on a cot in the offices on the street level, depending on where Dr. Taylor needed him on a given day.

"Why not come out with me and Thomas sometime?" Sally asked. "Thomas loves going to hear lectures and concerts and the like, and he is determined that I should learn to like such as well. Come along with us. You'd enjoy a night out now and then, wouldn't you?"

"You are thoughtful to include me. But Anne . . ."

"My sister would watch her and Dickie both. I know she would."

"Anne is still nursing. It is difficult to get away. You remember how it is."

"Aye." Sally's eyes clouded.

"I did not mean . . ."

"'Tis all right, Miss Charlotte. I remember my blunder whether anyone reminds me of it or not."

"It is forgotten, Sally."

"Not by the Harrises, 'tisn't. And not by me."

"Oh, Sally . . ." Charlotte reached over and squeezed her friend's hand. "Someday soon I should be delighted to accompany you for an evening out."

Charlotte glanced up and saw Dr. Taylor standing in the doorway, his expression dour. How much of their conversation had he overheard?

❧

A few days later, Dr. Taylor approached Charlotte as she sat spooning porridge into Anne's open, bird-like mouth. When she glanced up at him, he cleared his throat. "I've been wondering,

Miss Lamb, if it might not be time to wean Anne? She has begun eating other foods now."

She glanced at the spoon in her hand. "Yes, I know. But I had thought to nurse her for a full year or more."

"Ah, well. As you wish." He started for the door.

Charlotte turned, spoon still poised midair. "But if you want me to cease, then, of course, I shall."

"I was only wondering . . ."

Then it struck her. He wanted to be rid of her. Her heart pounded dully, painfully.

She would not overstay her welcome.

❧

She had not expected the process to be so difficult. In fact by the next morning, breasts full, she had already resigned herself to continuing on. But Anne was fussy and restless and wouldn't nurse properly. She pulled off again and again as Charlotte encouraged her to latch on.

"You must be hungry. . . ." What was the trouble? Had Charlotte eaten something that had spoilt her milk? She did not believe so. Charlotte grimaced. "One would almost think you understood your father's suggestion about weaning . . ." Finally Charlotte gave up, hoping the little girl wasn't coming down ill.

The next morning was much the same. Anne nursed fitfully, pulled away, tried again. Charlotte stroked her little tummy. "What is it, dear? What pains you?"

A sharp pain struck Charlotte's breast. Charlotte cried out and jerked back. Startled, Anne began to wail. Tears welled in Charlotte's eyes at the stinging pain. As Anne cried, mouth wide, Charlotte saw the white kernel protruding from her pink gums. Her first tooth. "Well, you needn't have bitten me. That hurt."

Anne cried louder yet.

"There, there now. It's all right. I know you did not mean to. At least I hope not."

After that, both of them seemed resigned to wean each other. Charlotte steeled herself for each of the few nursings that followed. Anne must have felt her apprehension, for she too seemed tense and nursed very poorly. Still, nights were the most difficult for Anne, when she rooted against Charlotte, wanting to nurse for comfort, to ease into sleep. Charlotte obliged her. Mornings were most difficult for Charlotte, when she longed for the relief of pressure nursing brought. Gradually she realized, however, that the morning fullness was diminishing. By evening, when Anne grew most fussy, it seemed Charlotte had very little milk to offer her, for Anne pulled away quickly.

Though she had set out to wean Anne, now that the reality of its imminence dawned on Charlotte, a strange panicked sadness stole over her. She knew once she was through, there was no going back. Her unique role in this child's life would be over. She would be more replaceable than ever. Anne would not need her anymore. How would Charlotte support herself now? True, she had never wanted this vocation, but what would she do?

Her breasts lost some of their fullness, which seemed sad too. She began to feel as empty as they. She would need to take in her gowns.

Knowing each might be her last, she began to cherish every nursing—and concerns for her livelihood were not uppermost in her mind. She would miss this. The warmth and satisfaction of holding this little one close to her body. Anne's little face relaxed and content, now and then opening her dark eyes to look up at Charlotte as if to greet her or thank her. Her little hand, lying against Charlotte's breast or stomach. The sweet sting of milk coursing through her, the tug of the curled tongue and rough-ridged mouth. The sounds of drawing, of swallowing, of nourishing. Of life.

Charlotte stroked Anne's hair, the soft curve of her neck. "Very soon, you will not even remember this time together. But I shall always remember. And I shall miss it. And you . . ."

Even as Charlotte's milk stopped flowing, her tears began, running over to take its place.

Two weeks after Sally's teatime visit, Charlotte stood before Dr. Taylor's desk, hands clenched together. "I will be leaving in a week's time, Dr. Taylor. Does that give you sufficient notice to make other arrangements for Anne's care?"

"Leaving? But why?"

"I have weaned Anne, as you requested."

"I only suggested it to afford you a bit of freedom."

"Well, I am free. You will not have need of me any longer."

"But we do. Anne is quite dependent on you."

"I am only the nurse, Dr. Taylor. My post here is finished."

"Well, that part may be ended. But there are other . . . capacities in which you might stay."

"Such as?"

"Well, however you like. That is . . . I know it's too soon to talk of . . . such things, and I haven't any right to presume on your time, but all I know is that, that . . ."

He stopped then, catching his breath and running his hand across his face.

"All you know is, what?" she prompted, trying to be gentle but feeling unaccountably frustrated.

He swallowed, then stuttered, "I want . . . I wish . . . I would like you to stay."

She was oddly touched by his stammering, his obvious nervousness. But no, she was foolish to read anything into his manner. His wife was not long in her grave, and he'd clearly loved her. Though the last years of their lives together had been wretched, that did not erase his pain, his mourning. He was not offering anything other than a position, and she'd do well to remember so.

"Do you wish me to be Anne's governess?" she suggested tentatively.

"Governess? She's a bit young for that, but...would you want that? I mean, eventually? Of course I would like you to keep caring for her as you do."

"Nursery maid, then?"

"Well, I don't like the sound of that. That's beneath you, Miss Lamb."

"No it isn't." *Not anymore.*

"What I mean to say, is that a woman of your character and education could do so much more, could be anything she wanted."

"But you need a nursemaid."

"Anne needs a nursemaid. I . . ."

"What?"

"For Anne's sake, I wish you would stay on as nursemaid, governess, what have you. But quite frankly, I don't."

"You don't want me to be Anne's nurse."

"No."

Charlotte felt as though she'd been slapped and drenched with icy water at the same time. She'd thought he admired her way with his daughter—that he admired her in general.

"I shall leave immediately."

"No!" he all but shouted.

She looked at him, stunned by his uncharacteristic outburst.

He sighed and said more gently, "Forgive me. I know I am a broken shell of a man with little to offer you. But still, I ask you."

"Ask me what?"

"To stay."

"As what?"

"Why must we define it? Can you not give me more time?"

"I'm afraid I do not understand, sir. I am an unmarried woman. I cannot stay under your roof unless I am employed by you in a legitimate capacity. Tell me you are not asking me to be your . . . to be your . . ."

"To be my what?" he said defensively.

"Do not make me say it."

"Say what?" He looked nearly angry now. "What is it that is so odious to you?"

"Dr. Taylor!"

"No, tell me. Be my what?"

She frowned, looked about her, then whispered tersely, "Mistress."

The man looked stricken. "Oh, Miss Lamb. Forgive me. No wonder you looked so ill. Certainly you know by now how highly I think of you. I would never make such a proposition to anyone, least of all to you."

She knew he meant it as a compliment; still, it hurt her feminine pride. She was not the sort of woman he would want for himself. At least, not anymore.

"Your friend Kendall had no such scruples, so I feared . . ." She let the mortifying words drift away.

"Yes, I am sorry for that. And I see why you might think—" He rose to his feet. "Miss Lamb, Charlotte, forgive me. I am handling this very poorly."

"No need to apologize. You are distraught. You still mourn your wife, and you have a young daughter to raise alone."

"Yes. But none of that changes the fact that I want you to stay. Anne and I would be adrift without you."

"As . . . ?"

He sighed. "I suppose I prefer the term nursery-governess. For now."

❧

Though she dreaded the possible repercussions, Charlotte decided she was obligated to write to apprise her cousin Katherine of her change in situation. She did not like the thought of placing Mrs. Dunweedy in an awkward predicament should Katherine write or call there. So she wrote a rather brief note to let her cousin know that she had taken a position as governess and was no longer residing in Crawley. She did not inform Katherine that she was in the employ of Daniel Taylor, for several reasons. She had seen the speculative gleam in Katherine's eyes when she had seen him arrive at her great-aunt's cottage. Though she might have imagined that. Worse, she had foolishly passed off Anne as her own daughter. If

Katherine were to inquire—or heaven forbid, take it upon herself to call upon the Taylor home—how would she explain that Anne was, after all, Dr. Taylor's daughter and not her own? Katherine's shock and censure would be too awful to imagine.

So Charlotte had omitted the name of her employer and his address on the first letter, only to be mortified when Daniel Taylor delivered a return letter from Katherine the following week.

"Lady Katherine asked me to give this to you when I saw you next," he said. "She came by the Manor today."

"She did?"

"Yes, she seemed certain I would know how to find you."

"Did you tell her . . . ?"

"I told her nothing. Knowing my shortcomings in the tact and discretion department, I thought it best."

"But she must know something, to ask you to deliver this to me."

"True. She did not seem surprised when I agreed to the task. I suppose she remembers that I had delivered that . . . other . . . parcel for her when last I was in Crawley."

Charlotte knew he was referring to the money he had long ago delivered to her on Katherine's behalf—most of which Charlotte had given to Margaret Dunweedy to cover her living expenses.

"She did mention she had stopped by the Manor on two other occasions with the intention of asking me to get some message to you, only to be told the first time that I was away on holiday, and on the second, that I had taken leave and no one knew when I would return. Must have been while we were on the coast."

She knew he did not like to recall that grim time. None of them did. Quietly, she thanked him for the letter and slipped up to her room before opening it. She held her breath as she read Katherine's curt reply.

> . . . I am trusting Dr. Taylor, who seems to know your where-abouts better than anyone, to get this to you. Goodness, Charlotte, why on earth did you not write to me sooner? I had grown con-

*cerned. I called round at Margaret Dunweedy's on Whitsunday,
but she could not—or would not—tell me where you had gone.
She said something about you being off on holiday, but of course,
given your situation, I did not believe it.*

Katherine went on to write several blunt questions.

*Governess? Could be worse, I suppose. In whose employ are
you? Do I know the family? I certainly hope they allow Anne to
stay with you. Where in the world am I to write you should the
need arise? Do not be foolish, Charlotte. Send me your directions
by return post.*

Did Katherine guess she had been with Dr. Taylor all along?
Was that why she was so certain he could contact her? But then,
why hadn't she acquired Dr. Taylor's home address—it would certainly not be difficult to discover, since he had a fairly well-known
medical practice. In any case, Charlotte knew she could not put her
cousin off any longer. And so, with no small trepidation, Charlotte
wrote back:

*I am in the employ of Dr. Daniel Taylor, with whom you
are some acquainted. I am content in my post, and the Taylors
are kind and generous employers, though Dr. Taylor is away a
great deal with his work as a physician. And, yes, Anne is here
and enjoying excellent health. I do hope the same is true for your
family. . . .*

After this, Charlotte and her cousin Katherine began exchang-
ing brief, occasional letters. Charlotte found it a mixed blessing
of pleasure and deprivation to read Katherine's chatty reports of
Edmund's growth and antics and "how dear Charles dotes on the
boy." Still, Katherine had not suggested paying a call, and Charlotte
had not offered.

And let this feeble body fail,
And let it faint or die;
My soul shall quit this mournful vale,
And soar to worlds on high.

—CHARLES WESLEY, *FUNERAL HYMNS*

CHAPTER 32

The Doddington churchyard was quiet in the late afternoon sun. White willow trees hung low in perpetual sorrow, paying homage to the departed. Field maples, whose leaves were just beginning to turn at the edges, shone orange-red. Blood-red too.

Charles Harris walked slowly through the churchyard, past the ancient yew tree and mottled graves whose inscriptions were worn unreadable, to a row of newer graves along the far wall.

Stepping over fallen leaves and yew needles, he stopped before a small grave. A child's grave. It was marked by a simple, handhewn cross. There was no inscription to give away the identity of the one buried there. But he knew who it was and mourned. Kneeling before the small marker, he reached out a trembling hand and gently touched the wooden surface, wondering again who had made it, who had placed it there, knowing such graves rarely had a marker of any kind.

Tears began flowing down his face, as they often did when in this place. When confronted with this loss.

"I shall never forget you," he whispered, then rose.

A door creaked open somewhere not far off. Charles turned sharply, startled. From around the corner of the church came Ben Higgins with a shovel over one shoulder and a bunch of chrysanthemums in his other hand.

The young man paused when he saw Charles Harris standing there.

"I'm sorry, sir," Ben Higgins said. "I didn't know anyone was about the place."

"Nor I. Did you put that cross there—on that grave?"

Charles pointed and the young man looked in the direction he indicated.

Ben nodded sheepishly. "That I did, sir. But on my own time."

"I am not reprimanding you. Merely asking."

Ben nodded again, standing there awkwardly, flowers drooping from his hand.

"Well, go about your work. Do not let me hinder you."

Still the young man hesitated.

Realization dawned, and Charles nodded toward the flowers. "Are those . . . for that grave?"

"Yes, sir," Ben admitted, still clearly uncomfortable.

Charles nodded, biting his lip. "You are a kind soul, Ben Higgins."

❧

Charlotte opened her eyes in the dim light and was surprised to see Dr. Taylor leaning over her bed. He held a candle lamp and wore his dressing gown. Startled, she instinctively pulled the blankets higher on her neck.

Daniel winced. "Forgive me. I had hoped not to wake you. I wanted to check on Anne."

Only then did she recall that little Anne was in bed beside her. "Oh. Of course." She remembered now. Anne's fitfulness, the burning skin—too hot to merely signal the emergence of more teeth.

"She cried so in her cradle," Charlotte whispered. "I finally brought her into bed with me."

Dr. Taylor pulled the baby blanket lower and tenderly felt Anne's forehead, cheeks, and chest.

"She is still warm. Too warm."

"I shall go fetch cloths . . ."

"Shh . . . stay as you are. Let Anne sleep. I shall fetch them."

He returned in a few minutes with a small ceramic basin and several face cloths. Gently he dipped one in the water, wrung it out, and laid it over his daughter's forehead.

"I'm afraid I shall get your sheets damp. I should have brought something to lay underneath her."

"I don't mind. I can do that if you like."

"Allow me. How many nights am I at the Manor and you must tend to her alone?"

"It is my responsibility."

"I'd say it is mine as well." He continued his ministrations, whispering more to sleeping Anne than to her, "What's the use of having a physician for a father if he cannot care for his own child?"

He untied his daughter's nightdress and laid another cool cloth across her chest. The little girl tossed her head, whining at the intrusion.

"If this doesn't work, we shall have to set her in a tub of cool water. She shall like that far less, I fear."

"What do you think is wrong?"

"Hard to tell at this point. Stomach is relaxed—no distension. Has she been pulling on her ears at all?"

"No."

"There is quite a lot of sickness going around. Hopefully nothing serious, just something that must run its course."

Charlotte watched him continue to touch a third cloth to his daughter's face and arms.

He looked at her suddenly. "How are you feeling, Miss Lamb? I do hope you are well."

"Yes, I think so. A bit tired, but that is to be expected."

He reached his hand toward her, then, seeing her surprise, hesitated, hand midair. "May I?"

"Oh, of course."

He gently touched her forehead, his fingers tracing down her cheeks before returning to the basin. "You feel fine. I never stopped to think Anne might have something contagious. Perhaps I ought to take her to my room."

"I do not think that necessary. And I am quite certain that if Anne has anything catching I should already have caught it in any case. Or perhaps even passed something along to her."

"I doubt that. You are so rarely out alone. When would you have occasion to come into contact with some ill person?"

"At the park or market, I suppose, though Anne is always with me. Or church. No, she goes with me there as well . . ."

"No wonder you are tired. It's amazing you are not exhausted."

"It is nothing compared to your days and nights. You so rarely sleep in your own bed, or at all for that matter."

"I usually find at least a few hours of sleep at the Manor. My own bed holds little appeal for me these days."

Charlotte could feel a blush warm her cheeks at the implication of his words. An awkward silence hung between them.

"Forgive me. I'm tired. I did not think. . . ."

"It is understandable," she whispered. "You miss Lizette, and no wonder."

"Perhaps. Still . . ." He shook his head.

Trying to lighten the tension, she said, "For my part, I rarely slept the night through at the Manor. All the noise and having to share my bed so."

"You—" he hesitated, eyes on his task—"object to sharing your bed?"

Her cheeks burned more furiously, and she was relieved he kept his gaze on his daughter.

"Not on principle, no. But before I moved to a private room, I slept with five others."

He looked up. "Five? Surely not as bad as all that?"

She smiled, "Two other women and three unborn children."

"Ah . . . crowded indeed." He returned her smile before again lowering his gaze. "At least here you have your own bed. Except when my daughter shares it with you. She has no idea how fortunate she is. . . ." He looked up, startled at his own words. "I mean, to have you care for her so. . . ."

She could not meet his eyes, nor stop the slight lift of her lips. "I know what you meant," she whispered.

❧

Walking with Anne through nearby Russell Square on a fine autumn afternoon, Charlotte almost collided with a young boy running past, pulling a Chinese-dragon kite behind him. "*Regardez-moi! Regardez-moi!*" the boy yelled in perfect French accent.

"*Très bien*, Jonathan."

Charlotte glanced over and saw an elegantly dressed young woman sitting on a park bench, her gaze fixed on the running boy.

Two finely dressed ladies walking together approached from the other direction. They, too, seemed to be watching the elegant young lady and her charge.

"I have contracted with an agency in Piccadilly to arrange for a French governess for Henry."

"I know you will be pleased. I would never go back to an English governess. They are so dour, and usually not as well educated as the French girls who come over."

Charlotte looked more closely at the elegant young woman. She had dark hair in a fashionable coil, and her dress seemed as fine as those the English ladies wore. As Charlotte passed by she looked at the woman's face more closely. She was reminded of Lizette Taylor.

❧

The next morning, as Charlotte sat at the kitchen table enjoying a cup of coffee and the quiet of a morning in which she had arisen before Anne, Marie dropped a section of newspaper before her.

"*Voilà*," the woman said, the paper slapping the tabletop. She had already turned back to the blood sausage and tomatoes she was frying before Charlotte could respond.

She looked at the paper. Folded in quarters as it was, she could not miss the bold print Marie wanted her to see.

French Governesses. Highest education.
Excellent references. Qualified to teach
literature, music, French, and etiquette.
Paris Agency, 212 George-court, Piccadilly

Charlotte knocked on Dr. Taylor's study door.

"Enter."

As she pushed the door open, he looked up from the thick book he was reading. "Hello, Miss Lamb."

"Have you a moment?"

"Of course." He closed his book, and as he did, she noticed it was a Bible.

Inclining her chin toward the volume, she asked, "Old Testament or New?"

He grinned. "Old. Someone once told me I should read it more often."

She smiled and then bit her lip, remembering her mission. "Dr. Taylor. It has come to my attention that many English families are hiring French governesses to care for their children."

He looked at her blankly.

"It seems the fashion now," Charlotte added.

"I care little for fashion, as you know."

"Yes. But I was thinking you might desire a French education for Anne."

He looked at her, clearly perplexed.

"She could grow up speaking both English and French," Charlotte continued. "Mrs. Taylor would have liked that."

He shrugged. "True. But you speak French."

"Very ill. My accent is far from authentic."

He stared at her, clearly unsure of her meaning.

"I understand there is an agency in Piccadilly for French governesses."

"Miss Lamb, I don't understand. Are you suggesting I replace you?"

"I am only thinking of Anne, what is best for her."

"What is best for her . . . or you?"

The implication stung.

He sighed. "I am only saying that if you wish to leave us, come out and say so."

"I do not wish to, but nor do I wish for you to feel obligated. You must think of Anne's future. Do what is in her best interests."

"I have. I believe *you*, Miss Lamb, are in Anne's best interests."

She lowered her head. "Thank you."

"But—"

She looked up. He was regarding her with an intensity that made her want to look away again. "There is another position I would offer you. If you were willing."

As she took in the longing, the trepidation, even the passion in his eyes, realization dawned. She had been a fool these last few months. He did want her, in every way a man wants a woman.

He rose and walked around his desk. Reaching past her, he shut the door quietly behind her. That done, he did not move away but stood close to her.

"You could become my wife."

For Anne's sake, for hers, for his own even, he would marry her. Even though he was not through mourning his wife. She ought to be relieved, she ought to be happy, but she was not. As the dread, the sudden irrational urge to turn and flee washed over her, she saw the reason clearly.

"What is it?" he asked, obviously not seeing the reaction he'd hoped for in her expression. "Have you no regard for me? Or is your father's approval still so important to you?"

"Of course not. I long ago gave up hope of winning Father's approval. As far as my regard for you, it is of the highest order."

"Then why do you hesitate? I realize it is too soon for me to make a proper offer, but I thought, in the circumstances—"

"You do me a great honor, Dr. Taylor. But—" And here she paused, taking a deep breath. "You see, as long as I can tell myself that I am in no suitable state to raise my son, then I can bear his absence. I can console myself with the wisdom that he is better off where he is, that I can barely provide for myself, let alone another. But if my situation were to suddenly change . . . if I were in a position where I could reasonably provide for him . . . and still . . . still I could not have him with me . . . that I could not bear. Do you understand? Does that make any sense at all?"

"I don't think . . . Are you saying that you must remain alone in order to bear his loss?"

She swallowed. "Yes."

"But would not the support of another make the loss more bearable? Or the possibility of another child someday?"

"I cannot think of that. He can never be replaced."

"Of course not. Still, the loneliness would be abated, would it not?"

"Perhaps. But I will always want him back. Always long for him."

"Perhaps there is something we can do. Your uncle is a solicitor. Perhaps—"

"No. I gave my word."

"Yes, but you were distraught, desperate. You thought you had no other choice, but now you do."

"Even if my circumstances change, I have not."

"But you have. You had just recently given birth. Changes occur in a mother's psyche, in her nerves, her mind, as I know all too well."

"But I knew what I was doing. Terrible as it was."

"Yes—then. But now—"

"I *gave* my word."

He opened his mouth as if to argue further, then closed it again. Frustration was evident in his stance and features.

"In any case, I could not do it to Edmund. How confusing and cruel it would be to rip his world, his very concept of himself, asunder. I cannot do it. I won't."

"But still . . . will you not reconsider . . . ?"

She looked at Daniel and felt tears filling her eyes. Slowly, she shook her head. "I cannot."

Was she making a terrible mistake? She remembered bemoaning the realization that she had let circumstances and the will of others set her course on many occasions. But now she had made a decision of her own, rejecting the only offer of marriage she had ever received, or was likely ever *to* receive. But she had made the only decision she could at present. She had chosen to stay her present course.

She could only hope fate would concur in the months and years ahead.

PART III

Surely 'tis better, when summer is over

To die when all fair things are fading away.

—THOMAS HAYNES BAYLY, *I'D BE A BUTTERFLY*

Monarch butterflies are not native to Great Britain,

but individuals are found in the south each year.

. . . blown there by strong winds.

—JOURNEY NORTH

The butterfly is at the center of numerous superstitions the world over,
and in some parts of Germany it is called "milk thief."

—ANATOLY LIBERMAN, *THE OXFORD ETYMOLOGIST*

CHAPTER 33

Two years had passed since Charlotte returned to London with the Taylors.

She walked slowly up the cobbled street toward the old Manor Home on Store Street. *Milkweed Manor*, she thought wryly of the moniker by which the place was infamously known. She could hardly believe it had been more than three years since she had first walked this way, carrying her child within her. This being autumn, the day was colder, and beneath Charlotte's wool cape, a bulge was mildly noticeable, much as it had been then.

She did not knock on the front door of the manor, but instead went around the back and let herself in the garden door. Gibbs looked up from her desk as she entered, then looked down at her rounded middle in question.

From beneath her cape, Charlotte retrieved her bulging reticule.

"Not safe to walk this neighborhood with one's purse dangling in plain sight," she said.

Gibbs gave her a rare grin. "It's good to see you, Miss Charlotte. Sally's expecting you."

"Charlotte. There you are," Sally called, coming down the corridor. "Right on time."

"Missy!" Anne Taylor shouted gleefully. The little girl, now nearly three years old, broke away from Sally's side to rush up and throw her arms around Charlotte's legs.

Charlotte bent to embrace her. "Goodness, I've only been gone an hour." She glanced up at her friend. "Thank you for watching her for me."

"I was pleased to."

"How is that new girl getting on?"

"The ginger-haired girl?"

"Yes—Meg."

"Oh, she has the way of it, she does. Nursin' her wee one like an old hand. Says you are a fine teacher."

"Good. I shall visit her tomorrow."

"And how did you fare shopping?" Sally asked.

"I found some fine new things for a girl who's growing far too fast."

"Let me see!" Anne cried.

"You shall, but let's wait until we get you home, all right?"

"Is Grandfather home?"

"I believe so."

"Then let us go, do!"

"In a moment . . ."

"That's all right, Miss Charlotte—you go on ahead. Thomas is off duty in a few minutes and we're to walk home together."

"How is Thomas?"

Sally smiled, her eyes glowing. "Wonderful, as you well know. Adores working for Dr. Taylor. Adores me." She sighed. "Never thought I'd have such a man for my husband—or any husband for that matter. And such a fine father he is to Dickie."

"I am so happy for you, Sally."

"As I always say, it's you I have to thank for it."

Charlotte shook her head. "I only introduced you."

"Still, I cannot help feeling guilty, Miss Charlotte. Should have been you before me. I cannot help thinking—"

"Go on, Sally. Do not worry about me."

Anne reached her hands high, wanting to be picked up.

"I am fine. We are fine." Charlotte held one of Anne's hands and put her other on top of the girl's head. "Is that not right, moppet?"

In the dining room of the Taylors' townhouse, Charlotte reigned over breakfast.

"Now, now, Mr. Taylor, sit down and have your porridge," Charlotte urged.

"Aw, Miss Charlotte," John Taylor said, "I haven't any appetite this morning."

"Breakfast is important, as you well know, being one of the most renowned surgeons in London. . . ."

"That was a long time ago."

"And becoming so again, to hear Mrs. Krebs tell it. Now, please sit with us and eat. We'd like that, Anne, would we not?"

"Yes, Grandfather. Eat! Eat!"

"Oh, very well. I cannot disappoint two such lovely girls."

Just as the three of them sat down to porridge and tea, Daniel Taylor walked in, rumpled and red-eyed from a long night of duty at the Manor Home.

"Good morning, Dr. Taylor," Charlotte said. "Did you have a pleasant evening?"

"Not at all."

"I am sorry to hear it."

"Finances at the Manor improving any?" his father asked.

"The pressure has let up some, yes."

"Capital!"

"I should not go that far."

"Here. Sit down." Charlotte spooned out another bowl of porridge. "Have some breakfast."

Dr. Taylor sat down with a grateful smile.

"Are you working in the foundling ward today, Father?"

"Yes. And Mrs. Moorling has asked me to look in on one of the new patients as well. Poor thing is frightened to death of Dr. Preston."

Shaking his head, Daniel Taylor shared a knowing look with Charlotte. Then he turned to his daughter. "And what will you two do today?" he asked, spooning treacle into his bowl.

"We're going to the *moo-zeeum*."

He chuckled. "How marvelous."

"I know she is too young to enjoy it," Charlotte explained. "But I have been longing to see the Egyptian exhibit."

"I hear it is impressive indeed."

"And we're to have cherry ices after. Do come with us, Papa!"

He smiled at his daughter's enthusiasm. "Not this time, I'm afraid. I did not manage much sleep last night. I am in great need of a nap before I see patients this afternoon."

"Missy says naps are good for you."

He smiled at Charlotte over Anne's head. "She is quite right."

❧

One afternoon in late September, Charlotte was playing backgammon with John Taylor during Anne's nap, when Marie handed her a letter from the day's post. From the return address, she saw it was from her cousin Katherine. She opened the letter and read it slowly. Then she glanced up and saw John Taylor looking at her with concern in his hound-dog eyes.

"Not bad news, I hope?"

"No. An invitation, actually."

"To a hanging?"

"No." She sighed. "To a birthday party."

"Well, then, that's cause for a smile, my dear, not a frown. Where is the party to be?"

"Manchester Square." What had prompted this sudden inclusion? Why had Charles not convinced Katherine to exclude her from the invitation list? Did he think that would rouse suspicion, after all this time? He certainly could not want her to attend.

"Worried about Anne, are you?" John Taylor asked. "Do not be. I shall watch over her myself."

"You are very kind."

What would it be like to see Edmund after all this time? Could she go and satisfy herself with a glimpse or two, or would the seeing only reignite the burning desire for more contact with him? Perhaps it was better to stay away.

"You have not had any entertainment in far too long, Miss Charlotte. You go and enjoy yourself. I shall pay for the hansom myself. I insist upon it." He beamed at her, and she felt she had little choice but to agree.

"When is the party to be?" he asked.

She looked again at the invitation. The date read *Friday the 7th.*

"On Saturday," she answered.

§

When Charlotte arrived, Katherine was reclining on the settee, one hand on her forehead, the other on her rounded abdomen. She glanced over at her guest before again closing her eyes.

"The party was yesterday, Charlotte," she said dully.

"Yes, I know."

"Forgive me for not standing to greet you. I am perfectly exhausted. I overdid yesterday—Charles is quite put out with me for it. This time is worse than the last. I suppose that means it is a girl. How was your lying-in with Anne?"

"Actually, Anne is not—"

"I am sorry you could not attend the party, Charlotte," Katherine interrupted. "What a to-do it was. Edmund was quite beside himself. Too many presents and too much cake. Went to bed with a tummy ache. And he's to have a pony when we return to Fawn-well besides."

"How exciting."

"Mrs. Harris came to town for the party, but she looked very ill indeed. What a wretched hat she wore. Oh, and William was here with his new wife—Amanda or Althea or something. I forget. Had you heard he married? I had thought he would marry you or your sister, and here neither one of you has wed. I must say Bea looked positively grim-faced upon seeing the two of them here together."

"Bea was here?"

"Yes. I suppose I hoped to throw the two of you together—force a reconciliation. Is that why you did not come—had you gotten word Bea planned to attend? I suppose your Aunt Tilney let it slip. . . ."

"I had not heard, actually."

Katherine rang a little bell beside her. "Celia!" she called. "Do bring me some ice, would you?" Then to Charlotte she explained, "It seems to help my headaches."

"Is . . . Edmund here?" Charlotte asked, palms damp. "I have a gift I hoped to give him."

"Oh . . ." Katherine waved her hand vaguely in the air before returning it to her forehead. "He's about the place somewhere. Do be a dear and find him, will you? My physician says I should keep off my feet as much as possible."

"Of course. I hope you feel better soon."

Charlotte walked out of the sitting room just as a maid was rushing up the stairs with an ice bucket.

"Have you seen Edmund?" she asked the girl.

"No, ma'am. But you might try the nursery upstairs."

"Thank you."

Charlotte trotted up the stairs to the third floor. As she looked in both directions, trying to decide which corridor to try first, she saw a red ball roll from an open doorway to her right.

The ball came to a stop beside a Greek statue, and Charlotte stooped to pick it up.

A little boy stepped into the corridor, then hesitated, clearly surprised to see her there.

"Hello," she said, suddenly breathless. "Could this be what you are looking for?" She held out the ball with a smile.

"Yes, thank you." He took the ball, then looked up at her with his father's brown eyes framed by a tousle of dark curly hair so like her own.

"You are very welcome, Edmund."

He cocked his head to one side. "Who are you?"

"I am your . . . your mother's cousin Charlotte."

"Cousin Charlotte?"

"Yes. And you are the birthday boy." She pulled a small wrapped rectangle from her reticule. "I have a gift for you."

"I know what that is—it's a book."

"Yes, and you probably already have it."

She stooped down, sitting on her heels, so that she was at eye level with him as he ripped open the paper and looked at the cover.

"Yes." He shrugged. "I do have it."

"Well, it is such a good book, it won't hurt to have another."

He looked up at her, little brows crinkling up—so like his father. "Why are you sad?"

"I don't know. I suppose it is because I cannot believe you are already three years old. It is silly, really. Birthdays are to be happy times, and you are a very happy boy, are you not?"

Again he shrugged. "Yes."

"I am so glad."

He lifted the book. "Read to me?" he asked.

Her heart fisted hard within her, and she bit her lip to hold back bittersweet tears. She opened her mouth to answer when a woman's voice called down the corridor, "Come now, master Edmund, your father will be home any moment." A prim-faced young woman in grey dress appeared, shaking out a miniature frock coat before her. "Time to dress."

Charlotte stood and the woman paused.

"Oh, pardon me I did not know Edmund had a guest."

"That's all right. I was just leaving."

The woman passed by them and into Edmund's room.

She felt Edmund tug at her sleeve. "Father is taking me to the circus."

"How nice."

"But you can read to me first."

She smiled at him. "I would love nothing more, but I am afraid I must take my leave."

"Oh. Then Papa shall read it. It's his favorite."

"Yes, I know," Charlotte said softly. She reached a tentative hand toward him and touched his shoulder briefly. "Happy birthday, dear Edmund."

Charlotte could not sleep. She turned over yet again. Her stomach growled. She should have eaten more at supper. Giving up, she reached for her dressing gown at the foot of her bed but could not find it. She must have kicked it to the floor with all her tossing and turning. Oh well. She wouldn't light a candle to find it and risk waking Anne. Besides, the house was warm and there was no one to see her at this time of night.

She tiptoed out of her room in her nightdress. In the corridor, she could hear John Taylor's soft snore as she passed his room. She picked up the candle lamp on the landing table and used it to guide her down the many stairs and into the kitchen. There, she set the lamp down and opened the icebox. She retrieved the bottle of milk and set about lighting a fire in the stove and pouring some milk into a pan to warm. Then she selected an apple from the vegetable bin. Taking it to the work table, she slid a sharp knife from its slot and set to work slicing off a few wedges of fruit.

The door opened behind her and Charlotte started. The knife sliced into her left index finger. She gave a little cry, more from fright than pain. She half-turned from the table, surprised and relieved to see Dr. Taylor standing there, medical bag in hand.

"You frightened me."

"Forgive me. I did not expect to find anyone up."

Charlotte became aware of throbbing in her finger. She put it to her mouth, tasting blood.

"I've cut myself."

"How badly?"

She stepped closer to the candle lamp and he did as well. Her relief that the late-night intruder was Dr. Taylor now faded as she remembered she wore nothing but a thin nightdress.

"Let me see it."

"I am sure it is nothing."

He took her left hand in his, her palm forward. With his free hand, he gently examined her index finger. Her heart pounded in time with its throbbing.

"Here, let's clean that." From his bag, he deftly retrieved a bottle of antiseptic. He held her hand over the basin, released her only long enough to open the bottle, then poured antiseptic over the wound. The stuff stung, and she wrinkled her nose at its smell.

"Let me wrap that for you," he said quietly.

He retrieved a small rolled bandage from his bag and then stood again before her. He guided her hand closer to the light and leaned near. She realized she was breathing in shallow, rapid breaths as he skillfully and gently wound the bandage around her finger and secured it. Still, the process seemed to take quite a long time, as he reexamined his work, still holding her hand in one of his. She hoped he did not guess how affected she was by his nearness.

Without releasing her hand, he looked up from her finger to her face. His eyes shone with intensity, his pupils large in the dim light.

Did she alone feel this tension, this delicious, terrifying ache?

To dispel it, she said shakily, "Who is minding the Manor?"

"Thomas is filling in. Said I looked dead on my feet."

She smiled and said awkwardly, "You do not . . . look so to me."

His eyes roamed over her features. "Nor you."

She swallowed and said needlessly, "I could not sleep."

He looked down at her hand again, as though just realizing he still held it.

"Will the patient live?" she asked lightly.

He did not smile. Instead he turned her hand over and lifted it to his cheek. He pressed his lips to the back of her hand and looked into her eyes. Charlotte could hardly breathe.

Without warning the kitchen door again opened, and they both turned to see John Taylor standing there, candlestick in hand. Charlotte took a sheepish step away from Daniel.

John Taylor looked from one to the other, a speculative gleam in his eyes. "I thought I smelled something burning," he said.

Charlotte turned. The milk was boiling out onto the stove.

Right after emergence from its chrysalis,
the Monarch is extremely vulnerable to predators
because it is not yet able to fly.

—Journey North

Chapter 34

At the breakfast table one morning in November, Charlotte announced to Dr. Taylor and his father, "Anne and I are planning quite the celebration tonight, and you are both invited."

"What is the occasion?" Dr. Taylor asked.

"Your birthday, silly!" Anne laughed.

"Today *is* your birthday, is it not?" Charlotte asked tentatively.

"Well, I guess it is. I had quite forgotten."

"I hope neither of you will have to work late tonight."

"I'm going to help make a cake!" Anne announced proudly. "Just like the one Missy made for my birthday!"

"How nice. I shall look forward to it."

"As will I," John Taylor said. "Though I'm afraid I haven't a gift for you, my boy. Unless you'd like a new ear horn or scalpel?" He winked.

"Do not trouble yourself, Father. You and I have gotten out of the habit of celebrating birthdays."

John Taylor folded his napkin and stood. "Well, I'm off. I promised Mrs. Krebs I'd be in early this morning."

His son turned his head to watch him leave. "If I did not know better, I would think he was taken with her." He looked at Charlotte and smiled self-consciously. "And I *would* recognize the symptoms."

Charlotte bit back a smile. "Do finish your breakfast, Anne, so we can begin our preparations."

Porridge dripped off Anne's chin as she said eagerly, "We are to wear our new gowns, and you must wear your green coat, Papa."

"Try not to speak with your mouth full, dear," Charlotte admonished.

Daniel bowed his head toward his daughter. "As my lady wishes."

"Do you not think Papa most handsome when he wears his green coat?"

Charlotte smiled, clearly embarrassed. "I . . . yes, quite handsome."

"Well, then"—he held her gaze—"your wish is my command."

How differently it all might have gone had he not stopped by the club on his way home. He had left the Manor sufficiently early, leaving Thomas and his father on duty, and only dropped by in hopes of finding Preston, who had not shown up to relieve them as scheduled. His father had insisted Daniel go home and not miss his own birthday celebration. He would stay until Preston arrived. Not seeing his colleague in the club, Daniel turned to leave. That's when he saw Lester Dawes. He might not have stopped at all, had his old acquaintance not looked so miserable, hands holding up his head, several empty tumblers before him.

"Dawes?"

The man looked up, bleary-eyed and desolate. "Hello, Taylor."

"What's wrong, man? You look dreadful."

"You haven't heard?"

Daniel shook his head.

"Lost a patient."

"I am sorry. I know how that feels."

"It's a double blow. I hate to be mercenary, but this will be death to my practice as well. It is always a gamble, having prominent patients."

"May I ask who?"

His answer hit Daniel like a fist. The sensation a sickening combination of true grief and pity along with several self-centered emotions far less noble.

"I am sorry," Daniel mumbled again, and ducked out of the room before the man could respond.

When he arrived home, Charlotte was there to greet him. "Happy birthday," she said shyly, adding tentatively, "Daniel."

She was dressed in a lovely rose-colored gown with a flattering, feminine neckline. Her hair was arranged in a pretty crown of curls, several framing her face, now flushed and expectant. He did not miss the intentional use of his Christian name, her attention to her appearance, nor the blush in her cheeks. No, he had not misread the situation. Her feelings had changed and she wanted him to know it. He should be relieved and pleased, but he felt a nauseating ball of dread in his stomach instead. Why did such a thing have to happen now? When she was finally ready to receive his affection? It seemed to Daniel a cruel and ironic twist of fate.

"You look beautiful," he said, an empty sadness stealing over him.

She smiled at his words, but her smile quickly faltered. "Is something wrong?"

He opened his mouth to answer. Must he tell her? Now? Could he not wait until . . . until there was an understanding between them?

"Happy birthday, Papa!" Anne shouted, running out to meet him, throwing her arms around his legs. "Doesn't Missy look like a princess?"

"Yes. She does. As do you." He smiled at his daughter, touching her fancy, curled hair and taking in her bright blue frock. "Your new gown is almost as lovely as you are."

Anne giggled and pulled his hand, urging him to follow her into the dining room. "I helped make the cake, but I fear the icing is rather a mess."

Daniel breathed a silent sigh. *A mess indeed.*

While Anne knelt on a chair at the dining room table, happily poking little sugar petals onto the icing of the cake, Charlotte joined Daniel in the sitting room. "Daniel, are you sure nothing is amiss? I hope I have not offended you."

"Offended me, how?"

"Well, by my presumption, my familiarity in arranging this birthday celebration. If I have overstepped—"

"I am the opposite of offended, Charlotte. I am pleased by your . . . familiarity, as you say. In my mind, you are part of this family already."

Even with her head bowed, he could see the pleasure in her pink cheeks and concealed smile.

"Charlotte," he said, suddenly intense, "my feelings for you, my intentions, remain unchanged."

Her head rose and she looked at him shyly, expectantly. How lovely she was, how fondly was she regarding him. Would it be so wrong to postpone the news that would wipe that look from her face forever?

"If your feelings," he added more gently, "were no longer hindered . . ."

"They are no longer hindered, Daniel," she whispered.

"Then I would ask you . . . what I have longed to ask you . . ."

She smiled warmly, her body leaning toward him ever so slightly. What agony this was. To be so close to her, to realize she was ready to accept him. But only because she remained in sweet ignorance.

He winced, then said, "But I cannot."

Her smile fell. "What has happened? Have I done something to . . . ?"

"You have done nothing. Nothing but make us all completely devoted to you. You have not only become beloved mother to my daughter, but beloved daughter to my father as well."

"But you do not share their . . . affliction?"

"Oh, I am indeed afflicted, Charlotte. But..."

"But?"

"I am afraid I have dreadful news. I thought to wait until after . . ." He waved his hand in direction of the dining room but guessed they both knew he included much more than the festivities in his statement. "But I find in good conscience that I cannot keep it from you a moment longer."

"What is it?"

"Your cousin Katherine is dead."

Charlotte gasped.

"She died in childbirth, her infant with her."

Charlotte sat, stunned, her hand covering her mouth.

After a few silent moments, Daniel rose. Charlotte still sat there, unmoving. She did not ask him to stay, nor assure him the news had no bearing. He knew too well that it had changed everything.

※

Although society did not expect women to attend funerals, Charlotte knew Katherine would expect her to be there. So, dressed in black, her face concealed behind a veiled hat and umbrella, Charlotte walked slowly past ranks of rain-speckled headstones, toward her cousin's gravesite. She watched from a distance as four black horses with black feathers on their heads brought the hearse into the churchyard, followed by a long procession of mourners. Six strapping men, William Bentley among them, carried the lacquered coffin to its final resting place. Charlotte slowly joined the rear of the congregation. In front of her, the mourners wore black—the few other women in black gowns and mantles and swarms of men bearing black armbands and gloves.

There were so many people in attendance that she barely caught a glimpse of Charles through the crowd and didn't see Edmund at all. The church bells tolled their sharp death knell, and with each clang, Charlotte felt her heart bang against her ribs. *Poor lamb*, she thought, the epitaph seeming to fit not only Edmund but Charles, and even Katherine as well. Her cousin wouldn't be there to nurture the little boy she loved, nor see him grow to manhood. And being so young, how much would Edmund even remember of the woman he'd called mother—a year from now? Five years hence? Charlotte's mother-heart grieved for Katherine's loss as well as that of Charles and Edmund.

The same priest who'd conducted Katherine's churching only a few years ago now officiated over her funeral. From her place in the back, Charlotte could not make out much of anything he said. A talented soprano sang a hymn so beautiful and haunting that the mourners wept more under its power than the cleric's words preceding it.

> *Why do we mourn departing friends?*
> *Or shake at death's alarms?*
> *'Tis but the voice that Jesus sends,*
> *To call them to His arms. . . .*

Charlotte wept as well.

She had not planned to go to Katherine's home in Manchester Square with the honored gentry, close friends, and family members who were traditionally invited to do so after the ceremony, to partake of a cold supper and a "cheerful glass." But she felt oddly compelled to do so. She was family, after all, a close cousin to Katherine. Tradition would expect her to wear black mourning clothes for six weeks for a first cousin; would it not expect her to pay her respects in person as well? Frankly, she was surprised she had the courage to ring the bell.

She certainly had no intention of approaching Charles. In fact her hands shook at the thought of it. She did not want him to think she was "waiting in the wings" nor expecting anything from him. She merely felt it was her duty, and yes, her right, to attend, if only for a few moments. Knowing her cousin as she had, she knew Katherine would be affronted beyond words if Charlotte did not at least make an appearance.

So with trembling hands she handed the butler her wrap and umbrella but kept on her veiled hat and followed the man up the stairs. Still holding her things, he said apologetically, "I'm afraid we've an overflow of coats, m'um. I shall have to put your things there, behind that screen, with the others. If you need help finding them again upon departure, I shall endeavor to aid you in your search."

"Thank you."

The drawing room was already filled with people huddled in small groups, some talking soberly and others less so, clearly enjoying the promised glass of cheer. Charlotte sat in a row of chairs near the door, content to observe the gathering. She did not see Charles or Edmund. They were perhaps in the adjoining sitting room. Nor did she see her father, which she found puzzling. She wondered if he was ill—could not imagine another reason why he would not attend. She recognized several people, but no one it seemed had recognized her. She breathed a sigh of relief.

Relaxing a bit, she allowed her head to swivel as she surveyed the remainder of the large room. Her heart pounded. There was her sister, Bea, holding Charles' arm as the two walked into the room. And there, his head barely visible through the assembled throng, was Edmund. Several mourners clustered around Charles as he entered, clearly offering condolences. Even from this distance, Charlotte could see there was a terrible pall over his features.

Bea leaned close to Edmund, her arm resting across his shoulders as she whispered some confidence. Her sister comforting *her* son? For some reason the idea of it—the reality of it—made her feel queasy. Edmund ran off suddenly, disappearing through the crowd, and Bea returned her attentions to Charles.

Charlotte realized she could walk right up to Charles and say a few kind words. If she could manage to ignore her sister's inevitable icy glare, she might even accomplish the feat with her emotions under rein. She sighed. Even if Bea were not standing guard at Charles' side, Charlotte knew she would not have the courage.

She rose from her chair and turned to leave. As she stepped briskly into the passage, she nearly ran right into Edmund. He looked at her, head cocked to one side.

"You're Cousin Charlotte."

She lifted her veil off her face. "That's right. What a wonderful memory you have."

"My mother died," he said somberly.

She nodded. "Yes, I know. I am very sorry."

"That's what everybody says."

Charlotte lowered herself to his eye level, sitting on her heels. "But even though she is gone, you are not alone."

"I know. I still have Father."

"Yes, and there are others, too, who love you."

"Do you mean Bea?"

Charlotte swallowed. "Bea?"

He shrugged and said matter-of-factly, "Mummy lives in heaven now."

"That's right. What a smart little boy you are."

"I am not little."

"All right, Edmund. You are very big. And far too wise."

"Haven't you any children?"

"I . . . not at present, no."

"You're crying."

"Am I?"

"Father cries sometimes. I do too."

"Of course you do."

She smiled at the boy through her tears and allowed herself to reach out and briefly touch his head. Then she retrieved her hand and stepped back.

She watched as Edmund walked through the doorway she had just exited—then realized he was heading directly toward his father and Bea. Charlotte quickly stepped behind the door. Out of sight but not out of earshot.

"Cousin Charlotte is here, Father," she heard Edmund say.

"Charlotte? Where?"

"Oh . . . I don't see her anymore."

"What did she say to you?" Charles asked.

She could not make out Edmund's reply.

Charlotte risked a glance back into the room and saw Charles bent over Edmund, his hand lying on his son's head, much as hers had done. When she saw Charles look abruptly in her direction, she instinctively ducked from view. Moving quickly to the temporary "coatroom" to retrieve her wrap, she stepped behind the oriental screen flanked by potted palms that served to conceal the untidy pile of coats from view. It concealed her as well.

Hearing footsteps nearby, she peeked from between the slats in the screen. From her hiding place, she watched Charles stride quickly into the passage and look in both directions. How foolish she felt behind the screen. Should she step out and offer her condolences?

But then Beatrice appeared beside him and took his arm. "Do not trouble yourself, Charles. I suppose she had the right to come and pay her respects, but I do wish she might have stayed away and not sullied the day for you. At least she had the decency to be unobtrusive. Though I wonder what she was thinking, speaking to Edmund?"

Charles stood still, alert without moving, as though trying to hear her . . . to sense her presence. Was he angry she had come?

Threatened that she would speak to his son? Afraid or furious she would dare make herself known to Edmund, and at such a vulnerable time?

I told him nothing, she thought defensively.

"Come, Charles. Come back in. There is no harm done. Forget about her."

He turned and gave Bea a brief smile, patting her hand, which was placed on his arm. "I am sure you are right. How good you are to us."

Yes, Charlotte thought. *Mr. Harris seems to have no problem following Bea's advice. No doubt I am long forgotten.*

She wondered if her sister would finally have what she'd always wanted. The thought depressed her. *I would not have chosen you to mother my son, but I have lost my say in the matter. You will do your best by him, I know—for Charles' sake, if nothing else. What would you say if you knew? Will Charles tell you, if he marries you? If he never told Katherine, I doubt he will. Probably best that way. You were never especially fond of me.*

Waiting a moment more, Charlotte stepped away from the screen and toward the stairs—just as William Bentley reached the landing.

"Miss Lamb!"

"Mr. Bentley," she answered, heart pounding dully. She wished she had remembered to reposition her veil.

"I am surprised to see you," he said with a knowing smile.

"Why should you be? Katherine was my cousin, as you must recall."

"Yes. And my uncle's wife." He cleared his throat. "You are here alone?"

"I am."

"Beatrice did not come?"

"She is inside. With your uncle."

"Ah, offering comfort. How good of her. I would have thought you—"

"I came only to pay my respects, Mr. Bentley. And now if you will excuse me." She quickly began to descend the stairs.

"Miss Lamb, forgive me. I did not mean . . ."

She turned back to face him. "Oh yes, Mr. Bentley. You most certainly did." With that, she smiled as knowingly as he had, she hoped, and walked sprightly away.

Charles watched his nephew stride toward him, eyes bright with some new trouble.

"I was surprised to see Charlotte Lamb here."

"You saw her?"

"Yes, she was leaving as I came in. First in line to offer comfort, I suppose?"

"William. I am tired of your innuendo and disrespect. Miss Lamb—Charlotte—did not even speak to me. I did not even know she had been here until Edmund mentioned it."

"Edmund knows her?"

"Apparently Katherine and Charlotte kept in contact over the last few years."

"I did not realize. And certainly I meant no disrespect to anyone. Especially at such a time. But do be warned, Uncle. The spinsters and widows are already lining up, ready to offer the grieving widower solace and care for his poor orphaned son."

"Edmund isn't an orphan."

"Motherless, then."

"You are a fool, William."

"Mr. Bentley." Beatrice came and stood at Charles' side, making her familiarity evident by her proximity and proprietary air. "How kind of you to come."

He bowed stiffly. "Beatrice . . . Miss Lamb. How pleasant to see you again."

"And what are you two gentlemen discussing?"

"Your sister, actually," his nephew said, clearly relishing her disapproval.

"Really."

"Yes, I have just seen her, and I must confess, I have never seen her looking lovelier. A bit tired perhaps—black doesn't really suit her. But still, as handsome as ever."

"Yes, well," Bea said briskly. "I must check on Edmund. Poor dear is exhausted with grief and attention."

She dipped her chin. "Mr. Bentley. Charles."

Both men bowed briefly as she walked away.

"My, my. That did not take long."

"William, please. Bea is like family."

"Or very much wished to be."

"Do shut up, William."

Grant us the pow'r of quick'ning grace,
To fit our souls to fly;
Then, when we drop this dying flesh,
We'll rise above the sky.

—ISAAC WATTS, *A FUNERAL THOUGHT*

CHAPTER 35

Months passed as Charles and Edmund grieved. They spent the Christmas holidays at Fawnwell before returning to London to begin the depressing task of going through Katherine's things and disposing of all but the most meaningful mementos. When they next visited Fawnwell in the spring, Charles brought several trunks of clothing to donate to Doddington Church for distribution to the poor. Leaving Edmund in the care of the boy's grandmother, Charles and his man drove over to the churchyard in a horse-drawn wagon.

Beatrice met him in the south porch of the church and in her sober and industrious fashion, helped direct the unloading. "This is very kind of you, Charles. I shall see to it that every piece is put to good use."

While his driver went back to the wagon for another load, Charles set a second trunk on top of the first. Bea opened the lid and pulled out several gowns—one with an expandable laced-vent bodice, and two others with billowing waistlines.

"These must be the gowns Katherine wore during her confinement."

"Yes, well . . . perhaps I will leave you to it."

"Of course, Charles. This is hard on you. Come to the vicarage for tea. I can do this later. Father, I know, will want to see you."

"Very well. Thank you."

He paused to direct his man to finish the unloading, then followed her across the churchyard and into the vicarage. There was no sign of Gareth Lamb. "I do not know where he has gotten to. I shall have Tibbets ask him to join us when he arrives."

They took chairs in the drawing room and Bea ordered tea. While they waited, Bea mused, "A whole trunk of gowns suitable for confinement. Perhaps I shall donate them to one of the lying-in hospitals." She added sardonically, "In honor of Charlotte."

"Beatrice . . ."

Tibbets entered with a tray, and when she had left again, Beatrice poured tea for the both of them. "I certainly hope she has not put in another appearance since the funeral, Charles."

"No, she has not."

"Thank goodness. I hate to think of her becoming a nuisance to you and Edmund, especially during your mourning period."

"Charlotte is not a nuisance, Beatrice." He hesitated, then turned to her, his face set. "What has your sister done to you to earn such bitter contempt?"

"I should think that obvious. She . . . she ruined my chances when she ruined herself."

"Come, come, Bea, you despised her long before that."

Beatrice shrugged her thin shoulders.

"One might almost assume you jealous of Charlotte."

"Jealous? Hardly."

"But of what?" Charles wondered aloud, as if he had not heard. "You are, classically speaking, more beautiful. You held your father's approval whereas Charlotte did not. William favored you, though that lad's opinion is worth less than I'd imagined. What is it you begrudge her?"

Bea's chin quivered.

"What did she have that you did not?"

Bea stared down at her hands, then lifted her gaze. "Your admiration."

He took a deep breath. "Beatrice." He sighed. "You have long held me in too high of a regard. And your sister in one too low."

"I do not think my opinion unjust. She has never named a villain in her fall. Can we not surmise his low status? We know he could not be a gentleman."

"Do we indeed? Did it never cross your mind that she might have another reason for withholding his name?"

"No."

"Beatrice. I know you foster some idea of a future alliance between the two of us."

She gasped. "I have never said—"

"Come, come. I tire of this game playing. You would have no objections to an alliance with me—is that not so?"

"I suppose, in theory, I would have no objections."

"Well, I do. And you should as well."

"What do you mean?"

"You despise Charlotte. But I admire her. You condemn the man responsible. But I am he."

"What?"

"Yes, Beatrice. I am that man. And Charlotte did not reveal my part in her fall because I had already chosen to marry Katherine. Needed to marry Katherine to keep Fawnwell afloat."

"You . . . and Charlotte . . . ?" Bea sputtered.

"Yes. And I could never join myself with a woman who despises someone I hold so dear. Someone *she* should hold dear as well." He sighed again and sat back. "Nor do I expect you will ever want to see me again now that you know."

Tears filled Beatrice's eyes. She squeezed them shut and the tears streamed down her pale cheeks. "Go," she said miserably.

It was the first time in twenty years he had seen her cry.

When Charles made his exit from the drawing room a few moments later, the vicar was sitting on the bench in the entry hall.

"So it was you all along," Gareth Lamb said flatly. "Yet you did nothing to help her."

Charles paused, realizing all that Charlotte's father had overheard. He took a deep breath, resigned. "Yes. I did nothing then. You and I have that in common. But now I can. And I will."

"Do not tell me you will marry my daughter in some foolhardy attempt to make restitution for past sins?"

Charles exhaled a dry puff of breath. "Is that not exactly what we are supposed to do—*Reverend*?"

※

When Charles returned with his young son to their London townhouse, he greeted the servants as politely as his exhaustion would allow and instructed the governess to put Edmund to bed straightaway. Weary from the journey and the encounters preceding it, Charles stepped toward the library, intending only to take a cursory look through the post to make sure nothing required his immediate attention before taking himself to bed. Passing by the sitting room doors, he was surprised to see his nephew William sprawled on the sofa, cravat askew and tumbler in hand. The young man did not bother to stand when Charles entered the room.

"William? I did not expect to find you here."

"That sweet housemaid of yours let me in. Said I could wait for you."

"I hope you've not been waiting long."

William shrugged. "Two days." He sipped from his glass.

"What do you want?"

"To help myself to your port, as you see. As well as a little holiday from the missus. I haven't the luxury of two dwellings as you do."

Charles bit back his annoyance. "I see."

"And how fares Fawnwell? I suppose you saw Beatrice Lamb?"

"I did."

"As cold and serious and delicious as always, I suppose?"

Charles sighed in frustration. "I do not understand you, William. You had your chance with her and gave it up."

"Yes. A pity. She is one of those rare women who is more attractive stern than smiling. Have you noticed that?"

Charles walked back to the doors and shut them carefully before turning again to face him. "Did you never have serious intentions toward Miss Lamb?" he demanded.

"Oh yes. I seriously intended to preempt your intentions."

"What do you mean?"

"I should think that evident. You know I had always counted on being your heir—back when I still thought you had something to inherit, that is." William reached for the bottle on the side table and refilled his glass. "I had believed you a confirmed bachelor, which was jolly good for me. But then I heard you were showing a great deal of interest in one of the vicar's daughters. Thus, I decided to deduce which of them it was and to win the lady—and keep the inheritance—for myself." He raised his glass in mock toast.

"Of all the presumptuous—"

"Yes, yes." He waved away Charles' censor with a casual flip of his free hand. "And I deduced it was young Charlotte you admired within ten minutes of stepping foot inside the vicarage."

Charles stared at him, silent anger building in his chest.

"You *did* plan to marry Charlotte Lamb, did you not?" William asked.

Charles made no answer.

"While I found Charlotte charming, with her lovely smile and generous . . . nature, I admit it was Beatrice I preferred. So prim. So tightly wound I was sure every moment she must come unsprung." He sighed wistfully. "How I miss those afternoons in Doddington, listening to beautiful Bea play. But of course, all that was before Fawnwell burned and I came to realize the dire straights you were in. Still, I must admit your marriage to Lady Katherine took us all by surprise. One of the Miss Lambs was especially devastated, as I am sure you know."

Charles clenched his fists at his sides.

"And after that I had no choice but to change course and begin pursuing a wealthy wife."

"But you still called on Bea after that, letting the poor girl think—"

"I deluded myself, hoping Lady Katherine might not be spring chicken enough to lay the golden egg. I was wrong—drunk on wishful thinking, I suppose."

"You're drunk now."

"Quite tolerably, yes. It's the only time I am this honest."

"So, when our son . . . when Edmund was born, you had no use for Bea anymore."

"Precisely. And regret it though I did, I would regret more being poor." He sighed theatrically. "Marrying the dreadfully cheerful Amanda Litchfield with her five hundred a year is a burden I must bear up under somehow. You know all about marrying for money, do you not, Uncle?"

❦

On a lovely summer day, Charlotte and Anne were sitting on a blanket in the small garden behind the London townhouse when Dr. Taylor came upon them.

"There you are," he said.

"We are having a picnic, as you can see," Charlotte explained.

A basket and Anne's miniature tea set were spread out neatly on the blanket.

"A picnic in the garden. How lovely. Might I join you?"

"Of course, Papa," Anne said. "But I shall have to fetch another cup. Constance is using the pink one, and Missy and I the other two."

"I do not believe Constance and I have been introduced," Daniel said, nodding toward the porcelain doll seated before the pink cup and saucer.

"Of course you have, Papa." The three-and-a-half-year-old sounded mildly peevish. "You see her every night when you tuck me in."

"Forgive me. My mistake."

Anne jumped to her feet. "I shan't be long. But do not blame me if the tea is cold, Papa. You did not tell me you would be joining us today."

"Do not hurry on my account, sweetheart. I am quite fond of cold tea." He sat down on the blanket and folded his long legs, knocking over the tiny sugar bowl as he did.

Charlotte righted it again and confided quietly, "The sugar is make-believe but the tea is quite real."

He grinned. "Then I shall endeavor to be more careful." He looked about him. "Such a small bit of earth we have here. Barely worth calling a garden."

"How fortunate, then, to have such a large plot at your disposal at the Manor."

"Yes." he said distractedly, then cleared his throat. "There is something I wish to discuss with you."

"Yes?"

"I've had a letter from our old friend, Dr. Webb."

"Dr. Webb? It is good news, I hope?"

"Yes, rather. He has decided to retire—plans to move north to be nearer his grown son and grandchildren." He plucked a forget-me-not from the grass and twirled the stem in his fingers. "He has offered me his practice. His home in Doddington, his offices, all for a very reasonable sum."

She stared at him, but he kept his gaze on the weed in his hand. "But—that would mean giving up your practice here and your work at the Manor."

"The Manor Home is my father's life's work. Not mine. I merely stepped in while he was unable. I can leave it in his hands now. He and Thomas can manage the place—and Preston—quite nicely without me."

"Have you told him yet—your father?"

"No, not yet. I wanted to speak with you first."

She was not prepared to ask why. "You would really leave London?"

"Yes. I tire of city life. And, in truth, there are too many memories here—in this house and at the Manor both—and not all of them pleasant. I quite enjoyed my time in Kent. It is so peaceful and lovely there on the north downs. So much open land. So much green." He lifted his face and smiled at her. "And, as you may recall, I was quite fond of its residents as well."

She smiled briefly in return, but felt a surge of fear rising within her. Were Dr. Taylor and his daughter leaving her behind? Or was he assuming she would return to Doddington with them?

"Your father will not be pleased at my return. But should I allow the opinion of one man to keep me from something which, I believe, will bring much happiness?"

She assumed it a rhetorical question, but then saw he was studying her, waiting for her response. Waiting for her to answer the same question of herself.

"Charlotte?"

She studied her hands, tightly clutched in her lap.

"Charlotte. I will not take you back to Doddington as Anne's governess."

She looked up at him, oddly relieved. She had inwardly cringed at the thought of returning to her home village as a servant. Of facing the disdain of her former acquaintance—especially her father and sister. Though at least governess was one of the more respectable positions of service. No, easier to remain in anonymity in London. Perhaps with Sally and Thomas, or Sally's sister. Or she could return to Crawley, as she had once thought she might do.

"You will find another governess, once you are settled in Kent?"

"Yes. I will."

"I understand."

"No, I do not think you do. I would not take you back to Doddington as a governess. But I would take you there—as my wife."

She stared at him, saw the grim determination on his face, and her heart pounded dully, a dozen different emotions flooding her mind.

"Here it is!" Anne sang, running back to them and plopping back down. "Now I shall pour you some tea."

As she did so, Charlotte felt Daniel's intense gaze on her profile.

"Will you, Charlotte?"

She looked up sharply from her thoughts. "Hmm?"

"Yes, Missy, will you have more tea?"

"Thank you."

As Anne refilled her cup, Charlotte glanced at Daniel, tilting her head in his daughter's direction, silently indicating that their conversation would have to wait.

That evening, after Charlotte had gotten Anne into her nightclothes and her teeth cleaned, Daniel came in as usual to tuck in his daughter and hear her prayers.

Charlotte silently hung the girl's dress in the wardrobe and gathered up her soiled stockings. As she did, she heard, without meaning to, Anne's sweet prayer:

"Thank you for Papa and Grandfather and Missy. And Constance too. Tell Mother not to be sad because we are all happy together. Amen."

His arm around his daughter's shoulders, Daniel looked at Charlotte over Anne's little bowed head. "Amen," he echoed, his gaze still holding hers.

After breakfast the next morning, Charlotte glanced at the mantel clock and saw it was nearly nine o'clock. Daniel sat at the head of the table still, nursing his third cup of coffee and rustling distractedly with the newspaper.

"May I be excused to go play, please?" Anne asked.

"Yes, you may," Charlotte answered and watched her skip from the room. She finished her tea, then looked at Daniel again. "Are you not seeing patients today?"

"Not as yet. I am certain I should not be able to concentrate in any case." He put down the paper. "I am still waiting for your answer."

She opened her mouth. Closed it. Then opened it again. "I—"

"Tell me you have not forgotten the question." He attempted a smile.

"No," she laughed weakly. "I have thought of little else since."

"And?"

"And, I think—"

A loud knock sounded on the door.

Charlotte rose to her feet. "I will answer that."

"There is no need for you—"

"Marie has the day off."

He sighed and rose. "Very well. But we *shall* discuss this tonight."

Charlotte went down and opened the door, expecting to find a messenger or delivery of some sort. She froze—except to quickly close her mouth, which had fallen open. Mr. Harris stood there, elegantly dressed as usual, but his eyes, which she remembered nearly always dancing with merry teasing, looked frightfully serious. He removed his hat and smiled at her, but his smile was brief and did not cheer his expression.

"Miss Lamb."

"Mr. Harris." She stood looking at him dumbly, and then the realization struck her that he wasn't there to see her at all and she felt mortified at her own presumption. "You are here to see Dr. Taylor?"

He shook his head. "No, Charlotte, I am here to see you."

She put her hand to her chest. "Is something wrong with Edmund?"

"No. He is fine—missing his mother, of course."

Charlotte swallowed. "Of course."

"Forgive me. I am handling this very ill."

"Do come in."

He followed her up the stairs to the sitting room. "Please, sit down."

"Thank you."

She sat in the chair opposite him. He crossed one leg over the other, then uncrossed his legs and spread his feet on the carpet before him, resting his elbows on his knees and playing with his hat. "I had every intention of merely paying a social call to begin. But . . ."

Sitting back, he ran his hand through his hair. "But, seeing you now, I cannot pretend to a casual call."

"Mr. Harris, you are frightening me. Are you certain Edmund is all right?"

"Well, fine in health and spirits. But it's no good. He needs . . . he needs a woman's influence."

"He has a governess. I met her once. She seemed quite capable."

"You know that isn't what I mean."

Did she? He could not mean— Her mouth felt instantly dry. "Mr. Harris. I am not sure my presence in your home would be in Edmund's best interest. I fear word about me has circulated, rumors at least. Many of your acquaintance do not hold me in the same esteem they once did."

"You do not suppose *my* esteem has been affected by all this. How could it be?"

She lowered her head. "No, but it might not reflect well on Edmund. Nor you."

"So be it. I refuse to be driven by the opinions of others any longer. You have no idea how often I have thought of you, grieved for you. Forced to work in a post beneath your station. Torn away from your family and friends—your child, worst of all. What a burden it has been, knowing it was all my doing. Do you think you might ever find it in your heart to forgive me?"

Charlotte answered quietly, "I have forgiven you. Long ago."

"Then, this is my chance—do you not see? At last I am able to right my wrongs as best as I can."

"You need not feel obligated. I have a comfortable place here."

"Charlotte, this is not about obligation."

She rose quickly, clutching her hands and walking away from him. She was trembling with nerves, afraid to presume. To hope. "Are you asking me to be Edmund's governess?"

She heard him bolt from his chair behind her. "Blast the governess, Charlotte. Edmund has that. He needs . . ."

She turned around to face him.

"He needs you."

Her heart ached at the words.

He stepped closer. "And not only Edmund. I—"

The sitting room door opened and Daniel strode in, pulling on a glove. "Charlotte, have you seen my other— Oh . . ." He glanced up and stopped abruptly, looking from Mr. Harris to Charlotte and back again.

When he said nothing for several awkward seconds, Mr. Harris said, "Hello, Taylor."

Daniel paused, breathed in and exhaled before responding. "Harris."

"Forgive the intrusion, old boy." Mr. Harris smiled and added lightly, "I have just been trying to persuade Miss Lamb here to make young Edmund and I the two happiest males on earth." His smile faded, and it was his turn to look from Charlotte to the other man. "That is, unless you . . ." He swung his gaze back to Charlotte. "You two are not . . . You have worked for him so long with no word, I just assumed . . . But . . . *is there* an understanding between you?"

Charlotte's face burned. She found it difficult to breathe. She could hardly raise her head, let alone meet the gaze of either man. It was not her right to speak first. But Daniel remained silent. Finally, she lifted her eyes to meet his. He looked at her a moment, his chest rising and falling in exaggerated effort. And although he answered Mr. Harris's question, his eyes remained fixed on hers when he said, "No. There is no understanding."

They stared at one another a moment longer. Then Daniel nodded curtly to Harris, said dully, "I wish you both the best," and quickly bowed and left the room.

Once he was gone, Charles said, "Forgive me. I did not intend to put you on the spot in that manner. I fear there is something between you after all."

"There is a great deal between us." Charlotte sighed, stepping to the window and watching as Dr. Taylor appeared on the street below and strode away. "We have been friends for nearly as long as you and I have been. I was there when his wife died, and I have nursed and cared for his daughter for more than three years. But he spoke the truth. There is no understanding between us."

"But there might be, someday?"

She hesitated only a moment. "Yes."

"Well, then, Charlotte. You have a choice to make. I am proposing marriage now, today. I am asking you to be my wife and Edmund's mother."

She looked at him.

"I suppose that last bit is quite ironic, since you have always been his mother."

"No. That was Katherine's privilege, in every way that counts. To Edmund, in any case."

"Yes. About that. I'm afraid I would have to ask you to keep the true nature of your relationship with Edmund a secret."

The statement felt like a blade between her ribs, but of course he was right.

"I am not saying we can *never* tell him, but . . . out of loyalty to Katherine's memory and sensitivity to Edmund's reputation and feelings . . ."

"Of course. I understand completely. I won't pretend it is not a painful mandate, but you know I want whatever is best for Edmund."

"Yes, I do know that. You have proven that over and over again. If only Bea could see—"

"Bea?"

"Yes. She, too, has taken quite an interest in Edmund. Though I am not convinced her motives are purely maternal."

"I take it she would not be pleased to know that you are here."

"You are quite right. She does not know I am here, but she does know . . . about us."

"She does?"

"Yes. I was quite tired of hearing her disparaging remarks about you, and the slanderous suppositions about the ill-bred scoundrel that must have ruined you. I confessed *I* was that man. Scoundrel, perhaps, but ill-bred on no account."

"You didn't."

"I did."

"Is that why you are here? Did she refuse you?"

"Bea refuse me? I asked nothing of her. It is you I am asking, Charlotte. You."

"Did you did tell her . . . everything?"

"I did not tell her about Edmund, for obvious reasons. She still believes your child passed on."

She touched his arm. "When it was your own son who died—yours and Katherine's—it must have been difficult for you, having to grieve in secret. Alone."

He nodded. "You know a great deal about that." He grasped her elbows. "Let us put an end to it, Charlotte. Let us neither one be alone anymore."

She looked up into the long-held-dear face of Charles Harris. He was still so very handsome. And he was, finally, offering his name, his protection. Perhaps even his love. She realized he hadn't mentioned that. But what did she expect? Outpourings of romance and devotion when his wife was not long in her grave? She knew he cared for her on some level. He always had. And oh! to be near Edmund. Her own son. To be his mother, whether he knew it or not.

But what about Daniel? She admired and respected him. Perhaps even loved him, his daughter as well. True, they had as yet no formal understanding, but he had made his desires clear enough. At least before today. Why had he not spoken? She could guess why. He knew how deeply she longed to be with Edmund.

Could she forego a future with Daniel in order to be stepmother to her own son?

But the alternative seemed even more difficult to conceive. For to refuse Mr. Harris would mean giving up Edmund all over again.

Oh, poor little butterfly, bound by so many fetters,
which prevent you from flying whithersoever you will!
Have pity on her, my God…so that she may be able
to fulfill her desires to Thy honour and glory.

—St. Teresa of Avila

Chapter 36

Time passed quickly, as time is wont to do.

Daniel Taylor worked alone in his garden in Dodding-ton, thinking back yet again to that day fifteen years ago when Charles Harris had come to his London home and changed his life forever.

Daniel had been aware, of course, of Charlotte's long affection for Harris, and knowing how she longed to be with her son, Daniel had despondently guessed which man she would choose. Loving her as he did, and wanting her much-deserved happiness, he had excused himself from the situation. He did not come home from the Manor all that day. He slept, albeit poorly, in his rooms there, knowing his absence would make things easier for Charlotte. And hopefully, less painful for him. He placed an ad in the newspaper for a new governess, confident Marie would suffice until one could be found. And he wrote to Dr. Webb, agreeing to take over his practice. He knew he might come into contact with the Harrises in Doddington, but since he surmised Charles would still be splitting his time between London and Fawnwell, he did not think it would be too often to be borne. He was ready to leave London and its memories behind. He would leave the Manor in the care of Thomas and his fine, understanding father.

Voices disturbed Daniel's memories, and he looked up to see a group of Doddington school children running onto the lawn nearby, kicking a ball. He hoped they would not trample his prized specimens nor his entire garden with it. He recognized most of the children and knew several by name. With the numbers of children scampering about the village these days, his practice stayed busy indeed.

He was on his knees beside a swamp milkweed plant, searching each leaf, when the ball flew over the low garden wall and landed with a puff of dust beside his patch of sciatic cress. A girl—his favorite among the village children—leapt the wall neatly and went in search of the ball. Watching her, he could not help but be reminded of Charlotte Lamb as a girl.

"Near the sciatic cress, Lucy," he said, returning to his examination of the chrysalis he had just found.

"The what?" she asked, bent low.

"The candytuft. There." He pointed toward the small bushy plants with clusters of flat white flowers.

"Voila!" The girl held up the ball triumphantly and tossed it back over the wall to her friends. But instead of clambering back over the wall herself, she came and squatted on her haunches near him.

"What are you doing?" she asked.

"Examining this chrysalis." After a moment he glanced at her. "Do you not wish to rejoin your chums?"

She shrugged. "Not especially." She knelt there beside him amid the milkweeds.

Now, close up, he thought Lucy reminded him a bit of Anne at that age, but Anne was all grown up now.

"You do know about milkweed, do you not?" he asked.

"I know Mr. Jarvis wishes you'd pull it from your garden."

"That's only because he doesn't understand how important milkweeds are. Besides a whole host of medicinal uses, monarch butterflies lay their eggs on milkweeds, which is the only plant the larva eat."

Lucy looked at him blankly, clearly not impressed.

"Monarchs are not native to England. But once in a while—every decade or so—they are sighted. Blown here by powerful winds."

"From where?"

"The Canary Islands, or even as far away as the Americas, where they are as common as black flies."

"From so far?"

"Yes. But look here—this is really amazing." He lifted another leaf, exposing a beautifully luminous jade-green pod. "I do believe this is a monarch chrysalis. Right here in my garden. If I am correct, some monarch stopped here long enough to lay her eggs on my milkweed. The caterpillars hatched, ate this bitter weed to grow—and for protection from those who would destroy them. Then hid themselves away."

"In a cocoon, right?"

"Yes, that is the common term."

"Is there really something growing in there?"

"Oh yes. It might appear lifeless or trapped, but only for a time. Inside it is secretly growing and changing until it will emerge strong enough to live in the world and ride the wind."

A magnificent black and orange butterfly alighted on a neighboring plant, and Lucy gasped in admiration.

"Is that a monarch?"

"Yes," he said, equally awed, and watched as it fluttered and rose in the air. They both looked up, following its flight. Over the girl's head, Daniel saw Charlotte, the former Miss Lamb, in the distance, walking down the lane from the direction of Fawnwell. Out paying calls, no doubt. Watching her, he said wistfully, "See how beautiful she is when she emerges."

Gaze still on the butterfly, Lucy asked, "How do you know it's a girl?"

Daniel shrugged, not shifting his focus. "She is a survivor. Strong and beautiful. A creature reborn."

Someone called out to Charlotte, and Daniel saw her pause and lift her hand in greeting. Eighteen-year-old Edmund Harris came trotting down the lane, smiling as he caught up with her.

Even from a distance, Daniel saw the way she looked at her son, her brilliant joy that they were together at last, and he thought his chest might break for the flood of gratitude and pain he felt.

At that very moment, Charlotte looked across the garden at him. Though they were far apart, they shared a knowing look filled with wistfulness and poignant understanding.

Daniel was happy for her. Truly happy. But with the happiness came the sting, the awareness of all Charlotte had sacrificed. How had she done it? Why?

He knew the why, but sometimes he still struggled to believe it.

❦

Charlotte, too, was thinking of that long ago day when Charles Harris had proposed to her. On this day of days, how could she not?

She still remembered Mr. Harris's earnest face as he awaited her answer. She remembered the surprise she had felt upon realizing her girlhood infatuation with him had faded. She had become too aware of his weaknesses, his previous, though regretted, betrayal. Still, she considered accepting Mr. Harris for Edmund's sake, if not her own.

When Daniel did not return home all that day, Charlotte realized he already supposed she had accepted Mr. Harris. After putting Anne to bed, Charlotte sat in the sitting room, waiting for him. At nine o'clock the door opened below and she heard footsteps on the stairs. She rose and went to the sitting room door.

But it was John Taylor who ascended. "Oh. Hello, my dear."

"You worked late." She forced a smile. "Was Daniel there?"

"Yes, shut away in his office."

"Do you know if he plans to remain at the manor all night?"

"No. I am afraid I don't know." He looked as though he might say something more, but did not. His weary face rose in a brief, sympathetic smile. "Well, good night, my dear."

"Good night."

She sat back in the armchair nearest the door.

Sometime later, she awoke suddenly. Dim light shone through the sitting room windows. The clock showed half past five. She heard cautious footsteps on the stairs, and with each step her heart seemed to beat faster. She rose and walked to the door, her hand on her stomach in an attempt to ease her nerves.

Daniel, drawn and tired, stepped onto the landing, loosening his cravat. When he looked up and saw her there, he hesitated. "Oh. Forgive me. I did not expect you up this early. I need only a clean shirt and I shall be gone again." He paused. "Tell me you have not been sitting there all night?"

She touched her hair self-consciously. "When you did not return, I grew anxious."

Daniel crossed his arms over his chest, his face wooden, eyes averted. "Is there something you needed to tell me?"

"Daniel," she began gently, moving closer. "If you are avoiding me because you think I shall marry Mr. Harris, then you are mistaken. I do not wish to marry him." How could she, when she loved Daniel, as well as Anne, so deeply?

Daniel stood frozen, clearly as stunned as Mr. Harris had been at her refusal. But though disappointed, Mr. Harris had wished her every happiness and assured her they parted friends.

Daniel's brow furrowed. "But . . . Edmund . . ."

"I know." She squeezed her eyes shut, then opened them again. "But it cannot be helped. I cannot have him and you both." She smiled tentatively. "And I want you."

When Daniel did not respond, she reached out and touched a button on his waistcoat, giving it a gentle tug. He released a long, jagged breath. "Charlotte . . . are you quite certain?"

She nodded.

Shaking his head in wonder, he slowly reached out and cradled her face with his long, sensitive fingers. He leaned close, his blue-green eyes wide through his spectacles. He whispered, "I am afraid to believe it."

She looked into those eyes and urged, *"Believe."*

His gaze melded with hers for a long moment before lowering to her mouth. His eyes drifted closed behind a curtain of golden eyelashes and he kissed her gently. Then more deeply. Then again.

＊

They were married by special license a mere fortnight later. Daniel's father was there with them, of course, proud and happy, Mrs. Krebs at his side. Aunt and Uncle Tilney also attended, as did Thomas and Sally, who smiled and wept throughout the entire ceremony.

Though invited, the Reverend Mr. Lamb did not attend, nor did Beatrice. Charlotte felt their absence, but not too keenly. She was busy embracing all the joy and passion of her wedding day and married life.

Even so, Charlotte regretted that she was never able to reconcile with her father. The Reverend, as distant and unforgiving as ever, died shortly after she and Daniel moved to Doddington. A kindly new vicar took his place and gladly welcomed Charlotte back into the church of her childhood.

Beatrice also remained distant. Through Mr. Harris, Charlotte learned that Bea married a naval officer many years her senior and resided in London. Bea did send a brief note one Christmas, enclosing their mother's butterfly brooch. Charlotte's thank-you note and other letters remained unanswered.

Charles Harris did not remarry. His mother, Mrs. Harris, rallied and provided Edmund a healthy regimen of maternal influence and nurturing over the years. Edmund spent a good deal of time with his grandmother in Doddington, and Charlotte was able to see him at village events or on the rare occasion Daniel was called upon to treat some childhood ailment or other.

Edmund had even played with Anne now and then when they were young and seemed to enjoy the company of Daniel and Charlotte as well. If he ever wondered at the reason for their heightened interest and many kindnesses, he never voiced the question.

He remained, of course, completely unaware of his relationship to Charlotte. Hearing her son call her merely "Mrs. Taylor" was always bittersweet, but she resigned herself to living with that particular ache for the rest of her days.

Charlotte's close relationship with Anne did a great deal to soothe that ache. Daniel's daughter knew about Lizette but had recently confided that Charlotte had always been mother to her, even before she and her father had married. At Daniel's encouragement, Anne had long ago stopped using the endearment "Missy" and began calling Charlotte "Mother." Every time she heard it, she paused to savor the sound and think, *What a lovely word.*

EPILOGUE

When Edmund Harris found me in my office and asked permission to marry my daughter Anne, I was at first astounded, then utterly amazed. The poor lad took my expression as hesitance and looked quite miserable. For one flicker of a moment I saw Charles Harris in the young man's face and thought of disappointing him in some sort of belated revenge for the obstacles his father had placed between Charlotte and me. But I quickly banished the petty thought. Thinking instead of Charlotte, as well as Anne, I warmly assured him of my blessing.

I follow behind now as Edmund goes to find Charlotte to tell her the news himself. I want to witness this moment from afar, so as not to intrude on their reunion.

I see them in the garden, standing close in conversation. Stepping nearer, I am just in time to hear Edmund's words to Charlotte.

"May I call you Mother now?"

She looks at him, stilled. Then her face blooms into a radiant smile. "Nothing would please me more."

Anne comes out of the house, and I blink away unexpected tears, stunned all over again at what a lovely young woman our daughter has become. She walks, tall and graceful, to join Charlotte and Edmund in the garden. She laces her arm through Edmund's, and Edmund offers his other arm to Charlotte.

"He's told you our news, then, Mother?" Anne asks.

Smiling, Charlotte nods. She links her arm through Edmund's, placing her free hand on his, as if drawing as much physical contact as possible deep into her healed but forever scarred soul.

Lucy, our youngest, comes up behind me and puts her hand in mine. "Why is Mummy crying?" she asks.

"Those are happy tears."

"She is happy?"

"Yes, she is soon to be the mother of the bride." To myself I add, *and groom.* . . .

So we are to be related to the Harrises after all. Not the relationship any of us anticipated all those years ago, but the one God saw, designed even.

Charlotte Taylor is my wife, my dearest friend. And as I stand here at the edge of the garden she has helped me tend so beautifully here in Kent, watching her bright eyes flit from daughter to son, son to daughter, I see joy transform her countenance, her spirit soar to heights beyond earlier imaginings. I see her lift her face to heaven and I know she is thanking God. From where I stand I join her prayer, thankful that He has transformed all the pain and sacrifice of the past into something so beautiful. I leave my solitary post and step into the garden, into the sunlight. Thankful, especially, that I am here with Charlotte, to watch her, finally, fly free.

AUTHOR'S NOTE

When I first began researching *Lady of Milkweed Manor*, I had never been to England. Through Web sites and old maps, I chose Doddington (Kent) as my character's birthplace—charmed by what I'd read about the place and how relatively unchanged it seemed (compared to say, London or Crawley). The old vicarage, however, had fallen out of church use by then and into private ownership. Even if I visited Doddington someday, I reasoned, I could do no more than look upon its exterior and try to imagine its rooms and what it might have been like to live there.

Two years later, when the book was finished and I learned it would be published, I decided I could finally justify my long desire to travel to England to see the places I'd written about. How serendipitous to discover that the old vicarage had just become a bed-and-breakfast! I could barely believe I would be able to stay in "Charlotte's childhood home." Nick and Claire Finley were wonderful hosts, and our stay with them was a highlight of our trip.

The people of Doddington were so kind and welcoming. Many thanks to you all—and especially to Pier Vousden, my first contact in the village, and the Rev. George Baisley, who graced us with a warm and inspiring Easter Sunday service that will long live in our memories.

Please note that while Chequers Inn, the Parish Church of Doddington (Dedicated to the Beheading of St. John the Baptist), and the old vicarage are real places, most of the other settings in the book are not. There are two fine manor houses in Doddington, but fictional Fawnwell is not among them. Nor are the book's characters based on real people.

There were several lying-in and foundling hospitals in London in the early 1800s, but Milkweed Manor is only a fictionalized composite of those real institutions. For those readers shocked by details like babies left in "the turn," and goats nursing syphilitic babies, be assured those details are all-too-real pieces of history. I found them fascinating and moving, and I hope you did as well.

In fact, I found the entire wet-nursing profession fascinating. The practice seems foreign to most of us now, but it was very common in the 1700s for infants to be sent away to be nursed, and in the 1800s for wet nurses to be brought into one's own home. Jane Austen herself was sent to live with (and be nursed by) a woman in the country for most of the first two years of her life!

While I enjoyed researching and writing about life in early 19th-century England, I no doubt made my share of errors. I am indebted to my talented editors, Rachelle Gardner and Karen Schurrer, for limiting these to as few as possible. Please forgive any remaining inaccuracies. One I am aware of is that the lambing season is actually earlier than I have it here, but I hope you will indulge the liberties I took to include it in the book's timeline. If you would like to read more about (and see photos of) the research and settings of *Lady of Milkweed Manor*, please visit my Web site at *www.julieklassen.com*.

In closing, I would like to thank my families—my husband and sons, and my Bethany House family, for all the support and encouragement that have made this book possible.

READING GROUP DISCUSSION QUESTIONS

1. After reading *Lady of Milkweed Manor,* do you view the foundling hospital "turn" as a compassionate practice, or one that was too easy on fallen ladies?

2. Was the topic of wet-nursing new to you? What surprised you about its history and practice? How would you have felt about having a stranger living in your home, nursing your infant for you?

3. Did you learn anything new about milkweeds or monarch butterflies? How did you feel about the imagery in this novel and epigraphs at the beginning of each chapter?

4. Reverend Lamb remained unforgiving, but did you notice a possible act of compassion toward Charlotte? How would it feel to grow up without a father's love and approval? How did

Charlotte's relationship with Daniel's father serve to fill this hole in her life?

5. How is the historical "puerperal insanity" Daniel's wife suffered from similar to or different from modern postpartum depression? Have you or someone you know suffered from this very real condition?

6. In the early 1800s there was much competition among medical practitioners for the delivery of infants (physicians, midwives, accoucheurs). Does this same competition exist today? Is competition in this field beneficial, or not?

7. It is much more common (and economically feasible) for a single mother to raise a child on her own today than it was in the 1800s. Faced with Charlotte's decision for the future of her infant son, what do you think you would you have done?

8. Which of Charlotte's various suitors throughout the novel did you like most? Would you have made the same choice Charlotte did?

9. Did the revelations about the character's lives in the final chapter and epilogue surprise you? Were you satisfied with the ending?

10. How would you describe the book's theme or message? What effect did the book have on you?

ABOUT THE AUTHOR

JULIE KLASSEN is a fiction editor with a background in advertising. She has worked in Christian publishing for more than twelve years, in both marketing and editorial capacities. This is her first novel.

Julie is a graduate of the University of Illinois. She enjoys travel, research, books, BBC period dramas, long hikes, short naps, and coffee with friends.

She and her husband have two sons and live in a suburb of St. Paul, Minnesota.

For more information about Julie, *Lady of Milkweed Manor*, and her upcoming books, visit *www.julieklassen.com*.

Looking for More Good Books to Read?

You can find out what is new and exciting with previews, descriptions, and reviews by signing up for Bethany House newsletters at

www.bethanynewsletters.com

We will send you updates for as many authors or categories as you desire so you get only the information you really want.

Sign up today!